I0818036

The Man at the End of the World

The Man at the End of the World

Published 2020 by Grunt, Ink.

ISBN-13: 978-1-7340884-1-0

Discover other titles by Chance Nix by visiting the author's website.
www.gruntink.com

This book contains mature language, humor, sexuality, and violence.

No animals were harmed in the making of this book.

246897531

FIRST EDITION

This book is for Grandma Carol,
for introducing me to Jaws and Universal Monsters.
Sorry I couldn't stay awake and you had to watch the scary parts by yourself.

Dedicated to:
Damien Wesley and Bastian Hardin
"Any bad day fishing beats any good day working."

And as always, to Jennifer
I love you, today.

GRUNT, INK.

Chance Nix

a novel

Canst thou not minister to a mind diseased, pluck
from the memory a rooted sorrow,
raze out the written troubles of the brain,
and with some sweet oblivious antidote,
cleanse the stuff'd bosom of that perilous stuff which
weighs upon the heart?

Macbeth Act 5, Scene 3

Part One

Chapter One

And the great marlin broke the restraints of the sea, capturing air, and stealing our breaths. The passengers aboard my ship crowded near the stern. Kojo, my first mate, shouted 'fish' as if I hadn't seen it. She broke headfirst, flying, suspended in the air, dragging her tail across the surface, then as quick as she rose, flopped back into the sea. There was life in our stream; today I'd earn my paycheck.

Any man can be at peace wherever the hunting is wild, and the fishing is good. That is until the world closes in, chokes the life from you, and leaves you with failed dreams and sad memories. Everyone has demons and sooner or later, the world unleashes those demons upon you. There's nothing you can do but buy the ticket and take the ride.

A cool breeze pressed against the ship, threatening to knock us off our current location. The anchor dug deep into the ocean floor, and the chain held true. With the breeze came a welcoming relief against the sun beating down on our shoulders. The blinding rays twinkling off the water reflected into a spectrum of colors. I pushed my sunglasses up the bridge of my nose and pulled down the brim of my woodland boonie cover.

The tide glimmered like the back of a speckled trout, masking my line. I lost it at the point where the vast ocean connected with the ample sky. Curling a finger around the 100-pound blue test line helped to determine if I had a bite or if the current alone moved my rod.

The wooden footrest of my fighting chair creaked as I adjusted my posture. The Indonesian wood shined under my feet and matched the rest of my chair. Its beauty betrayed me at the end of a long day with cramping and stiff joints. Four wooden slats across the back weren't extremely comfortable but did offer repose while waiting for a large catch. When there's no customers, I like to sit in my chair and stare out on the water.

The cost of such a chair escaped me. With the offset pedestal, wooden armrests, and custom rod holder between my legs, it was a pretty penny. Price is no consequence because this chair helped to bring in the big game. It was in this chair I caught the island's record for Atlantic white marlin; a 152-pounder which took three hours to reel in. A photo of it still hangs above the bar at my favorite pub.

I didn't keep that fish and the picture isn't one of me standing next to it with it hanging by its tail. That tradition died when commercial fishing killed the waters and threw off the balance of the sea life ecosystem. The monstrous fish of fifty years ago were a rarity, and the only way to preserve the sport and the sea life was to tag each fish. Some may find this ludicrous, but we weigh, tag, record, and release. This allows the fish to repopulate the ocean and grow bigger for another catch.

The AJAX, my tried-and-true fishing vessel, swayed with the tide. It rose over hills of water and skidded down the other side. This created a queasy roller coaster sensation to the three tourists who weren't accustomed to this life at sea. Seasickness cocooned me the first time I set sail on the open ocean and the constant motion battered me without mercy. Cramps and vertigo, which had once burdened me, waned with the passing of years, leaving only a vivid imprint on my brain. *Death would be a great relief,* I remember thinking.

Lost in the past, the ocean's mist kissed my face, bringing me back to the present. My line bobbed with the current, pulling tight then relaxing, a dance repeated over and over. Two more lines hung off the sides, and all three trolled behind my boat, baited with pinfish for big game.

CLICK. A foreign chatter broke the concentration I had on my rig. CLICK. An itch grew along my spine until I readjusted in my captain's chair to a proper sitting position. CLICK. The camera's automatic shutter echoed as a tall lanky man hunched forward, snapping pictures from starboard. When intercepting my glare, he stood erect, eyes wide and face scrunched-up as it rose from behind the camera.

"Oh my god. You haven't moved in fifteen minutes. You were so still and motionless I couldn't tell if you were breathing. I thought you were dead."

"I get that, but I ain't dead. I'm thirsty." With my free hand, I pulled a bottle of Krystal Ale beer from the drink holder attached to my armrest. Made locally on the island, no beverage had the same crisp and refreshing texture as Krystal Ale. The sun warmed the brown bottle and the remaining swallow of beer was bitter and flat. I grimaced and shouted, "Kojo!"

Throwing the name over my shoulder caught the attention of the dark island man on the flying bridge. Kojo leaned over the railing, blocking out the sun and turning him into a giant, featureless shadow. I liked Kojo. He's the only man I trusted with piloting my ship. It was he who taught me the ropes on my first fishing job, and when I built the AJAX, he came aboard. In that time, I watched his youthful black hair sprout streaks of salt and pepper. There had been other crewmen, but none were as trustworthy as Kojo. The man knew how to fish, how to read the waters, and was a hell of a guy to drink with.

"Beer."

Kojo nodded and fished a cold one from within the ice filled cooler. He kept it up on the flying bridge to prevent me from drinking them all in our first hour at sea. A fake leg gave him a limp disguised as stiffness, but he moved with the speed of a sailor twenty years his junior. Although the leg at times bothered him, Kojo never complained about it. He motioned to the cameraman, handing him the glass bottle of Krystal Ale.

"What happened to your hand?" The cameraman asked as I took the beer from him. I curled my left hand around to hide the missing pinky finger.

"Misfortune," I said. As I tore the top off, a splash followed a regurgitating sound coming from port side. One man stood leaning over the side of the AJAX, heaving his lunch into the sea, while a third man patted his back. I eyed these two for a moment, not sure what to make of them.

Three small dips and two hard tugs brought my attention back to my line. I squeezed my trigger finger, assuring myself nothing was there but the tide. Replenishing my thirst and still eyeing the end of my rod, I eased back into my previous slouched position. The enormous ocean captivated me, and I enjoyed the lack of ships in sight and the absence of land on the horizon.

Nothing felt more freeing than to be away from the things of man, out on the open ocean, amongst the last frontier. The beer was satisfying and as I placed it in the cup holder, another great splash echoed. I couldn't believe the sick college kid's stomach held so much substance. Hemingway created an interest in deep-sea fishing for most people even if the attraction was only a fantasy. The reality was those people weren't ready for the ocean's ride.

I couldn't deny that Hemingway's writings sparked my own interest in the sea, and lost in an epic daydream, my line zipped out. It wasn't the zip that startled me but a small cut that opened on my index finger. The line tightened, bending the rod, and I cradled the pole in both hands to keep it from ripping out of my harness.

"Kojo, it's a big bitch we got here."

Leaving his friend to his own demise, the healthy tourist rushed to the stern. The line moved at an invisible speed and the fool sprinting to the back of the ship almost caught it in the neck. I kicked at him, stopping him from a painful injury. The line ran on, and I allowed it without protest. To snag the fish when it wasn't ready would cause her to throw my hook.

This I didn't want.

I downed the last of my Krystal Ale, repositioned in my chair, and tossed the bottle to the deck. It rolled, smacking into some stored away equipment before disappearing from my story.

Adjusting the drag so the tension wasn't too tight, I readied my gear for battle. I didn't want the fish breaking my line before our dance even started. Two leather straps fastened the pole to the chair and the handle nestled tight into the rod cup between my legs. By the way the line screamed off the reel, a hell of a fight was brewing.

"Alright." My voice boomed from my chest, snatching the collective attention of the two tourists still standing. The sick tourist managed to look up, but another great descent rolled his stomach. I eyed the healthy friend in the striped blue and yellow rugby jersey not holding the camera, and said, "This is gonna be a long fight. I don't know if pukey over there has it in him, but you up for it?"

The college boy nodded his impatient head, licking his lips to get into my chair. The grandeur of the sea mesmerized him, stealing his ability to speak. I couldn't blame him, for the things entrancing him still held sway over myself.

I waited, allowing whatever clung to my line to think it had achieved victory. She swam, and I waited. The fish turned hard, not diving deep, but careened toward port side. I waited.

The rugby kid danced anxiously around like a child needing a bathroom. I waited. Their eyes shifted from the end of the rod to me, from the end of the rod to me, from the end of the rod to me. A feeling came traveling up the line, swimming down the pole, and vibrated into my body. It was the moment I had been waiting for.

My back flexed, teeth clenched, and I jerked the rod. Veins protruded under the skin of my arms, and my shoulders contracted with great tension. In my head, I could see the setting of the hook. The sharp silver point tore through the bait and ripped into the side of the fish's mouth. Water jettisoned through, shaking the hook, but its barbs held with the hope of not releasing. The force at which the mighty fish traveled pulled me forward in my chair as I snagged it.

"Fish on!" I shouted. Bolts anchoring the fighting chair to the deck strained. It bucked, cutting back toward starboard side.

Had I wrangled a fish or a whale? No matter how hard I cranked the reel or strained my back, the fish went whatever way it pleased. Shutter sounds from snapping pictures fired rapidly, hoping to catch something.

"Kojo, pull it." A simple phrase, an expression between us, started the engines. The anchor rose and the ship thrusted ahead. Pukey climbed to his knees, but the motion of the sea crumbled him to the deck once again. Both his friends watched the water intently. I feared a sudden lurch of the ship would knock them off-balance and at least one would fall overboard. Both braced themselves.

I didn't fight the fish as it moved but cranked the reel with sluggish, calculated rotations. The fish sailed out, but I drew it back to the boat, keeping it from pulling past 300 meters. We played this game of tug-o-war, me allowing it to go out, then bringing it back in.

"Hey, you," I shouted to the rugby tourist. I couldn't remember his name because all these college kids looked alike. "Are you ready to take over?"

I was reluctant to give up the reigns, but they did pay the bill, so I had to make it worth their money. With a frantic nod, and still without words, Rugby nearly leaped into my lap. I eased out of the fighting chair while coaching him into it, questioning the whole time whether he was mute. He looked nervous and as soon as his ass hit the seat, he cranked the reel with ferocious rotations. I seized his arm, willing to break it before he could break my line.

"Calm down. You fish like young people fuck, too quick and eager to get to the finish line. You don't wanna break the line. Focus. This is a fight, but not a slugfest. Feel the fish and allow her to surrender to you," I said, to which he nodded. I'm not sure if he understood what I meant, but it was his dime, so I didn't push the point. The angle of the rod curved, and the line ran straight out behind us. I watched the pole, reading the line, and analyzing the tide. To my surprise, Rugby was a good listener. He leaned back like a boxer slipping a jab, then slugged forward, reeling in upon my instructions. "She's running away, but we'll get her."

The sun beat heavy upon us. Burning exhaust fumes bellowed out where the propellers churned the sea white. Rugby relaxed, allowing the fish to drag, then reeled again. After ten minutes of instructions, he got the hang of it and I sat back with a cold Krystal Ale to watch the show.

His ill-friend snored in the corner and for at least a time, had ceased the expulsion of his stomach. Waves splashed against the hull, kicking up a spray that washed over Pukey. He woke swearing foul words with an arm draped over his face and eased himself into the shade of the compartment to cool himself. I troubled not with him.

Kojo kept the AJAX trudging forward at a steady pace, glancing back to ensure the fight was still on. Keeping an eye on Rugby's progress, I reeled in the other two lines. The small baitfish on each would keep on ice for a trip tomorrow. This day was over once this fish came in.

The fish coaxed the rod starboard and the chair followed. I instructed Kojo to stay with it. He eased up the throttle and the roar of the engine lowered. Rugby hunched over, the rod bent hard, and the line headed straight down.

"She's sounding," I said. He stared at me with a confused look. The spinning line decreased from the reel. "She's going down. Now the real fight starts. Tighten the drag."

"How do you know?" Photo Boy asked.

"Because I'm a fisherman. Now hit it." Rugby did, and the line slowed before stopping altogether. Slack appeared, and the rod relaxed.

"She's coming up. Hurry, reel, reel. Reel some of that slack in before she has a chance to head back out." Rugby paid attention. He caught as much line as he could before it moved off astern. I waited for the fish to leap out of the water, but she didn't. The line tightened, and Rugby got a few more feet. The thin braided line came closer to the back of the ship and the rod arched. "She's sounding again. Get ready."

Rugby pressed against the footrest and strained, keeping the fish from descending more. The line stopped, and he reeled as he leaned forward. An hour passed and both fish and foe continued this competition. I knew from my years of doing this job that the fish wasn't as big as some of my previous catches. Thirty minutes on the reel and she would've been mine, but Rugby wasn't seasoned for such a struggle.

"How are you doin'?" I asked.

"F…fine," Rugby stuttered. I had spent years away from the States and found it hard to place their accents. He wasn't from the South and damn sure wasn't from Texas. I was puzzling over this when, at once, all my thoughts ceased. I jumped to my feet like a man cheering a home run. A beautiful fish rocketed from the ocean a mere twenty meters away. The elongated snout penetrated the surface, followed by a glimmering head, and the hard shark-like hook of a dorsal fin.

Aside from Mr. Sick moaning on the floor, not one mouth had the ability to remain closed. Its pectoral fins flicked, brushing off a ray of water as its back stiffened. At the tip of its flight, the swordfish paused, almost freezing in mid-air. Instead of arching around to go in headfirst, the great swordfish flopped on its pale belly. The dark water exploded white as the magnificent creature disappeared into the ocean. The fishing line slacked, then jerked and grew taut again. Not once did the photographer snap a shot.

As the swordfish vanished, I careened my head about, scanning the rough waters for trouble. For more than a year now, that trouble came in the form of a massive bull shark with red scars on its dorsal fin. It had made a habit of attacking my catches. Already this morning, the shark stole a tuna, but some days it could be an insatiable enemy. This shark hated me, and I too hated it.

"Oh, she's trying to throw the line. Keep at it, boy." I attempted my best impression of an old sea captain with a gravel voice. Part of the experience these men pay for is the acting. They want adventure like the ones Hemingway wrote about and I was going to give it to them. Rugby reeled in hard and the fish followed. The camera steadily snapped as Photo Boy pressed the flash button rapidly with his index finger. The fish jumped, tugged, and fought, but no matter what she did, she couldn't resist the pull working her back to the boat.

"It's a monster," Rugby said. I wanted to disagree. In my experience, this was a young swordfish and nowhere near the monstrous size these beasts could grow to. I wanted to tell him this but instead, I lied.

"She sure is."

Time is a funny thing and what seemed like mere minutes had already turned into another half hour. The fish closed in on the boat and I grabbed the gaff to retrieve it.

"You OK?" I asked.

"My arms are cramping. They hurt a lot," he said.

Something surprising to me had kept happening as of late. Most of the men who came on these trips were quick to tell me how tired or hurt they felt. I grew up where men were men and didn't complain. You dealt with it, but the more college kids that came here on their parent's money, the more bellyaching I heard. I didn't want to judge them, but it was getting harder not to. Fighting a giant fish was hard work and it did cramp the arms and stiffen the back, but this was part of the trade.

"Do you want me to take over?" Photo Boy asked.

"No, I'm fine. Hey Billy, come look." Their ill friend, Billy, moaned and rocked at the invitation. Resting halfway in the hatch of the cabin, and with his arm still shielding his face, he made no attempt to get up. Rugby eased forward in the chair, giving slack to the line, then pulled the rod back close to his chest. Using the muscles in his back to do the work, he relieved some of the struggle from his arms. I laughed in silence, knowing how sore he would be in the morning.

"There you go. Reel her in. She's ours now." I shouted over the churning of the engine and splashing of the sea.

"Why do you call it a her?" Rugby asked. "Kind of sexist, you think? I mean, it could be a male."

"Old sea tradition. Doesn't matter, eye on the prize. Keep reeling."

The kid did and once again the fish jumped, shaking her head to throw the hook. She submerged, continuing the fight. Rugby pulled and reeled and worked until finally, the fish was at the stern of the boat. I went for the line's leader with the gaff to bring her aboard, but the next swell dipped our stern low. Water careened about the deck, surrounding our feet, but my mind focused on the fish.

Swordfish can be dangerous when provoked, or if in fear for their lives, will fight back. I've heard tales of small fishing boats punctured by the swordfish's massive bill. Kojo had a story from his youth about a fisherman harpooning a swordfish. Standing on the bow of his dingy, the man sank one harpoon into a fish that onlookers estimated at ten feet long. When the man reared back to cast another, the fish torpedoed out of the water and pierced his heart.

This wasn't a fish to take lightly, so when the boat dipped, and the swordfish leaped over the low platform, I panicked. Her slick body slid through the open hatch of the transom.

She was six feet long, and although small for her kind, was as aggressive as a tiger shark. She slapped and flopped, whipping about her tail fin. Her elongated bill sliced back and forth, burning to connect with some form of human flesh. I danced out of the way as the first real signs of life in the sick guy came to the surface. His body hung half out of the cabin, and one slap of the tail fin against the hull sent him scrambling for cover. He slammed the cabin hatch to keep the fish away.

Rugby drew his legs up and screamed in terror. Paparazzo cleared the ladder at light speed to take safety at the helm next to Kojo. I jumped over the fish, pushing around the rugby kid. The tail fin snapped out, striking my leg, tripping me. I crashed into the cabin's hatch that Pukey barricaded.

The fish bucked and broke one of my rods as the hook released its barbed hold from her mouth. I don't like hurting fish, but I'm not opposed to it either. This fish was dangerous and aboard my vessel, it could be deadly. Scuttling to my feet and holding hard to the gaff, I slapped it into her side. The two little hooks wouldn't hurt her but would allow me to control her better. I worked her back to the opening of the transom from which she had entered.

She flapped, her dark eyes stabbing at me with complete hatred. Blood from the small puncture wounds mixed with the water on the deck, but it was minimal, and disappeared quickly.

"Give me a hand," I cried out to Rugby, but he didn't move from the chair. Kojo slid down the ladder to help shove the fish overboard. It struggled but with the help of the slick deck, she went back into the briny blue. She jerked one way, then the other, unsure of which direction to go.

"What are you doing?" Rugby screamed, finally putting his feet down.

"Freeing the fish."

"That's my prize. How could you? I paid for that." Rugby snarled, eyes flaring with anger.

Who the fuck is he talking to? Smash this motherfucker.

I ignored the dark impulse in my mind. Sure, it would feel great to smash this guy in the nose for disrespecting me, but I'm not that young of a man anymore. The need to rush to violence wasn't a priority. I have thrown hands before, so there was nothing for me to prove. I took in a deep breath of ocean air to calm myself before saying, "You didn't pay for a kill, you paid for a trip. I don't kill catches, especially ones like this swordfish. Those are the rules."

"Fuck your rules. I paid for a trophy." A tear rolled out of the guy's eye and I stared at him without empathy. The cameraman snapped a couple of pictures, leaning into Kojo as he did, and Kojo shoved him away. Rugby's eyes never left me. "How could you throw it away?"

"This is a sports fishing vessel. There's no need to kill these creatures. Besides, now it will get bigger and make more fish."

"I wanted a trophy."

"Then have mommy buy you one. I'm not hurting the sea life for you."

"Fuck that, I want my trophy." Rugby shouted, rocketing up from the chair.

"Sheldon, what's going on?" Billy, the sick boy, groaned from within the cabin.

"He threw back my fish," Rugby whined. I didn't know if these two men were friends or lovers. They spoke gentle to one another, without masculinity. "Wait until my wife hears about this. We paid good money—"

"Your wife?" I asked with a genuine look of surprise that didn't go unnoticed. The look of his upset face caused a chuckle to cross my lips. One glance at his ring finger confirmed a golden band.

"You ponder something amusing?"

Oh my god, put this prissy motherfucker on his ass. Put him on his ass, right now.

"Ponder?" I laughed at him. He wasn't amused. "What? You keep a thesaurus in your back pocket?"

"We paid good money and my wife is gonna be highly distraught." He used ten-dollar words where two-dollar words would work. It made him look more like an ass than educated. The urge to punch him overwhelmed me, but I restrained myself. He fished out his touch screen phone and started texting. It wouldn't take much movement from the boat for that small black thing to go over the side. It looked expensive and I never wanted one. "God, why don't I have service?"

"Because you're at sea, dumbass."

"Excuse me?"

"No cell towers."

"I can't believe this," he said. I'm not sure what he was wanting to say.

"Look, this is how big game fishing's done. We tag and release. We didn't get to tag because of all—"

"Wait, you mean you do this all the time? You throw back perfectly good fish?"

"Look, man, it's not like you would have eaten that fish, anyhow. Let it live."

"Live? I wanted a trophy. So, you're telling me that I paid for something, you took my good money, and now you aren't going to give me what I paid for? Which are you, a barbarian or a thief, because I thought you were an American?"

"Watch what you say," I warned.

His face scrunched with a snide reply, "Oh yeah, why?"

"I am no thief, but I'm both an American and a barbarian." A twinkle of fear appeared in his eyes.

"You must dwell from an unincorporated part of the country, because in New York, we're civilized."

"I've never been to New York."

"You should cultivate yourself. This is highway robbery."

"Robbery?" I laughed. "This is to protect the ocean life."

"As I said, I don't care, I want my trophy."

"Why, to show off to your aristocratic friends? Fuck you." I smiled. His tongue gnawed at me and I liked him better when I mistook him for a mute.

"Take us back to the island. Wait until I speak with your boss. I know people."

He looked back at me with a glare and a schmuck snarl.

"You know people, but do you know how to swim?"

"Pardon?"

I calmed myself with a sigh and crossed my arms in front of my chest before saying, "Get off my boat."

"Oh, I will as soon as we—"

"No." My interruption was harsh, halting him at once. "Now."

His shoulders slumped at my order and I'm not sure he was still breathing. There was no land near us. His voice shook as he said, "You are not serious?"

"Do I look like a man who jokes?" I strolled over to the cabin and pulled a Louisville slugger from a pair of hooks above the door.

"Oh, Mr. Fancy-talker in deep shit now, mon." Kojo laughed, pushing the photographer toward the ladder and off the flying bridge.

"You can't throw me off," Rugby said. Photo Boy joined him, mean-mugging me, but gripping tight to his camera.

"Yes, I can. This is my ship." I patted the bat against my open palm and spoke softly. "You speak down to me again, and I'll throw your yuppie ass overboard, you understand me?"

What? No. Throw them off. Throw them off your boat. They disrespected you.

Rugby said nothing. His only gesture, a hard swallow on words never spoken. "You and your fairy fuckin' friends can sit down and shut the fuck up until we get back to the island."

I climbed the ladder, taking my place at the helm, and allowing Kojo to deal with our outraged customers. I didn't speak until we got back to port and only to laugh as birds dived in for scraps of dead fish, frightening the yuppies. Pulling the AJAX into her slit, I ordered them off my boat.

"Wait till we tell your boss how you treated us."

"Fuck off, douchebag." I hoisted a one-finger salute. By the shock on their faces, one would have thought I executed a baby dolphin in front of them.

"That word is offensive to women. I can't believe you would use such a derogatory form of speech. Welcome to the twenty-first century," Billy said, looking much better with dry land under his feet. He turned to give me one more insult before completely departing, "Savage."

They stuck their noses in the air at me. I could hurt all three of them if I wanted. They muttered something else but were already too far away to hear. I hated these types of guys, and they were one of the reasons I had come to the island. My home country was becoming pathetic.

"Jacob's gonna be upset," Kojo said.

"I ain't worried about it."

"I am."

Chapter Two

Covered in blood, seawater, and sprinkled with bits of fish, the AJAX desperately needed a swabbing. We took care of this bit of business before venturing to our favorite drinking establishment - the White Whale. It was a hole in the wall, a place with dirty floors and deafening music, but at least no one bothered you. Despite the small rotating group of energic tourists, a man could find a place to sit in the White Whale. They could drink away their days while contemplating life and worrying over mistakes.

Island Rum has a way of boarding the AJAX at times, but in most cases, I tend to save the hard drinking for the White Whale. Walking through the double doors, Kojo snatched a stool at the bar and ordered two beers. Sweat and the stale odor of hops wafted by my face as I cruised the length of the bar. The place was jumping for a weekday. More tourists meant more tourist women, and I enjoyed the atmosphere. Decorating the walls were pictures of amazing catches with many nameless fishermen.

I did recognize a few locals in some of the frames, but the two photos which always stole my attention were hanging behind the bar. Nailed to a beam separating the two mirrored sections of liquor was one black and white photo and one in color. The black and white one was a famous photo of Ernest Hemingway with a giant marlin. The colored photo below the Hemingway was of my recorded catch. The marlin laid along the deck of my ship and I carefully kneeled beside it. The fish was weighed, the picture taken, and she was returned to the sea.

I couldn't help but smile every time I saw this photo of me. King Louie, the hefty gentleman who owned this establishment, set me up a shot of Island Rum and a bottle of Krystal Ale - my usual.

By the time I took my seat at the bar, I was sure word had gotten back to our employer about the college kids. I use the term 'employer' loosely. Jacob Coke ran all the chartering businesses for the island, but he was an extortionist, not a boss. The thing is, unhappy customers were bad for business, and Jacob Coke hated bad business. My head napped on his chopping block, but I didn't care what Jacob had to say.

"Nicanor, why don't ya go home?" Kojo asked, wiping the excess beer from his lips.

"I just sat down and I'm far from being plastered." Static on the television created a fuzz, but I made out a caged octagon with three massive letters in the middle. Balancing on the counter, I cranked up the volume so I could hear it over the rest of the bar. I couldn't believe King Louie could get cable on such an old television. It looked like the one I used to play Nintendo on at my grandmother's house.

"Get da fook down, mon," King Louie said, not moving from his chair behind the register. I paused for a moment, ensuring the picture stayed, then plopped down on my stool. Satisfied with the clarity, I tossed back my shot. The harsh rum burnt my eyes, but I downed it and ordered another. UFC commentators, Joe Rogan and Daniel Cormier, were speaking, but I couldn't hear a thing.

"Well, turn it up," I shouted to King Louie. The stout, or should I say plump, man rolled his eyes.

"I got it." Her voice caught my ear, a familiar one that I was always glad to hear. Jazz, a beautiful waitress and good friend, patted King Louie on the shoulder as she squeezed around him.

"Nicanor. Kojo. How da hell are ya?" The island native greeted us while standing on her tiptoes to increase the volume on the old box television. My eyes couldn't escape the magnetic draw her long legs had when coming out of her short shorts.

"Hello, Jazz. How's it going?" I asked.

"Good, ya piece of shit." This sparked a burst of shared laughter among the three of us. "Which young bait ya got ya eye on tonight?"

We both scanned the bar, playfully searching for some young female prospect in need of a good evening. There were none.

"There'd be none if you'd come home with me." I clasped my pleading hands together.

"Oh no, not again." She shooed me with a flapping of her hand like I was a pestering fly.

"That's what you said last time." I grabbed at her hand and batted my pearly blues at her. "You know you love me. Come on, Jazz. You're the only one that can tame my tainted heart."

"It ain't ya tainted heart I worry about," she said to which Kojo spit his beer.

"Shut up, Kojo."

"Ya guys kill me." She laughed with that friendly smile. "I gotta work. Have fun."

"I love you, Jazz." Still keeping the tone of our playful banter.

"I know, ya damn fool." She flashed me her seductive smile, bumped her hip, and sauntered off to help some other patrons. Watching her walk away, my mind wandered back to the few nights Jazz spent under my sheets or I under hers. She was beautiful, lovely, but in no way did she want to settle down with me. Jazz wanted to leave the island, head for America, live the dream. Her goals weren't mine, and because of this, I couldn't be romantically set with her. Aside from Kojo, Jazz was one of the only islanders I cared to party with. I turned my attention back to my drinks, pleased with our good humor.

"Why ya stay here?" Kojo repeated his earlier question.

"I'm gonna watch the fight, drink some beer, then try to take some split tail home. Is that OK with you, ma?"

"No. I mean, why stay on da island? Why not go back to da States?"

"And leave all this," I swooped out my arm in a grand gesture and declared, "Never."

Besides, ain't like you got any family or friends to go back to the States for.

My smile dwindled. We drank.

The buzz of the bar drowned out the television and I stole the remote from behind the counter. Mashing the volume button down did little to increase the sound as the men entered the cage to their walkout songs.

"Damn it, King Louie. You need some speakers for this fight. How am I supposed to hear the commentators?"

"Ya could go watch it at ya house, ya cheap bastard."

"You know you'd miss me."

"I need a vacation," he said, flapping out his newspaper and returned to reading.

The Light Heavyweight Champion entered the octagon second, but it was the other fighter of the 205-pound division who I focused on. Henry 'Haymaker' Starr, the challenger, jogged around the ring, rotating his head, and swinging his arms. He loosened up as the champ, Viktor Silva, climbed the steel steps of the cage. Viktor squatted at the entrance and made a cross over his body. Then explosively, he sprinted, feet landing with heavy booms that vibrated the canvas as he crossed to the corner marked with a large red post. The two locked eyes across the ring, zoning out the rest of the world. The crowd stood to cheer.

"Why ya smilin'?" Kojo asked. I pointed at the television.

"Watch. See the guy in the green shorts? Watch this guy. He's gonna win tonight."

"Dis sport is too violent for me."

"Too violent for you?" I laughed. Either Kojo was lying, or he was getting old. "You watch and mark my words. You're gonna witness history. Haymaker will be the first man to beat Silva to become the UFC's Light Heavyweight Champion."

"Over Viktor Silva?" King Louie said, eavesdropping on our conversation, and rising from his chair. To the moans of a disappointed few, he yelled for one of his bartenders to kill the jukebox. "Man, ya crazy. Nobody beats Silva. Nobody."

“You watch, King Louie. You watch.” I reached over the counter and grabbed a mug. I poured a shot of rum into the glass, followed by an entire beer, and bit the bite of the first gulp. Wiping the excess foam from my beard and mustache, I continued to run my jaw. “Kojo, you’re right. We must go to America and watch one of these fights in person. We’ll get front row seats so close we can taste the iron in the air from all the blood.”

“Sounds appealing.” He mocked. “But I can’t go. I have a family. But I’m serious, why stay on dis island?”

“Yeah, da world is happenin’ in America,” said King Louie.

“Nothing’s happening in America,” I said into the froth of my glass. In two large gulps, I hit a pocket of rum that punched my throat. I winced but washed it down with more. “America’s not a place of happenings.”

On the television, a bell sounded, the clock started, and the two met with four-ounce gloves. Sizing one another up, the 205’ers held their respective stances. Henry’s arms squared up in a traditional boxing stance, while Silva’s hung loose and low. Viktor started the show, but Henry landed the first shot. Viktor threw a lazy low leg kick, and Henry made him pay for underestimating him.

He didn’t check it but came across the top with a right that sent Viktor wheeling back. The crowd erupted in a gasp, but Viktor regained himself and launched a jab forward, catching Henry sprinting in. The two squared up in the center, exchanging a fury of blows.

From Henry Starr’s corner, the microphones picked up his cornerman shouting, “Stick to the plan. Don’t rush it, Henry.”

Kojo took a swig of beer and cleared his throat while wiping away the drops from his upper lip.

“I’m serious, mon.” Not only did he overplay the island accent with the tourists, but it came out hard when Kojo drank. He pressed against the brass railing running at our feet and leaned back on his wooden stool. “Ya have no family here and no plans to tie ya down.”

A group of patrons at the rear of the bar exploded with laughter, but the fight and Kojo’s yapping masked the sound. I reached for a bowl on the bar, hoping to find a handful of salty peanuts, but to my disappointment, found only air. I occupied my tongue with another large gulp of my boilermaker.

“I have plans.” I forced another drink of booze down my throat. “I plan on drinking, fishing, and writing a novel.”

“Writing a novel?” Kojo laughed, making fun of me and half-choking on his drink. “Ya been writing dat novel for five years now.”

“Four years.” I protested.

Henry ‘Haymaker’ Starr caught Viktor with an overhand right, stumbling the champ. Those in the crowd not standing launched to their feet to join the rest in the arena. Some cheered and some booed. The bias of the crowd vanished as they cheered for a good punch or kick more than a fighter. Viktor rocked back against the cage, but Henry didn't rush in. Viktor had an uncanny ability to lure an opponent into his trap. His ground game was on a master's level, and if Henry rushed in, the fight would be over. Henry had done his homework.

"Who cares?" Kojo shouted, breaking my attention from the fight. He only ended up reminding me that I had a drink in my hand that needed my attending to. "Ya got nuttin' holdin' ya here. Why not go back?"

"I have no family there and no goals either. Why not stay here and have the same?" I hated talking about this. Kojo worried about my safety and thought I was reckless when it came to the matter of Jacob Coke. Most men on the island feared even the name of the Coke family, but I wasn't one of them. I took a hard swig from my beverage, never lifting my mouth from the rim until the glass was empty. "The water is better and so is the fishing. Terrible fishing back home. Small disgusting fish. No good."

"Yes, dis is true, but America's ya home."

"No, home is where the ass sits and right now, home is the White Whale." Slamming my hand down on the counter, causing bottles and glasses to leap, I demanded, "Where's my drink!"

King Louie waddled over a shot and beer, "Ya home? Den pay rent, ya cheap bastard."

I ignored the fat man.

"Besides, what's *your* goals?" I asked Kojo, ignoring King Louie.

"To be da Captain of me own ship." Kojo declared in a Napoleonic gesture with his hand over his heart and his head erect.

"Then fine." I slammed the counter again to the annoyance of King Louie and other patrons. Tiny droplets escaped the rim of my refilled mug. "My goal is to be your first mate."

"Dis is no good. I work ya too hard, mon. Why not go back to America and finish dat writing ya ramble on about?"

"Hey, I have sold stories to magazines, short stories, good stories."

"Good stories?"

"Did I say good. I meant great. Great stories to magazines and when I finish this novel, you'll see."

"Finish da novel," Kojo said. Another bellowing laugh followed. "Ya speak as if ya are da greatest writer of all time."

"Damn it." I hit the counter again, grinning, then holding my beer high in the air. "I am. You wait and see. Besides, you know I don't care to go back there. Why are you trying to get rid of me?"

"I'm not, but I tank for ya safety, ya should go."

"Safety, my ass. I can handle my own."

A man at the other end of the bar caught my attention. He hunched over his beer as if retrieving the secrets of the universe from within. I have stared into my own mug from time to time and not once have any secrets revealed themselves to me. This islander wasn't unfamiliar to me, although I couldn't recall his name and I can't say we were friends. He fishes another boat, so I see him at the dock almost every day.

"What's wrong with him?" I asked King Louie, trying not to draw the man's attention. By the way he lost himself in his beer, I doubted anyone could steal his attention. King Louie leaned in.

"Samuel lost his son in Queensbury." King Louie didn't have to say anymore. I knew what had happened to the man's son. Queensbury, the capital of the island, was in the midst of a hard-fought war. I positioned my back to Samuel, not wanting him to hear me and not wanting to see him.

"Crazy. War on the other side of paradise. It's so strange."

"Yeah, and tourists still flock here despite da fact a massive street battle is ragin'," King Louie said.

War? What does this place know of a real war? Only a little skirmish compared to what we saw. The cold, the dead, the rain. Remember it? Remember it? Remember it until it consumes you and you choke on it.

I shook my head to submerge the inner shouting voice with a gulp of beer.

"Poor sap." I no longer wanted to see the man's misery. I didn't need to see it or have it remind me of memories better left buried. I wished Samuel would go away. The television flashed, catching my eye, alleviating the dark cloud surrounding my mind. I forgot about Samuel, his dead son, and the war on the other side of the island.

The bell sounded for round two. Henry 'Haymaker' Starr shuffled back to the center of the octagon and Viktor mirrored. Neither man looked tired and had the energy of two fresh fighters only starting their bout. The two large men traded shots, with Viktor catching Henry on the temple. Henry's legs unhinged, and although he stumbled, he didn't fall.

Viktor rushed in for the kill, shooting low for a double leg takedown, but Henry scooted back. His arm shot out behind him, fingers searching for the cage to keep himself on his feet. Henry found the black-coated chain-link fence and managed to keep one leg from Viktor's range, but the champ wrapped his fingers around the other.

Henry stuffed Viktor's attempt at a takedown, pulled his leg free, and reset himself in the center of the octagon. This bought him time to recollect his head before Viktor continued his pursuit. The champ charged in and wrapped Henry, but Henry shoved his hooks under Viktor's arm. Viktor threw two quick elbows, snapping them off at a close range, but neither did any damage. Henry planted his feet and lifted Viktor. With a flashing spin, Viktor braced himself for a slam to the ground. Instead, Henry pivoted and smashed him against the cage.

The impact sent an earthquake across the ring. Henry pushed away, creating the distance best suited for his punching power. He loaded a right cross, but Viktor vanished, and Henry punched the air Viktor once occupied. His fist pummeled only the cage, as Viktor trotted back to the center of the ring. As Henry circled about, Viktor fired an inner mid-thigh kick that Henry ate.

Viktor followed Henry about, keeping the challenger in range for more leg kicks. The crowd hissed as Henry absorbed a series of thigh shots. Viktor trailed Henry like a tiger stalking its pray as he circled the perimeter of the octagon. A deep redness grew behind the snap of his kick. The clock counted down and everyone knew with the pain in his leg, Henry needed an end to the round.

One heartbeat passed; two heartbeats passed. Another kick stung Henry's leg. There came a hitch in his step, but he circled.

One heartbeat passed; two heartbeats passed. Another pinpoint kick. The clock sank.

One heartbeat, two heartbeats, another kick, and Henry stopped circling. Viktor sensed it and Joe Rogan called it.

"Haymaker's hurt. He's taken a lot of damage to that leg and I don't think he can stand much longer."

"I agree, Joe Rogan. You can't take those leg kicks from Silva and not suffer for it. He's gonna have to shoot for a takedown if he expects to survive this round," Daniel Cormier said.

"I don't know. The Champ's ground game is something else. I don't think the Haymaker has the skills to compete with Viktor on the ground."

He planted his feet, hands high, and bit into his mouthguard. Viktor loaded up for a crippling leg kick, and Henry smiled. Joe Rogan and Daniel Cormier spotted it and replays enjoyed highlighting it later. Henry's plan had come to fruition.

Henry had studied tape of Silva and had learned one small detail, a flaw in the champ's game. With each leg kick, Viktor lowered his right hand ever so slightly, leaving him open for a counter. If Viktor would have paid attention during weigh-ins or before the fight, he would have noticed Henry's thigh muscles were massive. Henry had spent the entire camp building his legs to be able to absorb Silva's kicks.

Viktor swung his right leg, and the hand lowered. Henry stepped forward, slamming a right counter hook into the Champ's jaw. The crowd roared as Viktor's legs went wobbly, shuffling back on unsteady feet, chicken dancing to regain his balance.

Now Henry gave chase, stepping forward without so much as a limp in his step. Viktor, the great champion he was, motioned Henry to attack, but this was all a façade. Henry didn't wrap him up or try to push him over but stepped in while punching. Viktor covered, but to no prevail did he stop Henry's shots. Henry landed seven unanswered left hooks and right uppercuts in a row. Still on rubber legs, Viktor shuffled out but didn't get far.

Henry pummeled with pinpoint accuracy, his arms pumping like pistons. Viktor tilted one way, then over-corrected with a looping right. It glanced off Henry's shoulder, who rolled under it and came up hard. The uppercut sent Viktor back into the cage and a frantic energy through the crowd. Henry lunged, planted, then torqued his hips to drive one last hard hook to the champ's chin.

I leaped to my feet, the barstool toppling over with a fearsome bang. In my excitement, I knocked my mug off the counter but caught it in mid-air with a swoop of my arm as if I had rehearsed the whole ordeal. I jerked the mug up to my lips, spilling foam onto the wooden counter, and took a deep swig. Eyes from the other bar patrons went from the television to me, but I didn't bother with them. My only concern was the fight.

Viktor's body buckled; he crumbled. Henry reared back with a left, ready to cement the champ into the floor, but the referee was on him. He grabbed Henry and rotated the sweating fighter away from his downed opponent. To Viktor's credit, he scrambled for a takedown, but there was nothing behind his attempt. As the referee moved Henry away, Viktor flattened on the canvas, defeated.

"Holy shit," said Joe Rogan.

"Haymaker. Haymaker. Haymaker." Daniel Cormier added with his hands pressed against the sides of his head in pure enjoyment and disbelief.

The crowd, and I, were on our feet while the announcers were shouting into their headpieces. Henry threw his arms up as he whirled around the octagon, screaming with joy and unsure of where to go. He had crossed a threshold that no other fighter had crossed before - defeating the legend. The man who came in as an underdog challenger was leaving the champion.

In all my crazy fight fan cheering, I hadn't noticed my overturned stool and would have fallen hard if Kojo hadn't picked it up for me. I threw a shot of liquor into my mouth, grimaced at the bite, and demanded another round to go with my beer. Other people in the bar, stained with my hysteria, were also appreciating the fight.

"God, is that not great? The Champion of the World." I could barely catch my breath and resisted the need to pull at my hair. Energy pumped through me without a serious outlet. Not sure if it was from the booze or the fight, but I felt elated. "Amazing. I love a good fight as much as I love a good woman and a good book. And to hell with you, Kojo, I will finish my book here."

"Yeah, but ya distract yaself too much with da fishing and da tourist women."

"I won't argue that."

"I fear, as my friend," Kojo started. I rolled my eyes at yet another parental speech. I didn't listen to my own father when he was alive, and so these tones rang deaf on my ears. "Ya wasting ya life here. Besides, after today, Jacob's gonna cut off ya business."

"My business?"

"Ya balls." King Louie injected, acting as if he wasn't eavesdropping.

Kojo nodded, adding, "And he's gonna fire ya, friend."

"And you." I pointed out.

"Yeah but dis don't matter. I be fine. Dis be my island." Then as if on cue, the double doors opened and in walked the round face of Jacob Coke. Sweat drooled down the sides of his obese cheeks and his clothes stuck to his massive body. Two men followed behind him and took seats at the bar. They did their best to look casual but appeared more like fish out of water.

"What in the hell are you doing?" Jacob shouted at me, getting the attention of everyone in the bar. Although born on the island, he fought hard to erase any notion of islander from his accent. His obtuse entry sucked the air from the bar, prompting the perversion of the patron's good time. My eyes never lifted from my drink to greet him. "I said, what the hell are—"

"I heard you." The tone in my voice silenced nearby conversations.

"Then answer."

"Answer? Who you talking to?"

"You. Now answer."

Fuck him. Who's he to talk to you like that? Tell this guy to go fuck himself.

"Fuck you." I'm not good with demands. He stepped one foot forward and my fist closed.

"What?" He asked, unaware of the danger he was in. I sipped on my drink, the joy I experienced earlier from the booze and the fight was fleeing me. "What did you say to me?"

"You heard me. I don't need this shit and I don't need those fuckin' yuppie college kids' shit. What more could I do?"

"You could do your job," he said.

"And what's that entail?"

"Show paying customers a good time. Not to drive them off." Jacob slammed his hand down on the counter. *How annoying?*

"I'm not killing a fish for sport. That's not how it's done anymore." My eyes drifted from my beer to the television to find the newly crowned Light Heavyweight Champion of the UFC standing in the center of the octagon. A team of men surrounded him as well as the color commentator, Joe Rogan, and a beautiful creature in a black dress. Her auburn hair hung long behind her back, enhancing the flawless features of her face. Alice Monroe was an apparition of Hollywood starlets from years ago and not even being marooned on a tropical island could hide her name from one's consciousness.

"I don't care how it's done." Jacob took another step forward and his two goons rose but kept their distance. "If they want a dead fish, then you give them a dead fish."

My spidey senses tingled. Trouble's brewing, so I chugged my beer. Kojo kept his eye on the television during all this. He sat calm and cool. Rising from my barstool like a gunfighter incarnate, I burned with intense hatred. My jaw clenched as he continued to flap his gums, "You work for me, so I tell you what to do and when to do it."

"I don't work for you. I captain my own ship."

"It's my charter."

Fuck him. Knock him out.

"I did my job," I said, ignoring the dark voice in my head.

"Fuck what you think. You don't think, you do what I tell you. If I tell you to show them a good time, you do that. If I tell you to shine my fuckin' boots, you do that." My knuckles turned white, and my heart rate elevated. I don't know if it was from my hatred or the adrenaline from the UFC match, but I wanted to fight.

This motherfucker told you to shine his fuckin' shoes like you're his bitch. You gonna take that? Gut him.

"Shine your shoes? Is that what you said?" I cracked my neck. Kojo decided it was time to intervene, putting himself between me and Jacob.

"Come on. Let's go." Kojo tried to shove me along, but I anchored in place.

"Oh, no." I moved him aside. "Shine your shoes? I'll shine your shoes when you go fuck yourself."

"That's twice you said that to me. Maybe you forget who you're talking to."

"I don't care who I'm talking to. I know who I am and what I can do and that's all I need to know. So, get out of my face before you can't regret this mistake. I'm warning you, this ain't a game you wanna play."

"Warning me? You warn me? I own you." He shoved a pudgy finger in my chest. As a knee jerk reaction, I palmed him back several feet. His two goons didn't react fast enough and only the counter stopped him from falling. They squared up, ready to jump at me, and Kojo stared over my shoulder, unimpressed by the commotion. Jacob acted disinterested as he pushed himself away from the bar, but there was panic in his eyes.

"Motherfucker, you don't own shit. Nobody owns me."

"You son of a bitch," he said, straightening out his sleeves. I'm sure he thought he was surprising me when he came with both fists raised. He halted abruptly at the tip of my blade which poked into the plump roll of abdomen bulging over his belt. His men moved, but he halted them.

Kill him. Stab that motherfucker. Come on, don't be a bitch.

A thrust of my wrist and he shrank back from the pressure of my knife. "I don't charter through you no more."

"I'm the only charter business here. You don't charter unless it's through me."

"The only thing going through you is my knife." Adjusting his shirt in some vain attempt to prove he wasn't scared, Jacob reversed. I eyed his men, twitching my knife and smiling.

"I'll have you *taken care of*," he said. My grin only infuriated him further.

"It's a small island." I sheathed the knife as he edged out the door, his girth rocking from side to side. His men followed, but I failed to see them out. My stool beckoned my returned and so I obliged. "Now, on top of no family or goals, I have no job."

"Told ya." Kojo sipped his beer and King Louie brought me another. "Why'd ya do dat? Ya cha'der ya own, he'll kill ya."

"I'm not worried."

"Day look mad. I tank ya a dead man," Kojo said.

"A dead man? I hear that a lot."

"Why did'ja bring out da knife?"

"Why do you ask so many questions?"

Why didn't you kill him? You're scared. You coward.

"I like to. Ya could've taken him wit'cha fists. Ya could've taken dem all. Ya a warfighter."

"I *was* a warfighter."

"And what'cha do now?"

"Like I said, I will write, and I will fish." The door opened again, and I half expected to see Jacob walking in with more armed thugs. My hand reached for my blade, but I stopped. Instead, a beautiful blonde strolled in. She surveyed the atmosphere before taking a seat at the bar. "And I'll still find tourist women to bed."

I finished my drink and abandoned my stool but stopped before leaving.

"I hope I didn't jeopardize your job."

"Please, dis is my island. I work wherever." I patted Kojo's shoulder, ordered him another round on me, then made my way to the long-legged blonde at the end of the bar. I pushed my sun-kissed hair behind my ear and brought forth a seductive smile that had a way of helping. Eyeing the absence of a wedding band around her finger, I moved in.

"Wanna dance?" I extended my hand. She tossed her long hair over her shoulder and cut her eyes at me, judging me, sizing me up as she took a swig from her drink. A debate waged in her mind, but the biting of her lower lip was her tell. Interested, her soft blue eyes smiled, making her even more desirable. She accepted.

"An American?" she asked.

"I don't know that dance."

She laughed and sat her hand in my extended palm. Her long bronze legs glimmered in the dull low hanging lights. We strolled onto what's considered the dance floor but was merely a section with tables pushed away. A man once told me the way to a woman's heart was by dancing because dancing was the imitation of lovemaking.

Now I'm not the best dancer, but I have a few tricks. Most of these female tourists, so young and ripe like freshly picked fruit, knew only how to bump and grind. While not exactly my forte, I didn't mind them grinding on my leg. She pressed up against me and we danced like two lovers. Her colorless shirt clung to her magnetic curves, and it wasn't long after we left that I was able to strip the clothing from her heated body.

Chapter Three

Seven days passed without retaliation from Jacob. Seven days of fishing on four different charters and seven days of not once looking over my shoulder. I refuse to fear any man, and although I doubt Jacob's anger will blow over, if there's no smoke, I won't look for fire.

A complete week of ease sailed by when on the eighth morning, I awoke in a frenzy. In these waning hours where the sun and moon plays tug-o-war with the sky and the entire island slept, my creative mind bloomed. Overtaken by an impulsive fever, I ripped the covers off while soaring out of bed with an ache to rush to my computer. This gripped me harder than any fear or any need of a drink ever had.

Naked, the blue light of my computer screen bathed me as I hammered the keys. Apart from starting the coffee maker, this incredible inspiration to work on my novel cast aside any usual morning routines. The hot steaming caffeinated drips created a melody to accompany the tapping of my keyboard. Although fishing provided me with funds to survive, writing fueled me. Well, writing and booze, but it's the writing which gives me purpose. It's the closest thing to a religious service I know.

My fingers, minus the missing pinky, jabbed down with little effort or interruption from my mind. They attacked like striking snakes. Words spat out on the screen faster than I could read them and the story, a memory, unfolded. This was my story; I lived it. I know it well but thinking of a novel and getting it on paper are two different things.

Nicanor's Shack

On most occasions, this task was like hammering a nail with a rubber mallet, but not this morning. Before the sun fully rose, the tale materialized as if on its own. I cranked out words on the fluorescent screen, pausing only to fill or sip my coffee. Daylight crept through the cracks of my shutters, but my eyes were oblivious to this act of nature. Although I live on a gorgeous island, I'm not a scenic writer who needs a beautiful landscape to inspire my muse.

No distractions allowed me to submerge into the depths of my story. I saw not the screen in front of me, nor did I smell the ocean air coming from the sea. Instead, the heat of a desert sun baked my face and the rhythmic pops of gunshots filled my ears.

Recalled nightmares funneled through my fingers, documenting my dread for all to read. Friends I had known, who died far too young, stood immortalized within my pages. Although their faces were the same in my mind, their names were different in the story. I did this out of respect and privacy. An asshole I may be, but a fucking asshole, I am not.

I banged out the keys until my backside ached from sitting, so I stood. Hunched over my desk with the steam of coffee lapping at my face, I carried on, pushing through the pain. I wrote until my fingers throbbed and my back burned, then wrote some more. In a lustful craze, I danced with a tale of war and friendship, bringing myself to kill men already dead. My stomach gnawed from mounting hunger but typing overpowered all worldly discomforts.

I wrote of men rescuing each other from horrors, torn to pieces by explosions while weaving a dreamcatcher of all things glorious and damning of battle. A group of fictional men, based on actual warriors, grew more real to me than the walls constructing my house. Their lives and their characters consumed me, but in the midst of all this writing, I found a problem. My typing halted. Something was lacking in my story that would draw a world of readership to it, but I didn't know what. Sure, it had brotherhood and war and death, but something basic was absent that I couldn't put a finger on.

It was in this thought that all my enthusiasm came to a full-tilt pause. Life vanished from my fingertips, leaving only a throbbing pulse of pain. I stood erect, staring at the screen dumbfounded. The words appeared foreign to me, even though I wrote them. There was nothing more in my gas tank, and so I returned to the coffee pot, only to find an empty canister.

I cherished coffee, and while waiting for it to refill, I slipped into a pair of boxers. Taking my fresh brewed cup, the eighth for the day, I stepped out the backdoor on the north side of the island. My white painted house reflected most of the heat from the sun, but neglect had chipped at its appearance. Despite this, I shielded my eyes from the beach's stunning bright glory.

The ocean smashed against the rocks and scampered upon the shore. A seagull sailed through the blue sky, trailing behind the echo of its own language. Surrounded by grass, my small house sat on a hill that sloped to the beach below. Cool wind against the backdrop of a warm day eased the pain in my muscles and fingers. No matter the magnitude of my drinking the night before, the ocean air reinvigorated me. I wished this scene wouldn't change, but I understood that the sun would sink, the waves would recede, and nothing lasts forever.

Emerging like a goddess from the sea, a woman sauntered upon my shore. The saltwater pulled back her brunette hair, giving the dark strands a metallic shine, and revealing its true length. A red bikini exposed her form and it was, from what I could see at this distance, without flaw. A beach towel laid pinned under a bag on the white sands of my beach, and she jogged to it.

I watched her, feeling at odds for staring, but not wanting to stop. I had been in love once, and not even that young beauty could match what stood before me. While drying her hair, her large round eyes scanned the shoreline, sensing someone watching. Not satisfied with her findings, she turned to me. A stark feeling of wanting to cower in my house crawled up my useless spine, but I didn't submit to it.

Playing it cool, I kept my stature, leaning against the back-porch railing with one arm crossed over my chest. Steam from my coffee warmed my face against the cool breeze from the ocean and I kept my deformed hand tucked away as not to draw her attention to it. To my relief, she smiled, and it burned brighter than any day. Her allure masked her true age and while squeezing the water from her hair, she waved.

"Hello there." Breath parted her full lips, but her beauty captivated me to the point that my ears were deaf to her words. She waved again, but still I didn't respond. The woman took a step closer. Her stern yet innocent face held hints of European aristocracy, and in her crystal blue eyes was a sparkle that questioned the world. She waved at me again while repeating her introduction, "Hello there."

There was a slight accent in her speech, which complimented her features, but I couldn't pinpoint from what region.

"Hello back," I replied. This eased the wonder in her eyes, and she gathered her things before walking up the small dune to my house. She didn't attempt to hide her body and held no shame in her appearance, and so she shouldn't.

"I'm sorry," she said, coming near.

"For what?"

"Is this your property?"

"The island is for everyone. My house happens to be here." This was a slight lie. I did own the property around my house and that included the beach my house backed up to.

"You hardly move, do you? You're like a statue."

"What do you mean?"

"I mean, when I said hello and you didn't respond, it kind of scared me."

"Why is that?"

"Because I thought you were dead."

"I get that," I said. She turned to spy the waterfront again as if climbing from it, she missed its radiance.

"It's so beautiful," she said. Waves tumbled into whitecaps as water rolled up the shore, then receded back. This endless process repeated for eternity. She had described the beach and yet, I heard only *beautiful*. Seawater trickled down the smooth skin of her long legs and a shallowness choked the air in my lungs. "So, you live here?"

"Yes."

"Your house is amazing. The view, incredible. Must be nice to wake to this," she said. I answered with a nod. I live in a dwelling a little larger than typical, but this is an unfair comparison to the islanders who live in huts. To tell the truth, most islanders would see my house as a luxury and nowhere near modest. Many of them ate and slept in a single room structure that housed many of their kin. Beds built in dirt and clothes worn for weeks, poor wasn't a word to them, but a way of life. Still, in the madness, they found love and joy and laughter. *Everything is in the eye of the beholder.*

"American?" she asked.

"Yeah. From Texas. You?"

"Not from Texas." She whipped her head to see something else that caught her fancy. Each syllable she muttered held a hint of gentle curiosity as if stepping out of the sea was the moment she was born. She observed things with the eyes of a child. I laughed at her answer, for it wasn't one. "Coffee?"

Her boldness to talk to a stranger, although refreshing, astonished me. Few held this confidence.

"Would you like a cup?" I asked.

"Yes."

"Cream?"

"Black." I stepped into the house and returned with her coffee. She took a seat on my wooden steps, eyeing the ocean. If someone had been walking by, they would have thought of us as old friends, or even a couple. Sitting on the stoop, we sipped our coffees, watching the boats sail across the horizon. The steam from our cups interlaced with the gentle breeze, weaving with the salty scent of the ocean. "No wonder people believed the world was flat, those boats look like they'd fall right off the edge."

I laughed heartily before the ocean's music and the chirping of birds returned me to silence. A ship's horn blew faint in the distance, doing little to disturb this scene. She moved her hair from her athletic shoulders, almost inviting me to nibble on them. I fought and won against the urge, but I couldn't deny the desire was there.

"So, is this a vacation house?"

"No. I've lived here for about a decade, year-round."

"Fascinating. How does an American come to live on this island?"

"By leaving America."

"Oh, secretive. OK."

"Are you on vacation?" I asked.

"Sort of. Working vacation, you could say. This is good coffee."

"Thanks. The beans grow on the mountain in the center of the island. They put it in the river and those that float, they keep and sale."

"Fascinating."

"You like that word."

"It's a fascinating word." Her snicker amused me. Her lips perched on the rim of the ceramic cup to sip the coffee and how I wished I was it. "What's fun to do on this island besides swimming?"

"There's great food and excellent bars."

"I don't want a tourist place. What's fun to do on this island that the tourists don't go to?"

"I know a restaurant not far from here that serves amazing jerk pork."

"Is there a dress code?"

"No."

"Then let's go. Do you have a car?"

"No. Do you have shoes?"

"Sandals."

"That'll work. Let me put something on besides my boxers and I'll take you there."

"Great," she said, pulling a pair of cut-off shorts from her bag. I slid into the house but took one peek back to see her pulling the shorts up over her butt. I don't know what I did to have such good fortune, but I hope I could keep it until morning.

Chapter Four

Café Dome wasn't much of a café or a dome. It was a hut on a pier. Enclosed by palm trees, massive bamboo shutters opened to allow guests a view of the lagoon bleeding into a raging ocean. Calm waters kept the pier and café steady as sea air ventilated the building that sat well off the beaten path. This place was renowned by islanders, for few tourists ventured here. Sad to say, because this was one of the most beautiful restaurants on the whole damn island.

Three piers stretched over the lagoon, jettisoning out from the café that connected them. Smaller fishing vessels, homemade canoes, and skiffs bobbed at the end of the piers.

We sat at the best table, with the sea to our side, and the bewitching aroma of the grill filling our nostrils. A scene like this would help to either break the ice or distract from a boring date, but neither was our case. Our conversation never wavered or faltered, and boredom never entered the equation.

"Do you always bring women here?" Her accent nipped at my mind, beckoning me to figure out where it originated from, but I couldn't place it. It wasn't quite Russian, but it wasn't English either.

"Only the strange ones who invade my property." I amused her, and while she was distracted, I tucked my deformed hand into my lap under the table.

"Oh, really?" She sat taller, back straight, breasts protruding. I pulled my eyes away.

"This way, if you're some psychopath and want to kill me, there's witnesses."

"Nicely planned, sir. And do you have many strange women *invading* your property, as you put it?"

"I will confess. You are the first."

"Good to hear. I don't want to move in on another psychopath's turf."

"Yeah, what self-respecting maniac would encroach on a fellow associate's area," I said. A small giggle escaped through her nose as she glanced over the menu.

"This place is beautiful," she said, admiring the scenery. It was simple, mainly faux bamboo constructed walls, but it filled the patrons with a time now forgotten with modern construction.

"It's the best little secret at the end of the world."

"The end of the world?"

"Oh, sorry. We have a little joke around here. People call this place the end of the world because everyone is running away from something when they come here."

"What are you running away from?"

"Who says I am running away from something?"

"You did."

"Nice ear." I adjusted in my seat, the reddening of foolishness coming over me. "I don't know if I'm running away from or to something, but either way it doesn't matter."

"Why's that?"

"Because this is paradise and your problems don't matter at the end of the world."

"I like that. What's good here?" she asked. I wasn't prepared for her question and although I had frequented this place before, I wasn't familiar with the selection.

"Jerk pork for sure, but aside from that, I don't know."

"What are you having?"

"The jerk pork." The waiter came, we ordered our food, jerk pork with vegetables, and topped off the meal with a pitcher of beer. It was too early in the day to cloud my thoughts with rum, but this didn't stop her from doing so. She asked for two shots of Island Rum, my favorite, and the waiter brought them with a pitcher of Krystal Ale. I stared at the off-brown liquid spilling out of the tiny glasses.

My novel came to mind as did my options. I could go back home and write or drink the rest of the day away with this lovely beauty before me. When she held up her shot, my decision was made.

"I'm sorry." She paused with her glass in the air. "Do you drink rum?"

Her statement wasn't actually a question but more of a challenge. My face scrunched with humor as I lifted the other shot glass. Light broke through a small cloud and strummed across a silver necklace hanging at the base of her throat. It struck me in the eyes, and I shifted away from it.

"Better than anyone else on the damn island. What should we drink to?"

"To the man at the end of the world."

"What?"

"To you."

"I've never toasted a drink to myself."

"Then to living at the end of the world."

"Sounds good. To the end of the world." We touched glasses. This marvelous woman threw back her shot without wincing, staring at me. She eyed me like a poker player reading their opponent, then eyed my drink. I knocked on the table with the bottom of my glass and tossed it back. After pausing for a moment to prove the harsh rum didn't bother me, I washed the taste away with a large gulp of beer.

"If anyone heard that, they'd think we're evil henchmen in some Bond movie," she said. My laugh caused her smile. "Has anyone ever told you, you look like a tall Shia LaBeouf?"

"I don't know, maybe."

"You do, especially when he grows out his beard. It suits you."

"Thanks."

"What happen to your hand?" she asked. My warning alarms went off, embarrassment flaring my insecurities. My shoulders ached to round, to encase me in an introvert's prison. I fought to prevent this and appear as normal as possible, but I'm sure my face hinted at my discomfort. I hide this by finishing off my mug. My deformed hand clamped my inner thigh, anchoring into place, unwilling to let go.

"It's embarrassing, really." I deflected.

"Do tell."

"Have you ever seen Tales from the Crypt?" I asked.

"No."

"It's an old horror show back in the day. There's an episode where two guys are gambling and if you lose, a finger gets cut off. Well, I played only one hand and was like, screw this." She inadvertently leaned closer, face captivated with fear and interest. Her wide eyes and open ears soaked up the story, lusting for more.

"Seriously?"

"No." The waiter sat our food down, stifling her protest, and allowing me a moment to refill our mugs. The alluring fragrance of the plates watered our mouths and pulled at our stomachs. I wanted to dive in, to engulf my entire self in the well-prepared food but restrained myself. Flipping open my napkin and placing it in my lap, I hoped to prove I had retained some class from the old world. The food locked my eyes in place, and I tried to recall the last time I had eaten.

Surely it hadn't been too long since my last meal for I hadn't felt the effects of starvation. Poking at it with my fork, I stabbed a piece of the jerk pork which oozed with seasonings. My taste buds stood on end and my stomach pleaded for substance.

"How's your—" I started but stopped. Bypassing the silverware, she lifted strands of pork with three fingers. Tilting back her head, her lips wrapped around her crane-like digits, devouring the meat.

The charred bark held the heavy flavor, but the juices ignited the essence of the meal. A high moan rattled in her throat and her head drooped at an angle. Her shoulders rolled back, her chest rose, and her eyes opened to find me watching. She was a woman in full ecstasy for all to see and she didn't give a damn. My fork hovered over my plate. I stood transfixed, engrossed by her.

"Oh my god. This *is* amazing," she said. The fingers of her free hand stroked the small jewelry attached to her silver necklace. Sunlight twinkled off the row of diamonds that started out small but grew in size. I cleared my throat before speaking.

"What's that?" I motioned with my fork at her necklace. She released it, not realizing she had been rubbing it.

"An infinity necklace."

"It's very beautiful."

"Thank you."

"Let me guess, Grandfather gave it to you?"

"No, someone I cared about very much did." Her face mirrored the discomfort I had when mentioning my deformed hand. "They're gone now."

I read the tone in her voice, the unwavering flatness of it, and knew what she meant by *gone.*

"That sucks." I took a large drink of cold, refreshing beer, trying to think of something to say while mentally kicking myself for having spoken in the first place. At last, I settled with simply saying, "I'm sorry."

"It was a long time ago." The solemn expression melted to bliss as she crammed another finger load of pork into her mouth. "My god, this pork is so good."

"Told you so." Then I joined her in the elation of our meal. As we dined and drank, three men in military fatigues walked in, carrying AK rifles. I wished they hadn't. They caught her eyes, filling them with questions, and stole the cheer from her.

"I didn't know this island was big enough for a military."

"This island is a chain of islands and they all share a military of sorts," I said.

"They come in here armed?"

"It's because of the war."

"What war?" she asked.

"The one in Queensbury."

"No one told me of this before I agreed to come here." She optioned for the fork instead of her fingers for the next bite.

"Yeah, it's on the other side of the island."

"That seems so absurd. Why is there a war here?"

"Drugs."

"Drugs?" She stared at me confused. "Isn't weed legal here?"

"No, it's illegal, but no one cares. The thing is a big-time drug dealer on this island ships drugs to America. The American government, well, let's say they're pissed about it."

"I bet they are. Those fat bastards don't like competition."

"Exactly. They don't like other dealers moving in on their territory. So, they propositioned the government here to extradite the drug lord."

"And this started a war?"

"Yeah. See, Christopher Coke, the drug dealer, runs one of the biggest gangs on this chain of islands. They call themselves the Pain Posse."

"Wait, excuse me. The Pain Pussies?" She leaned in to clarify what I said, unimpressed.

"Clever." We shared a nice laugh. "So, even though he's a drug dealer and a bad guy, to the community he's a Robin Hood-like figure. He gives back to the poor neighborhoods and in turn, they protect him. When word got out that the government was coming for him, the people took to the streets. Fighting broke out with the local police."

"So, they brought in the military?"

"The gangs and people were getting the best of the local authorities, so they brought in the Army."

"Wow. That's crazy." She eyed the military men sitting at the bar. They wore old green fatigues from the late 1970s or 1980s and two had on red berets. The last man took off his woodland boonie cover that matched his uniform and wiped away the sweat from his brow. Their rifles slung across their backs, and I doubt they had situational awareness on them. Someone knowing what to do could unhook their AK's and kill all three men with ease before they could react.

You could do that.

In another life…

Maybe.

"Scared of the military?" I asked, staring into her questioning eyes.

"No." She shook her head. "It's strange to see guys in uniform on a tropical island, is all."

"That's true. It is strange." I returned to my food. "Know anyone who served back home?"

"Yeah. I lost a…um…a close family member. It's just surprising to see here." I wanted to push the subject, to find where she was from, but my better instinct told me otherwise.

"I understand that. I lived here for years before I knew they had a military. It wasn't until my first mate's oldest son joined that I even knew about it."

"First mate? You're a fisherman?"

"I own my own boat and cast some lines."

"Like those." She pointed out the opening in the bamboo wall to one of the handmade canoes tied to the dock. This humored me.

"No. A larger fishing boat for a bigger group of people."

"How fascinating."

"Do you like to fish?"

"I don't know. Never have."

"You'll have to come out then, one day."

"Yes. One day. But today I wanna drink and dance. Do you know of any place like that?"

"Of course. But those kinds of places don't open until the sun goes down and there's still a few more hours before that."

"Well, I'm sure we can find something to do until then." Her seductive smile made me lightheaded. As she chewed, her smile never faded. A small bead of sweat rolled down the side of her face and I wanted to wipe it away, finding any excuse to touch her. My lips ached to kiss her, and I had to force myself to breathe. I don't know what it was about this chick, but she impressed me with her boldness. Her every movement, from the small twitches of her jaw muscles to the shifting of her feet, excited my blood vessels.

She looked at her food, then over to the weapons once again. Her chest rose and fell with a deep sigh and her eyes stared lazily at the rifles. In a somber, yet soft tone, she stated, "Isn't it astonishing?"

"What's that?" I asked. My mind, clouded with thoughts of touching her, forgot about the uniformed men at the bar.

"Even in paradise, war still finds a place. What a shame that is." Her face lowered to her plate, shaking her head while taking a bite. "What a shame."

Chapter Five

As fast as the clouds pass in front of the moon, the night slipped by us. Alcohol filled our lips and dancing busied our legs, but it was our hands which led us to the coolness of my bed. Our fingertips roamed with the sensual cravings to fondle one another. Our bodies melted as we tangled about, interlocking with intimate passion.

The windows, strategically arranged, cooled the house better than any air-conditioner. A breeze hissed in through the open windows, allowing crosswinds to fill the house with a chill. The rhythmic beating of air by the ceiling fan created a perfect duet of white noise with the roaring tide.

An hour passed and I watched her lively nature decline into sleep. Unable to welcome that great surrender, I stepped outside to stroll the shoreline for peace. My sole companion, a bitterly cheap bottle of rum strong enough to do the trick. The full moon hung high in its glory, giving the ocean a phosphorus glow to entice lovers and hypnotize drunks.

Driftwood tumbled in the continuous surf. Small ghost crabs skittered about, scurrying to clear a path. Farther inland, the thrum of indistinguishable insects created their own form of language. A stretch of beach ran along dense tropical forest, and I couldn't help but feel something stalking me. Branches bent and twigs snapped, but I carried on, paying only a mind to my drinking. Cool sand soothed my feet until I stumbled onto a pier near a resort.

A slow tide lapped against the rocks at the shoreline, caressing and washing the stones. I lost myself in its swaying motion. The ocean, which touched all oceans and thus was inseparable from one another, was without name to me. I wished to be on my ship, under the stars, to wake early in the morning to put down two thousand words and catch a great fish. My trophy was out there, somewhere, swimming among the blue waters.

Looking back across the island to the direction of Queensbury, I hoped to hear some commotion from the war. I focused as hard as I could, but only the tide was audible to me. In the distance, a storm churned over the dark sea. Manipulated by the drink, the rolling waves tricked my eyes, crafting a haunting face in the swells. The specter's familiar yet horrible features twisted in agony, creating a magnetic pull on my attention.

Memories plagued me. I couldn't run from them, or drink them away, or inflict enough pain upon myself to escape them. Rum helped to dull the senses, and so I took a long swig. Excess liquor accumulated on my blondish-brown mane and I wiped it free, continuously staring at the floating face which never ceased to garner my courtesy. It didn't retract nor advance.

The phantom's mouth gaped open but uttered no words. It didn't matter. I could still hear the screams from the now muted voice, and the worrying pleads that ushered out. This head wasn't a mere mirage, but a living, breathing creature. Like Scrooge had wished from Marley, I asked for words of comfort, but the face had none to give. As it wouldn't speak, I had no use for its haunting torment.

Another long swig drained the bottle and I heaved the empty glass container with all the strength my drunken arm could muster. The bottle splashed and resurfaced, then bobbed before the ocean sentenced my companion to its depths.

"Nicanor, ya blood clot." The floating face vanished at the first syllable from the island accent. Three men stood abreast at the entrance of the pier, blocking any dry escape route. Their presence annoyed me. I didn't recognize them, but of course the drink didn't improve my memory or vision. "My bro'da tells me bad tangs about ya."

"Save me the twenty questions. Who the fuck is your brother?"

"Da man ya stealing business from."

"I'm guessing you're referring to that fat piece of shit, Jacob." This didn't help my situation. The three took a step forward; the leader of the trio gritted his teeth. His knuckles cracked as his hands tightened into fists. I looked past the three but didn't see Jacob there.

Jacob - fat man, little balls, I thought.

I sighed, the fog of alcohol unyielding in my brain and preventing me from thinking of a way out of this predicament. These three men were threatening, but I'm not one to be intimidated. "And you are?"

"Finn." He pounded his solid chest, stating his name with pride. He stood in contrast of his brother, a mere meat head, the muscle of the family. The three men stepped forward, the dock groaning under their combined weight. The largest of them, Finn, pulled a step ahead of his pals, his strides echoing along the wooden planks. Their sense of security came from the fact that I was alone. People tend to not like me, but I do gather a sense of respect wherever I go. Most know me as a tough man or a great fisherman, but all knew crossing me could be fatal.

Finn's two lackies never introduced themselves. They stared with laughter on their lips, amused in the ass stomping I was sure to endure. The joints in my fingers popped as my hand curled to a fist which itched to greet their arrogant faces. I longed to smash in their noses like a drunk who longs for a drink or a promiscuous man longs for a woman of the night. I made note of both lackies, then returned my attention back to the hulking Finn.

"I don't know you, Finn, and can't see how my business is any concern to you," I said. Finn snarled at my questioning him. I looked past the three Islanders to see if there was anyone else nearby. It was late. No one was.

"Ya assaulted my bro'da."

With a drunken curtsy and an amusing smirk, I confessed. "That I did."

"No mon attacks my family and lives." His warning caused my jaw to stiffen, and I corrected my drunken stance to ready for an attack. Finn postured, trying to tower over me. I didn't enjoy the threat and my short fuse burned out.

"You threatening me?" I asked. He grinned. "I don't think you got the balls to jump."

"Ya a dead mon."

"People make that assumption of me." I paused, spitting into the ocean, then I flicked my hand, shooing him away like one would a child. "Fuck off, Finn."

"Oh yeah?" His eyes flared, and he stepped closer. With his index finger, he poked me in the chest. Being threatened with physical harm was annoying but putting a finger on me was downright stupid.

"Strike two, Finn. You threatened me and now you put your hand on me. Touch me again and I'm gonna cut ya from nuts to naval." This was a warning, and if he knew any better, he'd listen. Again, he placed the tip of his index finger to my chest and pushed.

"Blood clot." His insult flicked off his yellow teeth. From his hip he drew a flay knife, the handle wrapped in tape and the blade rusty from the lack of care. Finn was no fisherman, and although I'm not positive of the dullness, I doubt he knew how to sharpen the blade. He held it awkward, as if it was foreign to him, but his gravest mistake was assuming I didn't know knives.

Without hesitation, I unsheathed the Ka-bar from behind my back and lashed out with blinding speed, catching Finn off guard. A large laceration opened across his midsection and his white shirt morphed red. A trapped groan forced its exit from his mouth. His rusty knife bounced off a wooden plank and toppled into the water with a near inaudible splash. Finn stumbled back into the arms of his friends, grappling at his wound as blood stained his hands. Small droplets dotted the deck as fright and awe distorted his face.

I stood there, chest heaving, refusing to move another muscle. My blade held steady in my hand while my vision blurred again. Three men turned into six, then back to three. I forced my drunkenness away, tightening the grip around the custom-built handle of my Ka-bar. Carved out of wood and wrapped in small strips of leather, no other handle felt right in my calloused hands. The dock's light glimmered off the serrated shark tooth fastened to the end of the handle, catching Finn's attention as he eyed the blade I had carried in combat.

Kill him. Finish him. Finish them all. Don't let them get away or they'll come back stronger. They'll make your life a living hell. Kill them. Kill them all.

It had been ages since my razor-sharp blade kissed the flesh of an enemy. I lowered my arm, showing no threat, but ready to react if they moved. They hesitated with caution, and I welcomed them on. There was no fight in these men, and when I jumped, they flinched. Stumbling, they carried their bulky friend off, perhaps to an aid station or a hospital, I'm sure. I waited in that same stance until they disappeared, head slightly bowed, eyes forward with a stabbing gaze, and the blackening abyss of the sea behind me. I stood there until the moans of the ocean called me back.

I searched for the haunting face in the waves, but it was gone, only to be replaced by a pair of distant glowing eyes. A chill knifed my spine and confusion pounded my skull. I could have sworn a giant demon head rose from the dark ocean floor, ready to devour the entire island. The mixture of adrenaline and alcohol fogged my vision, and I shook my head to clear it.

The eyes were gone. They were never there, and what I assumed was a pair of evil eyes were two burning lights of a manor absorbed by shadows.

In my drunkenness, I found I wasn't looking out to sea, but in fact, peering across the grove to another spot on the island. Many nights I had spent on this spot and not once had I seen these lights burning. In the day, the manor sat back against a hill, but at night, the darkness consumed it. Once belonging to a famous writer, who was long since dead, it's beautiful décor now fell to ruins. Being a writer myself, I had always wanted to pilgrimage there, to see what this man had once found incredible about this spot. Maybe whatever magic he found was still there, and I could bottle it for myself.

But to my regret, I had never made that journey, and now know it's unlikely I ever will. The lights burning at the manor could only mean one thing. Someone was moving in.

Chapter Six

The week sailed by and the beautiful lady with the hint of a foreign language to her accent failed to emerge from the sea again. Watching the morning wakes capsize, I sipped at my steaming, brewed beverage while idly fiddling with a silver necklace in my other hand. After my confrontation with Finn, I returned to find her still sleeping in my bed, but upon my own awakening the following morning, she was gone. A ghost of her sweet scent lingered, and I touched the impression she had left in the sheets, finding a silver necklace hiding under the pillow.

At first, I believed this to be a parting gift, but with further inspection, I found the clasp bent at an odd angle. An easy fix. I confined it to my pocket daily, safe and sound, in hopes of her return. It held no significant charm to me, but each time I touched it, her essence entranced my memory. I could smell her hair and remember reading the braille of goosebumps across her arms as the night air kissed her skin. Every thought ended with us in bed, rivaling all other women I had ever slept with.

If daydreams of her occupied my mornings, then the manor on the hill captivated my evenings. Lights that I had assumed were two evil eyes multiplied each night until the silhouette of the manor materialized. Built with loose money and superb workmanship, the art deco style of bold geometric lines and patterns were accentuated with a flair of the Jazz Age elite. The large cliffs the manor sat upon kept the rising tides from damaging it.

What parties were held there when American liquor was outlawed, and money was plentiful?

The lights from the manor fabricated the illusion of a false day, filling in details of a structure built so strong, gale force winds did little to disturb it. A tall wall of hedges kept the world from seeing the grounds, concealing the majority of parties raging through the night. In the morning, all appeared abandoned and vacant. No lights burned, no vehicles populated the street, and nobody passed the windows. The desertion of inhabitants restored the manor to its former state of destitute and it was once again only a building which stood against sun and weather for almost a century.

Rumor has it some drug dealer recently bought the mansion as a front to hide and launder his dirty money. People on the island talk, but not one had been to the house or the extravagant parties thrown there. One tourist who chartered my boat said he had been but had never met the owner.

A reef enclosed a private beach well below the manor in a secluded cove. There were only two ways to the cove: by docking at the pier or taking the wooden staircase that zigzagged down the side of the hill like a lightning bolt. I fantasized about going over the reef at high tide and docking at that pier. I'd take the staircase and invite myself to whatever party was going on there.

Charters blurred together and the excitement of the tourists uninterested me, allowing this dream of grandeur to hold my fancy. My mind grew more distracted with the mansion on the hill and that night of unrestricted sex from the sea goddess. A school of flying fish cut the surface near us and my clients rushed to the side to watch. Kojo accompanied them and pointed out the large dark shadow swimming near.

"Is that a shark?" one of the tourists asked.

"Yea, mon. A damn demon who doesn't leave us alone," Kojo said. I didn't hear the conversation between the two tourists and Kojo. The shark swam near, but my attention remained on the mansion. It was the report of the pistol that jerked me back to my surroundings. My heart skipped and my muscles reacted to searching for a shooter and expecting an ambush. I reached for a rifle that hadn't hung from my shoulder in over a decade. Even with being on the open ocean, I knew an insurgent had come back to finish me after all these years.

"What the fuck?" I shouted, my eyes and nostrils flaring as blood throbbed in my carotid artery.

"It's dat damn red fin shark."

"What shark has a red fin?" a tourist asked. I came to the side of the boat to see fish scrambling away and the dark shadow receding back to the deep.

"It's a bull shark. The red marks are scars."

"How do you know?" the overweight tourist asked.

"Because I gave him those scars." Their imaginations took over as they wondered how I had done such a feat. They continued to search for a sign of the shark, but something else caught my eye. A small boat splashed against the surf, moving toward us.

"Trouble?" Kojo asked.

"Maybe," I took the pistol from him and stuffed it in the back of my pants. The boat, a motorized skiff, barely accommodated the five men on board. Kojo limped to the cabin as the tourists moved next to me at starboard, unaware of what was going on.

The approaching vessel slowed, then idled, allowing the motion of the water to ease them alongside us. Two of the five men held machetes at their sides. I had seen these men before. They worked for Jacob, but despite their intimidation tactics, I didn't fear them.

"Hey mon, ya be Nicanor?" the man with dreadlocks asked as he stepped on the gunwale of my ship. I held my hand up and placed a foot next to his, preventing him from crossing over.

"I am. And you are?"

"Eric, mon." He hammered a fist on his protruding chest. I sighed, not caring about his boasting, and crossed my arms. "To tell da tru'd, I figure ya be dead and dis trip be for nuttin'."

I rolled my eyes, and asked, "Why's that?"

"I figured Finn killed ya, mon."

"Not even close. Look, I don't know you, but I can tell you this. You never board a man's ship without asking." I knocked his foot off my gunwale with the toe of my combat boot. He caught his balance, eyeing me with questions while pushing his dreadlocks to the side. For a moment, I prepared for a punch, but got a smile instead.

"My apologies," he said, tipping his head. The side of his shirt slid up, revealing the handle of a knife stuffed in his belt. Another man, who sat at the bow of the tiny boat, kept his hand tucked behind his back. Although guns weren't outlawed on the island, few people bothered with them. Too much legality and all the red tape led to nothing more than a headache for most. At the back of the skiff, the helmsman kept his hand on the outboard motor, ready to pull away if needed. He appeared weaponless, but who knew what he could be harboring. "I'm here on business."

"I don't have business with you," I said. The overweight tourist shuffled into the cabin, ducking under the window, but peeking out to watch the action. The other man stood tall with eyes wide to suck in the commotion, secretly welcoming the train wreck.

"Oh, yea ya do, mon." Eric laid on the heaviness of his island accent to prove he belonged here, and I was an outsider, a visitor to his land. His lips stretched over a row of crooked, stained teeth and he scratched at his patchy beard. "I need to see ya cha'der papers."

"Cha'der papers?" I mocked.

"Yea, cha'der papers. Where day be?"

"Don't have them."

"Oh, bro'da. Dat's bad."

"Didn't need them before."

"But before, ya worked for Mr. Coke. He holds da papers. No longer working for him, no longer ya got cha'der papers. So, no longer ya cha'der." He motioned to board my ship again, but I planted a hand on his chest. My boldness impressed him.

"I doubt I can buy a charter license. So, I'm not gonna trouble myself with it. So, fuck him and fuck you."

"No, fu—" He reached for his knife, but I detained his arm, jerking him forward and thus off-balance. I halted his forward momentum by lodging the barrel of my 1911 under his chin. His crew made a motion to advance but stopped when Kojo leveled the twelve gauge. He pumped the forend of the shotgun, chambering a round. The thin tourist standing next to my fighting chair shot his hands in the air despite us having the upper hand.

"I do what I want. You *tell* Jacob that. And the next time he sends men for me, you tell them to bring their own body bags. Got me?" I paused, then provoked Eric with a snarl. "Blood clot."

Fear froze him. I shoved him back, causing him to trip and land hard.

"Get outta here," Kojo said, directing them with the trench gun. They waited for a minute longer, seeing if we meant business. Then Eric flicked his head and the helmsman pulled the ripcord and the tiny engine started up. The boat pulled away, fumes from their exhaust mixing with the saltwater air, creating an appealing odor. A fisherman's pheromone; a working man's scent. The boat slammed against the tide and the five men bounced upon their bench seats until they cruised around the point and disappeared. A victory.

"Holy shit, that was amazing," the tourist still standing outside said.

"Yeah," I handed the pistol over to Kojo, who carried both weapons into the cabin. I spun around, facing the shocked tourists with a large smile. They spooked at the clapping of my hands before I said, "Let's fish."

Chapter Seven

The two tourists departed the AJAX as the darkening sky pressed heavy on the remaining light. I must admit, I love this time of the day, when the cool winds from the east beat back the heat and the horizon's purple hue held highlights of burnt orange and reds. With the sun still a blub sinking over the side of the world, the manor resting on top of the cliffs glowed. Lights dotted the mansion and headlights roamed the serpent road leading to it.

"Kojo, there goes some more," I said. From inside the twin cabin compartment, Kojo peered out the port hole and shrugged.

"Why ya trouble yaself with dat stupid house?"

"Don't you wonder who's moving in?"

"Dat man's a fool, whoever he be. Dat house ain't been lived in for years, mon. Ya know it got problems. Floor falling in, lights don't work right. Day oughta tear down dat damn house. Damn fool he is, damn fool indeed." Kojo bent back down, cleaning up the mess left behind by the tourists. Tired from the work, he threw the rag on the deck. "I need a beer."

He opened the cooler but found it empty, another common bestowal from grateful tourists. Slamming the lid, Kojo jumped over the gunwale to the pier.

"I'm gonna get a beer. Ya want one?" he asked.

"Yeah. Bring some back. I'm gonna finish up here." Blood and fish guts streamed across my deck, moving freely with the seawater. Kojo hurried off while I continued to scrub until the cramping in my arms grew too great. I dropped into my fighting chair, exhausted from the long day, and closed my eyes. Time sailed by under the fading sky, and before long, I drifted off.

The rhythm of the ocean fogged my head with the sleep of unpleasant dreams. Visions of tormented horrors filled my mind. Forgotten explosions drummed my ears as haunted memories danced to the forefront of my brain. I no longer swayed with the ocean but stood firm upon a dirt covered floor painted by the desert sands. Shadows moved about, tricking the eyes to what was friend or foe.

My hands held not a fishing rod nor a scrub brush, but the hard texture of an M16's handle. Staring over the sights, I glided down the dark corridors of an unrecognizable house. Something moved ahead, and my trigger finger reacted. The blinding explosion at the end of my barrel robbed me of any night vision my eyes had acquired.

The figure, deeply absent of light and shrouded in a mist of all colors, toppled forward, slamming against a distant wall. My men moved up from behind me, clearing out the next room as I continued down the hall. A single bulb demystified the shadow, revealing a man dressed in an Iraqi thawb with two red holes decorating his chest.

I stepped over him and proceeded along, coming to –

"Excuse me." A soft voice ripped me from my nap. I jerked upright, almost tumbling out of my chair as a woman hopped away from me. The sun and the sea plagued my aching joints with stiffness, and I wondered how long I had been out. Rotating my head on my shoulders, I loosened my neck, then peered at the woman with one squinty eye like a pirate or a drunkard.

Blinded by the sun burning directly behind this intruder, I adjusted and in doing so, a pair of long legs came into focus. I followed them upward, but a halo of light obscured the woman's facial features. I wiped the work from my hands and moved to see her better. She leaned in with an extended hand and I shook it. "Oh good, I thought you might be dead."

"I get that a lot. How may I help you?" Standing, I collected myself to look less foolish in front of her. We both paused in mid-handshake as a spark of memory slammed us. She smiled with her eyes, holding me in them for a long moment.

"Hello there." Her polite words mimicked her introduction from the week before.

"Hello back," I said. A pit of embarrassment and fear opened in my stomach. Not once in the ten years loafing on this tropical island had I ever ran back into a tourist woman I had slept with, but I had also never been so spellbound by one.

Look at you clammin' up, chicken shit. Ain't like she came here for a relationship with you. Hell, she didn't even recognize you at first. Apparently, you didn't make an impression on her.

"Fisherman." Her mind pinpointed where she knew me from, and the pleasantness on her face informed me that she was pleased. "So, this is your ship?"

Fisherman? In our night of crazy drunken sex, this was the name she called me by. I can't recall what title I gave her, but neither one of us had cared to learn the other's real name.

"I'm the captain. How may I help you?" My face held stern, but my stomach feared her answer. Her very presence, beautiful and alarming, caused me to stop breathing. Sweat trickled down the side of my face, but even in my panicked state, her calm demeanor amused me.

"I'm looking to charter a boat for a day or so," she said. A serenity overcame me and the strength in my body returned. She wasn't here about personal business between us.

"For only you?" One side of my face smiled, lifting my eyebrow as to question her intent. She didn't appear seaworthy, wearing more clothes than the last time I saw her and far better dressed than the typical tourist. There was something about her that caused the currents in my mind to swirl. Her disposition screamed of education, but not the Stanford or Princeton type. The way in which she spoke revealed a worldly knowledge and her carefree attitude contradicted the graceful manners of her aristocratic traits.

"No, about four men and I or so," she said.

"Four men and you?" I weighed her statement, looking around my boat. That's a large party for my ship, but I was game.

"Yeah, that's how I like it." The fading sun burned hard and obstructed much of my vision, but I was quite certain she winked. A lump appeared in my throat. I scrambled.

"Are *you* gonna fish?"

"I'll be along just for the ride and the sights. I'll leave the fishing to the men."

"What kind of fishing do these men wanna do?"

"Deep sea, I'm guessing. I don't know, probably sharks, but I'm sure they'll want to drink and smoke cigars more than actually fish. Are you available?"

"Why did they not come see me themselves? Why send you?"

"Because they are on business slash vacation. So, if it doesn't pertain to their business, then they are on vacation. It's kind of like I'm earning their trust by doing a stupid task. Are you available?"

"When?"

"Tomorrow morning."

"I like to push out early, so be on the dock around eight." She agreed with my terms and price with a firm handshake. Her soft palm forced a memory of the night we spent together, and it was better than I had recalled. I caught her scent on the back of a breeze. "Were you looking for me?"

"No. Why?" she asked. I shook my head with no real answer, her hand not releasing my grip and mine doing the same. "I figured there'd be a captain on this dock I could ask about chartering his boat. Is there some agency I am supposed to go through?"

"No." I found myself hurrying to say. "We're good. I'll see you at eight."

"Eight o'clock then." Our hands parted, dragging across one another's flesh, sipping from the intimacy of our first encounter.

"What's your name?" I asked before she could turn away. "Or do I just charter the boat under beautiful lady?"

I flashed my million-dollar smile, masking the fear that she had heard all this before, and I was making a fool out of myself.

"Mabel."

"What resort are you staying at?"

"Why?"

"In case you try to stiff me on the bill."

"We're not at a resort. We're at the old Fletching Manor. I'm sure you've heard of it." And here she was, the reason the lights have been burning in the old manor. My caramel beard shielded the boy-like glee on my face. My heart quickened with each syllable she spoke, and my pent-up fear melted to affection. I wanted her again.

"Everyone has. Ian Fletching wrote some incredible action novels," I said as calmly as I could. "Well, if you stiff me, then I know where to go."

"You sure are worried about getting stiff?" I blushed at her seductive smile. I couldn't reply. "Eight o'clock."

"Yeah, eight o'clock." I stumbled over my words. She nodded, raising her hand, fingers mimicking the breaking of a wave as her palm transitioned from open to close, and she strolled down the dock. Her footsteps echoed against the wooden planks and I remained there staring. Her hour-glass figure swayed as she walked, and the wind ruffled the strands of her long brunette hair. She wasn't the typical vacationing girl. There was something more to her and I wanted to find out what.

We had spent an entire night together and it was only now I had learned her name. I wanted to kick myself for talking too much. Here was this beautiful lady and I had rambled on like a virgin boy seeing a naked woman for the first time. A laugh escaped me.

Why are you acting this way? You don't know her, and she doesn't know you. What? You think she came here for you, to engage you in some idiotic fantasy you've been having? Man, you're more fucked up in the head than I realized.

And in this was the problem. We slept together and knew nothing of one another except that our bodies were compatible. My internal temperature rose, and I reached into my pocket to fiddle with the object inside. *The small trinket.* My chest sunk, and I shot my gaze to the dock. Mabel was long gone.

I thought to run after her, to chase her down before she could get away again. A part of me knew she would never be back. I knew when eight in the morning rolled around, she would fail to show at the pier and be gone from my life forever.

Good, let her go. What? Are you having feelings for her? Remember the last time you had feelings? Remember how that ended? Do you want something more with her? You think you're gonna settle down with someone like her? She's a creature of the wind and you can't bottle that.

"Of course not," I said to myself. I pushed these thoughts aside and knew my irrational thinking was unproductive. She would be back in the morning and then I'd have another chance to give her what was hers. Thinking of her coming back brought my hand to my lip and I started to rub. An old habit I kicked many years ago.

When my nerves go bad, I tended to rub my lip with the first knuckle on my hand. At times, I rubbed so much I drew blood. To circumvent this, I bit down on the side of my index finger, flickering my tongue hard against it. This created a thud sound inside my head, distracting me. Pain kept my anxiety down until Kojo brought back a case of Krystal Ale and I could calm my nerves along with my thirst.

Part Two

Chapter Eight

The morning came in with the tide and by first light, I had written two thousand words on my novel, yet failed to tack down what was missing from my story. No matter because it had to wait. There were fish that needed to be caught and so I headed to the docks. The frosty morning held the reminiscence of a cold night the new spring heat had yet to burn off.

Inside the cabin of the AJAX, I brewed a pot of coffee which warmed my hands and belly while waiting for the party to arrive. The early morning fishermen moved about the dock, but the lack of sleep and the early hour prevented any conversation.

Things went quiet, so much so that you could hear the water slapping against the pillars of the dock. Only Kojo's snoring fought the gentle sounds of the tide for dominance. He sat in the fighting chair with his feet propped up on the transom, chin resting against his chest, fast asleep. The churning of the ocean's waves crashed in the distance, far from the inlet with the piers.

Impatient to get out on the open water, I shifted my weight between my eagerly tapping feet. If I wasn't writing, I was fishing, and to be waiting on a dock was neither. I fought my hand from rubbing my lips. To say I was anxious about seeing today's party was an understatement.

I needed to learn who had moved into the old rundown mansion. A desire overcame me, not only to find out who this person was, but to punch him in the face for invading my life. That old mansion stood on the hill, unchanged for decades, a beacon of a simple life. It was grand and beautiful in its solace, and the modern world was but an intruder. Now some stranger threatened all that, preying on my peace like a shark unaware of its own devastation.

From the moment the first pair of lights flickered in that damned old manor, it plagued me, and it's this man's fault. Whoever the hell he is, didn't matter. King or peasant, I had a desire to shake him, to scream in his face, to yell, *get out of here you foreigner, you modern invader.*

My blood boiled. The irritation in my body brought my finger up to my lip and I rubbed hard. I had the right mind to cancel the charter the moment this party came walking down the pier. I would shout, *go home, charter is over, you swine, you pig, you sonsofbitches. Go home and get off my island, you blood clots.*

I paused and closed my eyes. The waves crashing just past the lagoon extinguished my anger, and through my nostrils I drew in a long breath of sea air. It was here I remembered her, the beautiful woman named Mabel, the vixen of my affliction. She approached my daydream like an afternoon tide rolling in on the back of a breeze. My hand lowered from my lips to my pocket as an involuntary smile spread along the width of my face. I can't explain why I felt this way, but had to admit, it was welcoming.

You're embarrassing. Look at yourself, man. You're allowing this girl to consume you and you don't even know who she is. Cupid is bullshit, love is a lie, and you're being a jackass.

My skin itched with unease at my own thoughts. I had closed off these affectionate emotions long ago, but she sparked their renewal. Pulling my hand from my pocket, I stared down at the necklace interweaving between my fingers, wondering if this trinket was at the root of my meandering mind. It was the talisman that kept bringing her back.

You're pathetic.

The sun broke over the sea creating a horizontal rainbow of colors bleeding across the sky. Eight o'clock rolled by and still no party. Waiting and patience weren't two of my strong suits, but money is money. Besides, I had nothing else to do this day but watch the dock and fight off scavenging birds swooping in for pieces of fresh bait.

Around nine, the coolness of the night had melted, and the heat sweltered. I busied myself with prepping the gear, but this did little to stifle my rage at their tardiness. The ocean called to me and the fish beckoned for a fight. More fishermen came and went, some chartering groups, some venturing out on their own, but all gave me the eye of avoidance.

On such a small island, gossip is hard to hide from and once Jacob blacklisted someone, everyone knew it. I didn't care for their sideways glances or whispering words. I watched the dock for my party until all the other ships were out of the marina. Eight o'clock started the timer and I was on their time, no matter if they showed or not. If they stood me up, I'd march over to that mansion and give them a piece of my mind, and if they refused, then I'd give them a piece of my blade.

At five past nine, a few men approach the dock. I sighed, believing this to be the party, but on a closer look, I knew otherwise. The crew of three didn't have a fourth, and there was no woman with them. They closed the distance between the shore and the AJAX, and it was then I realized who they were. The man out front looked a lot different without my .45 jammed under his chin.

The wooden planks vibrated in unison as they marched my way. One had a bat, one a machete, and the leader with dreadlocks, Eric, carried a stained butcher knife. Blood or rust, I couldn't tell, but whatever it was, they didn't come to talk about a charter.

"Nicanor," Eric said. Without proper introductions, the other two remained anonymous to me.

"Kojo," I called. The man with the machete leaped onto my ship, detaining Kojo with the tip of his blade before he could wake. I contemplated attacking but didn't want to risk my friend's life. My life is irrelevant. His isn't. Besides, as he informs me most days, Kojo has kids. I reluctantly sighed.

"We bring word from da boss," Eric said.

"Bruce Springsteen?"

"What?" My joke went over his dreadlock-covered head. "Shut up."

I laughed, showing no interest in his threats. With a wave of my hand, I said, "Get the fuck outta here."

He fidgeted with his knife. "Ya assaulted his men and cut his bro'da. Get in ya ship and sail away from da island, or else."

"Or else what?"

"Dis is no plea. Dis is a warning. Ya go or ya die." His hand twitched. He was unsteady with his blade, rotating it nervously around in his hand, giving up his tale. He was an amateur with a knife. His eyes shifted, unable to hold contact with my own. I can't be positive, but I'm sure our last encounter frightened him. Eric looked like a gym rat, which to most may bring an air of intimidation. The thing is, I ain't most people, and when you come to fight me, you better ready yourself to die.

I couldn't control my chuckle at his twitchy movements. The disrespect at his authority didn't settle well with him. He clenched his jaw and stepped closer. So did I.

"I'm gonna die? That's funny. I tell you what," I scratched at my own beard, choosing my words carefully. "You tell that fat bastard to kiss my ass. I ain't scared of him. I ain't scared of no man. I'll stay and go where I choose. If he doesn't like that, tell him to come down here to speak with me again. But I don't like to be threatened."

"Or what?" Eric laughed, eyeing his two comrades who shared in his amusement. "Ya gonna kill us? Is dat it?"

"I didn't say that. I didn't say that at all. But I am saying, don't."

"Ya know who Jacob's family is?"

"Yeah, the Pain Pussies." I mispronounced the gang name on purpose, knowing it would stir these thugs up.

"Oh, funny guy. I'm sure his cousin Christopher tanks ya funny if he cuts ya neck," he said.

I sighed, taking in a deep breath through my nose before saying, "If."

His long dirty dreadlocks shook as he laughed, while generating the courage to do what he had to do. I knew what he was planning and was ready for it. When he lunged at me with the knife, I side-stepped, buying myself some time and distance to react. His arm shot straight out in front of him like a spartan thrusting his spear at an enemy.

I caught his wrist, twisting his arm up and over, before dropping him to his knees with a crushing stomp to the side of his kneecap. Broken teeth launched out of his mouth under the force of my elbow. Wrenching his arm back, I tore something in his shoulder socket, but refusing to release my grip. I'm glad the chartering party was late, and all the other captains had set off for the day. Eric's screams were too embarrassing for another grown man to hear. The knife fell to the deck and I kicked it into the water before his friend could retrieve it.

As the water gulped the metal blade, something hard struck me in the shoulder, shoving me into a pillar. The pain numbed my mind, but at least I didn't cry like Dreadlocks did. To be honest, I couldn't make any sound. The blow left me gasping, but I couldn't stand there wallowing in my own suffering.

As the wannabe ballplayer reared up for another swing, I moved. The bat echoed off the pillar and not only shook the pier but rattled the swinger. Before he could protest my movement, I lodged a formal complaint with a foot to his breadbasket. He puffed, doubled over, and flapped his lips like a fish in search of water.

Eric, despite the use of only one arm, nailed me with a shot to the liver. The cramp started immediately, and the agony flared. With quick reflexes, I broke

Eric's nose, sending his strength fleeing. He hung limp around my waist, and I shoved him off with little effort. Eric stumbled, but remained standing, and snapped out a nice right cross that cracked my head back.

A lump would grow under my beard, but I wasn't worried about the pain. With his left being no good, he threw another right, and I returned the favor with a healthy hook that stunned him. Eric tipped back, teetering near the edge of the dock, flabbergasted at my punching power.

Kojo flinched, wanting to get into the action but the machete pressed hard into him. The well-oiled blade held a clean sharpness and with a simple pound of pressure, it would slip through Kojo. He had no option but to raise his hands and surrender. I wanted to help my friend, but I was busy with my own problems.

The ballplayer readied himself to knock my head into orbit, but he never swung. A loud smack interrupted him. I flinched this time, mistaking the noise for a solid impact and puzzled that I felt nothing. Eric and I paused our battle to find four sharp dressed tourists standing on the pier. A hulking brute pulled the Louisville slugger from the islander's hands. A red handprint stained the ballplayer's face and hurt plagued his eyes.

"Now, two with weapons against one guy. That don't sound—" The ballplayer slugged him in the face before he could finish. The brute, standing five inches over six feet, ate the punch and barely moved. He took it on the chin like a champ because he was one. I recognized him at once, but I don't believe the ballplayer did. He was Henry 'Haymaker' Starr, the Light Heavyweight Champion of the UFC.

"That's cute." Henry chuckled and looked to his friends who seemed unfazed by the assault on their friend. They laughed as if knowing what was to come. "He thinks he's a puncher."

His good humor landed on the player, then morphed into a stern glare before breaking both the islander's nose and orbital bone with one thrust of his massive fist. The ballplayer crumbled to the dock. A splash came, and I looked at Kojo holding the machete, its former owner swimming for his life. Having been distracted with the prizefighter's punch, the machete guy panicked when Kojo attacked.

Eric, who was no longer staring at me, eyed the champ.

"Dis ain't none of ya business, tourist. Go now, before we fuck ya up," Eric said.

"We?" Comically, Henry looked around for Eric's friends who were no longer there. "I see only you."

Eric looked around and the disappointment of abandonment flared on his face.

"And yeah, I know I look busted," Henry touched the yellowish spots on his face, the healing of a hard fight, "but I'm down if you wanna throw hands."

Eric looked at the other three men, then surrendered with his palms raised.

"I get ya ano'da time." He informed me. I nodded, then catching him off guard, shoved him into the water to the delight of the tourists. Henry, along with the three men who accompanied him, held their sides from laughing. The wind kicked up from off the ocean, rocking the pier and swaying my own balance. This and the party of men standing near my boat faded from view as two women came down the dock.

Alice Monroe walked with her arm entwined in Mabel's while clutching an oversize sun hat flapping in the wind like the wings of a bird. Large white designer sunglasses shielded her face, protecting her eyes from the whipping of her hair darkened to the tinge of an aging rose. A tight-fitting blue romper hid an expensive bikini that cost more than I'd make in several months.

Everyone in their right mind eyed Alice as she made her descent to my boat; all but me. My eyes were glued onto the other female. They walked like schoolgirls, arms linked, pressing into one another, laughing at something I couldn't hear. A ping of jealously slapped me, and I wished it was my ear her breath was caressing. Mabel wore a more practical ball cap that kept her hair tucked in. Not to say she looked sloppy or plain because even in her casual attire, she held a grace and elegance meant for a queen.

With her opposite hand, she mirrored Alice's, trying to keep the hat from blowing away. Her long legs vanished into a pair of simple short shorts. Unlike Alice who wore heels, Mabel wore sensible shoes.

A large bag hung from Mabel's shoulder, and I couldn't think for the life of me what was in there. Where Alice appeared to have come to sunbathe, Mabel had the sense of work about her. The way she moved or talked was all for some goal she hid well with her pleasant demeanor. A pair of sunglasses, not designer but nice looking, concealed her brown eyes. I looked away, hoping she didn't catch me staring.

How did ya remember they were brown? Ya don't notice stuff like that. Geez, what a punk you're being.

"Wow fella, I thought you were a dead man," the chubby man said.

"I get that a lot." I turned back to Henry to break the hold Mabel held on me. Henry eyed me, a baffled looked draped over his face, as if he tried to recall where he had seen me before.

"Thanks Henry," I said, doing what many fighters couldn't, catching the champ by surprise.

Chapter Nine

His first glance was one of complete confusion. Of course, he didn't recognize me as my long beard distorted the old familiarity of my face. It didn't help that my skin was dark, tanned hard under the ocean sun. The years had been many since we last saw each other, but I smiled, and it was there in the arc of my grin that ignited an acorn of a memory.

"Nicanor?" My name stumbled out of his mouth. I scratched at my shaggy Viking-esque beard and nodded.

Henry marched at me; the nerves in my spine signaling me to shield away from a punch. I wondered if the years of estrangement warranted a beating. Despite being well-built, a life at sea has its perks, he dwarfed me in height and muscle. As he closed the distance, I held my posture, not backing or cowering. His feet fell heavy upon the deck, eyes cut razors, peeling away the hair and years to find the boy he once knew. Then his arms spread, and he wrapped me in an uncomfortable bear hug, while laughing my name.

"Is it really you, Nicky?" He pushed me away; he pulled me in again. "What the hell? How is this – how are you here? What the hell happened to you?"

"Went on vacation," I said, gasping for air.

"I thought you were dead."

"He gets that a lot," Kojo said with a belly laugh.

"Who is this?" One of the trio of men, with his gut bulging under his bright Hawaiian shirt, motioned to me. His puzzled pig-like face with an upturned nose said it all, *someone of my standards wasn't allowed to know the champ on a personal level.* He glared down the bridge of his pinkish snout and drew his chin back behind many layers, further cementing his barnyard image.

"This is Nicanor," Henry said, allowing my feet to touch the dock again. A rush of air flooded my lungs and the color returned to my face. He said my name as if they should have known who I was, but it didn't register with any of them. Henry didn't pay them any attention as he motioned for his wife to hurry over.

"Alice, come here. I want you to meet somebody." Alice pushed past the three men to study my face for a second, judging if I was worthy of her time. She shifted her weight, perching her lips, analyzing me as if I were a piece of art. Then one of the most gorgeous smiles materialized on her face. She extended her hand and I shook it, ashamed I hadn't cleaned my mitt before touching a creature of such beauty. "This is Nicanor."

"You have a nice face." This caught me off guard for I've never had such a compliment.

"Thank you." I stuttered. I wasn't sure what to say, but she nodded in acceptance.

"Are you a fighter too or something?" The markings on my face could allure to the misconception that I had seen the inside of a ring.

"No, we," Henry interrupted before I could say anything, "grew up together. I've told you about him."

"I'm sorry, I don't recall." A sheepish smirk slithered onto Henry's face as if embarrassment plagued him. She turned to me. "Did you corner my husband in his youth?"

Alice spoke with an air of elegance, not from a birthright but from lessons. I make this statement not out of spite but of observation.

"Finest cornerman I ever had." Henry carried on, squeezing me as he spoke. "Hell, he was the one who got me into boxing in the first place."

"No," I said. "Leslie Blackwell got us into boxing."

"Oh shit, that's right. Leslie Blackwell." A deep belly laugh exploded out of him, scaring me. "I wonder what happened to him?"

I could only shrug my shoulders at the memory of our childhood.

"So, you weren't a fighter?" Alice asked.

"A fighter? Hell yes, he's a fighter. A much better fighter than I could ever be. I get the privilege of using gloves. Nicky here, he went to war and fought for real, while I got the luxury of competing in the Olympics."

"Well, it's a pleasure to meet you," the famous Alice Monroe said.

"The pleasure is mine, Mrs. Alice Monroe." She couldn't hide her joy at my recognition of her name.

"Alice Monroe Starr, if you please." She squeezed Henry's arm. They took a moment to stare longingly at one another. There was love in their eyes or at least admiration for one another's social class. They were two people who were conquering the world.

"God, man." Henry planted his bear-like hand on my shoulder, clamping my collar bone and shoulder blade between his thick fingers. I forgot how big my old friend was and found it unsettling people wanted to stand in front of him and get punched for a living. "I still can't believe you're here. It's like a dream. What are the odds I'd run into you while trying to get away from everything in the world?"

"Well, people call this place the end of the world for a reason. A lot of folks come here to get away from it all," I said.

"You speakin' from experience?"

"Maybe."

"How long have you been here, Nicky?"

"About ten years on the island." I was so lost in the nostalgia of my old friend that I forgot others were watching.

"Geez, what happened to your hand?" Out of habit, I tucked my deformed hand away from view before looking at the insulting man in the fancy collared shirt. I own my own boat, my own house, I live a great life, but still one idiot's remark can cut me. My rage boiled. The yearning to punch him festered, but I kept my hands down and my face placid.

Henry intervened before I could do or say something. His tone changed from a loveable friend to a menacing giant. "Don't be a dick, Philip."

"What'd I say? It was only a question, Henry. No need to lose a limb over it." The expensive shirt guy snickered, making the other two rich men laugh. He looked familiar, like the guy in those Ocean's Eleven movies, but more gauntly. He pushed the sleeves of his expensive shirt up. Why he'd want to wear a long sleeve shirt to sea, stupefied me.

"Enough."

"Look," the fancy guy turned to me, "I'm sorry. No disrespect about it."

The salt and pepper streaks in his hair contrasted with his heated face. Why I mistook this scrawny man for George Clooney escaped me. For someone of such wealth, I don't understand why he didn't buy himself a steak and bulk up.

"Well, don't be curious. It ain't none of your business, you pompous ass." The others snickered at Henry's insult to their companion.

"OK, my bad."

"That's a nice shirt." I mocked. The frail man seemed to stand a little taller.

"Well, thank you."

"You do know we're going out to sea? It's probably gonna get ruined."

His eyes shot daggers at me before shifting away. Pushing his sleeves up his forearms, he carefully halted them below the elbow while saying, "Oh well. One shirt is as good as another. Who cares how much it cost?"

For some reason, I felt this was a dig at me, but he didn't push it and neither did I. Henry stepped into view, smiling at me as if nothing had happened with his accomplice.

"Came to a small, out in the middle of nowhere island and ended up running into my oldest friend. How crazy is that?" Henry repeated his earlier excitement while waving Mabel over. "Mabel. Here's a plot twist for your article. Champion of the World goes to an island for a little R and R and finds his long lost, and thought to be *dead*, friend."

"You're a writer?" I asked her.

She nodded. "I write for Spartan Men's magazine."

"Wow." Impressed was an understatement. Of course, she'd be a writer, but I started to question if she was real or plucked from my deepest fantasies.

"You know my magazine?"

"Like many men from my youth, I discovered it in Iraq." I wasn't a subscriber, but Spartan Men's magazine was popular among military guys during the war. It covered everything from sports to clothes to weapons, and even had scantily clad women in the articles. I hadn't read an issue since my deployment, but I had fond memories of them. "So, you're doing an article over this big ogre?"

The boyish insults and good-nature ribbing came back immediately. We were two brothers who had found one another and picked up where we left off.

"Haymaker has captivated the fight world. Everyone is simply enthralled with him."

"Why wouldn't they be, he just beat the best of all time," I said.

"Fight fans clamor for more. They want to know what his daily life is like. They're calling him the heart of the fight game," Mabel said. Henry shook his head, blushing. "People love him. The man who came up short every single time, but never quit."

"I got cheated those times." Henry snapped, a sore issue that even the championship belt had yet to remedy.

"And people know it." Alice wrapped one arm around his neck and ran her other hand across his chest, calming the large brute. "That's why they love you."

"The fact you won the title on a two-week notice. Fucking amazing," I said.

"You know." Mabel words lingered in the air as she faced me, the fuse to a burning question. "I think it would be cool to interview you, considering you knew him from before he started out."

She wants a private session with you?

My inner monologue nearly made me blush, but I kept my composure.

"We might wanna push off, mon," Kojo called out, already turning up the accent. "Fish be a waitin'."

"Yes," Henry bellowed. "Enough talk of work. Let's get on with the trip."

He draped his arm around my shoulder and led me onto my own ship as if he owned it.

Chapter Ten

The sun's rays touched the ocean's surface, imprinting colorful strokes of nature across the ripples that would be hard to capture on a canvas. Sea gulls, diving into the water for a late breakfast, faded away the farther from the island we sailed. Standing at the controls on the flying bridge, I read the current and aimed for a favorite stream of mine where the fish were plentiful. As the AJAX cut through the briny dark blue, I took notice of Alice and Mabel sitting on the starboard side. Clutching their hats, they bounced and laughed at each wave the AJAX slammed against.

Some folks get annoyed by the harsh motion, and although I didn't know exactly what they were laughing about, their bliss projected a welcoming glow. I wanted to be a part of their enjoyment. It had been nearly two years since a woman had boarded my ship, and what a shame, for their presence only heightened the grandeur of the sea.

I eased the throttle back, slowing the AJAX. There were no markers, no land masses, nothing to indicate we were in the spot I wanted, but I knew. I had fished these waters for a decade. Sure, I had a compass, but I didn't need it when heading out to my favorite locations. Kojo busied himself with baiting hooks and casting lines.

Henry, along with his three friends who he had failed to introduce me to, sat about the stern of the AJAX. Great puffs of white smoke rose with their laughing conversations. Only three of them smoked on cigars. The leaner and younger of Henry's accomplices, the one who took great care in his appearance, smoked on some device that nothing burned from. A strange device from the world I left behind. The heat of the day intensified, willing the young man to remove his shirt. I could be mistaken, but I thought I caught the fat guy eyeing him. Then again, with well-defined muscles, it was hard for one not to notice.

As always, Kojo's missing leg was of great concern to him, and he avoided the passengers unless they had a question. He didn't want to bother people, and because of this, most people paid him no mind. I caught the gauntly, salt and pepper guy eyeing Kojo's limp, and I bet it gnawed at him to not make a comment. If he did, Henry wouldn't be able to save him. I'd throw the bastard out to sea and leave.

Oh, how I'd love to see that. Yes, I would. Please say something. You felt it, when putting the hurt on Finn. You felt that raw power, that hunger. God, please let him slip up again.

I shook the thoughts from my head. Seeing Kojo hustling hit me with a sense of guilt. Here he was, doing all the grunt work, while I stood at the helm and eyed the scenery like some military officer I had despised during my service. On more than one occasion I told him to slow down, to ease up on his old bones, but his work ethic was rivaled by none. He enjoyed life at sea, telling me once that he was the luckiest man alive, getting paid for something he'd do for free.

Henry ascended the ladder behind me. Most boats had a chair on their flying bridge, but I preferred to stand at the top controls while piloting my ship. Inside the cabin was another set of controls to pilot the ship from during terrible weather.

Henry leaned over the railing, eyeing the two women making their way to the bow with extreme caution. The ladies crossed the gunwale on the leeward side, avoiding the wind to ease their journey. The bow had no chairs and was only a deck covering the sleeping quarters below. I had never had someone lounging on the deck, but the girls found it the perfect place to do so.

Mabel picked up Alice's pink cellphone and kneeled to capture Alice with the rest of the ship behind her. She studied the digital image on the phone's screen, and after being satisfied, looked up at me. We caught eyes, holding each other there for three beats of a heart. The corners of her lips curled ever so slightly before she looked away and stretched out next to Alice to soak up the sun.

Henry rocked back with a whistle and a grin, and the sense we were at a family reunion filled me. He patted me on the back in good nature, scanning the boundless ocean. I don't know what he was looking for, but I could bet money he was trying to find the island. We were away from the things of man. To the Universe, we were specks of dirt, dwarf micro-organisms on the open blue. Out here, a man learns how small he really is, even the Champion of the World.

"Man, I've never been on the ocean like this before," he said.

"Really?"

"Yeah. I've been fishing in several countries but never where I couldn't see land. This is fuckin' mind blowing to me."

"This is my normal."

"Now that's amazing." He chuckled a deep held breath and continued, "I have to say, I'm jealous."

"Jealous? Of me? Bullshit. You're a UFC champion." I brought the boat to a trolling speed and stepped away from the wheel. There was nothing to hit out here, and the speed was so slow that I didn't worry about holding the controls. When things got going, either Kojo or myself would get back to the helm to drag a large catch along. I paused to look around, pleased with the calmness of the ocean.

"Man, this is my idea of peace. I spend my work week rolling around with sweaty men, then I get punched in the face."

"Sounds painful."

"Can be. Look at all this. It's like you found Utopia or paradise."

"In a way, I guess I have."

"God, that's great. The peace you must have out here. I mean, look at this." His arms opened wide to showcase the vast horizon. Taking in a deep breath, he expanded his chest greater than figured possible. "The freedom you have here is priceless."

"Yeah, but I'm sure the gold around your waist pays a lot more."

Henry laughed at this.

"It pays good."

"Apparently. You bought that old mansion."

"Business, Nicky. I learned a while back ya gotta have many avenues of money coming in."

"Is that what those guys are around for? Avenues?" I motioned to his three companions lounging around the stern.

"Something like that. The guy who looks like a stockbroker from the 1980's, that's Philip Gables. He's like my business partner."

"Who's the other two then?"

"The big guy, that's Scott. He owns the agency I work for."

"Wait, don't you work for the UFC?"

"I do, but my management company is IFA." He said this as if I knew what he meant and when he saw I didn't, he elaborated. "International Fight Agency."

I shrugged my shoulders, never hearing those words before.

"It's one of the biggest agencies out there. Everyone knows it by its real name, Iron Fist Agency." He laughed at his own amusement. I grinned but didn't quite get his joke. "Scott is like the boss of my agent. He's a good dude. He and Philip go way back. They used to work together during the war."

"They were in the war?"

"Not like you were. No. They owned companies that had government contracts. Big money. Kind of boring if you ask me."

"Boring? It's kind of interesting if you ask me."

"It's not. We are basically business partners. But that's all work and I don't care to talk about work right now. I'm here on vacation and to my damnedest, I'm here seeing a ghost." He slapped his big palm against my shoulder. I wanted to lurch off-balance but stood my ground.

"So, who's the other guy?"

"Oh, that Nathan Spears, the mmoo-vie star." It wasn't a stutter but a slur that came out of nowhere. I wasn't sure if he was imitating the line from Gilligan's Island or if it was a real slip of the tongue, but I hurried along as to not draw attention to the slur.

"Never heard of him."

"Man, you have been gone a while. He's a big action star."

"No movie theaters, remember," I said. The trio of men cheered as the rude, fancy-shirted guy, I forgot his name, spun the reel. By the way the rod bent, the catch wasn't large, whatever it was, but it fought back and forth with him.

"But you do get the internet?"

"Kind of. But I'm too busy to watch movies. I use it for research, mainly."

"Research?"

"I still do a little writing."

"Seriously?" he asked. I nodded. "I remember you used to write back in the day. That's awesome, man. Make any money from it?"

"Not really. A few short stories in magazines. More of a hobby." Talking about my writing made me uncomfortable, and I normally refrain from it, but this was Henry. There was a connection between us, a bond that reappeared even after all the years we spent apart. I forgot how comfortable I could be around people, which was an alarming revelation.

"I bet it's a shark," the movie star said to his friends, breaking my conversation with Henry. Fancy shirt guy nodded while gritting his teeth and pulling back on the deep-sea fishing pole. Movie star bounced with anticipation behind him, patting the guy's shoulders. The fat guy sat back smoking a cigar like some mafioso. I surveyed the scene, studying how the line moved and fought; it wasn't a shark. A small tuna at best, but not a shark.

"Nathan's a big UFC fan," Henry said. I couldn't remember what we were talking about before the action started down below. The buzz of the line ripping from the reel was my drug, and fishing, my obsession.

"What?"

"Nathan. The movie star," he said, not slurring the word this time. "He came backstage after a fight one time and we hit it off. Became good friends after that. Alice loves him, and he's been helping her out with movie scripts. He's a cool guy."

"What the hell," Philip said as the rod went limp. He continued to reel in, and I could see a slight bend in the end. Something clung to the line, but it wasn't fighting. At once, I knew what happened. I motioned for Kojo to help.

"Cool. So, you married Alice Monroe? I'm sorry, Alice Monroe Starr." The name, Monroe Starr, hit a cord with me, but I couldn't remember why. I guess it doesn't matter.

"Yup, rich girl podcaster who landed on TV and now the movies."

"I've seen her on youtube. Any big movies?" I asked.

"Some but minor roles back in her twenties. It's a nightmare for us right now because she's pushing mid-thirties and with nothing coming along, she thinks the game's over. I keep telling her that streaming is the way to go nowadays." I didn't know what this 'streaming' word meant. The only stream I knew was the one my fish came out of.

"So, how'd y'all meet?"

"She was at a fight one night and we hit it off."

"Seems like you hit it off with people who come to your fights."

"I guess so. What can I say, winning a MMA fight is an incredible feeling, second only to sex. But yeah, we got married three years ago. Popped the question after that war I had with Edson Grossman."

"Oh, I remember that fight. That was a bad one. Your face opened up."

"You think that was bad, you should have seen the number I did on his knuckles with my chin. Wow, I know his hands were hurting the next day." This I laughed at. Henry took a drink and eyed his beautiful wife sunbathing at the front of my ship. "Shit, I guess I shouldn't say 'war' considering."

"Considering what?"

"Well, you've been in a real war."

"So? Ain't like I have a market on the word. Besides, that fight *was* a fuckin' war. A goddamn barn burner. Don't lie, you were going out, then somehow you fuckin' pulled that rear-naked out of nowhere."

"It's one of my highlight reels."

"What's Dana White like?" I asked.

"He's cool. The media doesn't get how cool and down to earth he is." I was a moment away from asking him to continue when a shot rang out, interrupting us. I flinched at the concussion and a large splash of beer jumped from my bottle, spilling down my knuckles. Shaking the beverage from my hand, I watched as white smoke kicked up near the starboard side of the ship, and the trio of rich men panicked.

"Get outta here, ya devil," Kojo shouted before firing off another blast with the trench gun. The water rippled with tiny splashes as a bluish gray fin streaked with red scars broke the surface. It circled about the stern irrationally, as if confused on which way to go. Kojo pumped the forend of the shotgun and fired again. Water wrapped around the fin and it vanished beneath the sea.

"You got'em," Nathan, the movie star, said. He rushed to the side of the boat in hopes of seeing the devil shark float to the surface. To his disappointment, it wasn't there.

"Only frightened him." I descended the ladder, scanning the water for signs of the shark's return. If Edson Grossman was Henry's war, this was mine. Our dance was simple: he'd eat a catch, we'd fire, and he'd swim off. A plague on only my life, for no other captain of any other ship seemed to be pestered by this fish. Many locals, full of backwoods superstition, believed this red fin shark to be a curse upon me. The Devil meant to drive my foreign ass away.

"I'll rebait the hooks," Kojo said, handing me the shotgun. I stashed the trench gun back in the rack above the cabin door and caught the trio whispering with concerned faces.

"Troubles?" I asked them as I exited the cabin. They looked to one another to see who would speak. Nathan did.

"Did you know you had a rifle aboard?" The excitement he had when watching Kojo blast at the shark was gone and in its place was a look of concern.

"Shotgun, and yeah, it's my ship. Why wouldn't I know?"

"Well, *we* didn't know."

"It's not your ship. Why *would* you know?"

"Don't you think that's kind of unnecessary?" Nathan asked.

"What?" I wasn't following.

"Don't you know how dangerous those things are?" His question led me to chuckle.

"Do you?" I mocked. I had carried a shotgun through the streets of Fallujah and knew full well the power they have. The other two men sipped on their drinks but eyed me with the same questioning demeanor as the movie star. He sucked on his electronic cigarette, blowing out a white cloud.

"They're unsafe, is all I'm saying."

"I'm unsafe."

"You are just a fisherman."

"Would you be willing to wager on that?" I said.

"He's got you there." Philip cracked and Scott followed. They laughed and pushed about the young Nathan. I started up the ladder to the flying bridge.

"You know I do my own stunts, right?" Nathan boasted, as if testing his manhood against me. I halted halfway up the ladder and turned back to him.

"So do I." I didn't flash it, but I didn't hide my deformed hand as I ascended the ladder. They caught my point. Philip and Scott couldn't contain themselves and ribbed the attractive young movie star.

"Do you think that shark will return?" Philip interrupted my ascent.

"I don't think so. The shotgun normally scares it off. It shouldn't steal any more of our catches today." The trio sat back with smug laughs, firing up cigars and telling stories. They tossed back whiskey and beer without care. None of this concerned me. I climbed to the helm and casted a glance over to the bow. Only Alice was there, lying back to catch the sun, the pink phone resting on a canvas bag next to her. I looked to the port side of my ship, but then brought my alarmed attention back to starboard as I heard the yelp and then a splash.

Chapter Eleven

The water kicked up, muting the yelp, and the sea sucked Mabel into its liquid embrace. Everyone on the AJAX rushed to starboard to see what had happened, but I didn't pay them any mind. I stood on the railing of the helm and dove overboard. The cold water came crashing in on me like an unexpected ice bath, stripping the oxygen from my lungs. I hurt to get back to the surface and when I did, I found Mabel treading water.

"You OK?" I asked.

She pushed the hair out of her face and smiled, laughing at the predicament she found herself in.

"I'm fine. I slipped. Why did you jump in?"

"Because I've never lost someone on a trip, and I'll be damned if I will now." She smiled and now I wasn't sure if it was the cold water or her beauty that stole my breath. "Let's get to the stern."

"Where?"

"The back of the boat."

"SHARK!" Kojo shouted from the flying bridge. He pointed out past us and I scanned in that direction. It took me a moment, for the surface of the ocean is great at camouflaging danger, but then I spotted it. Cutting across the small wakes, the red scarred fin of that damned ol' bull shark came straight for us.

Mabel treaded, searching for the shark, but as she had not seen the threat, she didn't hurry as most people would. She floated as if hypnotized, enthralled by the danger coming her way. Shoving her broke the trance and she kicked, swimming to the stern.

Kojo pumped and fired the trench gun, spraying the water with buckshot. This didn't stop that damn beast from coming. That fish and I had a long history with one another and so I guess this was his chance to finally get me back.

"Get up," I said, trying to push Mabel up on the transom. Henry was up on the flying bridge, watching without moving. I didn't know where Alice was, but I did know the trio of rich men stood there, not helping, amused by what was sure to happen. Mabel threw her leg up on the low platform and pulled. The rollers spun freely, and the water clung heavy to her body, causing her to slip back into the ocean.

The shark cut closer, picking up speed. Mabel shook the water from her face, and I wasn't sure if she understood the danger we were in.

"Someone help her!" I finally shouted, still trying to push her onto the platform. Henry flew down the ladder, but it was Nathan and Scott who took Mabel by the arms and lifted her out. I looked back. The shark was fifteen feet away and coming hard. Kojo fired again, peppering the water around the fin. This time he did hit the beast and perhaps slowed him some. I didn't wait for help or need it. I practically leapt out of the water as the red fin shark sailed by, aching to nip at my leg before I jerked it from the water.

"Holy shit, that was close," Philip said, then followed it with a laugh and a toke from his cigar. "I thought you said the shotgun scared it off."

I didn't look at him as I crossed over the transom and marched into the cabin for two towels.

"Thanks," Mabel said as I handed her one. "Can you believe how massive that shark was, baring down on us?"

"Yeah. That was mighty foolish of you." I tried to hide the anger in my voice, but I don't think I did a good job.

"I slipped. Scout's honor." She held up two fingers. The warmth in her face reflected that of the sun's. To ensure she had my attention, her fingertips grazed the wet hair on my forearm. My knees shook. I no longer felt the coldness of the ocean's water and looked away before she could read my thoughts any further.

"Scout's honor is with three fingers." I pointed out.

She corrected herself and kept that smile that could melt butter or the iciest heart before saying, "Honest. I slipped."

Before I could speak, Scott slapped me on the back. "Holy shit, that was exciting. You jumped in there after her despite the shark."

"Well, to be honest, I didn't know the shark was still there," I said, turning to scurry up the ladder to the flying bridge. Everyone was still delirious in what had played out, but I only looked to Kojo, pausing long enough to tell him I was fine.

I adjusted our course, keeping the speed at an easy pace as the wind kicked up. My wet clothes plastered to my body, but the chill offered a pleasant relief from the heat of the day. Everyone went back to water cooler gossip like chattering banshees, replaying and retelling what everyone had seen for themselves. Alice returned to her sunbathing, but it was Mabel that puzzled me the most. As soon as she was somewhat dry, she acted as if nothing had happened. I cut my eyes at her firing off pictures of Kojo and the others.

"Fascinating," she said looking over her camera.

"A fuckin' shark," Henry said, climbing the ladder. "That was some of the craziest shit I have ever seen."

"It happens."

"You get sharks a lot?"

"I don't like to catch sharks, but yeah, they like to come in after the catches."

"Ever get a great white?"

"No. I've seen them, but I've only caught tigers and bull sharks."

"I was down in South Africa and got to watch the great white sharks leaping."

"Are you serious?" There was no hiding my excitement. I had seen documentaries of this and had dreamed of going to see such an act. "I've always wanted to see that."

"It's amazing." Henry added. "The power and force they have is breathtaking."

"The great whites we get here don't really do that. Some claim they do, but I've never seen it."

"They do," Kojo called out.

"You lying bastard." I jested. Having lost my drink when I dove overboard, I fished two more from my little cooler, handing one to Henry. He accepted it.

"Wait, I thought you hadn't been on the ocean like this before?" I asked.

"I haven't. Not like this. Down in South Africa, we weren't far off from shore." He turned in a complete circle. "Out here, I don't even know where land is. Tell you the truth, this is kind of scary now that I think of it."

"Ports back that way." I threw a thumb over my shoulder.

"How can you tell?"

"I can feel it," I said. Henry stared in the direction I pointed, trying his hardest but failing at seeing any signs of land on the horizon. Nothing laid before him but an infinite blue ocean.

"I still can't believe I'm here talking to you." Henry popped the top on his Krystal Ale and took a long drink.

"Why's that?"

"Because I thought you died in Iraq."

"Really?"

"Yeah. When I didn't hear from you again, I got in touch with home, but no one knew anything about what happened to you."

"No real reason to go home. I mean, hell, you were in California, Dad was dead, Mom was a loon, and mentally, being back there wasn't good for me."

"Didn't you have a job lined up for when you got back?" Henry asked, leaning the small of his back against the railing.

"Yeah, I did. A bank job for my uncle."

"Good money, right?"

"I'm sure, but some nine to five job behind a desk would have driven me mad. Stiff tie, a clean shirt and shit. Naw, I was a field Marine. I couldn't have done that. I'd work there for five years, be attached to some annoying probably cheating chick who despised me anyway, then one day come home to put a gun in my mouth and end it all."

"Fuck." The word rolled out with a chuckle before he took a swig and wiped his mouth and said, "That's dark, but I get it."

"You ever go back home?"

"I had a fight in Dallas once, so I took a day to cruise the area. Saw Claire." A lump appeared in my throat. I wanted to change the subject.

"Oh yeah?" I faked my enthusiasm.

"Yeah, she said she wrote you overseas but never heard anything back." I shrugged my shoulders at this, not caring to hear about my ex. "I guess she thought you were dead, too."

"Times were tough over there and thinking about home only made it worse. You can't have your mind distracted by stuff at home, otherwise, you'll get your head blown off."

"I get that." Henry took a long drink to trod over the awkwardness of a touchy subject. "I tell you what was crazy, going back to our old high school."

"How was that?"

"So strange. It seemed smaller than I remember. They had a picture of me in the trophy case after I won the Olympics."

"That's bad ass." I remembered the trophy case in our high school's hallway and could imagine the picture he spoke of.

"Weird though. I mean, how many times were we told that we wouldn't amount to shit."

"True, but we did get caught ditching a lot to go get high or laid." I laughed into my beer. Those days, no matter how nice it was to remember, always brought back memories I cared not to see, and so I changed the topic. "So, she's writing a book about you?"

"Mabel? Well, now." He stood erect, clicking his tongue to the back of his teeth, gearing up to delight me in another tale of his exhilarating life. "It started out as an article when I fought Tunney."

"I saw that one. A slug fest from start to finish."

"Yeah, tough chin, but I knew he tended to drop that right hand."

"Yeah, but you took some shots. Both of you did. I remember thinking after that second round, how the hell were either of you standing or seeing for that matter."

"I was worried the doctor would stop us then, because my right eye was fucked. Anyway, Mabel stuck around because Dana White said I'd get a shot at number one contender. Mabel was gonna wrap it up after that, but then I had that quick turn-around for the title."

"I don't know if quick is the right word. I mean seventeen fuckin' days, that's lightspeed."

"Something like that. Anyway, she stayed on for that one as well, and here we are. One article turned into a few, and now with me winning the title, she wants to write a book about it. I couldn't say no. She's a part of my entourage now. She loves MMA, what can I say."

"That's pretty cool."

"She's a wild one, I tell you."

"What'd ya mean?"

"She lives by her own rules. Moves to her own beat, music only she can hear. She's a wild child, truly a free person in modern America. It's endearing. *She's* endearing."

"Shit, it looks like all of you are living by your own music."

"All of us?"

"Your entire entourage." I waved a hand down at the three men socializing below. "I guess having money allows you to do that."

"I guess so."

"Shit, man. Looks like you're living pretty good. You've come a long way since that poor kid on the streets I once knew."

"Yeah," Henry said with a hint of embarrassment behind his chuckle he was all too quick to hide with a drink. "Got a lot of rich friends these days. When I decided to get a vacation place, they were eager to join me. Besides, I hear the weather is great this time of the year."

"It is. Imagine your ass running with rich kids when we were young. It's laughable." My humor hit a nerve with Henry. All signs of good nature faded from his face. He smirked, but it was with uneasiness.

"I guess so." He drank. "New life. New friends."

"Guess so." I felt like we were battling to see who could make the conversation more awkward. Henry stood tall and downed the rest of his drink in one gulp, shaking off any agitation from his mind, as a delightful grin appeared.

"There's a party at my place tonight." He opened another Krystal Ale.

"There's a party at your place every night."

"This is true, and you should come. There's gonna be plenty of women there."

"I do well in that department, thank you."

"Mabel will be there." He teased with a poking elbow.

"Fuck you," I whispered comically, turning my attention back to the sea. Part of me was dying to tell him I had slept with her, but another part didn't want to let that cat out of the bag. Mabel stood near the starboard side, snapping a picture of another fish being reeled in.

"Come on. I see how you look at her. Why not, she's hot," Henry said.

"I ain't the kind of person that looks to settle down."

"Settle down? What the hell are you talking about? I'm talking about hooking up with a beautiful chick. I'm not propositioning you to marry the girl."

"I know, but y'all are gonna be here for the rest of the season and I don't want her to get attached to me. I'm a free man." I declared with a hand over my heart and my chin held high.

I couldn't deny the fact she was beautiful, and I did want to spend more time with her. As if hearing my thoughts, Mabel flashed a wide-eyed grin at us and snapped a photo. Joining us on the flying bridge, the clouds parted, and the sun boasted her appearance, announcing her arrival. She leaned against the handrail, looking sternward, casting her eyes down at the long fishing poles reaching out into the great unknown. Strands of hair, commanded by the wind, whipped at her face.

She warred with the free-flowing tresses, tucking them under the hat she wore. To me, she fought a losing battle.

"What are you two up to?" she asked, firing off another picture.

"Catching up," Henry said, and on that, he tipped his beer upward and popped his eyebrows at her. He gulped the beer and belched. I must admit, the Champ could drink.

"I'm ggoo-nna—" His face froze for an instant and the words drew long from his lips. His head glitched and he finished his sentence, "reel in something before this trip is over."

Henry climbed down, leaving Mabel and I alone. My palms started to sweat, and I chewed on the inside of my lip. I wanted to say something, but I feared I'd stumble over my words and make a fool of myself. I eyed her from my peripheral, scared she was staring at me, but to my relief, her look was on the ocean. I sighed and my shoulders unwound.

What are you scared of?

I wasn't in the market for a relationship and damn sure didn't need anyone to complicate my life. I enjoy what I do. The island, the fishing; drinking with tourist women who adored me. What more could a man ask for? And when not busy with these things, I had my writing.

Most people roll their eyes at struggling writers, but when I finish my war novel, it'll set this generation on fire. Men like Fitzgerald and Hemingway would be envious. Why should I risk paradise to get close to this girl? A bird in the hand is worth two in the bush.

Her hair smelled like lemons.

Relationships only end in misery.

Her toned skin appeared flawless.

You can trust nobody but yourself.

You're a freak with a deformed hand and a head full of issues. You can't even trust yourself. God, you're right, though. Her hair smells like lemons even after being in the sea.

Mabel was a riveting chick, and the sex was good. Hell, it was great, but why go back to it? I've conquered that mountain. There was no conquest there to be had, only heartache. My mind fired off warning signals, but my heart was deaf. Her bewitching aura held some supernatural grip on me.

Her face lingered on the group down below, but I found her eyes shifting to me. A smile followed and I think the attention was pleasing to her. I worked to pull my eyes from her but was unsuccessful. Her beauty shined brighter after her dip into the water. Aside from the moisture in her long hair and the darken color of her cutoff blue jean shorts, Mabel appeared completely dry. She was a tornado, dangerous in every aspect, yet simplistically beautiful.

Keep her away from you. It's for her own good. You know I'm right. You're a fucked-up individual who can't get over the past. You'll hurt her and she'll hurt you. You deserve nothing and no peace will greet you but death. Go on and take the AJAX out and leave everyone behind. It would be the best thing you can do for them. You only bring hurt and pain to everyone you know.

The tension torqued my shoulders, stringing a tight line of anxiety through my mind, and so I busied myself with the course of the AJAX to stifle the voice inside.

"She's beautiful," Mabel said.

"Pardon?"

"Your ship. She's beautiful."

"Thanks. It cost a pretty penny, but she's all mine. Spent a long eight years here. Long but wonderful eight years," I mumbled.

I wish you'd shut up.

"AJAX? You know it's meaning?" she asked. I chuckled at this.

"Of course, but do you?" I came back at her. She nodded her head, but I didn't believe her. "Enlighten me then."

"Oh, ye of little faith. Ajax was a Greek hero who was troubled by the events of the Trojan War."

"Impressive. But do you know what happened to him?"

"He slaughtered a herd of cattle, thinking they were soldiers, then killed himself."

"PTSD's a bitch. But good on you for knowing your history."

"You're not sore, are you?"

"Sore?" The speed in which she thought was fatiguing and tiresome to keep up with.

"Upset over falling into the water?"

"No, but I still think it was stupid of you to stick around to watch that shark. We could have been killed."

"I'm not scared to die."

"Everyone says that until death comes. And besides, you could of cost me my life. How does that set with you?" She didn't respond but looked out over the sea. Her mouth twisted as if pondering a question. A warmness worked through my bones and I wanted to kiss her. Our stalemate of silence broke when Henry released a deep and powerful laugh from down below. Mabel brought up her camera and fired away, catching the moment for some unseen purpose.

"This isn't awkward for you, is it?" she asked.

"Awkward?" I looked over the flying bridge at Henry, the subject of her pictures. "You mean you knowing my old friend and being on my ship? No, is it awkward for you?"

"I didn't mean the fact that I know Henry. I mean the fact that we had sex and now we are here." She spoke loud enough for all to hear, which alarmed me, but no one paid us any attention. "It was a one-night stand and normally, you don't see those people again."

"No, it's not awkward for me." I lied.

"I mean because, and don't take this the wrong way, but it was meaningless." The boldness in her tongue surprised and intrigued me. "It was two people satisfying one another with sex."

"So, you *were* satisfied?" I asked, my lips curling to one side as I reached into the cooler at my feet for two Krystal Ales. Finally catching her off-guard, her good-natured grin raised one of her eyebrows as she smirked. Popping the tops on both, I handed her a bottle.

"I guess it was good."

"Just good?" I teased.

"Geez, men and their fuckin' egos," she said, shaking her head and drinking her beer. Her tilted chin etched out her jaw line. I wanted to kiss it, to nibble on it, then nestle my head into that shoulder.

"You started it," I said. The wind kicked up again. Her hair, partially dried from the towel and with the help of the sun, slapped about.

"Ugh," she grunted. Her smile vanished. She thrust her beer at me, and I snatched it only a moment.before she released the bottle. At first, I thought I had insulted her. That pit, full of embarrassment and shame, opened in my stomach. She whipped her head over, gathering her hair. "This damn hair."

The tension eased in my shoulders. I had not been the subject of her irritation.

"I hate this hair." She cursed under her breath as she scurried down the ladder.

I casted a curious eye as she approached Kojo, who startled at her touch. Mabel whispered something into his ear, to which he nodded, then led her into the cabin. The wind died and the sun beat without blockage from the clouds. Her beer sweated in my palm. The trio, along with Henry, wrangled into the back of the boat. Henry was eyeing my selection of fishing rods and picked up the only one I had wished he didn't.

"I'm using this one."

"Hands off, Hoss," I said from above. Their collective attention rose to me.

"Why can't I use it?"

"It's my custom-built rod. Only I use it."

Henry eyed the rod, turning it over in his hand, and examining it more. "It looks good."

"It should," I said. "Damn thing was expensive. Hell, the terminator butt set me back about three hundred."

"Terminator butt?" Henry pressed a small button on the rod's butt and the handle bent, allowing to shift from standing to chair fighting style. "I can see that."

"Yeah, so put it back. It's mine and only mine." Henry did and backed away with his hands in the air as if the rod was a holy relic. He sat in the fighting chair, joining the trio in some mindless discussion.

"You know." Philip shouted up to catch my attention. "The last fishing trip I went on, they had all this modern gear that I don't see here. I mean, they had a line length counter and automatic reels and stuff like that."

"What are you getting at?"

"You don't have any of those things?"

"Because that's not fishing. Why would I want a machine to do all the work?"

"It's easier."

"Fishing isn't about easy. It's about the struggle, man verses nature. It's a fight."

"The only fight Philip cares about is the one that has dollar signs going into his bank account afterward," Nathan said. The others laughed and returned to their conversation, leaving me to my thoughts. Ten minutes passed before Kojo and Mabel re-emerged from the cabin.

My jaw hit the deck. Henry and the trio stopped fishing to gawk at Mabel. She thanked Kojo with a hug. Only Alice didn't pine over her because she still laid on the bow and couldn't see. Kojo returned to his work as Mabel climbed to the flying bridge. I handed her the lukewarm beer and she chugged it before grabbing another.

I wanted to speak but nothing came. The wind blew, fluttering her freshly bobbed hair. Mabel shook it, dislodging any loose, damp strands that didn't fall out during the cutting. Taking a long drink, she questioned my judgement.

"What? Is it uneven? You don't like it, do you?" She tried to examine her own hair. For a quick cut job, I must admit, the short style looked remarkable.

"You look like a flapper." My heart slowed and pained in my chest. I wanted to touch her, to bring her in close and kiss her. I had long been fascinated with the women of the 1920's and here this lady just upped the amazement and lust I had for her.

"A what?"

"It reminds me of a flapper girl from the 1920's."

"Oh yeah?" She ran her hand through her hair, tossing it about. "I could've been one of those girls back then. They were cool."

"I can see you at some speakeasy, dancing the Charleston with F. Scott or something."

"I don't know. Zelda would've cut me, I'm sure." I laughed at this and was glad she knew who I was talking about.

"You look good though."

"Feels good. God, it's like I cut off a ton of baggage. You have no idea how hot it can get under—" She paused at the sight of my long beard.

"I don't deny that." I scratched my hairy chin.

"That Kojo, he's nice."

"He's great. Taught me everything I know about the sea."

"How'd he lose his leg?"

"His leg?" I repeated, questioning the thought of him without a leg, but confirming it with one glance at him. I'm so use to the absence of his leg that I forget about it. His dark skin transformed into the light brown of plastic below his knee. "Bad times long ago."

"You were there?" she asked. I tucked my hand away as my throat went dry. Thinking of those times caused my finger to touch my bottom lip and I rubbed. Damned old habit, but it was my damned old habit. She asked again, snapping me out of my daydream.

"I was there."

She pushed it further, but I shut her down. Those were places I didn't care to go, and information I didn't care to divulge. I feared if I let more memories enter my mind, the flood gates would tear off their hinges. The aroma of burnt metal slapped my senses and my ears hummed from old explosions. I mentally sprawled, squashing the memories, and forcing them back from which they came.

She stared at me, reading my face and finding the answer to her question. Her creative mind ached to know more, wanting to paint a picture that I wouldn't give her.

"Look, Kojo's my dearest friend. If he wants you to know his story, he'll tell you."

"Oh, tell me," she pleaded. "I won't let it leave this ship, but I gotta know."

I sighed, knowing that if I didn't give her something, she'd pester me for the rest of the trip. I glanced down at the other occupants of my ship, and then said, "It was unfortunate circumstances."

A glow radiated from within her eyes, craving the story. She leaned in closer and as I mimicked this, I could hear the panting of her breath and the beating of her heart. The lust of a good story, to be the first to hear a tale few others knew, excited her even more than sex. My lips inched near her ear so my voice wouldn't rise more than a whisper. The fragrance coming off her neck triumphed over the smells of the ship and ocean. "What happened?"

"It was a freak accident. A freak *sexual* accident…with a midget."

She bounced away from me, an annoyed yet pleasant smirk on her face and slapped my shoulder. "Oh, you ass."

"I'm sorry, but I can't. Like I said, it's not my story to tell. Ask him if you want."

She thought it over for a moment, then nodded. "I guess that's cool. I understand. Loyalty is an honorable trait."

"Kojo's a great man. It would be a disservice to him." She stared at me. The wind, fearing her gaze, cowered away, and the tension between us vibrated until I cleared my throat. I sighed, breaking the stiffness, and bringing back the breeze. "So, what got you into the journalism and photography stuff?"

"Well, after the—" She paused, locating her words before continuing. "After having to do some growing up, I found I was intrigued with other people's stories."

"And what boss gave you the task of following around lug nuts there?"

"I asked for it. I love MMA and Haymaker's one of the biggest stories there is. And to cap it off, after nearly getting to the title on several occasions but coming up short, he finally does it."

There was a genuine joy in her when she spoke about the sport and her love for it.

"You know, I didn't know women enjoyed the sport."

"Geez, been living under a rock?"

"No, on a tropical island," I said, matter-of-factly, to which she mocked a gesture of being impressed with the shaking of her head and the rolling of her eyes.

"Well, for your information…" She poked me in the chest with her index finger. The spot warmed to her touch and I wish she would have left it there. "The sport has changed some in ten years."

"I've seen that. It was more ruthless back when I got into it."

"Why'd you leave?"

"The sport? I didn't really, only –"

"Why did you leave America?" The abrupt interruption surprised me. I opened my mouth to speak but stuck the rim of a bottle to it, mugging any words before they could escape. Still, she waited, and I gave her nothing. A cheer from the party broke our stalemate, but I knew she wouldn't relent so easily.

A great black marlin broke the surface with its dorsal fin expanded. The rich boys had caught nothing but tuna the entire day and a ping of excitement mixed with jealously hit them as the epic fish defied the laws of gravity. It snapped about, wanting to throw the hook, while the trio jested Henry about his luck. The champ leaned back, rejoicing in his moment.

"God, I love this," I said under my breath, but Mabel had great ears.

"Love what?" I had been holding the railing, searching the waters, when her hand graced the top of mine. It shocked me, and I feared I should pull away, but didn't dare to move. Did she do this on purpose or accident? I looked at her hand; she looked at me.

"There is no place more peaceful than a clear day on the open sea, fishing to no end." Mabel stepped back and took a picture of me and the water.

"You ever come out here on your own?"

"Sometimes."

"And that doesn't scare you?"

"No. If something happens, oh well. It's not like I'm leaving anyone behind."

Her head tilted, probing my statement, looking for any indication of truth or lie. Content with what she found, she nodded, believing my words. "I'd be scared."

"You should see what it's like. You get a new prospective of the sea, especially at night. You truly understand how small you are to the Universe."

"Who taught you to fish?" she asked.

"To deep sea fish? Kojo."

"Not your father?"

"Not really."

"What was your first catch?"

"You don't run out of questions, do you?"

"Of course not, I'm a writer."

"So, I hear."

"Well, I hear you're a writer, too."

"Hardly."

"Oh, don't be so modest. Henry said you've been published in magazines. What's your novel about?"

"How do you know I'm working on a novel?"

"Every writer is always working on a novel. What's yours about?" Mabel asked.

"The war." The word seemed to strike a chord with her, and a shadow fell over her eyes. I hurried along to push past any unpleasantness I may have created. "About the Battle of Fallujah in November of 2004."

"Is that why you left the States?"

"Because of the war? No."

"I meant to write?"

"Not entirely, no." Once again, she waited for me to continue, but I wouldn't. Aside from Kojo, talking about my writing felt unnatural and phony. Some things aren't meant for everyone and I had a strong feeling she was interviewing for her book more than having a general interest in my life.

"Good God, Henry, look at that thing," Nathan said. Everyone down below crowded to the stern to get a look at the fish Kojo pulled onto the transom.

"You should keep her." Philip commented. Henry looked over his shoulder at me and shook his head.

"I hear that's not how it's done anymore. But I do want a picture though." He held tight to the rod, fearing the fish would slip off the transom and run free. Quickly, Kojo measured, weighed, and tagged the fish.

"Mabel, get a shot." Henry, standing on the transom, leaned down next to the fish and Mabel snapped a few pictures as I searched the water for the red scarred fin. It had, I assume, ventured to new domains, for I saw nothing in our area. Once the photos were taken, Kojo released the black marlin back into the sea. She kicked, flipped her tail, and was gone.

Chapter Twelve

I had made up my mind, I wouldn't go to Henry's party. It wasn't my scene anyhow, and I knew I wouldn't be comfortable. There was plenty of work to do, like the novel or fishing repairs, and so I was content with not going. Although I'm sure those guys throw one hell of a party, I'd stay in and write, but when the burnt orange cab pulled up later that night, I climbed in.

Although the size of the island could warrant a vehicle, I've never needed a car while here. The dock wasn't far from the bar and the bar wasn't far from my house. Everything in my life was within walking distance, but the Fletching Manor wasn't a part of my everyday life. The cabbie presented a cheerful greeting as I climbed into his car.

It had been years since my last car ride, and I was curious on how it would be. The seat cushions were no different from the ones on the AJAX. Stuffing peeked through the cracks of the slightly torn upholstery like eviscerated intestines. I closed the door, encasing myself in the coffin-like space, and knew not what to do. The a/c didn't appear to be functioning, which answered for the stale smell of body odor, so I rolled down the window and allowed the cool night air to lap at my face.

We roared past the White Whale with music jamming from King Louie's jukebox. I didn't need to investigate the place to see in my head the men slumped at the bar. I had spent a decade among the stagnant beer and depressing scuttlebutt. It was as familiar to me as my own home and I knew the cracks in the ceiling as well as the nicks in the floor. I did wonder if Jazz was working this evening. The guilt of driving past wrecked my gut and I turned away from it with an odd sense of abandonment.

Behind the White Whale, the AJAX loomed like a puppy missing its absent master. The ocean wind moaned, pleading for me not to go, and I longed to be with my ship. We turned the opposite way; my body screaming as if I was being kidnapped.

Why are you going? No one wants you there. It's all a lie. They only want to make fun of you.

The road traveled inward through the island. Sandy beaches gave way to tall trees leaning seaward, reaching for the ocean, but restrained by their roots. A small ghetto nestled against a hill, with homes made from scraps of rubbish, blended with the surrounding forest. Their walls, a jigsaw puzzle of discarded lumber, cardboard, and rusted metal. Many doors were no more than curtains nailed over openings.

Inquisitive eyes studied the taxi, quickening the driver's speed. The beating of a steelpan drum echoed through the neighborhood. A group of children, no older than ten, chased after us. Their arms flapped back and forth in cheery waves and I could do nothing but smile and wave back. Most of these kids, if they lived to be adults, would never get to ride in a vehicle aside from a squad car.

The shantytown morphed back into a forest. The occasional shack or hut appeared, then vanished with the tick of a clock. It wasn't strange to see people walking the roadway, but not one stuck out their thumb or shook angry fists at us. It was always the same: a smile, a wave, a friendly head nod. All the while we drove, I could see the manor on top of the tallest hill growing ever larger in the windshield.

The forest thinned into a small town with grocery stores and businesses. Although I can't recall the town's name, it was far richer than the shantytown we passed before. No longer did the ragtag dwellings decorate the terrain, but instead, actual construction-built houses. This area reminded me more of a small suburban neighborhood back in the States.

The people who sat out on their front porches in this small town didn't wave or give a friendly greeting. Staring with the same prying eyes of the shantytown poor, these people weren't intrigued by the vehicle, but envious. They blinked eyes of hatred for not being inside it, and this saddened me. These people were far better off than the shack-dwellers, yet the poor seemed more content and jovial.

We drove on, tires beating the patchwork pavement, and I settled into the seat. I've long kept to the shoreline, and now, I no longer cared to see the island away from it. Whatever fruit that enriched the island grew rotten the wealthier the inhabitants became.

The rich will be at this party. The fruit will be diseased with the juices of death and gold.

The engine revved uphill, and by the way the car shook, I feared a piston would launch through the hood. The vibrations rattled me hard and the decayed cushion did little to protect my ass from its springs. The road twisted this way and that, cutting through large hills of trees. A convertible full of women, both islanders and tourists, careened around us. Each held a glass or bottle and celebrated as their car sped to the manor.

The wind enchanted their silk hair to flow like Medusa's snakes. Their perfectly applied makeup sparkled on their smooth skin, hiding any flaws they wished to cover. Youthful laughter which escaped their painted mouths, did so with heart and joy. Flashy evening gowns emphasized the tight curves of their bodies. They were women of the 21st century, free and full of life, and I wished I was with them.

I remembered being that young once, wrapped up in the moment and never once thinking of what was to be. Surrounded by friends, we were on top of the world, with nothing stopping us. But all who live, must age, and that exhilarated feeling of youth soon withers.

Where they are, I once was, and where I am, they soon will be.

Cars, taxis, Rolls-Royces and Bentleys, delivered loads of party goers eager to experience the thrill offered at Henry's mansion. The elite rich, whose mansions populated the island in various locations, arrived in fashion. Tailor-made suits and hand-stitched gowns were the envy of fashion for all those on lower pay scales.

Rising out of the two perimeter hedgerow fences was a heavy iron gate standing open to welcome in the guests. I have never been this close to the old Fletching Manor, but these iron gates had to be new. The bars were pristine without a hint of rust infecting them. Tall trees lined the drive, creating a natural tunnel of branches leading up to the manor like some antebellum plantation. Decorative lights, hidden among the limbs, illuminated the atmosphere.

Music boomed like a heartbeat from unseen speakers, pounding out a pulse for people to dance to. The drive split, wrapping around a rectangular fountain elongated to the point that people mistook it for a swimming pool. A musical array of water leapt upward from different spouts, mesmerizing all who looked upon it. At once, the fountain disappeared from my mind as we exited the tree tunnel and the manor exploded into view.

Chapter Thirteen

People moseyed to the glowing flame of the party. Green and white lights cast a holiday homesickness over my heart and for some strange reason I wanted eggnog at a fireplace despite the heat. Flashing strobes flickered in exterior windows, blinking out, then reawakening to the beat of the music.

My taxi stopped at the grand stone stairs leading up to the front porch, avoiding the rows of parked cars waiting for valet. I offered the driver some cash, but he declined, informing me that Henry had foot the bill. I thanked him and stepped out.

Call it age or experience, but unlike the other visitors rushing past me, I lacked the urgency to get inside. Eagerness nipped at the base of my skull, but I'm a fisherman whose patience has allotted a sense of pleasure in the little things. For years I have wanted to see this place and I took it all in because I'd never see this house for the first time again.

Pictures of this mansion from its heyday filled the internet and its glory was astonishing. Ian Fletching, the writer of adventure and action, loved the history of this island. An avid reader, Ian was said to have a library full of books on the subject and many more. One such historical topic worked its way into a popular series of his dealing with pirates. Ian collected pirate artifacts, but his true testament to his love of the swashbucklers was in the construction of his house.

Captured from above, the house held an odd design that no other house would dare to have. Four large buildings touched the corners of the main house in an implied 'X'. The mansion sat directly centered with curved walls creating an oblong shape contrasting with the sharp rectangular angles of the front porch. From the sky, the four diagonal structures and the large round house made up the intriguing architecture of a skull and cross bones.

From ground level, this buccaneer image wasn't noticeable, and I doubt many of the people running to get inside knew of the sinister design. Careening my

Mansion on the Hill

neck back, I counted three stories. A chill blasted my spine and a line from an old book popped into my head, *whatever walks these halls, walks alone.*

As the hypnotic young and wealthy old moved through the house, I found myself underdressed. Their glimmering gowns and fashionable tuxedos oozed with money and lust. Now, I didn't look like a hobo, but my clothes fit loose, and I lacked a shave. Give me a fruity umbrella drink and I could be mistaken for a guy in his mid-thirties on vacation alone who just so happened to wander into this party.

An old English Ivy pub cap pushed back my mess of hair and I found I was the only one wearing a hat. *At least I combed my beard.*

A beautifully decorated foyer, lined with freshly cut flowers, opened to a long hall cutting through the middle of the house. I couldn't help but wonder if the entrance to the White House looked like this. To my left stood the opening of a very fancy and very white dining room, fitted with an elongated table suited for thirty. People funneled past me, pushing to get through and around the barrier which was I.

Hypnotized by the music and river of bodies, I drifted through the house as the grandeur of the party swept me up. A row of doors lined the hall to my left, opening to rooms I could only wonder about. To my right descended an elegant rosewood staircase with ivory white balusters. I half expected to see a glamorous beauty coming down the stairs in an antebellum party dress.

A pair of French wooden doors ended the extra wide hall and beyond them stood a grand portico towering high over the backyard festivities. Whoever designed this place had a touch of English nobility in them. From afar, I had seen this manor in its ruins and couldn't believe it was the same place that sat abandoned for the better part of three decades.

Thirteen stone steps lowered the party goers down to the massive backyard, equipped with a stage for the band. Lights zipped and zapped about and past the dancing crowd. New stone lining shaped the pool without a single crack or chip to off put the work. The collective herd gravitated to the gigantic pool in the center of the lawn, where people swam and drank and danced around with little care. They twirled with one another, not caring who their partner was, only wanting more. The crowd swayed like the top of trees in a breeze to a rhythm that complimented the music.

Waiters balanced metal trays that surfed over the masses, providing booze for everyone. Among this sea of people, something moved against it like the fin of a shark cutting across the ocean's surface.

"Hello, fisherman." Mabel strolled angelically toward me and I almost didn't recognize her. The quick cut bob done on my boat was trimmed neater and the dark brunette hair dyed blonde.

"Hello, journalist," I replied. She sipped from a filled champagne glass, her black cocktail dress stopping at her knees with a matching pair of high heels that accentuated her calves. I recalled running my hands across that sweat-drenched muscle, streaming over her steaming thigh, and…

I stopped myself from conjuring any further memories. The obscenity of my own thoughts made me chuckle. She eyed the party; I eyed her. The beat of the music infected Mabel, taking her muscles hostage, and forcing her to sway in time with the rhythm. My breath shortened in my throat as my blood pressure elevated. Her hips thrusted, pulsing one way, gyrating back the other, capturing my lustful gaze.

She caught me staring and swayed harder, enticing me for her own amusement. Her shoulders torqued forward and back; her head angled to cast a spell with her bewitching eyes as she eased back into me. My rough callus hands were criminal against the expensive silk fabric of her dress. They glided around her curves without restraint. The dancing masses vanished, leaving us standing among the crowd alone. She brought the glass up to her lips, kissing the rim as the bubbly rose-colored liquid spilled over her tongue and down her throat.

I choked back the lump which had appeared, desperately hoping we didn't speak and break this moment. Although familiar, this woman was but a mystery to me and I was smitten.

Oh, you gonna run off with her? Leave everything and live happily ever after? She'll break you. You can't be loved because you don't love.

My movements ceased as my eyes sank to our feet. I held a deep breath.

Coming here was a mistake.

Her perfume weakened my knees and a nervousness plagued my stomach like that of a high school freshman. Before I could say or do something stupid, I snatched a glass of champagne from a waiter's tray, dropping the fizzing beverage down in one gulp.

"Nicely done," she said, facing me.

"Thanks. Nice hair."

"Alice and I found a stylist at the resort. They have everything there you could think of," she said. My mind went blank as her body continued to swing with the music. Her pause alarmed me. She waited for me to say something, but the only thing I wanted to speak was our body language. My hand fought to reach my lip, but I forced it into my pocket where the salvation to my situation laid.

"I have something for you," I said, breaking my moment of being mute. She stiffened, curious to see what I brought. She leaned in closer, her breath bathing my face, biting her bottom lip, and restraining her smile. I removed the silver necklace and dangled it from my fingers. Her smile dropped as a speechless look overcame her.

This was the first glimpse of her emotions that weren't somehow guarded. She hesitated, afraid to touch it in case it wasn't real, but then startling, her hand launched out to pluck it from my fingertips.

"Oh my god. I thought I lost it forever." Her voice quivered for a moment and I could have sworn she was near tears. She didn't cry, but she did cradle the necklace in her palms as if she caught a magical fairy and never wanted to release it.

"The clasp bent. I think I fixed it," I said. She held it up to study it.

"Where did you find it?"

"In my bedsheets." My teeth couldn't help but make a jester's appearance. She didn't respond to it. No look of embarrassment or reproach. Her eyes were calculated, as if trying to remember ever being at my house or gauging my words to find the truth in them. Without a single muscle movement, I felt her guard return. She handed the necklace back to me so I could put it around her neck.

"Did you know the clasp is called a boob?"

Nice one, dumbass. Like she doesn't think you're weird enough as it is.

"I did not and find it odd that you do." She gracefully touched the trinket, pressing it firmly to her chest to reassure herself it was there. Without warning, she assaulted my lips with her mouth. A waiter strolled by and I snatched two more glasses of champagne.

"This party looks expensive," I said, handing her a glass and drinking the other. "Does Henry pay for it all?"

"He doesn't really speak about money. He met Philip through Scott and invested in some companies, mostly online ones. They imply they all flip the bill for these parties, but mostly I think it's Henry." I could recall their faces, but not their names.

"Online companies? What kind of companies are online?" I asked.

"Most of them." So, it was true. I was out of touch with modern life. "The biggest company they invested in was the fight promotion, IFA."

"The one that manages Henry?" I asked. She nodded her head. "Henry told me about that. So, he invests in a company he works for?"

"Sure. He invested in himself. It's a smart move and they manage tons of other boxers and fighters."

"He said that's how he met…um…the Clooney looking guy," I said.

She laughed at this. "Clooney? You mean Philip. You think he looks like George Clooney?"

"He has that salt and pepper hair thing that Clooney made famous."

"I can see that, but Philip is no George." She paused, pulling a memory out of the ether. "Oh, George Clooney. I had such a big crush on him growing up."

"Where'd you grow up?"

"Lots of different places."

I'm not the brightest man in the world, but I knew when not to push a subject.

"If Henry's so rich, why does he still fight?"

"Because I love the game." Henry's voice boomed coming down the stairs. He arrived like a king ready to greet his subjects, pushing past as they tried to shake his hand or stop him for a picture. Henry nodded and kept a smile on his face but ignored them without being rude about it. He embraced me in a bear hug, lifting me off the ground. "I'm glad you came, brother."

"This is fuckin' cool, Henry." I spoke of his house and party to which he nodded as if seeing it for the first time.

"Yes," he said, then shrugged his shoulders as if he was bored with the whole scene. "Fuck it, come on."

Henry pulled me away and I caught a glimpse of Mabel following behind. I was glad she did.

"Where are we going?"

"For a drink. Ccoo-me on." His lip quivered with a slur. For some, I'm guessing, the party started much earlier.

Locking his arm around my neck, I found him much stouter than I had figured, and even if I wanted to protest, there was no escaping his clutches. He led me through the two French doors and into the large area where the base of the grand staircase stood directly in front of us. I wanted to go up them, to see the other floors, and venture throughout the house. Instead, we turned away from the stairs, but before heading down the hallway from which I had entered the house, we came to a pair of oak doors sliding open into a study.

Inside, people were socializing. Books adorned the walls and the hint of cigars, smoked long ago, lingered amongst the wood and leather furniture. I could only picture Ian Fletching writing in this room, sitting behind the desk with his famous scotch on the rocks and an endless pile of cigarettes, pounding the keys of his Royal Quiet Deluxe typewriter.

Women in elegant gowns perched upon armrests or in the laps of businessmen. They were nothing more than jewelry to these men. Philip Gables had two, one on each arm, and Scott Pound sat solo in the club chair which had no room for jewelry. A pair of love seats enclosed the sitting area centered in the room, and I couldn't help thinking whoever arranged this went for an oval office look.

Nathan Spears and Alice Monroe sat on one of the love seats. They carried on their own private conversation, away from the ears of the others. Alice popped up from her seat as we entered.

I assumed her attention fell on Henry, but I was wrong. With an elegance of a starlet from the golden age of movies, she gracefully wrapped her arms around Mabel. Mabel returned the welcome, and the two kissed on the cheek like Parisians, careful not to smear either's makeup. Henry released me from his choking grasp and headed over to a desk near the full-length window. From a decanter that sat there next to his championship belt, he poured three glasses, handing the first to Mabel, the second to me, and held up the third.

"To old and new friends," Henry said. As he spoke, his ice clanked against the glass half full of whiskey. Every lady and gentleman tipped their glasses to him.

"Pals." I locked eyes with Henry. A warming smile graced his face at a recalled memory. He nodded then drank. It was hard to believe that the guy in front of me was the Champion of the World and one of the richest guys in the room. To me, he was the poor kid from the trailer park who dreamed of glory in battle. It was Henry who wanted to join the Marines and asked me to follow along.

I took the shot and sat the glass down for Henry to refill.

"You drink whiskey?" Philip asked.

"I drink anything."

"I figured for an islander you'd be more prone to rum." He laughed, invoking humor from the others.

"I *do*, Island Rum preferably, but whiskey is fine. I mean, I'm from fuckin' Texas." There was a few looks of amusement and pleasant annoyance, but all in good humor. I picked up my freshly filled shot glass and touched the gold plate on the thick championship belt. "Now, this is impressive."

"I like it."

"He likes to take it out and wear it from time to time." Alice interjected.

"Quiet you." Henry teased from behind his drink. The look in his eyes shined with love for his wife and how could it not. She was the very definition of beauty. I was proud for my childhood friend.

"You *should* wear it. What an achievement. You don't put it up on a mantel or something?"

"I do. It sits there like a fish."

"A truly worthy catch, my friend." Something caught my eye on his belt. There was a small Marine Corps eagle, globe, and anchor attached to it. "What's this?"

"My boot camp EGA. The first thing I did was have that mounted on it. You like?"

"Yeah. Dana White was cool with you adding it to the belt?" My finger rubbed the small black emblem that meant so much to so many men.

"Dana is a big supporter of the Armed Forces, and a cool motherfucker."

"It's nice, brother. Real nice. I wear mine on my old boonie cover when I go out to sea."

"What about your medals?"

"In a box somewhere. I don't know." I lied. I knew where they were, buried in a closet with other forgotten memories.

"What do you mean, you don't know? I know you got the Purple Heart. That's not mounted somewhere?" He asked, remembering to refill my glass and hand it back to me. I accepted it with my good hand. Although I had already shown it off, I didn't care to draw further attention to the missing finger.

"No. They're not trophy fish," I said. Mabel took a seat in one of the reading club chairs and I took a place on the sofa next to Alice and Nathan. Philip sat across from us, a woman hanging around his shoulders, while Henry leaned against the front of his desk, more to be near his whiskey decanter than to be in the group.

"So, Nick." Philip addressed me, but I didn't realize this at first. I couldn't remember most of their names, and so I sipped my drink, waiting for someone else to respond. "How long have you been a fisherman here?"

"His name is Nicanor. Nic-a-nor. Not Nick," Henry warned into the rim of his glass. He sighed, sat the glass upon his desk, and rubbed his temples.

"I'm sure you called him Nick on his ship."

"That's different. If I did, that's between us and you're not me."

"Whatever." Philip shrugged.

He sighed again, regaining his calmness, and chuckled. "You're such a dick, Philip."

They shared the laugh and Philip seemed pleased with the insult as he turned his chin upward to the young lady sitting on the arm of the chair. She kissed the scotch off his lips. "Anyway, how long have you been out here, *Nic-a-nor*?"

"About ten years."

"Were you always a fisherman?"

"No."

"Not much for words, are you?" He jested and the others laughed.

"Why'd you leave though?" Mabel asked. She baited but there was no catch. Before the pause became awkward, Henry came to my rescue.

"Because, he does what he wants. He's Nicanor. He slays more bodies and more ass than all the men in this room."

Again, there were laughs and again there were eyerolls.

"Thanks, brother." I shied away.

"So, you were a Marine, too?" Scott asked.

"Still am." I corrected.

"You're still in?"

"No, but once a Marine, always a Marine." Henry added.

"So, why *did* you leave the States?" Scott insisted I answer. Everyone eyed me, but I said nothing.

"None of your fuckin' business," Henry shouted, coming to my rescue again. "Geez, you nosy motherfuckers. He left the States. End of chapter."

"Simple answer, I wanted to go fishing." This produced a belly shaking laugh from Henry. The others joined. "The world is too crazy. Out there, I'm free."

"*Out there, I'm free.*" Scott quoted. He whipped out his phone and started pushing the screen. "I like that. I'm going to post that on Facebook. It's cool, I'll tag you."

"I don't have a Facebook."

"Seriously?"

"Yeah. Don't you have to go to college to get one?"

"What?" Scott asked. All eyes were on me. They looked from one another, puzzled by what I was saying. Only Mabel didn't look at me. She examined the crowd, studying their reactions, collecting their characteristics.

"What does going to college have to do with anything?" Nathan asked.

"Oh yeah. Back in the day, you had to have a college email. That was like fifteen years ago, but my god, I forgot about that," Philip said. They laughed, exchanging glances; sympathetic looks for the idiot island man.

"Now anyone can get one." Nathan added.

"Oh my god," Alice Monroe said with a hand over her heart. "You're so cute. I have to snapchat this."

She did this on purpose to incite the crowd. They leaned in, waiting for my reaction as if I were an animal at the zoo. They exploded. Only Mabel and Henry didn't find anything amusing about my ignorance. Henry refilled his glass and stormed out of the room.

"Please sweetie," the auburn-haired actress said, chuckling. "You do know what Snapchat is, right?"

"Alice," Scott said. The fat in his cheeks jiggled as he laughed, giving it a strange hypnotic movement. It wasn't pleasant like Santa Claus and not as enjoyable as gelatin, but somewhat unsettling. "He didn't know about Facebook. I doubt he knows about Snapchat."

God, don't you wanna punch him in that fat face? Don'cha wanna? Don'cha wanna?

I shook my head, never hearing of Snapchat, but I figured it had to do with those stupid cellphones everyone was crazy about. More laughter caused my blood to boil. I didn't mind the humor, but the insults were a bit much, and I was ready to explode on their rude asses.

"Oh my god," Alice continued. "You're like, so primitive."

Fuck. Them. Up.

"Oh my god," Mabel mimicked in an airhead, valley-girl pitch. "You're like, such a bitch."

That silenced the room. Alice's jaw dropped and she stared hurt at Mabel. Mabel sat back in her seat and slurped at her drink, the ice rattling in the glass. Stares didn't bother her; another trait I admired.

"How rude, Mabel."

"Oh yes, I'm the rude one."

"Well, I didn't mean any offense by it," Alice justified herself, looking to Nathan for support.

"I need some air." Finishing my drink, I rose from my seat.

"I'll join you. It's kind of stuffy in here." Mabel smirked and followed me out of the house. We stood at the front fountain, watching drunks swim around the musical water jets.

"Those people are one of the reasons why I left. Guess you can't get away from assholes." The more they tiptoed through my mind, the angrier I got. The pent-up energy pulsated, and I had to pace to keep it under control.

"Yeah, they're everywhere," she said. I nodded in agreement and kicked at the stone wall of the house.

God, if they only knew what I could do to them, they'd never open their fuckin' mouths.

My fist clenched at the lust for blood.

"God, why didn't I?" I muttered, forgetting Mabel's excellent hearing.

"Why didn't you what?"

"Why didn't I knock their teeth in? Shove their fuckin' phones down their throats."

"A little hostile, are you?"

"Did you see all of them were on their cellphones? I mean, look at this," I swiped my hand over the crowd, many of them holding up phones to capture the moment instead of living it. "I fuckin' hate all them with their false sense of importance. They think their lives matter. They're meaningless."

She studied me, my words, my expressions, but once again, the sense of being a project came to me. I mentally kicked myself. I should know to keep my mouth shut and my temper in check.

"I have one."

"One what?"

"A cellphone," she replied. "But you're right. I hate it. My boss is always calling me about updates and I'm always holding it or looking for it. I'm a slave to it and you are completely correct. I hate it."

"That's why I love being out on my ship. On the AJAX, none of that shit works. The surrounding of the ocean shields you, forcing you to be in the present. No digital data, no pixels, just you and your surroundings. Nothing better than being out there by yourself."

"I would like to experience that."

"Yeah." I took a breath, my irritation calming. I hated this feeling even more than the hate I had for Jacob and his men. Jacob and his bullies were a problem, but one I welcomed. The people in that room were annoying, troublesome parasites.

An explosion erupted near us. My spine shivered, and a cold chill seized the muscles in my shoulders. All my recent aggravation returned, squashing my calm state. *Am I hit? Where is my rifle? Where are my men? How many were injured in the blast?*

These words funneled through me, rehearsed and worried over for years. I cited them as one would a song or a poem, as if remembering a phone number from childhood. The chill boiled to fury, and I turned to find a young man with a lighter, ready to spark another firecracker. My hand lashed out and snatched his throat. He dropped the items and scratched at my hand, but my grip held too tight for him to pull himself free.

His eyes bulged, and his face flushed for oxygen. I pushed forward, hinging him at the knees, leaning him back. My teeth mashed against one another as I squeezed. The boy of twenty was not a boy to me, but a man in a foreign uniform, ready to kill all I knew. My heart pounded in my ears and a harsh breath forced its way through my nostrils like a pissed off bull.

The kill was in reach, a pound or more of pressure would achieve it. The music from the house faded as the lights and people dissolved from my vision. In a world of bleak darkness, there was only him and I. His tongue protruded, and his grip weakened. I squeezed tighter, ready to increase my kill count. Mabel's hand rested on my shoulder, but she didn't pull me away. A peace swept over me, Hyde fleeing Jekyll, and I released. The young man flopped to the ground, gasping for air. A female I had not seen rushed to his side.

"Get away from me." I warned, my jaw tightened so hard it pained the muscles in my cheeks. The embarrassment of my action dawned on me and I feared to see the reaction on Mabel's face. I was a beast being confronted by the beauty. I had to face her; there was no way around it. An expressionless tone adorned her face. She blinked without care or worry. Her stare reflected my own sense of doubt and I wondered if what had happened with the young man was imagined.

I looked back to see the woman helping the boy into the house. It had happened, not some conjuring of my diseased mind, but a reality of my actions. When I looked back at Mabel, I found myself puzzled by her. She stood unfazed. It was a real moment that unfolded, but passed her like a cloud passes overhead, not warranting a response.

"I need a drink," I said.

"Let's have several." She mused.

"Hey there," A voice called from behind us. Nathan Spears and Scott Pound came down the stairs. Nathan continued, "I'm sorry about that."

I panicked. *Had he seen me choking that man and if so, why was he sorry about it?*

"Sorry for what?" I asked.

"About the teasing in there. Wasn't right. I wanted to apologize for that and show you we're not bad people," Scott said. I felt foolish and wondered if I had jumped to conclusions. I wasn't much of a social butterfly and perhaps judged people too harshly.

"It's OK. I'm not one who socializes much these days. It's cool though." I shook hands with them, and Nathan wrapped an arm around my shoulder.

"Good, because any friend of Haymaker is a friend of ours. I do believe I overheard you talking about going for a drink?"

"Yeah," Mabel said.

"Then let's drink until we can't feel feelings anymore." Nathan laughed, leading me back into the party.

Chapter Fourteen

And the beat dropped. The house vibrated from music and the good energy. I'd like to say couples danced but it was hard to tell who danced with whom as the massive crowd flowed together. The tunes morphed from one song to another and the crowd stayed in sync. With legs swinging and arms flailing, each face adorned a row of smiling teeth.

We started our descent into lavish madness by venturing into the kitchen. A team of island men, all dressed in white, cut fruit that came in large crates. All smiled, enjoying their work that filled the room with the pleasant smells of citrus. We grabbed drinks being prepared for distribution among the legions of pleasure seekers.

Scott cradled in both hands the most ungodly size drink overflowing with cuts of different fruits and who knows how much sugar. He jabbed a large straw into it and sucked. A loud smack followed.

"Heavenly. Want some?" He offered but I declined. I've never been one for fruity drinks. A little champagne and orange juice in the morning is fine, but the site of Scott's drink brought fears of heartburn to mind.

Mabel opened a thin door at the back of the large kitchen and the three of us followed onto an ancient elevator with accordion doors. With a loud clank, the elevator lowered us into the cool earth. What awaited me there? A dark occult in need of a sacrifice; perhaps some decaying corpse ready to tell me a story. The smell of damp soil and mud lingered in the air like that of a deep grave.

My irrational and child-like fears opened to nothing more than a wine cellar. Wine cellar is too modest and misleading a term, for it was more of a warehouse, running to what I estimated the length of the mansion. If I were a liquor baron, I'd see this place as a goldmine. Bottles adorned racks with names I couldn't pronounce, from places I've never heard of.

Mabel scanned the selection, shuffling her feet, never staying longer than a blink until she came across what she wanted. She pulled a dark bottle off a rack and smiled at us. To me, there was nothing unique about the bottle as it looked like any other wine bottle. The only thing I could read on the label was the year. 1925 – printed in gold lettering and with an art deco design. The date conjured up two things to me: the roaring twenties and the Great Gatsby. Both I was fond of.

"That's Philip's personal rack," Nathan said. I stared, not knowing the severity of his statement.

"I'm sure he'll suffer because of it." Mabel rolled her eyes and bounced over to a dry bar, searching the pullout draw for a corkscrew. She found it, expunging the cork with a loud pop. The air evacuating the bottle was the same air F. Scott had breathed. I wondered if he had drunk this brand of wine, but then remembered he was a gin man. Then again, he was an alcoholic, so it was conceivable that he did drink wine as well.

Mabel took a swig. The rose-colored liquid stained her lips and she smiled in delight before passing the bottle to me. I am not much of a wine drinker, but I couldn't refuse. It was sweeter than I thought and colder too. After my taste, the bottle went to Nathan, then Scott. As Mabel waited for the bottle to return to her, Nathan snatched another one from the rack.

"He won't miss this one either, I'm sure." He shrugged as we ventured up a set of stairs. The four of us ran out of the cellar like high school kids scoring a bottle from their parent's liquor cabinet. I expected the stone staircase to end at a pair of slanted cellar doors, but instead, we exited through a masonry artwork of an arch that was more suitable for an English castle instead of a beachfront mansion.

What kind of man was Ian Fletching, I thought.

Coming out into the night air, I found myself disoriented, but welcomed the pleasant aroma of freshly cut grass. We were on the other side of the house, opposite of the cliffs that faced my own home, but I had never seen this part of the property before. Directly in front of us, down a stone pathway, people ran about on a large tennis court. No one was playing the game, but simply frolicking about. This moment of concern for my location faded as Mabel led the group to our next destination.

Although still confused at where I was, the energy was intoxicating, and I didn't want it to end. I followed, allowing myself to lose control of my own course and let someone else take over. We cut between the house and a large two-story parking garage, moving our way to the backyard where the music was still playing. A man stood with a microphone, cohorting people to come on stage. Men and women, all too eager to oblige, came in pairs to preform whatever semi-sexual game the announcer had planned.

The band cranked up their music and the crowd cheered, dancing as the people on stage humped one another, trying to pop a balloon that separated their crotches. To me, every individual was there to further their own social status, but all of them shared the same desire – to have a good time, for a long as possible. We made our way through the crowd on the lawn. The band played a mix of reggae and modern pop, blending the two to create a sound that would arouse the masses.

Mabel took my hand, and while tilting back the century-old bottle, shimmied her way through an unseen path. Bodies dipped and swayed, gyrating to an insane pulse. Mabel spun and swirled, never releasing my hand that melted at her fingertips. Having recognized his star status, I looked back to see Nathan engulfed by a gaggle of females. He didn't disappoint them and collected the beauties in his outstretched arms.

Mabel stopped in the center of the dancing crowd and pulled me in. Her hips grinded with the beat and I welcomed it. Her heat excited me, and I pulled her in close by the small of her back. She turned, never breaking contact, and rubbed up against me. The lemon fragrance of her hair brushed my face and the glittering light glistened in a bead of sweat.

It slowly slipped down the smooth flesh of her neck, gliding along the curve to her shoulder, leaving a trail for my lips to follow. It stopped before continuing to her arm, and turned forward, sliding over her collar bone. I watched as it crawled at first, then plummeted under the folds of her dress. Without warning, she spun aggressively to face me, only our hands still engaged.

"There's Henry." I looked to see Henry and Alice standing under the back portico, lording over the gathering at the top of the stairs. "Let's go."

Off she went before I could protest, pulling me along. A hand grabbed my shoulder, not stopping me, but joining us. Scott smiled; I guess not wanting to be left behind. Butlers, carrying trays, continuously supplied the party with booze and I snatched a glass of champagne off one. A woman of dark beauty ran her hand over my chest and smiled, but I didn't engage her for she was heading into the crowd and I was heading out.

We three pushed our way up the stone steps to join the host and hostess. Alice kissed Mabel on the cheek, apparently forgetting the tiff they had earlier.

"Nicky. Enjoying yourself?" Henry asked, welcoming me with an arm around my shoulder. We stared over the crowd, our group, the rulers of all and Henry the leader of that.

"Indeed." I swallowed the full glass of champagne and handed the empty off to another butler.

"Good. Sorry about that in the study."

"Already forgotten," I lied. This pleased Henry who pulled me into him like an older brother sharing the world with a younger sibling.

"Oh, look Henry. It's the governor's wife," Alice said. I tracked to where she was pointing to discover a tall, elegant woman in the middle of three young, shirtless studs. One nipped at her neck from behind while the other two flanked her. Her hands surfed the curvatures of their muscles and they did the same to her. A row of large sparkling diamonds hung around her neck to show her wealth to all who gawked at her. "Looks like she's having a good time."

"I don't think the Governor minds." Henry pointed to a shrub of a man, portly and bald, engrossing himself with a drink and two young ladies.

"You know the Governor?" I asked.

"Recent acquaintance."

"Jesus, Henry. You've been here only a few weeks and already know everyone."

"I make it our business to know everyone." Philip interrupted, emerging with wide, shifty eyes. His teeth mashed together in a joker's smile and he clapped Henry on the back. "It's the same as in the States."

Henry leaned into me and whispered, "It's all for investments. Making money work for you."

He winked at me.

"So that's what these parties are all about? Investments." I asked. He touched his finger to his nose.

"It's the luxury of life I like."

"Funny. I believe in investing in freedom away from the restraints of man's money."

"Freedom? I like that," Philip said. "But you need money to be really free."

"For some." I corrected. Mabel stopped another butler and scored more drinks for us. Where her bottle of wine went, I didn't know, but I'm sure she didn't want Philip to see it. I turned my thoughts back to Henry. "This is crazy. Imagine if everyone from high school could see this."

"Fuck them." Henry tossed the champagne down his throat and said, "Come on."

And like Mabel before him, Henry pulled me along. Mabel grabbed my arm, Alice took hers, and we created a makeshift conga line, dancing through the house. We headed through two glass doors that opened to what was once a magnificent ballroom. The polished hardwood floor laid covered under sections of jiu jitsu mats. In the far corner stood a full-size octagon cage. Weightlifting equipment and heavy punching bags decorated a portion of the spacious room.

There were less people here, but still folks gathered, immersed in conversations of unimportance. Henry led the group to the far corner of the room where an iron spiral staircase spun up to a second-floor catwalk. I had no idea where we were going, but Henry was captain of this ship. We ran across the catwalk that looked down on the entire gym and entered another room.

The tall ceilings were held up by blue and white marble walls and pillars. At first, I believed this to be a small indoor pool.

"A pool on the second floor?"

"It's a Roman sauna. Steam valves there and there." He pointed to two round wheels built into the wall. "I love this room. One of the reasons I wanted the house. Great to relax in after a hard workout."

"But it's on the second floor?"

"So?"

"Don't you worry it might leak?"

"Not really. It's well built."

"Now you're just showing off your toys, Henry."

"I am." He laughed. "Impressed?"

"Thoroughly."

"Hang on," Philip said into the phone plastered to his ear. He cut through our group until he stood next to Henry. "We have a business call we need to take."

Henry rolled his eyes and sighed. I thought it strange to have a meeting during a party, but it was none of my business. I'm not rich and therefore, I didn't pretend to know how they operate.

"Alright. Sorry guys. I gotta go," Henry said to all of us, then turned to me and said, "Have a good time, amigo."

"Will do." The entourage departed, heading back through the gym, leaving Mabel and myself alone in the sauna. An awkward pause came between us. Feeling like a young man on his first date, I didn't know what to say or do. Then, of course not being one for awkwardness, she spoke.

"I don't know about you, but I'm in need of another bottle of wine. What do say you?"

"At Philip's expense?"

"Naturally."

"I'm down." And once again we were off, this time cutting through a maze of doors leading through not only a giant closet full of suits, dresses, and shoes, but everything else Henry and Alice or their guests would need. I couldn't believe the amount of clothes they had, as my own wardrobe consisted of four or five shirts, a few pairs of pants and shorts, and one suit I haven't put on in years.

We cut through *the* master bedroom of all master bedrooms. The bed alone was the size of my living room and as we made our way around it, Mabel pointed to the bed post and laughed.

"Kinky." Hanging from one of the tall bedframe posts was a strap and arm restraint. I wanted to laugh, my face frozen in hilarious shock, and that strange tinge crawled under my skin, warning me to get the hell out of there before someone saw. Again, Mabel came to my rescue, grabbing my arm and hurrying us out into the grand hallway as we giggled, wondering what escapades were held within those sheets.

We didn't make it back into the cellar for another bottle of wine. Instead, Mabel stole a bottle of champagne from the kitchen. With the popping of the cork, the rest of the night became a haze.

Chapter Fifteen

I awoke with the sudden sensation of falling in a dream, flinching at a woman stepping around me. The raising light of the sun peeked through rippling white curtains in a room I didn't know. I scanned my surroundings trying to recall where I was. The night before was only a patchwork of memories.

"Sorry." The woman who woke me whispered, then carried on. A pair of heels dangled from her fingers, matching the short cut red dress she fought to keep from riding up her thighs as she left the room.

Drinking glasses and bottles littered the floor amongst the sleeping bodies. A woman wearing a nude, sparkling thong, and nothing else, laid passed out over the arm of a chair with her ass in the air. I admit, despite the pressure of a hangover in my eyes, it was a beautiful sight, but the better part of me looked away. Regrettably, I dropped my gaze to the floor and at her feet, a man laid curled around the chair, naked. This sight was far easier to look away from. A drunken sleep incapacitated the room, and I didn't feel like waking them.

I sat up wearily, a foul breath clinging to my tongue, and the jabs of a hangover sticking my temples like an ice pick. A chill ruffled my leg hair. The pants I wore to the party were gone, replaced by a pair of blue swimming shorts. I puzzled over this, crawling through the dark recesses of my brain until a memory ignited. Under the fog of alcohol and after dancing relentlessly, Mabel and I stumbled back into the wardrobe room on the second floor.

We threw about clothes, playing dress up until finding suits to dive into the pool. My real clothes were a distant memory; I had no idea where they were. Upon standing, the pain dug into my skull and tilted the world. A drink would cure my problems and I found one downstairs in the kitchen.

The beer was warm but unopened, so I downed it and looked for another. Instead of booze, I found a grand breakfast displayed on the dining table. There was eggs and croissants, bacon and sausage, a various assortment of fruits, stacks of pancakes, and all the toppings and condiments one could imagine. Sunlight streamed through the window, hitting the table, making it hum and glow like a Christmas feast. Such a parting gift for those who decided to leave.

The party didn't die, and I'm not sure it ever did. It only changed locations and tempo. The house never seemed empty either, as those who stuck around to drain the vein of it refused to let it die. They took it in the pool or searched for things they had lost while finding new things to enjoy. I had a feeling that the party would continue whether Henry was here or not. All guests were uninformally invited to stay, but only a handful were awake that following morning when the party moved to the beach.

Age had a way of catching up with everyone, and it was there I realized father time was winning. Even a year ago, I'd be hanging with the best of these youngsters, but in my mid-thirties, not even the hair of the dog did the trick. My heart was ready to play, but my body and mind said otherwise.

I sat down the beer and picked up a glass of orange juice. It tasted strange without champagne, but I couldn't believe how refreshing it was. My stomach bellowed at the food laid out before me and I filled a plate faster than a mako shark swims. Stuffing my face, I concluded that my earlier assumption of the party was correct. It never ended at Henry's absence, only morphed into something new. What rages during the night could be found in the morning. No one is ever ushered away.

I patted my stomach, releasing a pleasant and satisfying burp. With the kitchen being one of the four connecting structures to the house, a side door allowed me to exit into the blinding light of morning. Outside, everything seemed clean, clear, and warm. Each blade of bright green grass stood no higher than the next and felt as soft as a mother's touch on my bare feet. I ventured out to investigate the luscious and pristine land. The hedges were clipped sharp and to perfection. An army of ground keepers and staff were hustling to clean the property without disturbing the guest still there.

I scrunched up my toes, then realized I was without shoes. I have never been so drunk as to have lost my shoes, but then again, there is a first time for everything. I scraped across the recesses of my mind but couldn't decipher where I had left them. They were lost to a wave of alcohol and the thrill of a good time. I didn't care though as I strolled around and found it remarkable that such a grand place lacked any weeds or imperfections.

I avoided the commotion about the pool and the hard cement pathways, sticking to the soft grass. Nestled in the corner of the deep green hedges, a wooden door opened to a long staircase zigzagging down the rocky cliff to a private cove below. I had seen this steep, lightning bolt staircase, but only from a distance.

Taking the steps one at a time, I worked my way back and forth across the cliff. The ocean blew a powerful breeze and the compulsion to be out on the sea, away from the things of man, pinged at my heart. From this height, the stairs seemed to drop into the ocean. Waves crashed against the rocks, easing my nerves, and soothing my headache. The tide broke itself against an old steamer, creating a smooth surf that washed up on the private beach nestled between two rock faces. Like the manor, I had longed to visit this beach. It was secluded; it was majestic.

The stairs ended at a pier where a small motorboat bobbed in the water. On the beach, people laid on blankets and towels, sharing laughter and drinks. They had no worries and ran about like children on vacation. Some headed into the surf while others greedily laid in the section where the sun hit the sand.

At last my toes pressed into the warm white sand of the secluded beach. The exotic beauty of this particular shoreline was unsurpassable even to the sands my house sat upon. I marveled at the contours of the rockface and unspoiled beach. No seaweeds saturated the area; no signs stood erected to distract. The area felt untouched by man and I hoped it always would.

It took a second to locate Henry and his entourage. Mabel laid shoulder to shoulder with Alice.

Henry called out my name, breaking the scenery's trance on me. I joined his group, and all were there: Philip, Scott, Nathan, Alice, and Mabel. A few other girls, who weren't permanent members of their tribe, sat with them. The chemical scent of sunscreen and suntan oil overpowered the salt in the air.

"There he is," Nathan said propped up on a single elbow in the sand. I gave a small wave of acknowledgement. "Thought you might have left?"

I shook my head, acting as cool as could be.

"How'd you sleep?"

"Rough."

"I don't doubt that. Especially after that lemon in the eye," Scott said.

"Lemon in the eye?" Alice asked.

"Some guy last night challenged people to a drinking contest. Nicanor accepted. The drunk went first. Then our boy here licks the salt and squeezes the lemon into his open eye." The collective group moaned with surprise. Until that moment, I didn't even remember that happening. I completely forgot that Mabel and I met back up with Scott amongst the dancing crowd. "Then to top it off, snorts the tequila. Craziest shit I've ever seen. Henry you should have seen it."

"I have." Henry bellowed with laughter and patted me on the back. "He used to do that to fuck with people in the Marines."

"Doesn't it hurt?" Alice asked.

"Painfully." I rubbed at my eyes, now understanding the reason for the pain, and regretting some life decisions.

"Wanna drink?" asked Henry.

"Not really." Sitting on a silver tray table were several glasses and a bottle of champagne and orange juice. I had to ask how they brought them down.

"We ain't carrying nothing down that embankment. I just call up to the house and they send it down on the dumbwaiter." A tiny metal door broke the natural contours of the rocks.

"Jesus, Henry. How rich are you?"

"Actually, this was already here. That writer who owned this place had it installed. It's old as shit, but pretty kick ass."

"No shit it is." I glanced down at the blue paint smudged on Henry's palms. "But not rich enough to get someone to paint the house for you?"

Henry stared at his hands and tried to wipe away the blue with no success.

"Henry? Paint houses?" The tribe exploded.

"Henry's an artist." Scott informed me. Some of the others chuckled to themselves, but Henry smirked, shaking his head. I could see he wanted to change the subject.

"Artist?"

"He has a room in the attic where he doodles."

"I don't doodle."

"He doesn't doodle, Scott. He's a serious painter who doesn't like to show people." Alice teased him, poking him in the side, then leaned up to kiss him. "But I've seen it."

"It's a stupid hobby and I'm not that good, but I still don't fuckin' doodle."

"He doodles." Scott assured me.

"Shut up." Henry crossed his arms over his chest as if insulted.

"He's modest." Alice draped her arm around his shoulders and kissed a ticklish spot on his neck. "He's really good, but he thinks painting isn't something a professional fighter should do."

"Or others should even know about," Henry jested.

"That's pretty cool, man," I said. Henry shrugged me off.

"It's dumb and a little sissy for a fighter." Henry remarked, but I knew he was lying about it. He tried to save face, but I didn't care about stuff like the others.

"Dude, you're talking to a combat vet Marine who's an aspiring writer. Sometimes I wanna kick my own ass. Not that macho."

"Hemingway was macho." He had a point.

"So." Alice directed her tone at me. "What caused you two to become friends? I know you were kids, but how did you meet?"

"How do any two boys meet? Circumstances."

"Circumstances?" They hung on every word, waiting to pass judgement, so I paused to select them carefully.

"Strength in numbers," I said. Henry laughed.

"What?" Alice wondered. "I'm confused. What am I missing?"

"We had a mutual bully in third grade."

"For real? You both got beat up together?"

"No. Leslie Blackwell would catch us alone and beat the shit out of us. I didn't even know Leslie was doing it to other kids. I thought I was alone," Henry said.

The very mention of the name struck like a tidal wave and still blistered hate beneath my skin.

"Wait, Leslie? A girl bullied you?" Alice asked.

"No. Leslie is a he." Henry informed her.

"Leslie Blackwell? I've heard this name before," Alice said, trying to recall from where.

"I'm sure I've mentioned it and I guess it was the name that ddrr-ove him to be a jerk." Henry frowned at the memory and took a drink.

"So, I went into the restroom and there Leslie was washing his hands. I was sick of him and welcomed a fight. About that time, Henry came in."

"So, I find Nicky standing there, mad-dogging *my* ttoorr-mentor washing his hands." Henry heisted my tale as he stood, jerking away the group's attention. "I was terrified of Leslie, but here was Nicanor ready to fuck shit up."

"Let me guess, this Leslie beat up both of you and you bonded over this," Philip said.

"No, we kicked the shit out of that guy."

"Damn right," I said, bumping knuckles with Henry. "Fucked him up good. He never messed with anyone again. That kid went his entire school life with his head down after that beating."

"That was back when you went by Nicky," Henry said, still laughing at our shared memory.

"Nicky?" Mabel scrunched her face, trying to understand.

"No one could figure out how to pronounce my name, so I let everyone call me Nick. Never Nicky though. Only this asshole."

"Hell yeah. After the beating we dished out, we were close as kin."

"Fascinating." Mabel cooed.

"May I ask you another question I've been dying to ask?" Alice asked.

"Sure," I replied. The sound of nostalgia in her tone lowered my guard.

"Did you lose your finger in the war?" She pounced, and I kicked myself for not being prepared to deflect such attacks.

"Alice!" Henry snapped.

"What?" She shot a look of bewilderment at him as if insulted he would try to chastise her. "I'm dying to know."

The others leaned in for my answer. As if operating on its own accord, my hand tucked under my arm. Time didn't heal all wounds. I still don't like people looking at it, and now everyone was staring.

Fuck that. Bust their faces. They want to mock you. Snap out a kick. Plant it in Alice's face. Let's see how her videos do with shattered orbital bones. Don'cha wanna fuck them up? Don'cha wanna? Don'cha wanna?

I sighed. Perhaps it was time to answer, to get them off my back, but before I spoke, Mabel stood. She dusted the sand off her legs as the coverup she wore flapped in the breeze. Its red lotus flowers swayed in a hypnotic pattern of blue coral print.

"I'm going snorkeling, wanna go?" She tossed me a pair of goggles and a snorkel from her bag.

"Hey, one of those are mine." Alice objected, but Mabel didn't acknowledge her so neither did I.

"Yeah."

"Hang on." Scott held up his hand as he puffed on his e-cigarette. "Kind of would like to know what happened, as well."

"Yeah." Philip chimed in. "You should answer Alice's question."

"I don't have to do shit," I said. Henry howled hysterically while the others looked on. I tore off my shirt, knowing the scars dotting my chest and back would spark more questions. Taking my hand, Mabel led me away from the group that Henry was scolding.

Before hitting the water, I could hear him say, "Y'all are fuckin' rude. I hope he snaps on you, dumbasses."

"Sure, Henry. Real scared," Philip said in a rolling pompous chuckle.

"You should be." His tone went calm and serious.

"Oh, sounds like a real man," Alice said.

"Oh no, Alice is in heat again." Nathan joked, to which the others teased her and angered Henry. I didn't hear what came after that as the tide washed over my ankles and drowned out their voices. The soothing water cooled my aching feet. Mabel swam out, and I followed, hurrying to pull my goggles over my eyes.

She sank, and the water swallowed her up without disturbing its surface. I dove into the crystal-clear surf and watched as she glided her hand across the sand of the rippled ocean floor. Her toned legs, which I desired to touch, kicked a steady rhythm, slowly propelling her forward. She looked over her shoulder as if knowing I was watching her and winked. I followed.

At fifty meters out, before the drastic drop of the ocean floor, Mabel stopped to tread water.

"You good?" I asked. Her wet hair plastered back like the day she emerged on my beach. She pulled the goggles over her eyes.

"God, this place is –" The words stopped in her throat. It was the first time I found her speechless. Words weren't needed; I knew the beauty of it all.

"Yeah, it is. Have you swum near the wreckage yet?" I pointed to the mostly sunken ship.

"No. I'm scared to go that far out alone."

"Let's go. Tide's low. Should be good."

"Why does it matter if the tide is low?"

"Less chance of sharks at low tide in this cove."

"Cove?"

"See those two cliffs?" I pointed to the two rockfaces coming down off the hill. They circled around, leaving an opening large enough for boats to come in. "They help block the hard current from the ocean and the steamer sits before the reef. At low tide, it's harder for sharks to cross it."

I examined her body and she leaned away from me with a near invisible seductive grin. "See something you like?"

"Checking for anything shiny," I said.

"Why?"

"Barracudas."

"Barracudas? Are they that dangerous?"

"They can be. They're fast and have a hell of a bite, but you're not wearing anything tempting, so we'll be OK." A look of concern came over her. "Don't worry, the water is clear. If it was murky and you had something reflective on, then we'd worry."

"Are there a lot of barracudas out here?"

"I'm sure you'll see one or two."

"Hmm," she said. I waited for her to utter her favorite word - *fascinating,* but she didn't. Instead she continued with, "Might be good to add in a book."

"So, you wanna go?"

"Do you?"

"Anything to get away from that crowd." I tossed a glanced over my shoulder, annoyed by their apparent good time.

"Sometimes they suck."

"Tell me about it. And thanks. I don't like talking about my hand."

"Well, I didn't do that for you. You looked as if you were about to spill it, and no way am I gonna let you tell them that story when you haven't even told me it yet. That's my scoop."

"Such a noble heart you have." This made her laugh and splash water at me.

"I know. Sometimes I don't know what to do with myself. How'd you lose it?"

"My finger?"

"Yeah."

"Ex-lover."

"Ass." She splashed me again. The water settled around us and we floated there, her waiting for me to divulge my secret; me refusing. "Fine, let's go to the wreckage."

"If you want." Before I could say anything else, she stuck her face into the water and swam off.

It had been a long time since I had looked at the sea from beneath the surface. What amazements it held. Bright and dark shafts of light filtered down from above. As far as the eye could see, the ivory sands blurred blue with the deep ocean. Pops of color revealed decorative fish swimming against a great copulation of coral.

Skirting from view, an octopus vanished beneath an algae-covered rock. We almost missed an invisible manta ray, small in stature, materialize from the sand as a common blue crab danced by it. I tapped Mabel's foot and pointed out the ice blue crab that shined in its own glory. The tiny shellfish poked at a spiky dark sea urchin, knocking it from its path as it hurried on thin legs to the coral.

Everything appeared bright and new. The sea had engulfed a small dinghy where, buried in the sand for decades, made a new home for nautical life. Circling about it, a school of clown fish played tag with one another. One broke off from the group and swam to us, stopping within arm's reach. It floated there, not frightened or aggressive, and studied us. To this small fish, we were massive, foreign figures, like gods coming to survey her life.

I floated, not wanting to spook the little creature, but simply wanting to watch it. Its small fins gracefully glided back and forth, keeping the fish steady. Her attention shifted from Mabel to me and back. The tiny clown fish twitched, turned, then swam away to rejoin its group. I imagine it went to tell its small friends of the two great travelers from the surface. My laugh bounded up the plastic tube lodged in my mouth, sounding odd underwater.

I looked to find Mabel much farther along and I kicked to catch up. Water fought to get inside my snorkel and choke off my air. It had been years since I swam, and the constant paddling strained my arms. I stopped only when Mabel's head resurfaced ten feet from the wreckage. The lifeless shell of the ship laid overgrown by rust and algae; a doomed skeleton shackled by the sea.

Mabel took a hard breath, smiled, and hand-combed her short, wet hair behind her head. Tiny fragments of light gleamed in the drops beading off her face, working their way down, seeping back into the ocean from which they came.

Her elongated lashes batted away any water clouding her vision, melting the stress and worries from her appearance, leaving her with a clarity and cleanliness that magnified her brown eyes. We hovered, not speaking but periodically making eye contact.

The tide lifted and lowered us like buoys as the water level rose more than I had anticipated. Mabel paddled her arms, projecting herself forward, swimming to the wreckage where I pointed out different parts that the ocean had transformed. Barnacles and rust painted a rough texture over the once sleek steel. In a hundred years, the entire ship would be some crustacean of the sea, eaten away by salt and time. Shadow and light battled through the iridescent water, disappearing and reappearing a world both foreign and familiar to us.

Small fish and other sea life scattered for shelter. I led her to a portion of the wreckage that rose out of the water. "Be careful now."

"This is beautiful," Mabel said. An out of place shadow appeared, giving me pause. I nudged Mabel, trying not to alarm her, but getting her to climb up on a rusty platform. She marveled at the ship, then gasped as a reddish gray fin broke the surface like a demented sail. Fear shocked her body. Her hands pushed at the railing, trying to get away from the water, but in doing so, snapped the rusty metal bar. It splashed into the water and Mabel went off-balance.

Before she could tumble forward and become lunch for that damn shark, I captured her arm, pulling her away from the edge. She snaked around my midsection, squeezing me tight, clinging on as if I was a life-preserver. "Oh my god. Oh my god."

"Bastard," I muttered under my breath.

"You said sharks wouldn't get in here at low tide." Her voice reached an octave higher and a tremor vibrated her body.

"The tide changed."

"What are we gonna do?" she asked. I scanned the beach and flapped my arms in the air to no prevail. The beach dwellers were too preoccupied with their own entertainment to notice us. Mabel shouted. I jumped, but the rusty grate we stood on groaned and we feared it would collapse.

I reached for my knife but touched only the skin on my backside.

"Damnit."

"What are we going to do?" Mabel asked. The water swelled, claiming more of the wreckage we stood on. I looked for a weapon, a sharp stick to jab at the beast, and drive it away.

"Let's shout for Henry at the same time," Mabel said.

The shark circled. On the count of three, we shouted and this time, over the rush of a breeze and the sounds of the surf, Henry heard us. He came to the shoreline and waved back as the bull shark cruised near. He was so close, I could touch him, so Mabel and I eased away from the water.

"Get the boat." I shouted, pointing at the small motorboat tied to the dock. He raised his arms out, not understanding what I was saying. We shouted together, "The boat!"

Then we pointed frantically at the fin in the water. I'm guessing he got my point, because he sprinted across the sand and leapt onto the pier.

"Holy shit, this is crazy," Mabel said. "I wish we had your boat."

"Me too," I paused, pulse pounding, and had to take several long breaths to calm myself. The iron grate moaned again. The tension of her grip eased, and she leaned forward near the missing railing to get a closer view of the beast. Vivid flashes of her plunging into the ocean, gone in a cloud of red water, spawned from the pit of my stomach and planted the seed of anxiety. "Now we wait. He won't be long."

"Good," she said, keeping an eye on the shark's fin. I had the strange feeling she wanted to reach out and touch the creature. She stepped closer to the ledge and a piece of rusty grate splashed into the sea. Mabel jerked backward into my arms. I tried to keep our movements shallow, fearing the entire platform would fall out from beneath us. Both our minds worked to neutralize the situation of fear.

"And you can't eat shark meat?" Her voice trembled, eyes watching the water.

"You can, but the meat isn't any good and most places have deemed it illegal." Our conversation kept our worries off the scarred fin. It circled in close to investigate, its flat head breaking the surface. We eyed each other, man and beast, and I knew one day I would kill that damn creature, or he would me. It wanted me as much as I wanted him. I'm sure if I dove off, the beast would have me, and leave Mabel completely alone. "Besides, marlins are more fun to catch. They can grow to incredible sizes. If you want, you can come out with me sometime and we can catch one."

"A big one?"

"We'll catch the biggest one out there."

"What about trying to catch that?" I looked at the scarred fin and my neck flexed. My teeth mashed into one another and the slits of my eyes sharpened to the edge of a dagger. The water lapped up through the fragile grate, splashing our feet.

"I'll kill that damn fish. It's been a thorn in my side for too long."

"How would you catch a shark like that?"

"There's several ways to catch a shark, but the size of that fish, I know it'll be one hell of a battle."

"Sounds like a date." I didn't know if this was a question or a statement. I started panicking for an excuse until she continued, "A personal fishing trip? I'm in. How about tomorrow morning at eight?"

The buzzing of a small motor broke the sound of the waves beyond the reef.

"Sounds good to me."

The red fin glided with grace into the water until nothing remained but a calm surf. I stared into the sea as the creature sank deep and swam away. Beams of stretching light crawled across the seabed and the love and fear I found in the water reflected at me. The ocean moved and lived around us and we were there, among it, one sea of consciousness.

Chapter Sixteen

From my previous experience, I wasn't expecting her to be at the dock by eight. At five past seven, the sun peeked over the horizon and she sauntered down in a pair of cutoff blue jeans shorts and a large hat. Simple clothes or elegant gowns, no one matched her stunning beauty. My own attire disappointed me and yet it was nothing I hadn't worn to sea before.

"Ahoy there," I called out, playing up the seaman jargon. She waved back.

"Am I too early?"

"Better early than late. Fish love breakfast." Taking her hand, I helped her over the gunwale. The boat rocked, shifting its weight, and Mabel stumbled. Digging her fingers into my bicep, a flash of fear popped in her eyes. Her body leaned away, and I caught her by one arm and the waist. I braced myself as her chest collided with the top of my midsection. Her head stood directly under my nose. My knees wanted to weaken. "You good?"

Her arms stayed wrapped around me as she looked up with 'thank you' written all over her face. She nodded, but I could still sense a hint of hesitation to let go. Her chest heaved one great breath for her to calm herself and we parted our embrace.

"I didn't know if you'd show," I said.

"Why not?"

"Well, an encounter with a shark is a scary thing."

"For you, sure, but I wasn't scared. Intrigued would be the proper word."

"Oh yeah? OK, that's, I don't know, crazy."

"I'm not scared of dying," she said in her blunt manner, surveying the AJAX. The wind shifted, threatening to blow her hat off as she crossed the deck to eye the ocean past the bay. The passion for adventure radiated off her. "Let's do this."

"Alright. Let's push off."

"Is your friend coming?"

"Kojo? No." I rushed up the ladder to the flying bridge and she followed.

"No first mate? Is this a ploy to get me all alone?" She asked. I kicked on the engine and pulled away from the dock. The AJAX cut through the smooth sheet of glass-like water of the bay.

"Damn, you figured out my master plan." I flicked my eyebrows playfully at her, flashing my seductive, half-smile. One of her eyebrows raised questioningly and her face scrunched up. Amused, she leaned back against the railing, bowing her spine, and allowing the breeze to kiss at the soft tissue of her neck. I piloted into the gulf stream on calm water and knew the fishing would be good today. "So, what do you feel like catching?"

"That shark from yesterday."

"Big ambitions."

"You think we'll see a fish like that today?"

The notion of the bull shark caused me to sigh and eye the sea. "Oh, we'll see him. Believe me, that bastard has a thing for me."

"Steals your bait?" she asked.

"Steals my catches is more like it. Never goes after my bait for some reason."

"Maybe you need better bait." She shouted over the loud engine and the rushing winds torpedoing around us. I couldn't help laughing. "Oh, I have something in mind for that one."

"Bait?"

"Yeah. Something he could never resist."

"Fascinating. You know what's strange?" There it was, her mind rushing from one idea to another. "Picturing you and Henry in the service together."

"Why?"

"He doesn't talk about it much. He said he met some trainer in the gym on base, but nothing else really. I guess it upsets him that he didn't go over." I remembered it all as she spoke but didn't care to get into that part of my life with anyone, even her.

"Go over? You know your slang."

"Been around plenty of military my whole life."

"Father?"

"Yeah. And other people. Spend enough time around them, you're kinda forced to pick up on the lingo." I nodded, understanding what she meant, and felt an uncomfortable pause coming on. Butterflies fluttered in my stomach. I didn't want a moment of awkwardness on this trip.

"Can't blame him though," I said. She looked at me as if forgetting what we were originally talking about. "Henry."

"Blame him for what?"

"You can't blame him for regretting not going to Iraq. Those were hard times and bad shit happens in war. He knew some of the guys that died over there."

"You could be right, but why hate himself?"

"It's hard for a man to miss out on his destiny."

"Destiny? What? Being champion of the world wasn't his destiny?"

"Growing up, Henry believed he'd distinguish himself in combat. His father received the Silver Star in Vietnam and his granddad, a Navy Cross on Iwo Jima."

"But that's not fair on him. Neither one of you knew he would be selected for the boxing team."

"Sure, but doesn't change things, though. His friends died. I know I'd hate myself for not being there. I'm sure he thinks that if he was there, some guys would be alive today."

"What happened though?" Mabel asked. I'm sure a look of confusion came across my face because she was forced to clarify. "Between you and Henry?"

"Why do you think something happened?"

"Because he thought you were dead for the last two decades. Friends don't do that to one another. So, what happened?" She caught me and I was stuck.

"Like I said, bad things happened over there, and I just didn't want to be around people anymore."

"So, that's why you left?" The tone in her voice was one of victory. She had been hounding me for that answer and although it was only part of the story, it was still enough to give her satisfaction.

"Mostly, yeah. I guess."

"Why didn't he try calling your parents?"

"Got no parents."

"Both dead?"

"Yeah."

"You're withholding." She glared at me with that faint seductive grin, hypnotizing me to speak. "Why didn't a childhood friend try to get in touch when he got back from the war? I mean, you obviously kept up with him. You've been watching his fights. It's not like you completely forget about him. What happened?"

"He wasn't my top priority. I got injured," I said, tucking my hand. "The world takes on a different view when all your friends are wasted, and you almost die. Besides, there were other things going on."

"Like what?" Mabel asked. I paused, wanting to tell her the real truth, the deep down hurt I had buried years ago. Instead, I came up with something much easier.

"Life." She read my face, digging for information, but my guard was up.

"There's something you're not saying."

"Geez, I don't know. Life has different journeys for us all and Henry and I went on two different paths. He went to the Olympics and I went to Hell. Do you know how to fish?"

"I've never been deep sea fishing before. It looked fun the other day."

"Why don't we head down to the stern and bait some hooks." I killed the engine and we scampered to the deck below. I instructed her how to rig the line with small tuna and how to hide the hook while giving it a good hold on the bait. Mabel hesitated to touch the dead tuna in the well, but taking a deep breath, she forced herself. She ran the hook through the bait, game at getting her hands dirty.

"There you go. Not bad." She baited her hook with a first timers' excitement, fantasizing about a large catch. The AJAX drifted, carrying our lines out with the current. The sun rose to paint the sky a clear blue with spots of white clouds as the ocean pitched and rolled around us.

"So, I was meaning to ask you something," she said, easing into the fighting chair and propping her feet up on the transom. Aviator sunglasses hid my eyes while I marveled at her long, toned, smooth legs glowing in the mid-day light. A ping of fear popped into my mind as her words echoed that of Alice who had started her own question the day before with a similar tone. I didn't know if I wanted to proceed with the conversation, but the top row of her ivory white teeth biting into her lower lip melted my borders.

Reluctantly, I said, "Go for it."

"What was that fight about?" she asked. I sighed, annoyed with the constant talk of Henry and myself.

"You have to be more specific. I get into a lot of arguments."

"On the dock the other day? Why did those guys want to kick the shit out of you?"

"Oh, that. I pissed off their boss and he wants me dead."

"Wants you dead, you can't be serious?"

"I am. I got into a scuffle with him. He's a douchebag who also sent his brother to rough me up and scare me off the island."

"How big is this brother?"

"Very big. Heavyweight, cut from stone."

"What'd you do?"

"I stabbed him."

"You stabbed him?" Her legs jumped off the transom as she sat straight up.

"Yeah. I sliced him open. Jacob wasn't too happy about that."

"Who's Jacob?"

"Jacob Coke. He's the boss. His cousin is the one I told you about, who runs the Pain Posse."

"Oh, yes, the Pain Pussies. Why does Jacob Coke want to hurt you? Besides you cutting up his brother."

"Why? You writin' a book?"

"Well, yeah." The word 'idiot' flashed across my face. "But not a book on you."

"Jacob's a rich man. He controls all the charters and if you charter your boat, you pay him. Everyone pretty much works for him. Except, I don't work for him no more and I still charter."

"And he doesn't like that."

"Not really."

"Aren't you afraid?"

"No." I left it at that. I didn't tell her of the years that had hardened me, the rough neighborhood I came from, the fourteen explosions, or the woes of direct combat fire. Only one man scares me, and it wasn't Jacob Coke. "Besides, it doesn't matter."

"Him wanting to kill you, doesn't matter?"

"Not really." I paused, watching the end of her line. It bobbed, then pulled tight as something took the bait and ran. "The only thing that matters to me is that."

Her eyes followed my finger to her spinning reel. She lunged for it, but I stopped her. The braided line would hold, but it could still break if not properly handled. I coached her, allowing her to fight the fish. It wasn't too big, but very feisty, perhaps a medium tuna or a mackerel.

She reeled and pulled, doing everything I instructed her to do until she didn't need me anymore. Mabel picked up the art like a natural, keeping the line tight as not to weaken the braid of it. I sat back happy to observe.

"It's coming toward the ship," she said. I stepped to the stern and readied the gaff to pull it in as it neared the rollers at the back. "When it gets up here, stay clear."

A ghost appeared in the water, a figure off-colored from the dark ocean, drifting about. I strained my eyes and removed my sunglasses but couldn't see what was on her line yet. It circled below the surface, heading starboard, then pulling back portside without fleeing. I kept clear of the rig as the rod bent.

She eased forward, then arching her back, pulled hard. I leaned closer to the stern, preparing the gaff to hook her catch, and leapt back. The words for her to stop reeling were barely out of my mouth when an endless row of teeth emerged, gapping, beckoning for me to slip and lose a limb.

Chapter Seventeen

The black eyes of a tiger shark glared at me while snapping its jaws. I set the gaff and pulled the shark half aboard my ship. It thrashed on the roller, threatening to teeter back into the ocean and pull me with it.

Its flesh looked slick like a marble countertop. The greenish gray body faded into a light-yellow underbelly. Black vertical lines ran in a row from the tip of its pointed caudal fin to the eyes. Its wedge-shaped head jerked about, attempting to throw its body back into the sea.

"Take this," I said. Mabel bounced from the chair, the rod and reel falling to the deck, and took the gaff's wooden handle. She stayed back, keeping clear in case the shark grew legs and attacked. Its head whipped about, but she kept a hard hold on the gaff. Slinging out my knife, I cut the line. The shark flopped, rolling backward into the ocean. The sea kicked up, turned over white, and masked the shark's retreat.

"What'd you do that for?" Mabel shouted, hurrying to the stern in time to see the shark swim away.

"I don't like sharks. All it takes is one misstep and you're in a world of trouble."

"God, that was scary. I thought that damn thing would leap up here like in Jaws and you'd be dead."

"What? Why just me?"

"Well, you're closer and I don't see me dying." She laughed and reclaimed the fighting chair. "Was that the one from yesterday?"

"No, that was a tiger shark. The red fin devil from yesterday is a bull shark. Both man-eaters."

"That thing was massive," Mabel said, looking overboard to see if the shark was still there.

"It was young."

"How can you tell?"

"The dark stripes. Those lines start to fade as it gets older."

"Which one is the worst, the bull shark or tiger?"

"To me, the damn bull shark. Tigers need to constantly move, but not the bull shark. They also go in salt or freshwater. Dangerous little buggers."

"Have you ever seen one attack someone?"

"Yeah."

"Fascinating. Was it Kojo?"

"What?"

"Was it Kojo? Is that how he lost his leg?"

"No," I said, reaching into the cooler for two beers. Distracted, I added, "Kojo lost his leg in Iraq."

If I could have, I would've thrown myself upon a sword at betraying my friend. Mabel took the beer from me and sat back in the fighting chair. No emotion crossed her face, but I could tell she was pleased in her victory. I busied myself with baiting and casting, avoiding the sense of delight I'm sure she was bottling inside.

"What happened?" she asked. I sighed. My finger reached my lips and rubbed in that old displeasing habit of mine. The pain felt right but I deserved to feel much worse.

"Bad times." I locked both rods into their holders and geared up the third, which I had cut the line. "That's what happens in war."

"Bad times happen all over, not just in war."

"It's worse in combat," I said.

"How? Tell me." She pushed on, not moving from the fighting chair as she leaned back. That old feeling of being one of her projects returned.

"You don't wanna know what real combat is like."

"Yes, I do. I want to write about it."

"You wanna write about combat? What? You wanna be Hemingway? Is that what you're after?" I asked. She shrugged her shoulders, not giving me a real answer. "Well hell, there's a fuckin' war happening on the other side of the island. Why not go check it out for yourself?"

"That might be something I should do. Might be good for my book."

My irritation worked its way up my body.

"Yeah and get your fool head shot off." I don't know why I was getting angry with her. She had no idea what she was asking for, but I did. I knew the true horrors of war. My finger returned to my lips. "Why not join the military?"

Then my stomach crawled up my throat as she said, "I would have if it wasn't for my husband."

Chapter Eighteen

Husband - the word clung in the air between us. Hurt replaced my annoyance at her probing into my life. I wished I hadn't heard her. Here she sat, a married woman, and yet, gallivanting with anyone she wanted. The pain in my heart prevented me from rigging the line and I couldn't face her either. I wanted to get away.

What an idiot.

From the corner of my eye I caught her staring. She hadn't moved except to drink her beer.

"You're married?" I steadied my voice while forcing out the question.

"Was."

"Divorced?" I hoped.

"Widowed." She answered. Regret stung. Anger turned to hurt that now morphed into guilt.

"I'm sorry. I didn't—"

"It's OK. I don't talk about it, I guess."

"He was a soldier?" Her early statement about knowing military people dawning on me.

"He was. He died in the war."

"Iraq?"

She slightly shook her head. "Different war."

I wanted to ask how, to know if it was like my men in Iraq. *Did he get shot or blown up? Was he alone like my friend, Carmichael, or did he get sniped standing between two guys like my friend, Dempsey?*

I instead said the only thing anyone can say, "I'm sorry."

"It's fine. He was a good man and we were married for five years."

"Kids?" I feared to ask. Again, she shook her head.

"No, but we planned to. I was in school for journalism. Another idea of his."

"His idea? You didn't want to be a writer?"

"Oh no. I did, but I was under the impression I needed to do something more secure. I was going into nursing, but he told me to go after my dream and pushed me to journalism. He was a good man that way."

"What was his name?"

"Dmitry," she said then paused. Her face scrunched up and a lite chuckle popped out. "I haven't spoken his name in years."

"Dmitry? Russian?" I tried picturing what this man looked like but could only imagine a burly Russian soldier in a cold war uniform.

"Ukraine." This also explained her slight accent I detected.

"I knew it. I knew you weren't from the States. I figured Russian."

"Not Russian. Never Russian." She was forceful, offended by my statement, but I made a note of it. Never call her Russian.

"He died in Russia." The root of her aggravation. "Like you said, life makes different paths for us all. We had a little house, a large backyard, planned on starting a family, but things went different for us."

"Was it quick?" To me, the scariest thing about war was a long drawn out death full of suffering. Dying men pleading with gods and crying for mommas. Late at night, in the comfort of my own home, the waves mimicked their screams. It brings about a fear that ordinary citizens don't understand. Suffering and dying all alone, far from home, in a foreign country. Talk of her husband only ignited memories I had suppressed for years.

"I doubt it was quick," she said. I didn't want to hear that as much as I'm sure she didn't want to speak it.

"Shit. I'm sorry. Mabel, you don't—"

"No. I should." I worried she would cry, but not a single tear filled her brown eyes. For some reason, it occurred to me that she had cried all she ever would. "He was an opponent of the Russian movement in Ukraine. A captain in the military, he spoke out against Vladimir Putin. When Putin stated that he wasn't going to get involved with Crimea, he secretly was setting a plan in motion for it. To help prevent a large uprising against Russian forces, many pieces had to be removed. Dmitry was one of those pieces."

My mouth hung open and the only thing I could say was, "Shit."

"We were making love one night in our quiet little house with the garden in the backyard." A small smile curled the edge of her lips as she pictured back on the house she once owned. It faded quickly as she continued, "We didn't hear anything when men in unmarked uniforms kicked open the door and jerked him from our marital bed. Dmitry screamed for me to flee. To get out, but I couldn't leave him."

"Did they kill him there?"

"They took Dmitry to a Gulag."

"Gulag? Didn't those things end when Stalin died?"

"Russia keeps up their old habits of showing the world only what they want to show. I don't care what people think or say, the old Soviet Union is still strong with Putin in office."

"Did you ever see him again?"

"I searched for him and found where he was. I found a lawyer who said he could help, but I had little money since Dmitry's bank accounts were frozen when he was arrested. The lawyer said he could help for special favors."

My index finger rose to my lip and I rubbed while transfixed by her story. The urge to hit something flared through me at the idea of some sleezy guy sitting behind a desk, a nauseating perverse individual with his gut hanging out and his dreary eyes gawking at her like a meal.

"It was what it was, and I was sure I would see Dmitry again. For three months this affair happened, and he did locate my husband, but it was too late. They had executed him as an enemy of the state. He was tossed into an unmarked grave with the rest of the captured men."

"How can you be sure it was even him if it was an unmarked grave?"

"The lawyer presented me with the official death certificate. He was shot on a firing line. Enemy of the state. When it all ended, his name wasn't remembered. The U.N. did nothing to Putin. The entire thing was simply overlooked, forgotten, swept under the rug. After that, life didn't seem as meaningful without him, so I drifted along. Writing pays the bills."

"How'd you end up in America?"

"My father was United States Air Force. My mother was French. They married then had me when he was stationed in Ukraine, so I spent most of my life speaking English or French at home, and Ukrainian elsewhere."

"That's why I couldn't figure out your accent. I'm normally good with placing people. I thought it was odd you didn't have the hard dialect in your English that most Europeans have."

"No. My father taught me a lot and we watched a lot of American movies. He loves Kurt Russell."

"Who doesn't?" We shared an agreeable nod. "Your parents are alive?"

"They live in California and after Dmitry died, I went to be with them."

"How did you get involved with Henry?"

"Dmitry loved MMA. We once got to meet Fedor Emelianenko when he fought Pedro Rizzo."

"You got to meet the Last Emperor? What was he like?" The elation in my voice couldn't be masked.

"A pure gentleman. So, after Dmitry was murdered, I found watching the sport made me feel closer to him. I figured why not be a sportswriter for the biggest growing, bloodiest sport in the world." One of the fishing rods hit and I hurried to get a hold of it. Mabel sat her beer down in anticipation.

"You think it could be another shark?"

"Doubt it."

"Could it be the same shark?"

"Could be but doesn't feel that way to me. Maybe a mackerel or tuna. Perfect fish to catch. Here, reel her in." I passed over the rod. The fight wasn't as hard as the tiger shark and Mabel worked the line accordingly.

"When did you witness the shark attack?" Mabel asked, pulling and relaxing, reeling and pausing.

"A long time ago. Reel."

"No fair. Spill it. What happened?" she asked while turning the crank. I knew she wouldn't relent and therefore, I told.

"You know that shark with the red scars on its fin?"

"Yeah."

"I gave him those scars."

"When it was attacking someone?"

"No. Kojo was reeling in a big marlin and the damn thing started eating it at the back of my boat. I grabbed the trench gun—"

"What's a trench gun?" she asked, still reeling.

"The shotgun in the cabin. I blasted the shark near point blank with three shots and thought I killed it."

"But you didn't." She mocked.

"No, I didn't." I rolled my eyes, playfully. "About a month later, he came back, killing at least one of my catches a day."

"Did anyone else have a problem with him?"

"No. I asked about the red fin, but most other fishermen thought I was just a crazy white guy."

"When did they start to believe you?" Mabel asked. She paused from reeling and sat up. She read my face, trying to make mental ticks so she could write about this later.

I sighed and said, "When the terror began."

Chapter Nineteen

She glared at me and I turned away. Reality set in and I found myself struggling to tell the story. Those were hard times and there was much death and suffering on the island. It was a period of my life I didn't care to relive, but the story was already cast, and she was hooked. I motioned for her to keep reeling while I studied the line, debating with my internal monologue on where I should begin. Her eyes burned into me.

"A couple of tourists got killed and everyone figured it was a random shark attack. Keep reeling." I pointed to her hands and she did. "Three men on a boat. Two were killed. The survivor couldn't identify the shark but did report the red scars on the fin."

"Jesus. Did they find the bodies of the other two?"

"The leg of one and head of the other."

"Good god," Mabel said, shocked and awed. She kept one eye on me and one eye on her reel, steadily bringing in the fish. The small fin of a tuna broke the water's surface behind the boat. "Imagine what that was like. Thrashing about in the dark water, eyes stricken with horror, filled with fear, sounds muffled."

Mabel's words painted a horrific image that movies couldn't do justice.

"Yeah, but attacks fade quickly on an island, especially during the summer."

"Why the summer?"

"Summer is normally storm season here. Best time to come to the islands is around November to April or May. By June, it rains a lot."

"What? That's weird to me. I figured it would be too cold to come here then?"

"Nope."

"OK. So, what about the shark?" She brought me back to my story.

"Like I said, shark attacks fade quickly. Then a man was walking his horse through the river and was attacked. The horse was killed but a boy saved the man and reported the same red fin seen at the tourists' attack. People started believing. Panic swept across the island."

Mabel continuously reeled.

"The fact that the same red fin was spotted in the freshwater river freaked everyone out."

"Why?" Mabel asked.

"Most sharks can't swim in fresh water, but bull sharks can."

"Damn."

"Indeed. Then all hell broke loose when the son of a rich resort owner got killed."

"How?"

"Spearfishing. The shark attacked him in front of his friends. The resort owner was this rich dickhead I used to work for."

"Seems like there's a common trend that you don't like your employers."

"I don't. Especially rich assholes. He put out a bounty on the shark and every fisherman became a hunter. There were people coming from other countries wanting to get famous by catching the newsworthy fish."

Mabel pulled back on the rod, working the antagonizing fish to the stern. As my own tale took over me, I had nearly forgotten she had a fish on the end of her line.

"How big was the bounty?"

"Big. The resort owner wanted the shark mounted. Everyone with a boat came out. Some didn't make it back. Place got crowded, gas prices skyrocketed, and fights happened all the time. It was a madhouse out here. People shooting out engines and sinking boats to stifle the competition." I continued speaking as she strained, cranking the reel. With a little help from me, a beautiful large tuna slapped the surface.

"Sounds crazy."

"A ship exploded, killing everyone onboard. We thought the shark had died with it, but obviously, we were wrong." Her line twitched and I snatched it, keeping it astern, and said, "Here she comes. Reel."

"So, the attacks stopped?"

"For the most part. I think it got hurt in the explosion. After that, it stayed out in deeper waters to torment my ship. Jesus Christ!" I shouted, leaping back, scaring Mabel as the head of the tuna broke surface. She kept reeling, alarmed when the body of the large tuna disappeared inside the mouth of the red fin shark. The shark's jaws closed over three-quarters of the tuna. I pulled my 1911 and fired three shots, striking the shark only once. It bucked and dashed away.

"Speak of the devil and he appears," I said. Mabel sat back and rubbed her arms, bringing blood back to the fatigued appendages. "He should stay gone now."

She exhaled breaths of exhaustion but didn't appeared troubled that the shark had eaten her catch. "How'd you save him?"

"Save who?" I pulled the hook from the decapitated fish before heaving the head into the water. The sea rose to intercept it and the head was no more.

"Kojo. You said you once saved each other. I always thought you meant on a ship or something, but I'm guessing you meant in Iraq. What happened?"

"Geez, all the questions. Now I really do think you're writing a book."

"Just not on you." She reminded me, but I had the strange hunch she wasn't being honest.

"That's right. I keep forgetting." I played, pausing to finish my beer, adding a slight touch of dramatic effect. I debated if I should continue. "Yeah, it was in Iraq."

I confessed, and without realizing it, a weight I didn't know I had been carrying vanished. I hesitated to go further, but she nudged me along.

"Come on. It's only us out here sharing stories. Tell."

"I joined the Marines after high school at the request of Henry. I didn't have any ambitions. 9/11 happened our senior year and the country was brewing for a fight."

"So, you joined after graduation?" Mabel asked, retrieving two fresh, cold Krystal Ales. I didn't bother with rigging another line. Two were already out there and this was story time. Fishing could wait.

"No." I chuckled as memories came flowing back to me of times before the Corps. It had been ages since I thought of those times: blue collar jobs, an apartment with endless parties, and a lifetime of hopes and dreams in front of me. "We had an apartment and worked in a warehouse. It was great. We were always having parties."

"I guess some things don't change."

"I guess, but those parties were nothing compared to what he throws nowadays."

"Was he boxing then?"

"Amateurs. Man, he was good."

"Still is."

"That's true."

"He's sick," Mabel said.

"What?" Her statement caught me off-guard. "What do you mean?"

"He gets these headaches and spends entire days in his room with the lights out. It's also why he likes to paint. He says it eases the headaches."

"Why? You think he's getting high on the fumes?"

"Maybe."

"Damn. I caught him slurring his speech a little, but I figured he was just drunk. Has he seen a doctor?"

"No. He says it'll pass. Says it always does. Anyway, Henry got discovered and you went to Iraq?"

"Yeah, you kinda know that part of the story."

"Kind of?"

"I went to Iraq a couple of months before Fallujah happened."

"I remember hearing about that battle. Dmitry was so enthralled by it all. He read about it every day and watched all the news reports. Was it as bad as they said?"

I drifted off, staring out to sea while recalling a section of time I'd purposely locked away.

"It was worse. Cold and wet. We got trapped in a house."

"How so?"

"Followed two insurgents and killed them. Before we knew it, the walls were peppered from outside enemy fire. We sprawled out on the floor, but it didn't help. One of my guys made a break for it. He took a round to the grape." Naturally, most people reacted to a young man dying. Not Mabel. To avoid interrupting my story, she moved not a single muscle.

"Three more insurgents," I continued, "rushed us. I don't know why the hell I did, but for some reason I threw my hand up to say stop. I guess they surprised me. I didn't feel it happen. One moment I had five digits; the next, I had four."

Now came the involuntary reaction. Her eyes widened as I willingly held up my hand to show her, letting my guard down in what felt like the first time since the ambush. The mismatching skin of the scar stood out and I couldn't recall the last time I had even looked at it.

Shut up, you fool. She is using you for information for her book. You're gonna be a character and nothing more.

The dark inner voice created the impulse for my hand to touch my lip and rub. Forceful breaths escaped my nose and I pushed forward.

"Then I made a terrible decision. I left my dead comrade there and got my guys out."

"How is that terrible?"

"You never leave a fallen brother behind."

"Yes, but you couldn't help that."

"Hindsight is 20/20. The city was getting darker and we scrambled. Getting into an apartment, we thought we were safe, but not so. My PFC walked right into an RPK. It riddled him. Then my other Lance Corporal took one to the shoulder, before kicking a grenade away from us. He took shrapnel in the neck."

Despite her wide eyes and intense stare, her expression remained somber where others would have given away to sorrow.

"My fireteam was wiped out. More insurgents flooded the apartment to kill me. I fought up three flights of stairs. I figured I was gonna die, but I wasn't gonna fuckin' die alone. It's kind of a blur, but running up those stairs, I don't think I wasted one round. Every shot made a mark. Fuckin' insurgents had to climb over their dead friends to get a chance at me."

I wasn't aware that I was pacing and shifting weight between my legs, stalking around like a boxer anticipating a rough bout before it began.

"I found an unlocked door and rushed in. The apartment was an ordinary unit: couch, table, family decorations, religious items. I knew I couldn't stay there and fight it out, so I climbed out the window to a fire escape. Problem was, the fuckin' rusty-ass fire escape broke, and threw me into the side of another building. The staircase collapsed onto itself, which helped with the fall, but I still broke my arm and a piece of metal stabbed me in the leg."

"You didn't black out or anything?" Mabel asked.

"Wanted to but couldn't. They'd fuckin' kill me if I did. So, running low on ammo and in a shit ton of pain, I pulled myself into a nearby alley. They came looking for me and I got three more before my rifle ran dry."

"What'd you do?"

"I readied my old hunting knife." I pulled the knife off my hip for a little dramatic effect. It worked. Waving it garnered a smile from Mabel. Danger and excitement of the blade fired inside her, arousing some animalistic lust, for I noticed her legs crossing and pressing firmly into one another. "And played coy."

"Coy?"

"Acted like I was dead. A haj came around the corner and I tripped him. I knew the next insurgent would get me, but I didn't care. I was gonna kill this one last guy with everything I had. Oh, how he screamed." I reveled in the memory of the blood splattering in my face and the fear in his eyes as I took his life. "Another man came but dropped back as rounds came over my head. The next thing I know, someone was dragging me."

"Kojo?"

"The noise of my gun battle I guess caught his ear. He shot with one hand and pulled me with the other. He said he came around the corner and thought I was dead." Recalling this part of Kojo's story caused me to chuckle. "He said I scared the shit out of him when I jumped up and killed that insurgent. We didn't know one another. Hell, we weren't even in the same unit. He had no cause to save my ass, but here he was, a stranger coming to rescue me because we wore the same uniform."

"Fascinating." She reached out and touched the shark tooth attached to the end of my knife. "Is that a real shark's tooth?"

"Yeah. I found it embedded in the lower platform at the stern." I motioned to the rollers. "It makes the knife look intimidating."

She pressed her fingertip against the tooth's point, then withdrew quickly. "It's sharp."

"Because it's real." I placed the knife back in its sheath and checked the lines that were out. The current took them out behind my ship. "It's a bull shark tooth."

"Do you think it's from the red fin shark?"

"I do."

"Well, maybe that's why he keeps coming at you. He wants his tooth back." She amused herself, but I couldn't help thinking there could be some truth to her backwoods superstition. "So, you're the one hurt and Kojo's saving you. What happened next?"

"He's pulling me along, then he falls. In my mind, I remember him falling before the explosion, but it couldn't have happened that way. It was indirect fire, maybe a mortar but could have been a rocket. Anyway, the explosion was large and rocked the area. Kojo didn't scream out. That's how I knew he was in bad shape. Blood pooled all around. I had to act fast."

"The leg injury." She nodded knowingly.

"I tourniquet his leg, slung him over my shoulder, and carried on."

"With a broken arm?"

"Yep, fuckin' adrenaline. Not being able to wield my rifle and with Kojo passing out, I hobbled along with a piece of metal in my leg. I waited for another insurgent to find us, but I never stopped. Luckily, none did. I found this guy's unit and they called in an evac."

"Did you know his name?"

"Nope."

"How did you two stay in touch?"

"Truth be told, I'd be damned if we didn't end up in the beds next to each other in Germany. I didn't know it then, but the explosion that took his leg, also dusted me with little bits of shrapnel. The doctors couldn't believe I had carried him out. We were bonded from that day on."

"Why'd you come down here? Besides your parents dying, why'd you leave the States?" I finished off my beer and instinctively went in search of another.

"It wasn't one thing or another that sent me down here," I said. I happened upon a bottle of rum before a beer, and since it felt fitting for the situation, I took a swig and held it out to her. To my surprise, she accepted. My stories of Iraq reawakened the memories of her dead husband. Picking up on her pain, I attempted to change the mood, but found I didn't need to. Something bit down on the line and hurried away with it.

Mabel grabbed the reel and started cranking, the quickest learner I ever instructed. Determination scrunched up her face as she pulled and reeled.

"She's coming up," I said, helping the line to the back of the boat. The moment of struggle and hardship evaporated as the fish came free from the ocean and landed on the deck. Seven long spines created a beautiful dorsal fin and the teal and white colors of the body were separated by four curving lines.

"What is it?"

"A roosterfish."

"What?"

"A roosterfish. It's very beautiful. You have to get a picture of this," I said. She grabbed her camera and shot a photo of me. "No. It's not my catch. You hold it and I'll take a picture."

"I don't want to hold it."

"It's very easy. Here." I instructed her how to hold the fish and readied her camera. "Now smile."

Her grimace turned to joy and I captured the moment forever. Her body was frozen, and she didn't know what to do.

"What now?"

"We throw her back."

"She is very beautiful, isn't she?"

"Yes, she is." I wasn't looking at the fish.

"Do you want to keep her for your mantel?"

"Not my catch." We tossed her back and Mabel waved to the departing fish. I grabbed the bottle of rum and we shared it.

"So, it wasn't just one thing that brought you to the island?"

"Jesus, just pick right back up, don't you?"

"Yes, I do."

"No, it wasn't just one thing that brought me here. Hell, I didn't come straight to the island anyway."

"I figured you left the States for here," she said, catching her breath from the fight. A satisfying glow, like the one achieved after a good night of sex, enveloped her. She sat back in the fighting chair and drank from the bottle of rum. She was beauty in all its form.

"Kind of. I traveled for a bit first. I wanted to explore. After a couple of years, I sort of ended up here."

For a long time, I had seen war as my own personal tragedy, never crediting how combat trickles down to affect others who weren't present during the gun battle. We passed the bottle back and forth until the rum numbed our feelings.

Chapter Twenty

Strong pinks and purples shot through the clouds, battling for the sky until the night swallowed it up. The moon twinkled off the wakes slapping against the hull of the AJAX. There's no place I'd rather be than here watching her, cross-armed, staring at the end of the world from my stern. I reeled in the lines.

I suggested to go back to port, but she insisted on staying out longer. The stars dotted the sea, and in the distance, a whale moaned. I wanted to spend more time with her and so I offered dinner on the ship.

"Do you like chicken?" I asked, dropping anchor not far from the shoreline in front of my house. The water was calmer here, making dining out on the deck a pleasurable experience.

"Yes."

"Do you like cheese and bacon?"

"Of course." Eagerness and pride went into my cooking, which was apparent as I marched into the cabin. She followed, sitting at the small table in the galley. "It's nice in here."

"Thanks." I readied the food and prepared the small, portable grill. My normal culinary routine was a solo meal, so I had to get crafty for a side dish. A can of green beans would have to do, something simple with a hint of salt – delicious.

"Oh, cool." Mabel spotted the record player mounted to a small shelf. I pulled out a small box of vinyl from under the bed at the front of the boat. Taking the small grill out to the stern, I fired it up, tossing on the two pieces of cheese stuffed chicken wrapped in bacon. While I worked over the steps needed for this meal, a wave of music rushed from within the cabin. She sat at the cramped table with an assortment of vinyl records, studying them with the enthusiasm of a teenager.

"Man, these are cool. You only have vinyl?"

"No cd player here," I said, coming back in to hand her a drink.

"I like it." She picked up a few, turned them over to glance at the track list, then moved on to another. Frank Sinatra, Ol' Blue Eyes, came booming out of the speakers and even at the compact table, Mabel rocked her hips. "Vinyl's making a huge comeback. Even modern artists are putting things out on vinyl."

"I can't say I'd know a modern artist even if you played them for me."

"There aren't many good ones. Not like this." She held up a Dean Martin album. A quick chuckle escaped her while she sorted through the pile, picking up another album. "What is this?"

"Robin Hood: Prince of Thieves soundtrack," I said. She gave me a humorous look of suspicion and disapproval. "What? Bryan Adam's *Everything I do* is one of the greatest love songs ever."

Still laughing, she picked up another.

"And *Legends of the Fall* soundtrack as well?"

"Another great one. Those songs are all instrumental and kick ass. Put it on," I said. She sat it down to pick up one more.

"Oh my god, we have to play this."

She removed Frank from the player and replaced it with Bob Marley's *Legends*. The track played as she accompanied me outside. A gentle breeze blew in from the sea, and Mabel stood behind the fighting chair, crossing her arms in front of her chest, rubbing them for warmth.

"Want a blanket?" I asked.

"No. I'm fine." She moved closer to the grill, absorbing the heat. A small amount of cheese bubbled between two crisping pieces of bacon. My sense of smell was in a tug of war over which would reign supreme, the chicken or the bacon. "This is so amazing."

Fittingly, she whispered her words. Nights in front of the ocean felt silent to me, as if the need to whisper was in order. With the meal finished, I prepared our plates and we took a seat on the padded benches under the flying bridge. I figured she'd sit opposite of me, so we'd face one another, but instead, she scooched in close, sopping up my body heat.

"I can't believe you're able to go to bed to this."

"On good nights," I said. Melted cheese oozed from where her knife sliced through the tender chicken meat and moaned with delight when it touched her tongue. I smiled. "Come hurricane season, things get a little more hectic."

"I don't doubt that. Sounds scary." She wrapped her tongue around another piece of chicken. Another moan seeped out; a sound I adored. She pressed into me, the bare flesh of her arm rubbing against mine while the volatile sensation of her taste buds overwhelmed the rest of her body. "God, this is good."

"Thank you." These were the last words said between us for the remainder of the meal. The surf rolled in, receded out, synching to our breathing. Observing her enthralled by the ocean, I wondered why she was here. *Is this still some part of her research or does she genuinely enjoy my company?* I thought.

The surf grew into a gentle calming roll, and blue sparks flared across the shoreline, swirling into the small waves washing ashore, illuminated by millions of tiny bioluminescent phytoplankton.

"Check it out," I said, nearly leaping off my seat to point this rare occasion out to her.

"What is that?" Her posture stiffened, and leaning forward, she marveled at the blue glow of the microorganisms.

"Dinoflagellate."

"What?"

"I'm sure I screwed up the pronunciation of that, but it's tiny organisms, that when disturbed, glow blue."

"Why does it happen?"

"I don't know, but this time of the year it makes the beaches look beautiful."

"It is beautiful," she said. I grabbed a spare blanket to drape over her shoulders and returned to my spot. "Thank you."

We watched the magical algae floating like settled stars drifting on the water's surface. A pile of Krystal Ale bottles accumulated nearby.

"You get to see this almost any time you want."

"Whenever they're here. They don't last year long."

"Yeah, but still. You get to see this view. God, people would pay a fortune for this."

"I don't doubt that. I love it. It helps to center the soul. Kind of brings you back down from all the stressors in life."

"Very Buddhist sounding of you," she said.

"More Taoist than Buddhist, but I've dabbled a bit in the teachings. Meditation helps calm me down, but I don't do it as often as I should." This realization saddened me. I couldn't remember the last time I had meditated and knew that it would do me good to get back into the practice.

"Centers the soul? Do you believe in a soul?"

"Not really. You?"

"I'm not sure. Becoming a widow changed me." She spooked herself saying the words out loud. In her eyes, she wanted nothing more than to take the words back. "I don't have the answers but when I look up in the sky, I feel very small and my problems seem insignificant."

"That's how I feel on the ocean. You're so small and you have this minor problem of struggling with nature, but it's the most magnificent thing in the world."

"I find comfort in understanding not all things need a deeper meaning. I flow where life takes me."

Her words echoed my own belief. A life I did not take flashed through my mind, gripping my heart with equal amounts of pain, fear, and delight. Had the war not happen, and the events in my youth, who knows what mundane life I would've lived, never to see the sights before me now. My hands patted my pockets for something I knew couldn't be there.

An urge, so strong it caused my legs to shake, cycled through my system. I hadn't touched a cigarette in ten years, but some things never change. The very notion of the war made my nerves itch for a drag of that sweet nicotine.

"What do you want out of life?" She flipped the channel on me, and the abrupt change caused me to choke on a swallow of beer. I admired her mind and the speed at which it worked. She had an insatiable appetite for a story as if nothing quenched her thirst and she was left always wanting more.

Her question rolled around in my head. I was a child the last time someone asked me this. My hand rose to my mouth and I rubbed my lip as I contemplated. A hard sigh preceded my truth. "I don't want anything, I suppose. I'd like for the world to leave me alone, you know, not to be bothered."

"But you like to write, so you have something you'd like to say."

"Not really. I enjoy writing, but I don't care for the world to encroach on me. Kind of like J.D. Salinger."

"You're more educated then you let on?"

"Thanks, I think. Pretty sure that was an insult, though?"

"Not at all, but Salinger, Hemingway…you play that not-so-informed Marine fisherman but there's something deeper to you."

"Whatever, look, I wanna write but I don't want questions about it. I wanna fish and live on the island. I wanna watch the sun rise with a steaming cup of coffee and see it set with some rum."

"Does it get lonely?"

"No. I find company when it comes, like now." I nudged her with my elbow to her delight. "I'm fine with solitude. What do you want?"

The words were burning on the edge of her lips. "To feel something real."

I was taken aback, not knowing how to respond. She didn't look at me but watched the bioluminescence in the tide. The chilled wind blew hard and she tightened the blanket around her shoulders.

"What do you mean?" I asked.

"Can I be honest with you?" This was a rhetorical question. She was going to tell me what was on her mind regardless of how I answered. "I honestly haven't felt anything real in a long time."

"I take offense to that."

She ribbed me with the point of her elbow.

"I mean, emotionally. Remember being a teenager and everything being so new. I haven't felt like that in a long time. Not since the—"

She hesitated, but I finished it as kindly as I could.

"The war."

"Yeah, the war." She lost a lover, her husband, a man she promised to spend the rest of her life with; a bond not easily broken. I wasn't trying to make a move or capitalize off her vulnerability, but my arm draped over her shoulder. One human being giving support to another. Some people, no matter how troubled, are at home in their pain and we recognized that in each other. "Why did you leave?"

That same question still burned in her and I figured I'd give her something.

"A few different reasons. For one, my father died before I went overseas."

"Oh, I'm sorry."

"When I came home, everything was different. I had that compulsion to call him when something funny happened or when I had a question, but he wasn't there anymore. I had no direction in life, I felt abandoned."

"By your dad?"

"No. Not by him."

"Then by who?"

"When you're fit and able—" I paused, mustering the strength to speak once I knew my voice wouldn't quiver. "When you're fit and able, the Corps loves you. When you're hurt, the powers that be like to put you on the back burner and forget all about you. With everything else going on in my life, I felt like I was standing in water up to my nose."

"Depression."

"Badly."

"The powers that be?"

"It's not the guys you serve with. What I mean is, it's the desk pilots, the admin guys who sit in their air-conditioned office and lose your paperwork over and over again."

"That's terrible. What about your mother?"

"She loved me. At least, I think she did, but she was lost in her own sorrow. I can't blame her. A part of me knows she didn't even notice I was gone. Besides, I was in the Marines then, and we weren't close. Neither was my father and me. I was an accident at the end of a loveless marriage."

"Oh, come on." She nudged me, but I didn't budge. The good humor faded from her face.

"It's true. They told me."

"That's a horrible thing to tell a child."

"I'm fine with it. It taught me at a young age to rely only on myself. It's what got me into writing."

"Did you go home for her funeral?"

"I was in Germany and didn't find out until a month afterward."

"Have you gone back at all since being down here?"

"No. There's nothing there for me now. Besides, I don't go to graveyards. They only remind me of things that don't matter anymore. My parents are in my memories now and I rather them be there than to remember them as stones."

"What about a girlfriend?"

"I had a girlfriend, and that brings us to reason number two of why I left." My lips loose from the liquor.

"Oh." She leaned in, her eyes glowing with anticipation, wanting every drop of pain and misery I had stored within. "Please tell."

"No. You don't wanna hear about that." I teased, brushing her off, denying her lust.

"Yes, I do. It's the steak and I'm a starving woman. Tell."

"I found out she cheated on me before I deployed. In fact, she cheated on me a lot."

"Oh, shit. What did you do?" Mabel licked her lips.

"Nothing," I said. Her disappointment was prevalent in the way her shoulders slouched. I'm sure she expected me to spin a tale of the crazed Marine going ballistic because of his broken heart. "Well, nothing at the time."

She perked back up.

"What a bitch. I can't stand cheaters. Please tell me you at the very least beat someone's ass?"

"No. While deployed I stopped writing her, hoping that she might worry while I was in Iraq. I doubt she did."

"That's it. You ghosted her? There's gotta be something more. How'd you get her back for cheating on you? Come on, give me something good." She reached out at me, gobbling up my story like a shark devouring a small fish, wanting something bigger.

"Ghosted?" I smiled, learning a new slang term. "Her name was Claire and she's a woman who thinks she deserves a life of glamour."

"A stuck-up bitch, is more like it."

"Yeah, she acts like the Queen of the World and everyone needs to bow to her presence. She wanted everything her way, a life of leisure. When I came back to the States after Germany, I was at my lowest. I almost went to see her but couldn't do it. I took off, promising never to acknowledge her existence again and avoiding my hometown. Time went by, I roamed and came down to the island.

Then about a year ago, I had a charter and there was this guy I knew from the old neighborhood."

I drew the story out, gathering her attention and building on the suspense. Mabel loved it.

"We talked about old times, about Henry making it big in the UFC. It was after the Bedford loss, where Bedford afterward got popped on PED's."

"Oh yeah. Big controversy. Back to Claire." She halted me before we got off track.

"Anyway, without asking, he told me about Claire. Said she was on her third marriage with three kids, living in a trailer. This made me laugh because Claire hated trailers, and swore she'd never live in one. She even made fun of the other kids in school who did live in them. Thinking back on it, she was a bitch even then. I don't know what I saw in her."

"Oh, karma got her. That's awesome," Mabel said with a smile, but by her body language, she wasn't happy with the outcome of this story.

"Oh, it gets better," I said, arousing her attention again.

"Her mom still lived in their old house. I sent Claire a picture of me standing in front of my beach house with the ocean behind me. On the back I wrote, *good people end up in great places, cheaters end up in trailer parks.*"

Mabel ripped into laughter, slapping at her leg, and spilling her drink. I savored the moment of watching her gloom fade into hysteria. I was cracking her code.

"Slightly demented, but what a great way to get back at someone. Revenge at its finest. Man, I wish I could have seen her face when she opened that letter," Mabel said.

"Me, too."

"If she knows you're alive, how come Henry didn't find out?"

"This was only last year. I'm sure Henry had put me out of his mind by then, thinking I'm dead and all."

"See, if you had a Facebook account, you could go and check out how miserable her life is."

"I don't need to do that. I got my closure; besides I live in a great place, doing what I want. If I allow social media to enter my world, it could strip away the very thing I want most."

"Peace and solitude?"

"Indeed," I said, and tapped the tip of her nose.

"You want absolute freedom."

"The only absolute freedom is death, but in the meantime, I'll take what I can get. Hence, I live alone. When you don't have anyone counting on you, then you don't have anything troubling you. Kojo is the only one I worry about."

"You worry about someone?" she asked sarcastically.

"Yes, but I don't care for it and I don't care for anyone worrying over me. When I die, I don't want it to be in a hospital bed with people surrounding me, crying. My ship is where I want to be when my time is up." She met my eyes with complete understanding. What she said next almost felt recited.

"I hope I die after I write that one great book everyone remembers me for. Fitzgerald had *Gatsby*, Hemingway - *Old Man and the Sea*, Bradbury had *451*," she said each while ticking them off with her fingers. She continued naming authors and book titles until all ten digits were used. Her passion for writing was clear and ignited the inspiration in me to finish the latest draft of my Iraq novel. Mabel continued, "All I want is that one book that people will think about for all time. After I do that, I can die happy."

"Happy?"

"Well, at least satisfied."

Intoxicated by her monologue, I joined in. "I too want the best seller."

"I'd love to read your work." I clammed up at her suggestion. I hardly let anyone read my work, knowing it was no good. I could see her reading it, contemplating why she was wasting her time with it, and this would only break my heart.

"Shut up. No, you don't. Besides, it's not that good." I tried to play it off, hoping the subject would change.

"How do you know?" Mabel verbally jabbed me, and I admit, she was right. Her brown eyes stared intently at me, real and interested. She was a complete mystery to me.

"Maybe." We clinked beer bottles against one another.

"Here's to us both getting what we want in life." We drank. A warmth overcame me for the first time in a decade. I never told anyone about the picture I had sent Claire and by Mabel's reaction, I'm satisfied I did.

We stayed there, watching the night, counting the stars, dreaming upon the waves.

Chapter Twenty-One

I could hardly sleep the week since Mabel left my ship after her personal fishing trip. We fished, then wined and dined, then made love under the song of the sea, but a week had passed and now the sounds of the crashing ocean no longer held a melody. I tried my damnedest to work and push Henry's epic party from my mind, but no matter what I did, the thrill I knew in my youth at experiencing new things kept nipping at me.

The weekend seemed ever drifting, pulling away from me, never to be caught up with. Each night I spent staring at the mansion on the cliff, wondering what fun I was missing out on. I wanted to bolt for a cab and head there. The mystery of the grand illusion captivated me, and I wanted to reside among those walls. Henry would welcome me.

Three charters in five days kept me busy, but I'd be lying if I didn't say as Friday afternoon became evening, I bounced off the AJAX. The lights in the mansion were glowing not as they had done during the week, but as they had done on the weekends. That meant only one thing – the party was starting. Excitement bit, and I tried not to show it on my face. Kojo swabbed the deck as I set off.

"Where ya goin'?"

"I'll see you tomorrow." I never slowed my stride.

"Ya want me to finish up?"

"Do what you want. I'll see you tomorrow."

"Doubt that," he muttered, but I still didn't stop. I sped around the White Whale, not thinking twice of the music and laughter inside. The joy happening at my old bar was in no comparison to the lavishness of what was at Henry's place. Energy and anticipation brewed in me, and I nearly jogged to my house. I showered, cleaned up my appearance, and planned to catch a cab at the White Whale.

This wasn't warranted. As I exited my house, a green Porsche convertible pulled into my drive. I had never seen this car before but knew the driver.

"Hello, Fisherman," Mabel said, stepping from the driver door.

"Hello back." I whistled at the car, wondering where on the island did she get such a ride. "Nice car."

"You look good," she said at my pressed shirt and slacks. "Jump in."

"How do you know I'm going to the party?"

One of her eyebrows raised at me before she said, "Where else would you be going, Fisherman?"

"Again, with the insults."

"Oh," she mocked. "Did I hurt your feelings?"

"Maybe you did."

"Well," she said, stepping a leg back into the car. "Maybe you can punish me for it later."

"Maybe I'll use Henry and Alice's cuffs." This tickled Mabel and our banter pleased me as I joined her in the car. "Damn, this is the nicest car I've ever been in."

"It's a Porsche Boxster." I didn't know what that meant or why it was different from any other Porsche. The only thing I knew was that it was extremely expensive, and I didn't need a price tag to tell me that. I kept my hands in my lap, afraid to touch or break anything. She pulled out of my drive and headed toward Henry's. "How's things?"

"Fine. Fishing and writing."

"Any trophies?"

"No, but they're out there."

"How's the book?"

"It's missing something, but I can't put a finger on it," I said. Mabel snickered. "What?"

"Nothing." She tried to wipe the smile from her face.

"It's because I'm missing a finger, isn't it?"

"No. No." Her eyes tried to remain on the road, but they kept shifting to me until she finally relented. "Yeah."

I couldn't help but laugh. I had set myself up for that one. "That's fucked up."

"You said it." Mabel protested. "You want me to take a look at your story?"

"I don't know." I sighed, wanting to readjust in my seat but fearing any movement I did could damage something I couldn't pay for. "How's your writing going?"

"Just preforming the mundane task of documenting the Champ's life. Although I must confess, it's hard to get a personal interview with him."

"Why's that? Y'all live in the same house."

"True, but every time I do get alone time with him, Philip or Scott needs him for something. Or some new business partner is on the phone. It's annoying."

Chapter Twenty-Two

The small talk continued as she pulled through the iron gates of Henry's mansion and circled around to the back. We entered the largest of the four buildings surrounding the main structure of the house. Many cars stood in nice rows in the multilevel garage. Classics, sports, and luxury vehicles, each shining, each expensive. I couldn't imagine how rich my old friend was or how he came about accumulating so much wealth. These thoughts led to more questions about his business partners and their dealings.

We stepped out of the garage and into the open air. On the other side of the house, the sea roared beyond the cliffs. Overhead, the stars lacked in appearance. No storms lingered over the island and my mind hurt staring at the blank, dark sky, barely a twinkle visible due to the festival of lights at this party. Mabel didn't take notice but pulled me along. Music bumped from where it had the week prior and I envisioned a gaggle of people bumping into one another.

A path led us from the garage to a side entrance of the house. Although the music outside was loud, there was a different loudness coming from within. I looked with eyes unadjusted to the new atmosphere and registered a unique vibe. Mabel didn't stop but marched on through two doors that opened to the gym. A crowd, much larger than expected, stood shoulder to shoulder, wall to wall, straining to see in the center.

The cage, which a week before had been in the far corner, was now situated in the middle of the former ballroom. Two men, both island youthfuls, threw hands inside. A referee accompanied the sluggers, judging every movement.

Mabel didn't need to stop to look around. She led us over to the iron spiral staircase, where for safety, a security guard stood at the bottom to prevent overcrowding. He knew Mabel, allowing us up as the crowd roared from one good punch to another. Seats, padded with green cushions and reinforced with strong metal frames, lined the railing of the catwalk and two chairs waited near the champ. *The best seats in the house*, I presumed.

"Nicky," Henry rose to welcome me with a hug and offered us the two chairs. Mabel sat next to Philip and I took the chair next to Henry. Alice sat on the opposite side and I felt as if we were with the King and Queen of England.

"What the hell is going on here?" I asked, amazed at the spectacle.

"Fight night."

"We went into Queensbury," Philip chimed in, "and Henry found a gym. After meeting several of the fighters, he got the wild idea of having his own amateur night."

"Do they get anything?" I asked.

"Fight for five hundred. Win, another five," Henry said never removing his interest from the fight down below.

"Damn Henry, starting your own UFC island?"

"There's talent here. I've been thinking of contacting Dana to come see."

"Dana White?"

"No, Dana Carvey. Of course, Dana White. He's always looking for a fight."

Henry's words cut short as the crowd roared. One fighter in blue shorts stumbled against the cage and his opponent rushed in for the kill. Henry was on his feet, leaning over the railing to get a better view.

"Heard y'all had fun last weekend," Henry said. I wasn't sure what he was talking about but wondered if he was implying that Mabel and I had slept with one another. It's not that I mind if people knew, but I'm not one to kiss and tell. He looked at me and picked up on my concern. "Fishing. Mabel told Alice you guys had fun fishing last weekend."

"Oh yeah. It was a good time."

"Yeah, Henry," Mabel shouted over the noise of the crowd. "I *had* caught a shark."

"Wow, what kind?"

"I forget." She shrugged her shoulders. "What kind was it, Nicanor?"

"A tiger shark," I yelled as the audience cheered another good shot.

"No shit," Henry said, eyebrows raising. His mouth gaped open but stayed silent. There was little he could do to conceal his excitement or his desire to have been there in person. "Did you keep it?"

"No," she said, squeezing my shoulder. "Fearless here threw it back. Said he didn't like those things."

"I *don't* like those things."

"Damn. That would've been cool to see. I wanna get me a set of shark jaws to hang up; the biggest shark out there," Henry said.

"Be careful what you wish for, darling. Why would you want that anyway?" Alice asked.

"Because it'd be cool. A set of jaws hanging in my painting room, man, I'd like that. Maybe we can go out and catch that one your boy was shooting at the other day. You know, the one you told me about."

"The red fin shark?" Mabel asked.

"Yeah, that one. We should catch it."

"Me and that fish will have our day, but today isn't that day. We did catch some other fish. Some bluefin tuna and some tarpon and a crazy roosterfish."

"Roosterfish?"

"Yeah, a beautiful fish."

"Oh, you should have seen it, Henry. One of the fish got eaten while I was reeling it in. We pulled only the head aboard." Mabel added.

"Its head?" Alice asked without interest, only to hear herself speak.

"Yeah." With Henry not obstructing my view of her, I stared at Alice. Her dyed blonde hair matched that of Mabel's and the two could be mistaken as sisters if one didn't know better. "Sharks like to wait for the tuna to get tired and then as they're heading to the boat, BAM, the sonsofbitches attack."

"Damn, that's crazy. We'll have to go back out," Henry said.

"Any time." The fighter in green camo shorts threw a hard-left hook but Blue Shorts covered, blocked, and returned with a flying knee. His kneecap struck the opponent's face and dropped him stiff. His ankles curled inward, his arms crossed over one another, and eyes stared into the back of his head. The referee dove in between the downed fighter and his attacker before more damage could be suffered.

A shock ran through Henry and he clapped his hands so hard together the pops of air exploding between his palms hurt my ears. "Hell, yeah. Philip. Give that guy an extra hundred. Fuck yeah."

A waiter appeared with a silver tray and several drinks on it. I took a glass full of ice and Henry's own whiskey brand. It was strong, biting at my lips, tongue, and throat, but did the job at easing me into the night.

"We should do this every Friday. Friday Night Fights, what do you think?" Henry said.

"Sure, love," Alice began, "but soon there won't be any fighters left on the island if you do that."

"Then we'll import." Henry leaned over and kissed his famous wife.

"If I didn't know any better, Henry, I'd swear you were in the drug business."

"Drug business? Why's that?"

"You're the richest man I know. I mean, this house alone makes Scarface's look like a shack on the island."

"There's no money in drugs." Henry boomed over the cheering, watching two new fighters enter the ring. "The real criminals are on Wall Street."

"You a criminal, Henry?"

"Investments. I'm into investments." He turned away from the ring and the crowd and leaned into me, his voice lowering as if a secret would expel from him for only I to hear. "I make money work for me."

He jabbed a finger in his own chest.

"Instead of you working for money?"

"Correct."

The drinks came as quick as punches, always an ever-rotating staff of waiters carrying silver trays with booze. The two fighters, one in black shorts, the other in white, met in the center of the octagon. Good vs Evil in the Devil's playground. White Shorts, head shaven with the face of a brawler, snapped out a kick to the much bigger, pretty boy wearing the black shorts. Pretty Boy came back with a lead leg kick of his own. The slap of his foot could be heard over the crowd. Onlookers went wild.

I winced.

Pretty Boy twitched his nose as if itching for a real fight, bored with this one. Brawler answered this smug look with a quick right cross. Pretty Boy's poker face flushed red and charged in with a counter but missed. Annoyance clenched his teeth as Brawler circled away. The two followed each other around the center of the cage, throwing shots, landing some, missing few, but nothing with substantial damage.

The fights were impressive. The grandeur of it all only caused my mind to wonder how Henry made this kind of money. An unpleasant feeling kept pestering me. Fighting doesn't pay these kinds of bills unless you're a *reigning* boxing champion, not a newly crowned MMA champ.

"If we make this a regular thing, we may need to charge admissions. Make some money from all this."

"Good idea, Philip. Making money moves." The champ laughed, never wavering from the action down below. He leaned into me again and said, "That guy in the black shorts, the good-looking fella, he's holding that right hand really low."

"I've noticed. I think the other guy has noticed too. He keeps going for that looping left and is just short each time." As if hearing our conversation, Brawler stepped in and missed again with a left hook. Pretty Boy dodged it, slipped a quick right, but ate a second left hook. He reacted with a right hook of his own. Brawler backed away and Pretty Boy followed. This was his mistake. Brawler planted his feet and threw fists. Pretty Boy, overconfident, lobbed a right hook that Brawler eased away from.

"Remember when we used to do this? Call fights?" Henry asked.

"I do. Those were fun days." We drank and toasted one another.

Pretty Boy overreached on that right hook. Brawler's left foot came to the outside as he tossed in a right to the body, then snapped a left hook over Pretty Boy's shoulder. His first two knuckles landed with a crushing thud. Pretty Boy staggered, hurt, and went flat on his ass. He had enough sense about him to roll and get up, but Brawler was waiting. Patiently and catching him in reach, Brawler smashed another left hook that dropped Pretty Boy against the cage, legs reaching up from muscle memory to snatch his attacker in a jiu jitsu move.

Brawler wasn't naïve enough to fall for it and although Pretty Boy was stunned, he was still dangerous. Instead, the pouncing Brawler stepped to the side of Pretty Boy's legs and torqued three hooks: left, right, left. A massive forearm from the referee ripped Brawler from the assault. Everyone went wild; none more so than Henry.

Mabel leaned forward, captivated by the action. Her love for the sport poured out in placid ecstasy and if asked, I'm sure she would fail to find the right words to describe this experience. Watching the fight filled her with a warmth that only the grandest of memories could do. She sat back, pausing from the thrill of the sport.

"Wow, first round knockout. Wonderful." She ran her hand through her hair and exhaled heavily, a woman lost in the throes.

"You gotta come to my next fight," Henry crashed back into his chair.

"When is it?"

"Don't know yet. I'll be calling Dana next week to talk." His words amused me. I had seen Dana White on the television so many times, but to sit here with someone who actually dealt with him on a normal basis, to the extent that he had his personal number, was astonishing.

"Dude, your fuckin' life is unbelievable."

"I know." A ringing interrupted before he could say anything else. We both turned to see Philip reach into his pocket and pull out his cellphone. Henry sighed from the other side of me, knowing what was to come.

"What's up?" I asked.

"Nothing." He rolled his eyes with displeasure.

"I'm guessing that's for you."

"I'm sure of it."

"Don't you have your own phone?"

"I hardly use it. I keep it in case Dana or the UFC matchmakers call me. I don't ccaa-re for them. They interrupt everything."

"Dana White?"

"What? No. The phones interrupt everything."

"I feel you. It's like a leash." And with that, Philip stood and came over to Henry, whispering in his ear. Frustration brewed upon Henry's face. He pointed to the cage, but Philip shook his head.

"Goddamnit, alright." Henry snatched the phone from Philip. He cut to me and said, "I'll be back."

Henry vacated the noise of the gym for the quietness of his sauna.

"Let's go get a drink," Mabel said, startling me as she stood next to my chair, towering over my shoulder. I didn't protest as my own throat needed refreshment.

"What's up?" I asked.

"Nothing. I hate all the business talk during a fight. Spoils it for me." I figured we'd head off to the kitchen as we had the previous weekend. Instead, Mabel grabbed a bottle of champagne from a butler and we found ourselves outside, looming over the dancing crowd.

"Does Henry do that a lot?"

"What?"

"Get pulled away for a secretive phone call?"

"All the time. It's irritating."

"Who are these business partners?"

"Don't know. He doesn't really talk about the business with me. Henry's first love is fighting and that's what he stays focused on. It's Philip and Scott's job to handle the other businesses but everyone wants to talk to the champ."

"Do you think he's into something illegal?" I asked. She laughed.

"No. Why?"

"Look at all of this. He's living like a multimillionaire."

"Because he is."

"But no way from small stocks and fights could he afford all of this."

"I think Philip and Scott pay for it, too." Mabel looked up at the sky and now noticed what I had earlier. Her shoulders slacked and her mouth turned to a frown. "I hate that you can't see the stars out here. It's like in New York. You can't see shit for the night sky. I guess when we left the big city, we brought some of it with us."

I looked up, feeling too the disappointment she felt. Then my spirits brightened as she said, "Let's get the fuck out of here and go for a ride."

I agreed and we quickly left the jazz of the party for the rocking of my bedroom.

Chapter Twenty-Three

Around the time when the middle of the night became early morning, the passion to write pulled me from my slumber. During the rejuvenating peace of my sleep, I stumbled upon the missing key to my Iraq novel. An element that would flush out my story, giving it the depth it lacked. A compulsive force pulled me from the bed, completely nude, to assault my keyboard with no regards to the woman sleeping there. Thank god I had prepared the coffee maker the night before, a nightly ritual.

I nailed the brew button as I passed by without pausing. Hissing coffee struck the heated glass pot, disturbing the silence of my beach bungalow. My finger rubbed furiously at my bottom lip while waiting for my story to load on the screen. I fought the desire to shake the laptop in hopes it would work faster.

I feared any moment lost to time without touching the keys would cause the story to fade from existence. A dream sparked this revelation, filling my mind with the missing theme. I had a platoon of men waging war upon the streets of Fallujah. The story had death of enemy combatants, the fall of friendly troops, laughter, tears, and all that goes with young men in battle, but the one thing it was missing was a female lead.

The main antagonist had a wife back home, but there wasn't a female character to relate to. Although it is fashionable for women to be in combat roles now, in 2004, it was debated, aside from Navy Corpsmen or Army medics. My fingers didn't fly across the keyboard but soared without missing a stroke. I knew where her character needed to go, what she looked like, and her drive. Her character arc was the easiest of all the people I have ever written. I wrote as fast as I could, trying to get it all out on the screen before it evaporated like the morning mist.

I paused only to sip the coffee I didn't remember pouring. The transition from night to dawn happened before blinded eyes. I saw nothing change, heard no morning waves or squawking birds. Aside from my keyboard, my monitor, and my story, I was completely dumb to all existence around me. I wrote until my muscles ached from sitting, and forced me to stand, writing hunched over. Possessed, my story grew, and captured the thing for which I was missing.

Any issues arising from adding a female character to my war saga were easily smoothed out. I found myself in love with her and feared how the war would shape her. In all my published short stories, I had never written of love. It was a territory unfamiliar to me, but easy to navigate once I tried.

I continued to strike at the keys until the tips of my fingers burned and slowed me. I had lost track of time in my fury of writing, but in three hours, I wrote over three thousand words. I'm not the quickest writer, and I know for some this is a small amount, but for me, it was astronomical.

Slurping at my coffee and surprised that it was still hot, I turned to find Mabel in the kitchen. She leaned against the open back door, standing in a pair of pink panties hidden by one of my long tank tops. The beach shined behind her with crashing waves of white caps and a swirl of steam rising from the mug held near her chin. She smiled at me and I stretched my throbbing body before the hint of embarrassment washed over me.

"Good morning," I said with a yawn.

"Good morning."

"Did you give me this?" I asked holding up my mug.

"Yeah. I didn't want to bother you. You were in the zone."

"No, that's great. I spooked myself because I couldn't remember getting up. How long have you been watching me?"

"Not long," she said. I shied away.

"Well, I feel stupid."

"Why?"

"Didn't know anyone was watching me write. Kind of dumb, I guess."

"Not at all. I'm impressed, actually. You were a man on a mission. Did you get what you were fishing for?"

"I think I did. Hopefully, it freshens out my story."

"That's great. God, I love that sound."

"The surf?" I nodded out the door, assuming she was talking about the tide coming in, a true force of nature.

"Striking keys on a keyboard. It's like music to me. When I'm deep into it, all things fade from me, but that sound stays. It's like white noise or something."

"I know what you mean." I stood to top off my cup. The morning breeze from the ocean made me aware that I was without clothes. I rushed to cover myself with a pair of lounge shorts I found carelessly tossed over the back of a chair in the living room. I could hear Mabel snickering at my plight.

"What draft is this?" Mabel looked over my shoulder at the computer. My anxiety rose. Anyone stealing a peek of my work unnerved me and I wanted to slam the laptop closed but didn't.

"Umm, I don't know. Twentieth, maybe?" I jested.

"Email it to me. I'll read it and see if I can't give you a few pointers. It's funny how many times you go over a story and still find little errors."

"Maybe I will."

"Maybe you should now before you get cold feet."

"Maybe I already have cold feet?"

"Then do it. Be a man and send it to me. I thought Marines were tough and not scared?"

"Marines are tough and not scared, but the writer in me is terrified." This made her laugh, easing the anxiety in my bones. I came back into the area where my desk sat between the kitchen and living room. I attached a copy to an email and sent it to the address she wrote down for me. "Are you hungry? I could whip up something for breakfast."

"I could eat." I ventured over to the refrigerator and as I readied to open it, a breeze came in behind me. Mabel stood at the back door, sipping on her coffee, watching the waves crash against the beach, the cusp of her butt poking out from beneath the hem of my tank top shirt. The wind ruffled her short blonde hair and a glow wrapped her in an exterior light. I could have stood there forever, but the hypnotizing scene broke with a knock at my front door.

Chapter Twenty-Four

To our surprise, Henry stood at the door. Parked in front of my house was a candy apple red, 1956 two-door Bel-Air with white trim, white wall tires, and Alice sitting in the front. The car was a convertible to boot. The morning heat rushed into my cold house and I wanted to shut the door to keep it out.

"You two have fun?" He snickered.

"What are you doin' here?" I asked, slipping on a shirt and a pair of shoes.

"Get ready." He motioned to the car. "We're going out."

"Holy shit, where did you get that car?" The assortment of cars in his garage impressed me, but I hadn't seen this one and it was the crème de la crème.

"Motherfucker, I'm the Champion of the World. I want something," his eyes flicked to Mabel, then back to me, "I get it."

"Where's your friends at?"

"Standing in front of me. Get in." Daylight magnified the brilliant colors of the convertible. The whites, reds, and chrome exterior gleamed in the early morning, beckoning us to take a ride. Before I could answer, Mabel, already throwing on a pair of cut-off shorts, led me by the hand down the walk, joining Alice in the back. I climbed into the passenger seat, marveling at the matching two tone color leather interior.

The main road we drove ran the circumference of the island, with cliffs and ocean to one side, hills and trees towering over the other. We cruised through ghettos of beach front shanty huts and zoomed past strolling pedestrians.

"So, you two have fun last night?" Again, the way Henry phrased his sentence implied he knew something about Mabel and me. I casted a sideways glance at him and suspected Mabel did the same. He looked from me to her, then back to the road. "The fights. You two have fun watching the fights?"

Henry shouted into the wind with the speedometer reaching fifty. He zipped around one car, narrowly avoiding a head-on collision. The approaching driver tensed, and I matched his angst, readying myself for disaster. Henry jerked the wheel to swerve back into his own lane. The opposing car's horn blew but it was too late to flip us off.

"Yeah, they were great. It was a lot of fun." I looked over my shoulder to find Mabel sitting forward, her face a short distance from my head. Although my own face contorted at the near-death crash, she remained calm, without a hint of disruption to her demeanor, as if it was all natural and planned out. Alice sat with her head back, soaking in the sun, also not a care in the world.

"Sorry I had to bail like that. Business, you know." It took me a moment to remember what he was talking about.

"What kind of business makes you leave your own party, Henry?"

"Money business," he said, sternly. Then a smile replaced his expression and he added, "First world problems of the champ."

"I guess it's good business if it affords the life you're living."

"Are you implying that my money is dirty?"

"I didn't say that."

"Stocks." He shouted abruptly. I didn't understand what he meant and again he repeated himself. "I make my money from the stock market."

"Where the real criminals lie?" I shook my head, understanding the statement he had made the night before. "So that's the investments you spoke of?"

"No. Not really. There's other things I invest in, but big stocks make big risk with big rewards."

"So, why keep fighting?"

"Like I've said before, I love the sport." I looked to Mabel once again and her expression was one of inquiry. I feared that she would resent me for nonchalantly divulging Henry's stock secrets when she had been trying to get him to tell her this in an interview for months now.

"Where are we going?" Mabel asked, wanting to change the subject.

"You guys hungry?" asked Henry.

"Hell yeah. Starving," Mabel said.

"Good. I wanna eat. I'm hungry and there are too many people at my house right now. Too noisy. I wanna get away and have breakfast and see ssoo-me sights."

"So where too?" I asked, ignoring the slurring of his words.

"Queensbury," Alice said.

"Queensbury? Isn't there a war going on there?" The delight in Mabel's eyes flamed with the kernel of a story rolling in her mind.

"Kind of. But we'll be on the better side of town," Alice said, unsure of herself.

"Why Queensbury?"

"It has an amazing art exhibit. Mainly nautical theme, but still, I've been dying to see it. Figured you guys would like to come, too." We passed cars and people in a blur, and I sat back to enjoy the wind and sun against my face, unaware of what was to come.

Chapter Twenty-Five

We arrived at the Shanty Shake faster than I had expected. I'd never heard of this establishment, but it held the nostalgic reminiscence of a restaurant from back in the States. Pictures and antique décor from the 1950s and 1960s cluttered the walls while the floor shined with black and white checkered tiles. Each booth felt ripped from a hopping malt shop and should be filled with teenagers wearing black jackets, letterman sweaters, or poodle skirts.

A small patio, lining the street, stared out over the city strips of small shops. The walk from the parking lot was short, but the sweltering heat confirmed our choice to take a corner booth in the air-conditioning.

"God, I'm hung over." Henry's lips stuck to one another as he spoke and sweat clung to his brow. "How the hell is it so hot at the beginning of March? Haven't these people heard of winter?"

"Southern hemisphere, Henry. It's summertime now here."

"Hello." A young woman, her nametag reading 'Amelia', approached our table with four menus. Her dark skin, reflecting the sun's glory, shimmered with hints of rosy pinks and rouge. The sight of her pinged my heart with homesickness for her very stride mimicked that of Jazz. Surely my absence from the White Whale had my old comrades and drinking buddies missing me. From a three-pocketed waist apron, she pulled a small pad of paper and a pencil. "What can I get'cha?"

Henry pushed his sunglasses up his nose. "Four glasses of water and four cups of coffee, and what will y'all have to drink?"

A lame joke from the big ogre, but it did cause us all, including Amelia, to smile. She hurried off, leaving us to look over the menus. Before long she returned with our drinks, placing them in front of us along with sugar and milk. Henry jabbed a straw into his water, sucking it down until the ice rattled in the bottom. Amelia chuckled.

"I'll bring da pitcha," she said and walked away after taking our orders. Henry huddled over his ceramic cup, washing his face in the steam of coffee.

"Hard night?" I asked. "You didn't seem this bad on the drive in."

"The rushing wind helps, but when I sit still, it starts to hit me." He sighed, his heavy eyes fighting the good fight to stay open.

"Haymaker here decided to out drink everyone at the party," Alice said in a neutral tone while patting her husband on the back. He smirked at her and rolled his eyes, not caring to relive his debauchery from the night before.

"Our parties tend to dive into a crazy festival, but last night went even wilder. At one point, in front of everyone, some chick stripped down naked and went swimming in the pool. It incited others to do the same."

"Is that surprising? I mean last week I woke up at your place in a room with mostly naked people," I said. Henry gave me a confused look like he couldn't recall me ever coming to a prior party.

"Well, things like that happen, but not when the party is in full swing. Normally, as the crowd starts to thin out, people go wild or hook up with someone, but never to the extent it was last night. I think there was thirty or forty people in the buff."

"Sounds like full hedonism."

"A whole pool of hedonism." Alice added.

"Exactly. It was wild. I couldn't even find any of my normal—"

Before Henry could finish, I interrupted coldly, "Leaches?"

"Friends." He corrected with a grin. "Everyone seemed to go wild."

"I retired earlier than most," Alice said. Something bounced in her eyes and I caught it.

"I swear each party gets crazier and crazier. But they're lots of fun." Henry dumped several spoonfuls of sugar and a steady stream of milk into his coffee, matching Alice's coffee perfectly.

"Sounds loud," I said into my own cup of black coffee. He offered me the milk and I refused. To me, a man's coffee should be black as midnight coal, with no additives, and I find it odd when it's not.

"That they are. Remember the parties at our old apartment?"

"Yeah, but those were minor parties of poor eighteen-year-olds, drinking illegally compared to the ragers you throw now."

"But how fun were those parties? You coming tonight?"

"I don't know, Henry." Despite how fun the parties were, my aching body told me I had grown too old for this kind of lifestyle, no matter how much I wanted to be a part of it.

"Come on. It'll give me an escape from my business partners."

"But I thought you loved those *friends*?"

"I do, but it's nice to hang out with someone from back in the day." The waitress returned with our meals and we devoured them. I didn't realize how famished I had been until the plate stared up at me. My stomach moaned a dying death and I dug in. Hardly a word passed between the four of us as we ate.

"I find you interesting," Alice said. I glanced at her sideways, not understanding her angle.

"Why's that?" Mabel asked, marveling. I figure she had the same suspicions I did.

"He's like a wild animal coming into the fold. Rough and dangerous. I'm waiting to see what he'll do or say next."

"So, I'm an animal?"

"No, darling. Not like that. You amaze me is all. I've never met someone like you."

"Well, I've never met someone who got famous on the internet. That's gotta be cool." She cast her eyes away. I didn't mean to insult her, but I do believe she took a slight offense.

"Yes, but it was only a launching platform for my career."

"I heard you've done movies. Where did you go from here?" I asked.

"Silver screen stardom. Nathan is working with me to perfect my acting."

"That's good. I hope it pays off and you're the next Audrey Hepburn." I nodded in approval.

"Well, thank you." She returned my nod, any awkwardness between us vanishing as she took a drink to clear her throat. She looked over my shoulder at the hustling street beyond. "I can't believe the news is saying this is a war zone. Is this what one looks like?"

She asked Henry who shook his head.

"I don't know. Ask him." He pointed his fork across the table and all eyes moved to me, waiting for an answer to a question I didn't hear.

"Well, is it?"

"Is what?"

"Is this what a real war zone looks like? I thought it would be different," Alice said. I turned to see what she saw, to compare it with the horrors in my memories. To me, mortars and rockets, bullets and explosions were the bristles dipped in blood that painted the scene. The image of a street in Fallujah blurred with the street I saw from the diner's booth. I didn't see a war zone, but a city alive with the activity of a civilian world.

"A war zone has many faces. The one I'd seen was ugly and barren. The only flower which grows in such a place is the flower of death."

"How poetic." Alice added before nibbling on her food.

"God, I wish I had been there with yyoouu, brother." Henry stared at me and in his eyes, I could see he wanted to say something more but was afraid his stuttering would trip him up. He squashed the words with a long drink of water and simply said, "I wanted nothing more than that glory."

"Why would you care about such things?" Alice asked.

"Umm…a family tradition, you could say. I figured it was my destiny or some shit."

"Yeah, but you're the Champion of the World. People love you," I said.

"Ahh." He flicked his hand at me, shooing away my talk. "That don't matter. I'm champion now, someone will be champion later. It is what it is, but what you have is something I'll never have. The testament that said you stood in the *real* combat zone and succeeded."

"Oh, horseshit. All that combat romanticism is crap for the movies. Real war ain't like that."

"Still, I wanted that test. It was my dream."

"Your dream, my nightmare."

"Yeah, Henry. You could have died in Iraq. Then you'd never have been champion of the world," Mabel said.

"Or met me." Alice kissed his cheek.

"No, that's where you're wrong." He ignored Alice and beamed his interest at Mabel. "Dying in combat is the greatest thing in the world. It's the biggest achievement a man can have in life. To die for your country is the greatest glory a man can have."

"Now who's poetic?" I pointed at Henry while looking at Alice. She agreed.

"To tell you the truth, sometimes I kick myself for having been in the gym that day when I got discovered. I never wanted to be champion, I wanted to be a hero in the Marines. I wanted to be somebody the world would thank." I had to look away from him. Remorse pried at my brain, but there were other things unspoken between us that extinguished these feelings. I didn't need to hear this nor did I care too.

"You think too much about shit that don't matter." I told him.

"Oh yeah? What do you think about?"

"I think about that damn shark out there."

"The shark with the red fin?"

"Damn right. That shark is a killer and I want to catch it more than anything else in the world. To me, that's glory." The chaotic flare in my eyes made the three of them laugh.

"It's good to spend time with you again," Henry said. I sighed, feeling brushed off after enduring his monologue of self-pity.

"Hell, I can't believe I'm sitting here eating with the UFC Light Heavyweight Champion." I recalled the details of his fight with vigor and enthusiasm. "A thing of beauty."

"Thanks." Henry touched his napkin to the corner of his mouth, then readied his fork. "You know that feeling when you hit the perfect shot and it lands solid? I had it then. I knew it was over before I even started pouring on the combinations."

"Could you see it in Silva's eyes?" Mabel asked.

"Oh yeah. His eyes glistened over, and he was done." Henry scooped up a fork full of eggs and stuffed them into his mouth. Mabel fished a small notebook out of her handbag and jotted down some sentences. This action stirred something inside Henry, for he sat taller and poured on the dramatics, "It's strange, looking back on it now. Real strange."

"What is?"

"It's like life slowed to a crawl. The left came and I rolled under it, thinking that I need to pop in a hook. That landed, and Viktor stood lazily for a moment. I reset my position and was like, hell, might as well throw another one. I've watched the replay and there's no way you could believe I had enough time to think that clearly, but it's true. Time slowed. When he landed, I reared back with a left, but there was nothing in it. I was gonna tag him a soft one until the ref stopped it. I knew he would. I mean, I didn't want to hurt the guy. Silva's a legend, I respect him."

"Well, my friend," I held up my glass of water to him. "It was beautifully done. Congrats, Champ."

"Thanks."

"You speak about fighting in such an artistic manner," Mabel said.

"Well, he is a painter." Alice added.

"That's right," I said, interested. "What kind of stuff do you paint?"

"Stupid stuff."

"Bull, tell him." Alice punched him on the shoulder. I couldn't recall a time in my life that I had seen Henry so silent and embarrassed. "Fine, I will. Lately, he's been painting the island. Beautiful scenes of the sea."

"Really? I'd like to see them."

"They're not good."

"Yes, they are. He's shy." Henry rolled his eyes at Alice's bragging. This humored Mabel and me, but I remembered my own feelings at Mabel asking to see my novel and felt for Henry.

"For real. I want to see it. Maybe you can paint me one to hang on my mantel."

"Maybe I will." He stared at me for a moment longer then said, "I've miss you, bro."

"I've missed you, too."

"Oh, I've missed you, too." The mocking voice announced as the figure approached our table.

Chapter Twenty-Six

Philip strolled leisurely to our table as if his presence was not only welcomed but appreciated. As hot as the day was, it still surprised me to see him in a long sleeve dress shirt. The cuffs rolled and pushed up his forearms, but still, he had to be hot under it. Of course, the rest of the trio, Scott and Nathan, came in too, accompanied by the day's set of groupies. Scott nodded at us, but continued walking, exiting out a side door and taking up a seat on the patio.

"What are you doing here?" Mabel asked.

"Alice told us you were all coming into Queensbury for breakfast. Thought we'd join you for some mid-morning drinks," Philip said. Nathan winked at Alice and followed the other females out the door to join Scott. Despite the scorn in Henry's eyes, Alice stood from the table with a delighted bounce.

"Sounds great. I wanna mimosa," she said, wiping her mouth and grabbing her purse. Henry's eyes glistened over, turning to disappointment. His shoulders slumped with the force of a heavy sigh, breaking eye contact with everyone.

"Alice, we're in the middle of breakfast."

"So? Bring it outside," Philip said, and started to the door. Alice moved to follow but Henry took her arm.

"I wanna eat in here." His voice was softer, pleading with her through the faint frown at the corner of his mouth.

"OK. Eat and then come join us. I'm wanting a drink." She paused as they exchanged looks, and I knew what Henry would say next. With another sigh, he stood from the table.

"Fine. Let's go."

He instructed Amelia of our plans and she said it was alright. Although I was hesitant to go, Mabel clutched my arm and drug me along. Two of the women sitting on either side of Philip didn't look up to acknowledge us as Mabel and I came to the table. Like the last set of ladies, he flaunted them as if I should know who his trophies were. I didn't. It puzzled me that a man like him still managed to get beautiful women. We passed them on the other side of the table, and I caught his cross look at me. It was only briefly, but it was there, glaring at me as if disapproving of my presence.

Money, Nicanor. Money.

We sat at the end of the wooden bench, the railing separating me from the street beyond. Their conversation never seemed to change or end. It rolled from one topic to another, keeping good humor present and business at bay. Amelia came to the head of the table, suppressing the look of being overwhelmed at the addition to our party. Many spoke but Henry's massive voice interrupted all.

"You know what sounds good," Henry said, flashing his seductive smirk to Amelia. As soon as he was around the trio, his demeanor completely changed. An aristocratic air radiated out of him. "How about a pitcher of mimosas? Hell, bring two and we'll pour our own."

He tossed cash on the tray she balanced at shoulder height. Amelia smiled and disappeared into the restaurant.

You fool, you stupid, stupid fool. What made you think that these guys wouldn't show up? Why are you still in their company? Did you forget what Henry did? You remember the agony and what you did. Yeah, you do. You remember, you sly bastard.

I clamped down on the inside of my lower lip. Pain dulled the dark voice and I eased into the conversation. Stories tossed about like a hot potato and I laughed along with the others. My annoyance and rage at the intrusion on our breakfast faded and I found myself enjoying the party around us. Scott stood up to take center stage.

"And the bastard had me on that goddamn treadmill and jacked up the speed and elevation. Next thing I know, I'm faceplanting and being launched out the back, slamming into a wall. The fuckin' machine is still running and burning the hell out of me and my good friend, Philip," He slapped Philip on the back, "videoed the entire thing, then posted it."

"Yeah, I did." The table jumped with laughter.

"Last time I exercise with you, you Jewish bastard." The drinks poured and the conversation got louder. Any tension I felt, drained away with the emptying of my glass. Mabel refilled her own, then topped off my drink without me having to ask. Talk bounced around the table and I sat back, not wanting to interrupt it, but to marvel at it. I laughed when others did and found myself having a real good time.

Then the outside speakers caught my ear to a song both sad and sweet, and one I knew long ago. It filled me with memories although I couldn't recall the song's name. I drifted away from the pleasantries of the conversation while marveling at the structure of it all. Friends, known and unknown, sharing a good time with one another, not caring about any troubles that may be present in their lives.

The song flared the thoughts of old times with friends of my own. Some without Henry, several with, but all much like this one, with good friends simply enjoying one another's company. An artificial family of one's own creation. A tear of happiness stung behind my eye as the years that flooded my mind had been many. These people sat here, not realizing that it was all a fading moment that moved too quick.

One day, many years from now, they would all be in different places. One may be walking down the snow-covered streets in New York City while another is watching the sun set over the Pacific Ocean. Some will be with growing families or passionate lovers, but at one point, each one of them would look back at this moment and remember the joy and love they had for one another.

The drinks circulated, the laughs captivated, and it all made me miss friends who were no longer in my life.

Then the music faded, and the conversation became lost on me. The air shifted and the energy of danger heightened my senses. Something tingled at the base of my skull and darting my eyes across the neighboring rooftops, I scanned for signs of threats. My laughter died. My heart raced, heightening my ears to any sounds of aggression. A car zipped by. I didn't jump or startle but analyzed. This was a condition I couldn't turn off, nurtured by the years of training and fighting in combat.

Each alley cutting between two buildings held high probability of an ambush point. Every window, a nest for a sniper. I envisioned men stampeding from an alley with AK rifles firing, destroying the harmony of the chaotic breakfast. I hated this feeling. I hated this place, and this was why I never came into the humming city.

Alice laughed at something Henry said. The others did as well as the sun warmed my shoulders, fighting off the cold growing inside my mind. Good nature and drinks flowed wildly.

Look at their casual position of comfort. I wish the war would hit them, so they could feel the intense flaring of nerves.

I chuckled, trying to suppress the dark voice, and fighting the urge to slip away from the good time. As if hearing my inner darkness, one of Philip's *remoras* pointed at a green jeep driving past with three men in woodland fatigues.

A military officer sat in the passenger seat, shiny rank on his collar, while one soldier drove and a third stood manning a machine gun in the back. A belt of ammunition fell into an unseen ammo can. I know this weapon, a M249 SAW, but it wasn't designed for a vehicle mount. It was a personal assault weapon, carried by a member of a squad. Many smaller countries, to peacock their power to larger nations, put on such foolish shows.

No one at our table appeared to be alarmed by the jeep except for Mabel. She took her phone and snapped a picture. On the table sat everyone's cellphones and I learned fast I was the only one without. One by one, they checked their devices, hoping some important notice was waiting for them.

No calls rang out and no text messages beeped, but still they checked as if life hung in the balance. The only one who didn't look at his phone was Henry. Henry stood at the head of the table, his back to the diner, bellowing some story. Like Lon Chaney Jr. in the *Wolfman*, I watched him morph from a quiet man of artistic desire to a monster of unrestrained consumption.

How long could he keep this going and if the party died, would he too? I wasn't in the mood to drink, but the glasses filled and dispersed around the table, so I partook. The two women on Philip's arm danced to music coming from hidden speakers.

The awning that covered the patio did little to protect us from the sun's rays. With blue eyes and years of explosions, the sun completed a triple threat to my light sensitivity. Only a good pair of sunglasses eased my ever-growing headache. The sweetness of the mimosas didn't help, and I motioned for Amelia's attention.

She filled glasses and moved along. With the chatter reaching a deafening volume, I found it impossible to get a glass of water. The conversation marred with their cackling until I couldn't make out one word from another. I joined the laughter, but I hardly spoke. Twice Mabel glanced at me to reassure my presence and twice I faked pleasantries.

Henry never sat while wrangling all eyes to his every word. This was Henry in his element, taking center stage for all to adore him. The wind cut across the patio and I caught a hint of the sea. Images of marlins and sailfish took me away from the party and I wished we were aboard my ship. I wouldn't even mind if the trio were with us.

"Well, Mabel would know about that," Scott said, to the amusement of the others. At the sound of her name, my attention came spiraling back to the table. I didn't catch what was said beforehand and so I wasn't in on the joke.

"What was that?" I asked.

"The mile-high club. Ever join it?" Nathan asked. It took me a moment to figure out what they were talking about.

"I tried once," I said. The table leaned my way, eager to hear my addition, and accepting the anticipation I allowed to grow. "But they don't let you in solo."

The table leapt back with laughter and I even caught a smile on Philip's face.

"Nicely done." Mabel whispered to me through her own chuckles, then loudly proclaimed, "I almost joined but got caught."

Thinking of Mabel in a sexual situation excited me. I envisioned I was her partner, stuffed into the cramped quarters of the airplane restroom, the heat coming off her body. Unaware, I shifted closer to her to feel the same heat my mind conceived. Mabel casted a seductive half smile as if questioning how far she could take her story. My face told her to continue, but my heart soon regretted it.

"Not my fault we got caught, was it, Nathan?" Mabel said. At once my stomach dropped, knotting in pain. I like Nathan, but the thought of him sleeping with Mabel irked me. A grainy picture of their sweaty bodies rubbing against one another brought about a headache that neither sunglasses nor mimosas could touch. My biceps tensed, and my forearms flexed, causing my fists to clench under the table. Four fingernails dug into one of my palms; three in the other, leaving red marks.

Nathan's laughing face aggravated me more as Mabel continued with her story. I wanted to lunge across the table and nail him to the floor. She spoke as if this information was public knowledge. Despite my madness, I didn't react, but instead, faked a good-humored expression.

"Seriously, how?" I found myself asking. I couldn't stop it. It came out on its own.

"Those damn restrooms are too small. Ain't my fault. They always look so much bigger in the movies," Nathan said. The chuckles bounced around the table as slippery as the drinks.

"Doesn't everything?" Mabel snapped, and the laughter elevated. Bile joined the knots and alcohol building in my stomach, burning my throat. I did the foolish thing and tried to extinguish it with more alcohol. It didn't help. Mabel, still laughing, bumped into me. My skin crawled, repulsed by her touch. *How could she sleep with that guy?*

A hollowness blanketed the partygoers who yelped like hyenas. I could see them chopping at bits of meat, pulling and tearing it free from whatever rotting carcass was there for their enjoyment. The burning in my chest was nothing more than heartburn but felt more like a heart attack.

"Are you alright?" Mabel asked, leaning in to whisper, gently stroking my arm. I nodded, a lie. I'm not too foolish to misunderstand what this is between Mabel and me. She's not a woman looking for love or a relationship. She's a woman of her time and that is all she wants. For her, emotions aren't a part of our unspoken agreement, but I'm afraid they were for me.

"Heartburn. I get it when drinking too much orange juice."

"I may have tums in my purse."

"It's fine," I didn't want anything from her. The emptiness inside me grew with each word she uttered. "It'll pass. I'm about to go."

"Go? Why?"

"I have charter parties tomorrow. Gotta get back to work."

"Aw, don't say that word here," Scott said to the other's delight. Mabel inched closer, her words tickling the hairs in my ear.

"You're not upset, are you?"

"No." Another fib. "It's been a wild weekend and I need to get –"

KA-COW. My spine arched and my shoulders tried to cover my ears. Everything stopped as the snap of a bullet broke the awkwardness of my exit strategy.

Chapter Twenty-Seven

This wasn't a car backfire or a figment of my imagination. The others at the table heard it as well, but while they paused with smiles of wonderment, I moved.

"Get inside," I ordered, shouting while jerking Mabel from her seat. A convoy of three military jeeps slid to a halt. Soldiers, armed with M16s, bounced from the vehicles as automatic gunfire replaced the fading echo of the first shot. Pieces of wood from the railing splintered as we ran in. The soldiers directed their arms at an apartment building across the street. Henry grabbed Alice and slung her inside the restaurant, pushing the others to join her.

Everyone cowered behind tables, keeping beneath windows while trying to view the action. A flood of screams joined the choir of gunfire as the diner's glass window, wall length in height, shattered by a stray bullet. We rose enough to see a group of rebels sending a volley of rounds at the soldiers. Mabel sat higher than the rest, higher than myself, and shrugged off my attempts to pull her down. She snapped pictures, then paused.

"Oh god," she said. A boy ran across the street, stuck in the middle of a crossfire. Soldiers took cover behind their vehicles, rebels hid behind walls, but nothing protected this boy. My finger rubbed against my lip as I prayed he made it to safety. Those prayers went unanswered and his cries went unheard. His sandals flew into the air, swirling distractedly into spirals, pulling eyes away from the boy as bullets slammed into him.

He tumbled barefooted through the street, leaving his blood to paint the ground. From knee to hip – hip to shoulder, the force of the bullet twisted his little body, slinging him down. A collective gasp rang out behind me.

"We have to do something." Mabel moved but I forced her into cover.

"I ain't going out there," Philip said, to which his friends agreed. They cowered with gawking eyes, fearing the death outside would bring an end to their party. Scott, who didn't spill a single drop of his drink, flicked a piece of dirt from the top and finished it off. He frowned at his own predicament, unsatisfied with his current circumstances.

"What do we do?" Mabel asked.

"That kid's dead. Why risk our lives for him?" Philip reasoned. The two unfamiliar girls crouched in close to Philip who in turn, moved in closer to Henry behind an overturned table. Henry pulled Alice in close, his arms wrapped her head to shield her from the violence and the sounds. She screamed, shaking her head uncontrollably. More shards from the windows exploded, followed by another eruption of collective screams.

I didn't like what I saw, disapproving of them and disgusted with being a part of their group.

"Cowards." I exhaled through clenched teeth.

And who are you to judge them? Look where you sit. Out there is the death you crave. The honorable death you deserve. The death that will end all your suffering. But you're too comfortable to take that chance. You're a part of them now.

Gnawing sensations clawed at my neck and back and the very air these people exhaled seemed tainted. No matter the work they had done or the makeup they wore, these were the ugliest people I had the displeasure of knowing, yet I was accepting them as friends. I shared laughs, drinks, and stories with them.

My inner battle dissipated over the barrage of gunfire. The boy cried out. People scattered in all directions but not one came to his aid.

Pathetic. Grovel at their feet for their scraps and maybe they will accept you.

"Fuck that." I stood at the protest of everyone around me and stepped through the broken window of the door.

"Nicky, stop."

There you go. Can you feel it? Can you feel that old notion of strength? This is your world. This is what you're good for.

"Stay down, you fool," someone called out behind me. I don't know who it was and I didn't care. I picked up the pace and vaulted over the wooden railing, landing on the hard street with surprising agility, and moved unnoticed by both shooting parties. I wasn't a target for them, but if I stepped into a bullet's path, it would be of my fate and fault alone.

I hustled, keeping my profile low to avoid the crossfire, gliding across the street as I had done in Fallujah. The memory in my muscles was remarkably strong and I moved as only a man who'd been in combat could. I didn't zig or zag, but beelined to the boy, who laid as all boys wounded in battle lay, in a blanket of their own blood.

Painful tears sealed his eyes and without moaning, he took a breath. With my first aid skills being rusty, I knew I couldn't do anything for the kid here. I heaved him into my arms and threw him over my shoulders. Warm blood saturated my chest and back. Three rounds, from either soldier or rebel, I didn't know which, sparked off the ground near my feet.

A soldier stepped in my path. I expected help, but instead, he shoved his rifle barrel in my face and ordered me to drop the boy. The kid had no weapons and no gear to identify him as a rebel, but the soldier perceived him to be. I snapped out a kick, planting my foot on the soldier's kneecap, buckling him. With my free hand, I ripped the rifle away from his hands and tossed it away while running for the diner.

I waited for a shot to the back. Surely, another soldier witnessed the assault on his friend and assumed I too was a rebel, but this didn't happen. Mabel held open the front door, ushering me in. I ran past her and carried the kid into the kitchen. Henry's party followed Mabel in behind me to witness the fate of the war-torn child.

"God, I thought you were a dead man," one of the unknown females said to me. I didn't acknowledge her. With the help of Mabel and Amelia, I laid the kid on the metal counter and shouted for towels, but they did no good. The kid bled out, leaving his face pallid and body ridged. The kid died there with strangers staring at him, like so many young men before him, and I saw all their faces in his.

"Well, that sucks," Scott said, without a hint of compassion. Alice cried and wrapped her arms around Mabel who watched indifferently.

"That sucks?" I said. My hands, still drenched in the kid's warm blood, tightened into fists.

"Yeah. You went through all that trouble to save him and look what happened. Kind of pointless when you think about it. Imagine if you would have gotten killed too." I stood speechless, not sure where to go from there. I wanted to hit him, but I felt sorry for him as well. He lacked the basic human trait for sympathy. Henry placed his hand on my shoulder, and I wanted to shrug it off.

Although the fighting carried on outside, the firing dwindled. With each waning pop, the group flinched. One of the unknown women tried to leave in a sudden wave of hysteria, but Philip restrained her. The dead kid, whose body grew colder, became a metaphorical expression of life and death to come. I could read it in their faces, but only had contempt for them. They'd spent their self-indulgent lives disregarding the fact that the world didn't revolve around their good fortune. Violence was the ruling class, no matter if the elite liked it or not.

Part Three

Chapter Twenty-Eight

A week passed again without interruption from Henry or his socialite friends. Not even Mabel visited, which pleased me as I returned to my natural state of isolation. I clammed up, avoiding almost everyone besides Kojo and only talked to my chartering party when it was essential. Old waves of emotion brewed and burst inside me, bringing with it a heart gripping terror that disturbed my nights and filled my dreams with memories of war and young children cut down by faceless figures.

Two charters occupied my week; not once did Jacob's men trouble me. I doubt he forgot about me, but the truth was, I didn't care. His threats felt meaningless to me in my dejected state, but I did plead with Kojo to board another ship. My troubles didn't need to interfere with his life. He refused at first, but with work dwindling, he took what he could after checking in with me each day.

The time off from chartering trips was good for my writing. Fishing for pleasure without work re-energized my brain, allowing me to focus on the problems with my novel. With last weekend's antics fresh in my mind, the developed arc for my new female character fully formed. I played around with her backstory for days until my fingers ached to get it on digital paper. It gave my novel more substance, for all good stories should have a love interest and I had finally found mine.

Through the blinds of my window, in front of my desk, the sun rose and fell, but I paid it no mind. I wrote, fueled on coffee and little else, until my story concluded. It ended not how I had planned, but sometimes a story has a life all its own and the writer can only buy a ticket to take the ride. By the time my stomach grumbled, night had consumed the island. Exhausted from a day of writing, I sat out on the beach with a cold bottle of Krystal Ale.

Stars twinkled above, but my eyes only gravitated to the lights coming from Henry's mansion. Day or night, weekend or weekday, the festivals continued. There was no denying the alluring power it held, tempting me to show up and enjoy the life others were living. I didn't, but I couldn't deny the luring power of being among them, fun to excess, but the more time spent with them was less time spent in my own private paradise.

They broke you. All these years on your own and now you risk it all for some glimmer of acceptance from these yuppies. You're soft. You lost your edge.

I didn't want to listen to this darkness, but like everyone, I was doomed to be trapped with my own white noise.

Pathetic. Why don't you kill yourself and put everyone out of your misery?

No amount of shaking could rid me of the negative banter, so I did the next best thing, I drowned it in booze.

"Been wondering about you?" Her voice jolted me. I'd been so wrapped up in my own mind that I had failed to hear the soft sand crushing beneath her smooth feet as she rounded the corner of my house. My drunkenness interrupted my attempts at being presentable. At last, I subsided to being a likeable drunk by offering her a beer and seat on the cool sand. She accepted.

"How's it going?"

"Just got back," she said, as if I knew what she was talking about. From my expression, she realized I didn't. "I had to see my publisher in New York. Been gone a few days. You haven't been to Henry's?"

"Nope. Been working."

"That's good. On your novel?"

"Some."

"I read the chapters you gave me on the plane. Pretty good. How much of it is true?"

"Most of it."

"Well, I like it. Send me the rest. You got something here. I told my publisher about it." Part of me wanted to kiss her until a knot built in my stomach and I wish she hadn't read it. This novel was my life, my child, and I don't think I was at a place where I could accept someone reading and judging it even if it was a good judgement. My nerves settled and I asked her to repeat herself because I was six beers deep.

She's just being polite. Your work sucks, you fuckin' poser. She's just boosting you up to ridicule you later. They're all gonna laugh at you. You can never be one of them.

The mocking voice poked, but my good mood won over, drowning out what the beer could not. As it subdued, I had to admit, the mocking voice held some truth. I didn't need to be around the people at Henry's mansion, but I was still drawn back to her, which would eventually lead back to the mansion.

"Wow, that's amazing," is all I could say. Looking out over the ocean, my mind filled with dreams of signing a publishing contract, envisioning what the cover would look like, and the texture of a hard copy in my hand. I pictured cameras snapping in my face and a movie starring that kid from the Transformer films. Big dreams under a big sky. "How long were you gone?"

"Three days. Nothing big, but it's nice to be back here. God, you leave this place and you forget how beautiful it is. This really is paradise at the end of the world."

"I don't think I could ever leave this place." I finished off one bottle and fetched another from the small red cooler sitting next to me. Mabel was still nursing her first and didn't accept the offer for another one. "How's Henry?"

"I haven't seen him," she said.

"Really?" I knew his house was large, but I didn't think it was so large you wouldn't run into another occupant.

"If he's not in his bed, he's in his painting room. Alice said he's been having bad headaches and light sensitivity." I knew that wasn't good. I worried that with his career, there could be some underlying issues he needed to address. "She says it's from all the drinking and he wants to take a break to focus on his paintings."

"Maybe that's for the best."

"You should come by tomorrow. He enjoys being around you. I can tell."

He wouldn't if he knew your secret.

"I'd like that, too." The words that came out weren't entirely a lie. The parties at Henry's were amazing and addicting. Although if asked, I'd deny it. Seeing the parties rage every night was near maddening, because a good time was slipping past my eyes.

"Good. I'd like to see you there."

"I'd like to see you there, too."

"Good. It's a date then," she said. We sat for a moment, drinking our beers and watching the stars reflect off the waves.

What are you doing? You're allowing them to invade. You know it's a mistake.

"Well, do you wanna go have sex now?" Her boldness, although refreshing, was still something I had to get used to. I didn't decline her offer.

Chapter Twenty-Nine

I didn't decline her offer to the party either. Something inside me told me not to go, but then the notion of missing what could be a fantastic time gnawed at my brain. I had never been to parties like the ones at Henry's mansion. There was dancing, drinking, exploring, a swimming pool, a rock stage, cage fighting, and Mabel. Reluctantly, I went.

The house jumped with an overwhelming magnitude that was mysteriously captivating. Lights, as green as money, throbbed, pulsing with the boom of the music. As before, people flowed through the doors and drunken bodies filled the front fountain. With the nearest neighbor miles away, the noise freely expanded.

I stood on the front lawn and stared up at the structure, but something was not right. Previously, the culture of the crowd could be described as women decked out in expensive jewelry and designer gowns with men dressed fit for any charity ball or dinner. I still found some of those people here, but the majority looked as if they were going to a college frat party, dressed for comfort more so than class. Although I'm not one who should be talking, for my own clothes weren't that fashionable, the change in attire unnerved me.

Aside from Kojo, I thought of myself as a solo guy, a loner who didn't need that kind of human connection. I need the written word, the open ocean, a full bottle of booze, but not the compassion of another. A good lay, an occasional handshake, and a drunk friend sustained my needs, but the world, no matter how far to the end of it you reach, finds a way to pester you. It tracks you down and puts a hurting on you. I escaped it once, fleeing from my home country which only held pain and misery, and now it was back, stalking me.

The fine hair on my neck stood on end and my shoulders drew forward. An emptiness encompassed my chest and from these dark recesses of my mind slipped the demented voice.

Because you're weak. You're a sadist who secretly enjoys the pain they are inflicting.

The word sadist tossed about in my mind and I wondered if this voice, crawling out from some cesspool of horrors, was right, yet my feet remained planted in front of the mansion, staring up with all the wonders my mind could create. There was some magnetic attraction that pulled me to Henry and his entourage. Deep down inside, I hungered to know them, who they were, why they lived the way they did. Perhaps I wanted to write about them, but I couldn't deny my skin flared with warnings for my departure.

Then go. Why endure the misery that is their company? Get on your boat and get the hell out of here, even though we both know you won't. You revel in this pain because you haven't felt it in a long time, and that pain makes you feel alive.

The doors parted for all guest to enter and I proceeded. Upon crossing the threshold, I halted at the overall vibe seeping from the plaster of the house. People funneled past my stationary position, hurrying with the impatience to catch a subway train instead of joining a party. I assumed they worried that each minute spent away would be a missed minute of pure pleasure.

Their need for excess was not on my radar. Overhead, a poor wattage bulb hung from a long extension rod, transfixing my eyes. I recalled the first time I entered the hall; the lights were bright and warming. Now a dimness emanated from the centers. Only I seemed to take notice.

Squeezing by me, a sublime creature entered the tide. Her long, straight auburn hair trailed down her tanned back to a white thong bikini, complimenting her complexion. Even other women stared in envy as the smoothness of her back only accentuated the firmness of her butt.

On the second-floor landing, leaning against the banister, Nathan and Philip stood drooling over an attractive woman. She gave sly glances between the two, impressed with Nathan's stardom and Philip's fortune. I continued using the white thong as a guiding light, passing the study, and expecting to see men sitting in the leather chairs, but only books occupied the room.

The thong disappeared into the army of fun-seekers as we dared to go out back. A massive gathering littered the landscape. The wandering eyes of partygoers scattered and bounced between people leaping into the pool, dancing wildly throughout the yard, or on the band rocking out on a small stage. No face was familiar, and I wondered who the tourists were and who were islanders.

A selected few smiled genuinely, but most held stern looks of seriousness stitched to their features. Despite the laughing and cheering, the element of joy which engulfed the previous parties was missing. The crowd's dancing mimicked a sexual nature more vulgar than I cared to see. A man and a woman ran by, stark-raving naked, and leapt into the pool to the massive approval of others.

A tap rapped upon my shoulder and I turned, expecting Mabel or Henry. Instead, a butler in a penguin suit stood, face expressionless, and said, "Nicanor?"

"Yes." He pointed upward where Henry stood on the balcony of the third floor, overseeing the party. Mabel was with him and together they waved down at me. I waved back, glad to have an excuse to vacate the area and head back inside.

The grand staircase split off in two directions on the second floor. Several doors lined the walls, stoking my imagination at what stories they held. Philip and Nathan were no longer there, and I wondered who had got the girl. A sick image of both assaulted my mind and I rushed to swat it away. Another stairway continued to the third floor, crossing over the length of the house. It was a strange design if I have ever seen one, but then, I've only been in one mansion - this one.

Once on the third floor, I found Henry and Mabel leaning against the railing, chatting. The air felt lighter up here, lessening the gravitational pull emitted from the party down below. Even this floor held couples or small gatherings, but they were spread out far enough not to bother one another. To the left of the balcony, and shielded in shadows, a doorway concealed a set of stairs leading up to the attic. Up there, among the cobwebs and ghosts, one could find Henry's painting room.

I envisioned a wooden tripod easel facing an open window, overlooking the ocean. The thought made me want to go home and move my own writing desk out back, so the ocean could engulf me as I wrote. A foolish notion of a young romantic writer for one couldn't write with the wind blasting their face and the thunderous crashing of waves interrupting their thoughts. A painter creates what he sees in the world, but a writer creates what he sees in his mind.

With beaming excitement, Henry welcomed me, meeting me halfway. Mabel trailed him from the balcony. He wore a suit, dressed dapper as always, but it was Mabel who stole the air from the room. Her dark dress, hemmed to her knees, shined green in the reflection of light. I realized something about Mabel I hadn't noticed before. She wore dark colors more than anyone else, like a woman in mourning, which contrasted her good-natured tone. I greeted them with a hearty handshake for Henry, and a hug and a kiss on the cheek for Mabel.

Her nose tickled my beard and I pulled her in closer to inhale her intoxicating perfume. I could have melted in her arms if she would have only wrapped both of them around me. She didn't, but not out of cruelty. Mabel, as I had learned, was not a romantic person. She hugged me with one arm as two old friends would.

"How's it going?" Henry asked with a robust grin. His large hand pounded a thud against my back, breaking the trance she held on me.

"Fine, what are y'all doing up here?"

"Finally getting more interview time with the champ." Mabel punched him in the arm to which Henry played the fool, rubbing it and wincing in imaginary pain.

"Talk, talk, talk. That's all you ever want to do." Henry jested.

"That's not all I do." She countered. Henry and I shared a glance then broke into laughter, taking what she meant as perverse. Mabel rolled her eyes, but a smile broke through before she could suppress it. "I have work to do. I'll see you boys later."

"If I'm interrupting, I can come back."

"No. I'm done with him for now." Mabel's touch went from Henry's shoulder to my arm as she ventured down the stairs. Although Henry didn't, I watched as she continued onto the second floor and vanished behind a closed door.

"That's her room."

"It's late. She normally works this late?" A beat went by after the door closed and part of me yearned for her to come back. As I readied to turn, the door reopened, and I found myself not breathing, anticipating her appearance. Instead, a down trotted Alice exited the room, closing the door behind her. She adjusted her shining silver evening gown and strolled out of sight. I'm glad Henry didn't see the look of disappointment on his wife's face. I wondered what her and Mabel could have talked about in such a short time.

"She likes to ttyy-pe up the interview while it's still fresh in her head. Come on." Henry led me outside to the spot where he and Mabel stood moments before. A whiskey decanter sat on a small table with four glasses. Two crystal glasses were used, two not, and Henry poured us each a drink. We stood watching the party goers and sipping our drinks. "Nicky, I'm glad you came. Mabel said you would."

"Is that so? She said you've been a little antisocial as of late."

"Antisocial? Naw, just painting a lot. Haven't been in the mood to party since—"

"Yeah, me neither," I quickly said to avoid any mention of Queensbury.

"Anyway," he said, turning me to the view. He waved his hand to the island, to the beach, to the sea. "I can't believe this is your home."

"I love the island. You don't need much. Life is simple."

"Must be nice." Henry finished his entire drink and poured another.

"What's that mean?"

"You know, things get complicated. I feel oovveerr-whelmed—" He snapped his head to the side before he continued, "half the time."

"Is that why you took up painting?"

"It calms me. This might sound crazy, but I miss life in the Corps. You know, before I got spotted at that gym."

"I know. It's funny how tough life in the Corps can be, yet so simple. Do your job, make a little money, then have fun. No added stress, except for that whole dying part."

"Yeah, but I didn't even ggee-t a chance at that." He took a long gulp of whiskey, the ice rattling in the glass, and refilled. He spoke slower and I half-expected to see him stumble soon. "God, I hated myself when I found out you guys had deployed. I tried to get back, but my new command wouldn't allow it. They couldn't understand why I'd want to give up the chance to go to the Olympics in order to go to war. They said I was more valuable to the war effort and the Corps as a prizefighter going for Olympic gold. They weren't real Marines."

I couldn't find the words to comfort him. I wanted to spill the truth, the reason behind it all, but I couldn't bring myself to it. Instead, I said, "Things happen, man. You didn't know we were deploying."

"No, but it's crazy how qquuii-ck after I got picked up by the boxing team that y'all were given your oorr-ders." He rubbed at his temples, then clamped his teeth down on his knuckle to smother his quivering tongue.

Empty glass, filled glass, empty glass, filled glass. The routine worked over and over before my eyes. He swayed lightly, and I wished he'd slow down, but it's not my place to tell anyone how to live.

"Life is crazy, man. But you're the Champion of the World. Look at all this," I motioned to the grounds the mansion stood on. "All this is yours."

"Kind of, but whatever. Come check this out," he said with the glee of a schoolboy eager to show off a new toy. I expected for him to lead me to his painting room, but instead we proceeded into the master bedroom. I faked like I had never seen the room before. The cuffs and restraints no longer hung from the bed post, but I didn't let on that I knew about those. Resting on top of the bed was the cold steel of what I first thought was a shotgun. "Look at this."

He picked it up and handed it to me, a double barrel that wasn't a shotgun, but an old game rifle known as a .450 express.

"Man, this is a beauty."

"Just got it in. Check out the inscription." On the bottom side of the rifle was an engraving that read, '*LtCol. Henry James Patterson.*'

"Patterson? Patterson?" I racked my brain but couldn't recall why the name rung such a bell.

"Think lions," Henry said. Then it hit me. Henry James Patterson was the bridge builder who had killed the lions in Tsavo back in the late nineteenth century.

"Are you shitting me?" I couldn't believe I was holding the rifle of legend.

"Not at all. This is the rifle that killed the last lion."

"From Ghost and the Darkness?"

"Fuck yeah, but not the movie. This is the real rifle. Ain't she a beaut? Oh, and check these out." He stepped over to a cabinet and pulled out two ivory handle revolvers.

"Both .45's?" I asked, marveling over the beauties.

"Indeed. What do you think?"

"I think you have 'fuck you' money."

"You'd think." A dark veil fell over his face. He took the twin revolvers and stored them back in the cabinet. We walked back to the balcony where his drink was waiting. "I hardly get time to myself without someone knocking on the door, needing me to sign my name to this or that. And as for 'fuck you' money, not really. I'm kind of banking on my stocks and investments right now."

"Why's that? You're the champ. Look at this place."

"Everything's expensive and I pay for it."

"Don't they also pay for it?" Referring to Philip and Scott.

"They pay for some things, but the majority of everything falls on me."

"Well, that's bullshit. Fuck that. Flip the bill on them."

"Can't really. All my money is tied up in them. That's why I envy your life."

"Don't," I said.

"Naw, it's true. I envy your life. Man, you get to go fishing, hang out on your bboo-at." He snapped his head again, whipping it violently to the side to shake the word loose from his tongue. He took a second and a hard breath then continued, "You do whatever you want. Sit around and soak up the grandeur of it all."

"Ain't easy during hurricane season and there's no tourists. I survive but just barely. But compared to most people on the island, I'm well off."

Part of this statement was a lie. I didn't barely survive and felt awful at this fib for my bank account held no concern to me. Owning both my house and boat and with a monthly pension for my wounds, I maintain a very modest, but well-off living. I don't know why I said that lie, but it weighed heavy upon my shoulders and pained at my neck.

You dishonest piece of trash. Look at you. Now, you're lying for no reason? What happened to you? Pathetic.

"Still, you get to wake up without the commotion of the big modern world. Hell, you don't even have a cellphone. How cool." He was right. For years my life held the simplicity of a bird's flight when the winds lift its wings and it soars with little effort. This isn't always the case and in recent days, complications mounted. Gone was the carefree bird and my mind felt like a sailor caught in a hurricane with raging winds and pelting rain. Any corrections I did seemed fruitless against nature's will.

"The grass is always greener," I said, holding up my deformed hand. "I wish I still had all my digits or that some of the guys from back then were still around. Can I tell you something I haven't told hardly anyone?"

He nodded his head, secretly pleading for me to share like we had when we were kids.

"I see them almost every night. I close my eyes and there they are. I hear their screams on the back of waves. It's my biggest regret."

"We all have regrets," he said, staring out into the night. "We all have demons."

I finished my drink and motioned for another.

"Yeah, I guess the grass is greener," he said. "I tell you what I want."

"What's that?" I asked, taking a sip. The liquor was smooth and tasted of money.

"I would love to sleep an entire day without someone bothering me." I couldn't help but laugh at this. Here stood the Champion of the World, the richest man I knew, who seemed to have every plaything at his fingertips, yet the only thing he wanted was uninterrupted sleep.

"You're the champ. Can't you tell people to fuck off for a moment?"

"You'd think that, but it's not that easy. Even here, in this paradise, I'm constantly working on my side businesses or being asked questions about my ffii-ghting career. I'd rather hit the bag or practice some rolling drills on the mats without onlookers in suits. It seems like everybody wants to pull me in so many different directions." He paused to take a drink. "You know I own a whiskey distillery?"

He shook his glass in front of me, rattling the cubes of ice inside.

"No, I didn't."

"It's another reason why I'm on the island. There's the whiskey company, some other businesses, and with people wanting my pic for pprroo-ducts, I can't sleep or think. Hell, I can barely speak with Mabel for her interviews and I really want to do that. That's the whole reason Philip and Scott are here."

"They're here so you can sleep and do interviews?"

"No. I'm the face, and they're the money. I mean I own this place, but it's sucking my bank account dry. I said Philip and Scott help when they want, but if they wanted, they'd stop the money and I'd be finished. Luckily, I have several stocks I can fall back on. It's nerve racking to constantly think of my money and how it could all go away in the blink of an eye. I'm counting on a few of these businesses and my stocks."

"So, why not cut them off and strike out on your own?" I asked. He looked over his shoulder to ensure no one was there.

"Eventually I wwaa-nt to. Like I said, if these stocks and businesses take off, I'm gonna try. Might lose a lot at first, but hopefully it will be OK. It's just hard to."

"Hard to what? Lose a lot at first?"

"No, striking out on my own. I'm their cash cow. There's contracts and shit that are hhoo-lding me in place and no one wants to lose when I'm winning. Hell, I think I'm getting screw by a lot of people, but I just don't know who or if they really are. Maybe I'm just going crazy and sometimes I just wanna stop everything."

"Then stop everything."

"Maybe I will one day." A dark, sinister gaze crossed his eyes and I didn't like the vibe he was giving off.

"So why is Nathan here?" I asked, hoping to change the subject to something more pleasant without being noticeable. I failed.

"That's for Alice. He's here to help her with her career." There was something else he wanted to say, but he kept his mouth shut. It's for the better. A marriage is no place for a third wheel.

"Why not come on the boat with me? Just you and me. We can get away and no one can reach you there."

You wanna take him out with you? You are soft and I guess you forget a lot of things. Pathetic.

"I'm sure some way the world would find me out there. Besides, I'd feel guilty for encroaching on your paradise, Nicky."

"Nothing's encroaching on me out there. Out there, I leave all my troubles behind and simply fish. One of the oldest tasks known to man. I cast a line and hope for a fight. The smell of the ocean helps fight off depression," I said. I rubbed my lip, wishing I hadn't said that word.

"Depression?"

"Umm, yeah," I said sheepishly. "War shit, you know."

"No, I don't," he said regrettably. "But I do know about depression. Sucks. I wish you could bottle up that essence of the ocean, that part that takes away all the worries. I wish you could bottle that up and give it to me."

"I can't bottle it up, but I can give it to you. Just get on the boat."

"Maybe soon." He said, but something in me knew he didn't mean it.

"Don't make excuses, motherfucker." He wouldn't look at me. The world I was handing him was outside his mental grasp. He couldn't see how to live without the trappings of life, and under the weight of success, he forgot the trick of being free. Empty glass, full glass.

"The only absolute peace I'll get is death," he said.

"Perhaps that's the only peace any of us gets. But for clarity of mind, you gotta get away from all this shit. Get on the boat."

"That's easy for you to say. I know Philip and Scott and Nathan would all expect to go." Henry slouched forward from inebriation and despair, resting his forearms on the railing.

"Fuck them. What? Are they your mother? You're the fuckin' champ, act like it. Take control of your life like you take control of the cage. All that shit, it's only agreements and business. It's not your life."

"It *is* my life." He snapped. "It's agreements wwoorr-th millions."

"No, it's not your life. It's your job, and if you don't learn to separate the two, you'll find that *absolute* peace."

"Maybe that's for the best."

"Shut up. Don't talk like that."

"Yeah, you're right," he said, correcting his slouch and polishing off one more drink. I couldn't believe how much he could put away. "So, you and Mabel been seeing a lot of each other."

"Not a lot. Why?"

"Nothing. She's a cool chick. Very iinnddee-pendent, but what a minx." I got the feeling everyone knew something about her I didn't.

"What aren't you saying?"

"Nothing." We turned to rest the small of our backs against the stone railing of the balcony. A cool wind blew in and a deep horn from a passing ocean liner moaned in the distance. "Look, she's awesome, just watch yourself. Don't get too attached. It's not her game."

"Not her game?"

"She enjoys a good time, don't get me wr-oonn-g, she's cool as shit, but she's not one for emotions or connections. She's looking for a warm body to fill her cold heart if you get me."

"You saying she swings both ways?"

"That's not what I was getting at, but yeah, sometimes. I don't want you to fall for her and expect s-oomm-ething serious."

"Fall for her?" I don't know if it was the drink or not, but I took offense at the suggestion I wasn't in control of my own desires. "Look, I have a great life here and I don't plan on having anyone interfere with it."

"I'm not trying to up-sseett you." The habit of snapping his head was something I was realizing he was all too familiar with. "I'm only saying that most women get att-aa-ched. Especially in a sexual relationship, but she's blank. I know it has something to do with her husband dying, but still, she can be cold at times."

"We all have a past, and we all have our issues. Like I said, though, I'm not looking for a nuclear family. I enjoy my life." The anger in my veins expanded.

"Let's get out of here," he said, forcefully changing the subject and slapping me in the chest with the back of his hand.

"Why?" I asked.

"I wanna go for a drink." I eyed his glass. "Some place else."

"Where? The biggest party on the island is down there." On the ground below, young people danced, intoxicated on both liquor and good times. There were rich and poor, tourist and islander, young and old. No one was denied.

"I don't care. The party will go on with or without me. Let's go. Know of any place with some real music, something besides island music?" I did and immediately the White Whale came to mind. It had been weeks since I had visited my old stomping grounds.

"I do."

"What are you guys talking about?" Mabel startled us.

"Wanna get outta here, toots?" Henry tried to persuade Mabel. It worked. "So, where's this music at?"

"Near my place." Henry cheered at this, pumping his fist in front of him. Without another word, and filled with youthful excitement, he took off down the stairs. Mabel and I worked to catch up. As we pushed through thriving bodies, a halting voice caught us before we reached the front door. If I'd known what was to follow, I would've shoved Henry out the door. But things unfolded the way they were meant to.

Chapter Thirty

Reverberant voices of the horde masked the shouter's location. Scanning faces revealed nothing until Philip emerged from a previously empty study. I guess Nathan took the girl. Two men accompanied Philip and their presence sounded my alarms. I readied myself for battle by reaching behind my back for my blade but grazed only a patch of my own flesh.

So many distractions lately left me off my guard, but I kept my hand in place to at least give Finn and Jacob the illusion I carried. The taller of the two brothers lunged forward, but the shorter, fatter man held him back. Party goers nearby shuffled out of the way but stayed close enough to witness. Henry and Philip split their attention between the two men and I, scrutinizing the mounting tension.

"Do you know one another?" Philip asked. Jacob Coke fired up a fat cigar as Finn cracked his knuckles in anticipation. Damage from our previous encounter remained hidden under his t-shirt.

"We are former associates," Jacob said.

"That's a nice way of putting it. I'd say you were more of a slave master than an associate."

"Hang on there," Philip stepped forward with his palm up to me. "You can't say that here."

"Fuck off." I warned through gritted teeth. My eyes never left Finn or Jacob. Philip didn't know what he was inserting himself in to.

"I kill ya, mon." Finn threatened.

"Keep talking. I'll finish my design on your chest." I flexed the muscles in my arm to imply I was pulling my knife. The twitching of the fibers kept their attention. Jacob's cigar burned bright with listless puffs. Henry stood between the others and I, while Mabel stood to the side, doing her best to soak in each word spoken, never intervening as was her nature. She waited for the speculative outcome, which would go into the pages of a story.

"I hear you're still chartering." It never ceased to amaze me how American Jacob could sound when he wanted.

"That's right."

"Then you owe me money."

"I don't owe you shit," I thrusted a finger in his direction, "and send your boys at me again, I'll carve them up worse than I did your brother."

Finn made a motion to advance on me, but Jacob raised his hand, restraining him again.

"You don't understand. I'm not doing this for money."

"Oh yeah, then what's it about?"

"For the good of the people. Not all are fortunate enough to have such big boats to charter all day on. I do this so everyone gets a piece of the pie. It's only fair."

"It's only communism. You give out scraps to these junkies while others work their asses off for meager pay. I ain't no fuckin' commie, so I'll go my own way."

"I can't have that. You do it, then others might think it's OK to do the same, then where will that leave the real poor at?"

"I guess without a meal ticket. I've seen those *real poor* you talk about. Those junkies that do your bidding for that poison you keep feeding them," I said. Finn stepped forward, but Henry checked him back.

"Watch yourself," Henry said. "No fighting unless it's with me."

"And who ya be?" Finn asked.

"Henry," Philip interrupted before the conversation escalated any further. "This is the gentleman we've been arranging to meet with about the distillery."

At once Henry's shoulders slacked, and as if nothing had happened, Henry extended his hand. "That's right. Mr. Coke, how are you?"

His voice changed from rough fighter to Wall Street businessman.

"Fine, if not for this little trouble." He pointed at me.

"Oh, I'm big trouble." I corrected.

"Enough," Henry demanded. "I'm sorry, Mr. Coke, but I must leave. Philip can assist you in anything you need."

It was nails on a chalkboard each time Henry called him, Mr. Coke. Giving that kind of respect to a piece of shit like Jacob brought bile to the back of my throat. Henry touched my shoulder and said, "Let's go."

I shrugged him off.

"You're gonna deal business with this commie fuckin' pig?"

"That's no way to speak to our guest," Alice said, coming down the stairs and taking a place next to Mabel. Henry and I ignored her.

"Come on, man. It's business. I'm not caring about it right now."

"Henry, business." Philip made an attempt to direct him into the study.

"Handle it." He instructed, then directed me toward the front door. "Let's go."

"Where are we going?" Alice asked.

"Places. Can we please go?" Henry tried once more to usher me to the door. Jacob, Finn, and Philip returned to the study, with Jacob lagging slightly behind to eye me. Against my better judgement, I followed with Mabel and Alice in tow. Henry hurried out to his red Bel-Air and started it before Mabel, Alice, or I were off the front steps. The girls climbed into the back and me in the front. Henry sped away with us leaving behind the party and all who dwelled inside.

Chapter Thirty-One

"Sorry about that," Henry said, cutting the wheel and swinging the large metal car around the front fountain. People howled, not knowing who they shouted at. I was still gritting my teeth as the massive car snaked down the winding road. I had the right mind to leave them once we arrived at our destination. "I just want to hang out with you guys tonight."

I took a breath, calming down. Everyone had the right to get away from their troubles and by the look of it, Henry was due this more than most.

"Yeah, let's drink," I said. Mabel howled at the moon, the wind rushing by, beating at our faces.

"Where to?"

"The White Whale. It's by my house."

"House? You live in a shack," Henry said. A cheap shot, but a good one.

"Oh, sorry it ain't a mansion for his majesty." I rolled my hand and bowed as if he was a member of the royal family.

"It's a nice shack." Mabel's face appeared between Henry and me.

"Thanks, Mabel, you're a lot of help."

"Any time." She patted me.

"So, what's your deal with that Jacob guy?" Henry asked. My rage flared and my first instinct was to yell at him, to chastise him, but this wasn't his world, and this wasn't his fight. He knew nothing of my troubles with Jacob and it was wrong of me to act so offended by his intended partnership. I sighed, releasing the anger I felt.

"Well, remember those guys I was fighting on my dock?" Henry nodded his head. "Those were his men. What I wanna know, what business do you have with him?"

"My whiskey company is wanting to open a distillery here near the river."

"Whiskey, here? Island Rum and Krystal Ale are the main drinks on this island. I don't know if a whiskey company will do well."

"It will and Philip found out that Jacob's the guy we have to talk to."

"He's a crook."

"Aren't they all?"

"Deal with the devil, you gonna get burned."

"Thanks, mom. Look, I get that you have beef with him, but business is business, man."

"Funny, how things change."

"Yup, the world changes when you alienate yourself from it." His bold statement slapped me in the face.

"Alienate? I didn't alienate myself."

"Then why didn't you get in touch with anyone again."

"Because I don't fuckin' have to."

"You took off, leaving everything and everyone behind." The wind whipped at us as we cut through the island.

"You can't understand," I said.

"Enlighten me then." Henry drove the large metal car into the curiously full parking lot of the White Whale. It appeared that his house wasn't the only party in town.

"Guys, can we forget about all that and go have a good time? Let's go get naked," Mabel wailed as she stood up in the back of the convertible. Two couples heading toward the rambling establishment turned and cheered.

The jukebox boomed like I had never heard before and I couldn't believe my eyes. Nearly every table bloomed with occupants and each person held a drink. A space void of tables populated with couples dancing to the tunes. Henry beelined for the bar, taking an empty seat that a gentleman had deserted.

I stood dumbfounded, astonished at all the people in my old bar. It had never been this busy and a sadness struck my heart. It had changed in the time since I'd last been here and I feared I had as well and that neither of us could be who nor what we once were. An emptiness consumed me. I wanted to run, to get back to the only sure comfort I had left in this world – the AJAX. As always, Mabel pulled me along.

"*Las cuatro cervasas* and whiskeys, *por favor.*" Henry mispronounced it as *poor fa-vor.* King Louie blinked blankly at him.

"This ain't Texas, Hoss. They don't speak Spanish 'round here."

"Oh, my apologies," Henry said. He knocked on the hard wood of the counter and held up four fingers. "Four Krystal Ales and four top shelf whiskeys, please sir."

"I need a vacation." King Louie mumbled under his breath and got the order.

"King Louie, what's going on here?" I asked.

"Business, mon. Some big tourist came one night and da place ain't been da same since. I had to hire some help." He didn't stay to chat but instead, hurried off to help someone else waiting at the bar. It all seemed different and even his old stools were gone, replaced by leather ones with backing. Quickly, my eyes shot up to the beam that separated the two mirrored sections of liquor bottles.

Thankfully, despite all the changes, the two photos, one black and white, one colored, still hung. Perhaps forgotten during the upgrades to the bar.

"Is that you?" Henry asked.

"Yeah. That fish still holds the record on the island."

"Holy shit," Mabel said, leaning over the bar to get a better look at the six by nine photo. "Why didn't you keep it for your mantel?"

"I caught it years ago. I didn't realize it would be my best catch or a record setter. The guys on the ship told me to tag it and throw it back and so I did."

"Damn, what a beauty."

"That's true."

Henry held up his shot, pulling me away from the photo, and said, "Pals."

I picked up the tiny glass but didn't repeat the toast. The ladies paid us no mind, but they touched glasses with ours and downed their drinks. Henry winced at the liquor burning its way down his throat.

"I asked for whiskey, not rum."

"If you don't name the whiskey, they assume you mean rum in a shot glass," I explained, humored.

"What the fuck for?"

"It's de islands," I said in my best, horrible island accent.

"Screw that, another shot and this time, real whiskey." Before I could protest, he spun around and ordered. I threw back the rum and caught sight of someone amongst the chaos that remained unchanged as much as the pictures behind the bar had. Sitting at the end of the counter, leaking a repulsive aura, Samuel huddled over a beer, apparently unfazed by this new atmosphere.

Even though I pitied Samuel, his very presence was unsettling. The sight of him brought up a memory of the boy dying in Queensbury. He conjured all the images of the dead I had known. Pain wrecked my stomach, twisting my insides with agony and sorrow. I never cared to seek another death again.

I rapped once on the bar top to order another shot and beer. Henry glared at the full ones sitting in front of me with questioning eyes. This had nothing to do with him and so I didn't feel obligated to explain. He shrugged with his face and took a long pull off his beer as King Louie brought both drinks to me. I separated from my group.

Pushing through the crowd, I made my way to Samuel who didn't pry his eyes away from the empty mug clamped inside his interwoven fingers. His memories filled the capacity of his being, lost in a thought I'd never experience. I sat both drinks down in front of him and with dried tears clinging to his corneas, he glanced at me. No words passed between us, only a nod, and I left him there, never to see him again.

As I returned, Henry downed a shot of Jameson whiskey and spotted a vacated table in the back. He pushed his way through the crowd, worming around the tables, never looking over his shoulder. Accustomed to people in his footsteps, he didn't doubt we were following. Henry pulled out a chair to sit when a young man snatched one of ours, adding it to the several already filling his own table.

"Put that back," Henry ordered.

"No one's sitting there," the young man argued, smiling arrogantly.

"There is now. Put it back." The young man hesitated, sizing up Henry, deciding if he could take the well-dressed man. His drunken mind worked this over until his friend whispered into his ear. The young man returned the chair with an apology.

"You sonofabitch," an island woman shouted, stopping at our table. She balanced a waiter's tray at shoulder height, and I rose to give her a hug.

"Jazz." The long-legged beauty ignited a warm welcome. "How's it going?"

"Pretty good," she said as Henry leaned back in his chair, eyeing her without any concern of Alice sitting next to him.

"What happened here?" I asked, glancing around.

"Place is full of terrorists almost every night."

"Tourists." Alice corrected.

"I know what I said." Jazz snapped back. "College kids mainly. One of dem blogged about it and it went viral. I don't know what day see in dis place, but day love comin' here."

I introduced Jazz to my company, and we ordered more drinks. Mabel motioned her over and whispered something in her ear. The tall black beauty smiled, nodded, then left our table. We carried on, observing the atmosphere without speaking. This continued until Jazz brought back four glasses of some bluish liquid. I eyed it with suspicion and even flicked the rim of the glass to see if something moved in the cloudy substance.

"Cheers." Mabel picked up her glass and tossed it back. She slammed the shot glass on the counter and waited on us. Henry shrugged his shoulders and together we drank the fruity, sugary drink. It wasn't pleasing.

"What the hell is that?" Henry grimaced. I wanted to vomit.

"Blue raspberry vodka." Mabel informed us.

"It's delicious." Alice licked her lips.

"God, I hate vodka. Nearly died from it one night," Henry said.

"Fuck yeah, you did." I wiped the repulsive drink from my mouth, while simultaneously laughing and gagging. "Shit, that's gross. How dare you, Mabel."

The horrible drink brought us a bout of good humor, but we ordered something more appealing. Time rolled on and we drank, carrying on a great ramble. Henry ordered shot after shot, loading them up and knocking them down, while I stayed more with beer. The hangovers were killing me as of late and I figured if I stuck to beer, I could wake in the morning and work.

"Slow down, Henry. What are you trying to do, break some record?"

"I am the Light Heavyweight Champion of the World." He boasted, slapping at his chest. "I can out drink, out fight, and out fuck any man on the island."

His eyes landed on Mabel, attempting to replace drunkenness with seduction.

"Well," Mabel took a swig from her beer and leaned in, mimicking his own gaze. They swayed together like two magnets repealing one another around an invisible field. "I'll let you know when I fuck the rest of the men on the island."

"That's why I love you, Mabel. You're like oonn-e of the guys. You drink and ttaa-lk dirty. Hell, you would have fit right in with us back in the day." Henry snapped out his hand and slapped my shoulder. I jerked, not at the pain but at the unexpectedness of it. "Back when we tore up the streets. Damn, what good times those wweerr-e—"

A burp interrupted his slur. His face drooped, eyelids heavy, the picturesque features of a man on the verge of a drunken slumber. He shifted in his seat. The alcohol accumulated in his system, hitting the right blood vessels, and hitching a ride to his brain. The lightness in his tone vanished, "Then you left wwiitt-thout a fuckin' word to tell anyone if you were alive or not. I thought you wweerree ddee-ead."

"I get that."

"You think I'm laughing!" His palm slapped the table. A few surrounding patrons looked at us, then subconsciously inched their chairs away. "I grieved for y-oouu, man. I thought you had died in Iraq. I searched for your name on the internet but couldn't find anything. Ya got no social media."

"Don't need it. Don't want it. Had no one to stay social with."

"Fuck you. Didn't you even care about me?"

"I saw you on the television. I knew how you were doing."

"But you didn't ccaa-re that I thought you might be dead."

"Didn't really think about it."

"No, you didn't. I spoke to Claire and she didn't even hear from you while you were over there." With each word, he wobbled, and I figured he would soon fall from the table.

"Who's Claire?" Alice probed Mabel, both girls listening intently to our conversation.

"His ex-girlfriend."

"Didn't even have the nerve to write her." Henry asserted, staring into his beer before taking a gulp.

"Well, you'll have to excuse me. I was a little busy fighting a *war.* Not exactly a lot of time left for dealing with whores."

"Oh shit." Alice surprised herself with saying. It was one of the only times she let her guard down and I believe her real voice came out. Absent were the pretentious syllables and snobbish attire of her speech. She seemed normal, appearing human.

"That ain't cool, man. She was your woman. She was good to you."

I cracked up at this, leaning back in my seat and bellowing a hearty chuckle.

"Good to me? That's rich. If you have a problem with what I did, go call her yourself. But since you're here, how about another drink?" I proposed, trying to change the subject. Henry shrugged his shoulders and laid his forehead on the table.

"Too much testosterone. Let's go dance, Mabel." Alice stood, pulling at Mabel unsuccessfully.

"What time is it?" Mabel asked.

"Time to dance, come on." Alice tried again, but Mabel refused.

"It's late. You got somewhere to be?" I said.

"Not really." With a startling surprise, Henry rocketed to a sitting position, looking about with renewed energy.

"Shit," he said, slapping at his shirt as if it was on fire or he was looking for something that was lost. "Let's take a shot."

"Calm down, killer."

"Fuck that, let's take a shot."

"I don't want another shot," Alice complained. "I wanna dance. Mabel?"

"Oh, come on, pussy," Henry said with a stretch and Alice scrutinized his disgusting insult.

"Man, it's like 3:30 in the morning. You can't drink like that here. The island sun will get you." I told him.

"Fuck you, I'll drink any way I want."

"Hey mon." Henry looked up at the bouncer standing by our table. I sighed again with frustration, knowing none of this would lead to anything good. "Ya fall asleep again, ya out."

"I didn't fall asleep."

"Don't put'cha head on da table."

"Fuck you." Henry tossed back his shot that had been sitting there for some time.

"Henry, calm down." I warned.

"Fuck you too, bro."

"Man, chill out. Look, it's late. How about we leave?"

"Hell no. I'm drinking. Fuck you guys." He placed the rim of his warm Krystal Ale to his lips and finished the thought on his mind. "You run away, I don't."

"What does that mean?" I asked.

"I didn't slur my speech, motherfucker."

"Yeah, for once."

"Whatever. You wanna run away, go. I'm here though." He flicked his hand at Jazz for her to bring him another shot and beer.

"Henry, stop this. Let's go," Alice said.

"Oh, like you even care."

"You know what, I'm gonna go." I stood, ready to leave, but then he continued.

"Good, go." The better part of me told me to get out of there, but I hardly listen to that part of me.

"You know, you're starting to act like those fuckin' assholes friends of yours."

"At least I have friends."

"Yeah, until your money's gone or you lose that title. Then let's see where those *friends* will be."

"Fuck you, you don't know them. What gives you the right to talk shit? Why, because they're rich and didn't struggle like you? Those are my friends, don't disrespect them."

My flippant attitude annoyed him. "Or what?"

"I'll show you why I'm the Light Heavyweight Champion of the World." I knew I couldn't take him in a fight, but I wasn't going to back down either. I may not throw gloves like Henry, but my mental game's on point. I could hurt Henry better than anyone.

"What? You gonna beat me into submission? Knock me out? Well, I tell ya, you better fuckin' kill me, because I play for keeps, remember. I don't play knock out. I put you down for good, motherfucker, but you wouldn't know anything about that, would ya?"

"Fuck you. You'll nnee-ver be what I am or have the money and friends I do."

"Those aren't your friends, Henry. Those guys are leeches, parasites, and when they suck you dry, you'll be out on your own with nothing but your fucking belt."

"Yeah, but I'll still be the guy who held the belt and you'll sstt-ill be a fisherman."

"Henry, come on, stop." Alice intervened, but Henry shooed her off.

"Oh, so you know me?" He eyed his wife. "You don't. Shit, none of you know me."

"I don't know you?" I was offended. "We were friends once, but that was a long time ago. Different lifetime, motherfucker."

"Yeah, long ago."

"Ya need to settle down." The bouncer interrupted.

"Or what?" Henry held a confidence few men could understand. I couldn't imagine how it must be to know that you are the best fighter in the world. Henry didn't bother to look back at the man who hulked over him.

"Henry, stop it," Alice demanded.

"Or what? I'm the champ, but that's not good enough for some people. I'm the champ. I'm the motherfuckin' champ. Doesn't that matter to anyone?"

"What's your problem?" I asked.

"I ain't got a ffuu-ckin' problem. You do. I thought you were dead, man. No word in like fifteen…sixteen years."

"I ain't gotta explain myself to you."

"Oh, big bad Marine, ran from the world when things –"

"Henry, stop it, now!" Alice stomped her foot, but it did little to command his obedience.

"Or what? You'll go cry to Mabel or Nathan? Don't think I don't see shit." Mabel perked at the sound of her name. "Oh, look, Mabel's with us now that her name is mentioned."

"Shut up, Henry," I said.

"What, bro? Did that upset you? You think Mabel's into you?" Henry mocked in a patronizing tone. Everyone at the table shifted uncomfortably. "Mabel's into everyone. Ain't that right, Mabel?"

She didn't defend herself.

"Mabel likes anything with two legs that talks. Especially two at the same time." He aimed his words to hurt me but stared at Alice while speaking. Neither woman said a word. "She didn't tell you that story yet? Yeah, the first week we knew Mabel she was crawling into our bed."

Mabel brought her beer up to her lips and took a long drink with an unapologetic gaze. She had nothing to be ashamed of or sorry for, but it hurt, nonetheless.

You better say something, or I'll push you until you kill yourself. Say something. Say something. SAY SOMETHING!

I knew Henry was drunk and said things he wouldn't say sober, but I was mad, and now I wanted to be even.

"Well, apparently she's so good your wife still wants some." I jabbed back. Henry didn't laugh. His smile melted with distain. "I see things, too, bro."

Henry stood first, but only by a second. Our chairs launched out like two Old West gamblers ready to draw down on one another.

"Screw you," he shouted, thrusting a finger in my face, getting the attention of others at the bar. The bouncer stepped away, heading back the way he came, for what I was sure was additional support. He'd be a fool to think he could handle a man like Henry on his own. "You left me alone. By myself. I had no body. I had nobody to watch my back. You were family and you bailed and didn't even tell me you were still alive."

"Watching your back? I'm the one who went to war. You went to the fuckin' Olympics. No one was trying to kill you there."

"Screw you, Nicky."

"Thanks, but I'll pass. One screw over from you is enough." A weight lifted and I settled back into my chair. He stayed standing, breathing steadily, staring at me.

"What's that mean?" His tone went somber.

"Claire." At the mention of her name, a deep secret he had kept bubbled to the surface. He sank, returning to eye level with the rest of us.

"Y-oouu kn-ooww ab-oouutt th-aatt?" The shock delighted me, and I took pleasure in his discomfort. The moment lingered there while I slowly sipped my beer, and sitting down my mug, I wiped my mouth and glared.

"I would've taken a bullet for you. How could you?"

"It was –"

"Don't say it was one time. Don't you fuckin' dare," I shouted. Alice and Mabel leaned in, eyes wide, darting between the two of us.

"So what? You wanna hit me for it? Go ahead," Henry said.

"You dumb bastard." I couldn't control my snickering. "I already got you back and you never even knew it."

"Oh yeah, how?"

"How many times did you go to that gym on base and how many times did that manager show up? He only came once, right? He didn't know you from Adam."

"You arranged that meeting?" Now he was catching on. Every moment of his life since that day was being played in his head and I stood there smiling. An odd feeling of satisfaction came over me like when I sent Claire the photo of me living in paradise.

"What did you say back in Queensbury? Your biggest regret in life is that you didn't go to combat like your grandfather and dad. Man, I had to hear that shit my entire life. The glory of combat, bullshit."

"What happened?" Mabel asked.

"The NCO's got warning orders, but guess who wasn't there?" No one spoke and all eyes were on me, so I continued, "I was frantic. Finally going to war. My dad had died not too long before that and I was itching to go. I couldn't wait to tell Haymaker that we were finally getting our chance, but I couldn't find him. So, I did the next best thing, I called my girlfriend."

"What did she have to say?"

"Couldn't get ahold of her at first, but when I did, boy did she open the fuck up. I guess at the news of us going to war and possibly dying in Iraq, her conscious got the better of her. She needed to get some stuff off her chest."

"She confessed about Henry and her?" Mabel was getting the picture.

"Oh yeah," I said. Henry's drunken stare lingered on me. I leaned in so I could be sure Henry could see my face. "She told me about her affair."

His dull, unenthusiastic eyes infuriated me. I wanted to reach over the table and punch him. My voice rose as I continued, "We were best friends! Since childhood. I wanted to kill you."

"Why didn't you?" Henry asked.

"Because I loved you. I loved you and you betrayed me." I shouted then regressed, hoping to lose the interest of the onlookers. "You were my brother. I couldn't kill you, but I didn't want to be around you either. Instead, I took away the one thing you wanted most in life; the chance to prove yourself in combat. So as ordered, I kept the deployment news a secret and made some calls. I knew you wouldn't pass up a chance to fight for a living."

Henry's hand tightened around his bottle.

"Jokes on me though, I didn't think you'd go on to be one of the best fighters in the world. Even if you are the champ, and claim the title Marine, you're no combat vet. You weren't there when the bullets flew, and our friends died. You weren't there to get a kill and you've been living with that defeat ever since. You knock out people. I've put dozens in the fuckin' grave."

I sucked in a deep breath through my nose and my lips pulled back over my teeth. I won.

"How could you?" Henry exhaled the words with a softness I didn't know his voice was capable of.

"I was avoiding this because I moved on, bro. But since you're hellbent on bringing up the past, fuck it. Get your pencil out, Mabel. Here's one for your book on this fearless fighter. When my father was dying, I thought the two people I could turn to were you and Claire. Imagine what I felt when I found out the reason Claire left my side at his fuckin' deathbed." Alice and Mabel's mouths hung open and both refused to blink. Henry sat back and snorted like a tough guy unamused by my tale.

"Did you know his father was dying?" Alice asked. Henry shrugged his shoulders, still unfazed.

"Doesn't matter."

"He knew and she called him up to get away from the problems of *Nicanor's life*," I said, blocking out Mabel and Alice from my attention, focusing only on Henry. "She called you and instead of saying, what the fuck or no, Nicky's my best friend, you said come on over. She called you and you two fucked while my dad was dying. A guy that was like your own father. I called her, and I called you and neither answered. I needed you."

I held up my drink and tipped it in his direction. "Fuck you, Champ."

"Fuck this." Henry pushed away from the table and stood. "I'm out."

"Who's running now?" I shouted. "Good, go. Get the fuck off my island. I forgot my golden rule. I don't drink with men who haven't been in combat. Go back to those other pussies at your mansion. Oh, my bad. Their mansion, right? Or at least they'll take it when you go broke."

"You aren't driving." Alice snatched the keys.

"Don't fuckin' tell me what I can and can't do."

"Calm down, Henry. I'm driving you. Mabel, can you help me."

"Fuck y'all." He stuttered and stumbled.

"I'm going home," I said, offering Mabel to come with me. She declined.

"Like I give a shit what you do," Henry said to me as if I had spoken to him. "We ain't friends, motherfucker. We're acquaintances at best."

"I don't even give a fuck if we're that."

"Ya two need to calm down," a larger bounce, much bigger than the first, said while approaching our table.

"Sorry," Alice said.

"Sorry?" Henry faced the bouncer. "Fuck you. I ain't calming shit."

"Then I'll throw ya out." The bouncer loomed over Henry, but Henry only laughed at his size.

"Bbii-itch, I'd like to see you t-rryy. You know who I am? I'm the motherfuckin' Haymaker." The name didn't register with the bouncers.

"Henry, let's go." Alice demanded.

"I ain't running from no motherfucker. Fuck you." He pointed at the bouncer. "And fuck you, too"

He pointed at me. My fist clenched, but I refrained from throwing it.

"Henry, that's enough." Mabel protested.

"Oh, what Mabel? You no longer on my side? What, you ssllee-ep with me and my wife and then ventured into his bed and now you're with him?" My face remained stern, but my heart went hollow. A touch of sympathy in Mabel's eyes was for me, and I couldn't help thinking that she had it bad tonight. Then she blinked with her normal callus expression. His words cut like a thorn in my side as he said, "Nicanor, you ain't shit."

"And you're the champ, but what do you have? Nothing."

"I'm fuckin' rich. Millions, about to be billions, motherfucker. I got three large houses, cars, and the fuckin' world."

"All that glitter, but no real gold. No peace on this earth. You can't buy the freedom you want. You can't change the past. You got no stroke, motherfucker."

"At least I don't live in a fuckin' shack, forced to fish for a living, and running from some ppuu-nk ass island gangsters. I ain't got no stroke? Where's your balls, motherfucker?"

"I fish for a living because I'm free out there. I ain't got some rich guys with their hands up my ass like a fuckin' puppet."

"You had a great job, a girl, and you threw it all away because daddy died, and she hurt you."

A thought dawned on me and I sat back, feeling sublime at my own revelation. The hate and rage I held fled with this single reflection. I pitied Henry.

"You dumb bastard. You don't get it. I didn't leave because of her. I had a great job lined up when I got back, and I could have had a house and a car and married that bitch, but I didn't want that. I don't want the mansions and the cars and all that crap. I don't care about that stuff. That's why I left, Henry. When our friends died in Iraq, I realized something you never will. Life is so little and there's more to it than the lies sold in magazines and on TV."

"Had to go find the meaning of life? Bullshit. You ccaa-n't hack rree-al life. You can't hack it."

"You still don't get it, Henry. You simply don't get it."

"Then explain it to me, Ol' Great One. Fuckin' fisherman. You think you're so special, you're so woke, right? You ain't special."

"You're right. I'm not special and I don't wanna be. You spend so much of your life worrying about what everyone else thinks."

"Bullshit. You do. You care just like everyone else cares. Don't fuckin' lie."

"I'm not lying, Henry. I don't care what people think about me because I can't change that, and I have no control over it, so why worry about it. I'm slave to no master except nature. I don't hate you, Henry. I pity you."

"So, that's the ssee-crets of life you found out? That you can't control it. Wow, fuckin' impressive, buddy. Maybe you *should* worry about it. Maybe you sh-oouu-ld've wwoorr-ied about it with Claire. Then she wouldn't have went after other men." That dig hurt, but I dug back.

"Hmm, how about instead of worrying about me, you worry about that fuckin' slur in your speech you got goin' on. Are you trying to drink yourself to death? Go see a doctor before you go full-on stumble bum."

"Guys, calm down," Mabel said, but we weren't listening.

"I may have some lloo-ose wiring from big shots, but everyone knows who I am. Everyone likes me and wwaa-nts to be me."

"Keep telling yourself that, champ. You call those guys your friends, those smug ass motherfuckers? You're a *cash cow* for'em, remember?" I repeated the words Henry uttered earlier.

"Let's go." Alice pulled at his arm, but Henry jerked away from her.

"You're right. I ain't shit, but I am the champ. I'm the Champion of the World. I'm the Light Heavyweight Champion of the World." The large bouncer grabbed Henry by the shoulder. "Did you hear me or are you deaf, motherfucker? I'm the Light Heavyweight Champion of the World. Get your fucking hands off me."

The anger and adrenaline kept Henry from stuttering or slurring. He shoved the bouncer and I grabbed at him only to get pushed too. I banged into a door, forcing it open and me out into the parking lot. Several people followed, but Henry strolled past me without so much as a glance. Mabel helped me to my feet; my pride hurt more than my body. Alice assisted the drunken Henry to his car, putting him in the passenger seat.

"You OK?" Mabel asked.

"Sure," I said, brushing off my arms and legs.

"He's just drunk, you know. I doubt he'll remember this tomorrow."

"I know. You good to drive?"

"Sure," she said, holding up the keys she had taken from Alice. Embarrassed and hurt, and although I didn't welcome the affection, I allowed her to kiss me on the cheek. She hesitated, questioning me, then climbed into the car and pulled away. Their departure pleased me until a gravel voice shouted my name.

Chapter Thirty-Two

A sliver of light slit the night veil and the sea hollered a breeze from some dark abyss, pulling my old bones back to it. In the house upon the shore, I slept and wrote, but my true home floated upon the waves. I took a single step in the direction of the dock when the calling of my name stopped me. Three men cut across the White Whale's parking lot with a march of trouble.

"Look at dis bitch," Eric, the dreadlock man who I fought on the pier, amused himself at my aloneness. I didn't recognize the other two goons, and this caused me to wonder how many men Jacob had on his payroll.

"Listen guys, I'm tired and not in the mood to kick the shit out of y'all. Go away before something bad happens." This wasn't the movies and I wasn't about to Bruce Lee these men. I knew an ass-whipping was in my future, but it was in their future, too.

Their shadows stretched along the cold concrete, encroaching on me. I reached for my blade but once again felt only by bare skin above my waistline. For over a decade I had grown accustomed to my knife, but now, for the second time in one evening, I found myself without.

A gunfighter missing his weapon.

I shuffled, backing against a wall to cut down their avenues of approach while tucking my elbows in tight and raising my fists. If battle was what they wanted, then I was prepared to give them one hell of a fight. Eric stood directly in front of me while his cronies closed in on the flanks. To my left, one of his stupid friends cackled at my stance.

"Dis fool danks he knows how to fight," the cackling man said. I couldn't help grinning as I pivoted toward him, torqueing my hips to generate a massive surge of power. The force traveled up through my right side, into my shoulder, and into my arm. My fist connected with a solid thump to his nose. Some bone crunched and warm fluid saturated my fist and forearm. His head snapped back, and his knees buckled before he grabbed his face.

I was allotted a moment of glory, for Eric and the other guy paused to see their friend fall. The look on their faces registered shock and disbelief. They couldn't believe I had dropped their friend with one shot, but this didn't last. With his friend in tow, Eric speared me against the wall, slamming his shoulder into my gut. I responded with a downward elbow between his shoulder blades, hoping to break his spinal cord.

His other friend, a bulky fella with a bad receding hairline, sucker punched me. I didn't see it and although I've been hit harder, it was a good shot. Heat and pain flared, and my cheek flashed red. Ignoring his friend, I sunk my underhooks in on Eric, trying to toss the stout, shorter man. He sank his weight into his hips and drove into my mid-section like a linebacker, banging my head against the bricks and pinning me to the wall.

Another jab caught me in the ear. I wanted to scream in pain, but I needed to move. With Eric bent over, I drove a knee into his sternum. He coughed but didn't let go. Three more unanswered punches came from Baldy and I slapped him across the face, a move straight out of Nate Diaz's playbook.

Stockton Motherfucker.

Before I could verbalize this out loud, another punch closed my lips. Eric pushed off, but staying in tight, threw a hook that bounced off my shoulder and hit me in the neck. I grunted and returned with my own hook to his jaw.

Eric struggled to balance, wobbling back with his hands up, giving me more room to work. I readied to strike and although they didn't realize it, both men switched to defense. I pivoted to Eric but shifted and planted my foot into Baldy's knee. He hitched, but this didn't deter my overhand right from sending him to the ground. Eric, alone, rushed in with his last chance. He caught me with a solid left hook, and I admit, it stunned me for a second. Old Broken Nose, the cackling guy I had dropped first, kicked me in the ribs.

I fell to one knee.

Eric arranged the meeting between my face and his kneecap which sprawled me out on the cold damp pavement. The kicks came in a fury, but I rolled to my stomach and pushed myself up despite the hits coming. I'm a fighter and I believe in winning, and if that means fighting dirty, then I fight dirty. I drove an uppercut from my kneeling position into the nuts of Broken Nose. He yelped, then collapsed, holding himself as he went down. I struggled to get to my feet.

I saw red and went to work. Every problem, every bit of anger I had, be it with Jacob, Henry, Claire, the trio, or even Mabel, I mustered into each punch I threw.

God, how I love this shit.

There came an impact that stopped me. A white fire burned a hollow flame in my stomach. The warmth of my own blood stained the front of my pants and I felt empty as if I couldn't catch my breath. My arms stretched back, ripping at my shoulders as an unseen person forced me to stand.

"Jacob sends his regards." Eric held up a blade, glimmering in the light with my blood. "And his farewells."

His pungent breath rolled over his bloodstained teeth, saturated with hints of bad rum and iron. He drove his blade back into my stomach. I couldn't escape the searing pain or the vacuum-like sensation that sucked the breath from my lungs. I fought to draw in air as the knife slid from my belly.

Another terrible pain exploded in me, but different from the first two stabbings. This time, a vibration screamed through my side with blinding agony. The knife deflected off a rib, chipping at the bone that prevented it from diving deeper into my vital organs. A thick taste of copper coated the back of my mouth and my strength evaporated. I didn't need any help to the ground, but the goons threw me down anyway.

I imagined I heard my name, calling out from faraway, every-so-faintly, but it faded to the sweet embrace of death.

Chapter Thirty-Three

I'm a hard man to kill. Death, no matter how much I craved it, was always fleeing from my grasp. I don't know how long I laid there, or who rescued me, but I did open my eyes again. A room, awash in white and painfully gleaming, burned my retinas. I searched the bedside table for my sunglasses, but no luck. In fact, it wasn't my bed at all, nor my room. Consciousness returned to me in waves.

My vision blurred with a cloudy haze as a figure stepped into view. I tensed, expecting one of Jacob's men, but instead, my old friend stood there. Perhaps the only friend I ever really had. His eyes shined the reassurance that I was alive.

"Why is your arm bandaged?" I asked, throat tight and pleading for a drink of water to rid myself of the sandpaper in the back of my mouth.

"What happened to your stomach?"

"I got stabbed," I said matter-of-factly.

"Me too," he replied. I tried to sit up, but an excruciating tightness torqued my intestines.

"Who stabbed you?" I asked between moments of pain that robbed me from my ability to breath. I tugged at the surgical bandages wrapping around my mid-section, expecting to find barbed wire instead of cloth. I wanted to release the tourniquet they had on me, to alleviate the pressure on my ribs, but Kojo stopped me.

"Same guys who stabbed ya." A puzzled looked must have crossed my face because before I could ask, he explained. "Found ya near the bar. This damn ol' leg don't let me run as fast as I'd like, but I got there before they could kill ya. Took one in the arm before they fled."

"Sonsofbitches. Help me up so I can go get them."

"No need, bro'da. I took care of dem. At least da one with da dreadlocks."

"Dead?"

"I don't know, but I took his nose off," Kojo flicked his wrist as if he had a knife in it. "I sure he be wishin' he was."

Laughing hurt, breathing hurt, speaking hurt, but it felt good to see my friend. I truly had missed him. The grandeur of a life I never wanted and friends I didn't care for filled my head with noise and drowned out what was important to me. My eyes burned with tears, but I extinguished them before they fell.

Having been tempted and swayed by all that dwelled within the mansion, I damned myself and damned all near me.

You know he set you up. Henry had those guys waiting. That's why Jacob was at the party. I bet you are a part of the deal. He wants the distillery and Jacob wants you dead for the disrespect you've given him. He planned on getting you hammered, then having you killed.

I shifted in my bed, hoping to relieve the stiffness in my body, but the only thing I did was bring on more pain.

Pain. That's what it is. Pain, and now you need to bring it to them. Bring that whole fuckin' house down on them. Crash their party and show them what you do best. Can you see it? Can you see them standing around in that fuckin' study, sipping drinks and laughing at how great it was that they got one over on you? Bring on the hurt. Kill them all. Wreak havoc and kill'em all.

"Where the hell am I?" I asked looking at the pure white of everything.

"Queensbury. They took you to a local doctor who had you rushed here for surgery," he said. I didn't know I had surgery, but looking at my wrappings, I could have been mistaken for a mummy.

"Thanks for coming, but you don't have to stay."

"I ain't goin' nowhere."

"I'll be fine, Kojo."

"I ain't goin' nowhere," he repeated. "Some guys tried to kill ya and I swore when ya drug me out of dat war, dat I'd watch ya back forever."

"You drug me out that alley first, remember?"

"Sure, but ya carried me out. We bro'das. I stay." I'm glad he said this. I couldn't keep my eyes open, but my mind still wandered. I thought of Jacob Coke and his men and how after I healed, I'd get them all. I'd make them all pay for what they did, and I'd bring their entire empire down to the ground. I'd stock up on ammo and go all Rambo or Bruce Willis on those motherfuckers. My strength depleted, and I didn't drift, but plunged into a realm of nightmares and revenge.

Chapter Thirty-Four

After three days of tearing stitches and reopening wounds, my fever broke, and I was released. Once during my delirium, I envisioned Mabel and Henry outside my room. Two people I didn't care to see and thankfully, in my vision, Kojo kept them at bay.

He set you up. Kill him.

At home, I locked my doors, latched the shutters, and blinked the world away from my very existence. In less than a month, my world had collapsed in on itself. I lost my job, pissed off my gangster boss, and endangered the only real friend I had. All this while subjecting myself to a group of people I'd never be caught dead with.

I blamed everything and everybody. I blamed Henry for sleeping with my high school sweetheart, which led us to this point. I blamed Mabel for bringing Henry and his friends to my boat that first day.

Amazing how Mabel and Henry both left a moment before those guys jumped you.

All of them would pay. I took on the enemy in the streets of Fallujah, and I'd take them all on as well. I'd show all of them what kind of Marine I was and still am. Jacob Coke and his men will feel what true terror is before I end their lives.

My sanity, fragmented with bothersome images, maddening thoughts, and depressive suggestions, battered me without restraint. A lone bottle of Island Rum sat on the top shelf, tempting me, but the wounds in my stomach prevented my partaking.

Large surfs broke outside the wall that entombed me. The sirens of the ocean beckoned me and after three days, I needed escape. Broken body be damned, I headed for the AJAX, salvation within walking distance. The perfect place to clear my head of Henry and my heart of Mabel.

As I reached the ocean's edge, all my worries shrank in size. It's the immenseness of it all that does this to a person. Mabel wasn't to blame for my misfortunes, no more than the wind is to blame for knocking over an old building. It's the foundation which is at fault, and my own foundation seemed unleveled.

I allowed the AJAX to wade with the evening tide while I sat on the stern, wishing away my troubles. As good as it had been at first to see Henry, I wanted him gone. There was no place on my island and no room in my life for him. I wish he'd leave and take his asshole friends with him.

Mabel kept coming to the forefront of my mind, and as hard as it was for me to say, I wanted her gone too. The deep seeded instinct boiled up from my core, urging me to leave. It said to shift the throttle of the AJAX forward and leave it all behind. Henry wasn't leaving this island and Mabel wasn't going as long as Henry was at the top of the MMA game. The trio of douchebags weren't leaving when the money was still flowing.

I baited a hook and hoped for relief from the nagging in my brain. *Should I stay? Should I go?* I didn't know. What I did know was fishing. Fishing had a way of carrying my mind away. As the line drifted astern, I eased back into my fighting chair, ready to reel in something for dinner. I was no academic scholar, so when mental dilemmas bore down on me, it helped to transform them into physical ones. Fishing does this for me.

Manifesting my problems into the catch held more therapeutic charm than any shrink could. My line hit, pulling taut and heading deep. The fish wasn't big, a small mackerel or tuna, nothing noteworthy. This wasn't the fight I was hoping for, but even a bad day of catching fish was better than any good day doing anything else.

I pulled back on my rod and at once regretted it. For a decade I had been a professional fisherman, taking charters out to sea, and the task of cranking a reel was as casual as breathing, but something was different now. My thoughts were adrift somewhere else, and the pain of three knife wounds in my stomach came surging back to my anxiety. The agony was so unexpected, I almost lost my grip on the reel.

Clenching my teeth, I bore down. My attention pivoted to the pull and swaying of my line. Lightning jolts rushed through my wounds; nerve endings forcefully trying to heal themselves and causing me great agony. Through the pain, I played tug of war with the fish that would give up before I would. At times I released the drag, not fearing the breaking of my line, but of my stitches.

Before I became a human pincushion, a fish this size would take me ten minutes to reel in. Time passed unknowingly, but it must have been well over an hour when the fish gave in. I flicked a switch on my fighting chair which triggered the underwater lights at the back of the boat to illuminate. A yellowish green hue flowered out before surrendering to the darkness.

I reeled, effortlessly, and soon a figure appeared in the yellow glow of the spotlight. I stood at the transom, rod bending at a hard angle, and brought up the fish. I love this moment in the sport, where the fish emerges from the invisible depths, its glimmering beauty shining with the light reflecting off its scales. The dark water morphing with the reds and greens, silvers and blues, before the fish dulls with oxygen and slime.

I wished I could release the fish while it's true glory still shined, allowing it to go back, but once on the hook, neither of us are the same and the dance must finish. I stood there for a moment, allowing the tuna to swim back and forth, until it bucked, and pulled to run again. I held true to my line, but something grabbed it and pulled hard. Its fin, both tail and dorsal, cut the surface as blood blanketed the yellow glow. To my horror, the fin held the same hue as the water – red.

Anger pulsed in my veins.

Oh, you forgot, didn't you? Pathetic.

Seawater slapped against the hull while the unrelenting shark violently slipped in and out of the surface. The strange sound of my own laughter erupted deep from within my throat. Distracted with the rest of the world, I forgot about this one nuisance. He was still here, waiting for me as if saying he'd never leave me. Perhaps the one constant in my life. The fish slid down the shark's gullet and I pulled hard on the line, hoping to set the hook and do battle. I did.

The hook, although small and not meant for such large game, did find something to hold to, but as the line held, a stitch did not. Pain burned in my side at the open wounds and a small trickle of blood stained my shirt. The square gray head of the bull shark rose from the water, grinning at me, mocking me. I gritted my teeth with adrenaline pumping intensely, but I wasn't ready for this battle. My stomach flared, and I crumbled into my fighting chair.

The line spinning off my reel popped at the touch of my blade. I couldn't fight this shark no matter how much I wanted to.

"Choke on it." I cursed. Placing a hand over my bleeding side, the wound burned hot and I feared infection. "I hope you choke on it, you fuckin' fish."

Chapter Thirty-Five

Oh, wicked world, how you trouble me still. Mounted stress eroded as I trolled through the harbor, freeing me from some mental exhaustion and for the first time, my lungs drew in a breath of ease. What I had hoped for had worked. The fishing, the dark ocean, and even the shark brought a warm familiarity. The world seemed fresh, renewed, less polluted, and I rejoiced in the clarity bestowed upon me.

I envisioned my life returning to normal, determined to steer clear of Henry and his friends, but as the AJAX neared shoreside, I realized this peace was a delusion of a struggling mind.

You think you can run away from them? You foolish bastard. You'd be better off taking this boat out and sinking it with you on board.

All my troubles, all my worries were waiting on the dock as I eased the AJAX into the slit. My shoulders torqued inward, rounding my back. Standing only pained my knees and I regretted not installing seats on the flying bridge. A weakness overtook my stomach.

You need a drink.

I need a drink.

You need food.

I need food.

You need pain relief.

I need something to relieve the pain, if only the pain in my mind.

Shoot yourself.

I pressed one of the wounds on my stomach, igniting every nerve in my body and drowning out all other ailments that plagued me. She stood in sandals, arms crossed over her chest, nervously twirling a strand of hair. Mabel shifted her weight, anxiously waiting for my arrival. Before I could kill the engine, she hopped aboard.

"Welcome aboard." The irritation being present in my voice. "It's impolite to board someone's ship without permission."

"Where have you been?" Mabel asked.

"What are you, my mother?"

"We found out you were out of the hospital."

"We?" I over-exaggerated my looking about as if I was truly expecting to find someone with her.

"Yeah, Henry, myself. We called to check on you and they said you had left already." I killed the engine and the deafness of the night tumbled in on us. I pushed past her to tie off the cleats to the dock.

"So, what do you want, Mabel?" With each passing second, her presence irritated me more.

"He's gonna kill himself." Her words were blunt. I was sure she hadn't said what I thought she said, but when I asked her to repeat herself, she did. There was a real sincerity in her voice, but this didn't stop me from sighing with annoyance. No remorse or sympathy came over me. I had allowed myself to be wrapped up in their worries for weeks and for the first time since, I felt like myself again, free from their bullshit.

"That's his problem. Don't bring it to me."

"Henry won't see anyone. He doesn't come out. He feels horrible about what happened. He tried to see you in the hospital, but your friend wouldn't let him in."

"That's right. My friend. The only fuckin' friend I ever had." She followed my every move, never more than three feet from me.

"Please, you're being unreasonable."

"Oh, you care about something now? Bullshit."

"He hates himself. Believes he's the one who got you stabbed." At this, I turned quickly, scaring her as I stuck my face a mere inch from hers so she could see the anger in my eyes.

"That makes two of us."

Fuck yeah. Tell her off.

"What's that mean?"

"Don't act like he ain't at fault. It was a set up from the start. Business deal I'm sure, a way to show Jacob Coke his good faith."

"That is not true. He wouldn't."

"Because you know him? Lady, I was his closest friend and he slept with my girl. He fuckin' stabbed me in the back." I paused to lift my shirt. "Then got me stabbed in the front."

She sighed and for the first time struggled to find words.

"I'm serious, I'm worried Henry will kill himself."

"I don't care."

"How can you say that? Something's not right with his head. He's been getting more headaches and his speech is getting worse. I don't know if it's a concussion or a mini-stroke, but something's not right with him."

"Like I said, I don't care. He's punch-drunk, the piece of shit." I finished tying off my ship and headed up the dock with her echoing my footsteps. I thought my frustration was obvious, but apparently, she couldn't take a hint.

"You're bleeding."

"I know," I said bluntly.

"What do you plan on doing?"

"I can't really do shit, right now, so I plan on going to bed, then getting up tomorrow and going fishing again. You know, rehab my injuries. Why?"

"Curious, is all. Those men tried to kill you and you're going to stick around?"

"Don't be curious." I snapped. "I ain't a chapter for your book."

The hurt was prevalent. "I didn't say you were."

"Good. Don't wanna be."

"But what if they come for you?"

"Then they come for me. What concern is it of yours?"

"I don't want to see you hurt"

"Umm, yeah, I'm sure."

"What are you gonna do, take on Jacob Coke? Guns blazing?"

"Maybe. I don't know, but if they come at me, I'm gonna put them down."

"You're willing to kill people?"

"Won't be my first time."

"Why don't you leave the island?" She asked as we left the docks and rounded the White Whale. I had half a mind to go into that bar and see if I could find any of Jacob's associates, but I wasn't at a hundred percent yet. Mabel had my rage firing but now wasn't the time. We came around the side where a red stain painted the sidewalk.

"Why would I leave the island?" I diverted my attention to the direction of my house.

"Those guys meant to kill you. They want you gone."

"Yeah, well a lot of people have tried to kill me. Don't mean shit."

"This is stupid," she said, hitching her step to keep pace.

"This isn't your life. It's mine. It's my dream. This is what I wanted and I ain't letting nobody take it from me."

"What does it matter? If you stay you could get killed."

"You think we're getting out of this life alive? Death comes to everyone, but not everyone gets to live their dreams. My entire life I wanted to own a boat, to fish and write for a living and that's what I'm doing. And I'll be damned if I let someone push me out."

"You act like this is the only place for you to have that dream. There's other islands. Go to another."

"And what, cut bait and run? Fuck that." I unlocked my door and stepped inside to a dark house. The hair on my neck stood on end. The profound nothingness allowed paranoia to seep through the cobwebs of my situational awareness. Mabel followed onto my porch, but I blocked the entrance, filling the gap of the door. "I stand and fight. I'm not one to be hauled off and executed without putting up a resistance."

The words cut her deep and a part of me wished I could have taken them back. It was wrong of me, but all is fair in war. Having her against the ropes, I dug in deeper. "As for *your* friend, if he gets better or not, doesn't really matter to me."

I closed the door on her, not letting her speak another word. Leaning against the cool wooden frame of my home, an elation washed over me, riddling my arms with goosebumps. Her power weakened me on many nights, but tonight, I prevailed. Her footsteps strained the wooden planks of my steps and part of me wanted to fling open the door. I wanted to chase after her, to pull her into my house and stay in bed with her for days on end.

Fuck that, let that twat go. She doesn't care about you, only about her story. She'd watch Henry blow his brains out and not think twice about it until she typed it out on her computer. I doubt she'd shed a tear. She only needs you for a story arc.

That nagging voice in my head was right. She only brought trouble.

Chapter Thirty-Six

I woke to the next day with a song in my heart and a spring in my step. I felt strong. With my wounds still throbbing and rum out of the question, I dropped a few pills to help dull the pain. I hate medicine, but every drink I took felt like fire eating through my insides. I planned on getting some fishing in, but the AJAX was low on supplies for the kind of fishing I had in mind.

I went to the local markets, got what I needed, and as I circled around the White Whale, I found Jazz sitting on the back steps.

"Hello, bruiser," she said, catching me off-guard. With my hands full, I was a split second away from dumping the supplies and going for my knife.

"Damn, Jazz. Scared the shit out of me." My heart knocked against my ribcage. "How you doin'?"

"I be fine, how ya be?"

"Been better. Feeling decent."

"Ya face paints a different picture." She puffed on a cigarette. It was true. My fresh bruises showed a hint of yellowing and the soreness in my right eye hurt to even blink. I sat down my stuff, aching for a drag from her cigarette, but refrained myself. I had plenty of bad habits and could do without another.

"What are you doin' here so early?"

"Openin' up da place."

"King Louie finally go on that vacation he's always going on about?"

"Naw, he ain't feelin' good."

"What's wrong with him?"

"Got brea-ding issues."

"Huh?" I asked, not quite sure what she said.

"No air. Too fat. Did'ja hear?"

"That he's too fat? I can see that."

"No, did'ja hear about Christopher and Jacob Coke?" The mention of their names sent my blood boiling.

“No, they get arrested?” I said, not caring to hear about any member of the Coke family.

“Day dead.” Her words slapped me, and I wasn’t sure I heard her correctly. Asking her to repeat, she did. “Da whole damn island is talkin’ about it. Da army finally got dem. Shot Chris on his roof and Jacob in da pool.”

“What about Jacob’s brother, Finn?”

“Day shot him on da toilet.”

My heart sank, not out of sadness for lives lost, but out of disappointment. I owed them one. I owed them a beating that now I would never give. I felt robbed. With Christopher and Jacob out of the picture, they had no one to take over their world, and their gang would dissolve. My rage felt like a match that had burned out with no further purpose than to be flicked away.

In the Corps, my anger was pointed at my enemy, the insurgency, and since most of their faces were covered, it was easy to transplant that fury from one person to another. Here, I had no obscured adversaries, and now with this news, I had no enemies.

I took a breath and settled with the thought I couldn’t control the entire world. That all debts don’t get paid. I smiled at Jazz to mask my true disappointment.

“Crazy how the world goes.”

“Yeah, mon. One moment ya takin’ a shit, next moment, ya dead. Like fuckin’ Elvis,” Jazz said, shaking her head.

“Fuckin’ Elvis.” I picked up my stuff. There was something different about her. Something seemed off that I couldn’t put my finger on. “You good, Jazz?”

“I’m leaving, you ol’ bastard.”

“Leaving? Where to?”

“Da States. Going to da States.”

“No shit?”

“Yeah. Told ya I was.”

“Shit. Damn.” I didn’t know what to really say. “You have a good one, Jazz.”

“Ya too. And keep up da right.” She held up her hands like a boxer, furthering my laughter. I carried on my way, listening gleefully to the water caressing the dock. A strange sensation took over. I felt at ease. For the first time in a real long time, I felt like no one was waiting to get me. My head was in the clouds until I saw *him* standing at the AJAX’s slit.

Chapter Thirty-Seven

"Hey," Henry said with a slight wave. He looked like shit, as if he hadn't slept in a few days. His hair was unkempt, he lacked a shave, and his clothes were wrecked with wrinkles and stale odors. A film of plaque coated his teeth and his skin held a tint of yellow, a sure sign of jaundice. I eyed him for a moment, then boarded my ship and sat my gear down.

"What do you want?"

"To talk, man." It was a plead, not a statement.

"Yeah? What do we have to talk about?"

"I ccaa-me to see you, you know, in the hhooss-pital." He stuffed his hands in his pockets and eyed the deck while rocking from heel to toe, heel to toe.

"That's nice. Thanks," I said, showing no interest in his words. He looked for acceptance with his apology, but I had none to give. Instead, I was listening thoroughly and waited for him to slip. One word in the wrong direction and it wouldn't matter if he was the Champion of the World, I'd smash his face in.

My breathing shortened, narrowing my vision, and the pressure building behind my teeth unnerved me. This form of rage scared me, for I know what I can do when I get to this point. Filling my lungs with long, controlled breaths, I distracted my anger with my bait box.

The greenish, gray water of the harbor splashed against the dock's pillars, slapping the hull of the AJAX. Henry stumbled while standing still, clinging to a tall lamp post to keep from falling. No sea legs. I don't know if it was the wake of the boats moving out of the harbor, or if Henry was as bad as Mabel had said. I didn't care. I didn't want to see him, because if we did throw hands, I wouldn't stop at putting him down or getting a tap out. He or I would have to die.

The wind kissed the rolling water. I could imagine hearing the marlin leaping in the great distance. Somewhere, among the massive blue, a shark swam, waiting for the sounds of my engines, ready to harass me. Sitting here and talking gnawed at the skin on my neck.

“What’s in the white buckets?” Henry pointed at the two five-gallon buckets I stowed away.

“Chum.”

“Chum?”

“Yep.” I busied myself, hoping he could take the hint.

“You know, I didn’t hhaa-ve anything to do with–”

“Don’t,” I interrupted, slamming the lid of my bait cooler. “I don’t care.”

I tossed the empty carton to the deck, hoping Henry would drift off with the echo of the empty box. I wanted him gone, for a different predator stalked me now, one of the aquatic variety, and this revelation excited me. The shark filled me with a purpose and pushed out the need for acceptance from Henry and his friends. The old me settled in my skin once again like wearing a favorite jacket that had been missing for years. I had no need to go back to Henry’s mansion or attend his parties. I had no need for Henry.

“Don’t you have a party to be getting to or something? Isn’t there some asshole that needs your help? I’m sorry, I mean your money.” This dig hurt him.

“Ccoo-me on, man. Don’t be that way.” Henry stepped his expensive shoe on my gunwale. I cut my eyes at his foot and he paused.

“You know on this island you can still kill a man for boarding your boat without permission.” The snarl on my face told him all he needed to know, but it was reaching for my blade that caused him to remove his shoe without scuffing the paint. Under the bandages wrapping around my torso, my three wounds pained and itched. I wanted to scratch at them, but the smallest amount of touching brought more pain than I cared to bare.

“Did you hear about Jacob Coke?” Henry asked, keeping the conversation friendly.

“I heard. I guess that spoils your business plans for the island.”

“Maybe it does, but it doesn’t matter. I don’t care about that right now.”

“Yeah, you do.” I latched down all things that needed securing.

“What’s your problem?” He had the audacity to ask.

“My problem?” I looked around in disbelief. Here he was, coming to my boat after I had been left for dead and asking me what my problem is. “My problem is none of your fuckin’ business. Remember what you said, we ain’t friends, remember?”

He shook his head as the memory came to the forefront of his brain. “I was drunk.”

“Don’t matter. You said it. You said it right before I got stabbed.”

“I didn’t have nothing to do with that.”

“I bet. Why are you here?”

“Mabel said she tried to see you, but you gave her the cold shoulder.”

"And? What's that matter to you? I didn't give her anything." I untied the ropes from my cleats and climbed the ladder to the flying bridge. "I ain't married to her, I ain't kin to her, and I ain't got no loyalty to her."

I started the engines.

"Where *do* your loyalties lie then?" He asked, thinking somehow this was a burn against me.

"Out there," I cast a finger to the horizon. I could see the whitecaps in the sea as the waves turned over and brought an unrest to the tranquility. "And with any man who can make it out there. Not some loafer wearing city folk who comes to my island and has poorer men do everything for them. Out there, when the tide turns and the sea decides to hate you, that's when you get tested and find out what kind of man you are."

"It's like being in the ring."

"But in the ring, there's a referee to save you. Out there, ain't nobody but yourself. When's the last time you had to rely on just yourself?" I shouted to him while pulling out of the slit. He said something, but the AJAX exited the harbor and its twin engines drowned him out. A man in a skiff waved at me and I returned it, but not once did I look back to see if Henry still remained there. I didn't care and as I broke out into the open ocean, Henry was far from my mind. The sea kissed me with its salty brine, welcoming me home once again.

Chapter Thirty-Eight

Deep sea fishing is hard to do, but much harder when you do it solo, and injured. I rigged up two rods and allowed the lines to sink overboard while tending to some maintenance. Hooks need sharpening, reels need respooling, and the boat needed a good scrubbing. I did all this with one eye on my work, and one eye on my rods. Nothing was biting, but the sea was calm, so I wasn't complaining.

The sea swayed the boat, rocking it like a baby's cradle, keeping in sync with the cool breeze. I swabbed the flying bridge, pausing several times to simply look around. The ocean stretched far, uninterrupted by anything of man. I breathed easy, content with life. With the sun overhead and the peace of the day, I longed to stretch out for a mid-day nap, but the ocean opened its brilliance to me, washing all thoughts and worries away.

A school of porpoises breached twenty meters off the bow, and I watched with child-like enthusiasm. An hour later, a fin as tall as a billboard broke the waves. Gliding through the current, one could've mistaken it as the sail of a skiff cutting through the tides. No red markings decorated the fin.

Although my mind filled with gleeful amusement, I didn't forget about that particular fish lurking in the deep, watching my every move.

The sun reached its peak above the white clouds, rushing in a northwestern path.

Focused on swabbing the flying bridge, my ears perked up to the clicking of my rotating reel. Careful not to pull a stitch, I shuffled down the ladder and to my gear. The line didn't zip out but rolled lethargically off the reel. Once I got a feel for the fish, I hit her, setting the hook. The fight wasn't much, a small grouper, to which I pulled in with little effort.

The day crawled on, but this wasn't a displeasure. On the contrary, this was what I needed, the rest and recovery granted by the sea gods. I sat there, breathing in the salty air and soaking in the healthy sun. The static of everyday life was absent and the need for company never entered my mind. I watched the sea, rising and falling at the horizon, and breathed.

I didn't slip into sleep but succumbed to a simple peace until an itch came over me. I baited the line with a bonito and tossed it in. I knew what I was aching for and I didn't care about the pain. Not a single black cloud disturbed the serenity of the scene, and the world stood with a pureness I had never fully recognized nor respected.

A small patch of blood dotted the bandages on my anterior. I couldn't believe how close to death I had come again, kissing it with tongue, and still surviving. Better men than I had succumbed far easier to death and for reasons unknown to me, I was still here.

The longing to pour myself a drink grew. My hand shook until I clamped my teeth down on it, keeping me from the rum, and instead, I had a cola. My taste buds exploded, not only from the sharp and refreshing carbonation, but at the lack of alcohol. The cool liquid in the lone glass bottle was as good as I remembered from my youth. I smacked my lips with delight and eased into my fighting chair with the warming memories of home to comfort me.

I wished my father could have seen all this. Sitting there, I understood how people could believe in a heaven. If there was such a place, it was among the tides.

Eyeing the grand ocean and sipping the cold beverage, I surrendered to it. Nothing sat upon the calm and steady horizon. Alone. All alone.

The rod in front of me bent and in a frightening hiss, zipped out. I fumbled with my drink, trying to get it in the cupholder while reaching for the rod. The screws holding the rod holder in place strained and couldn't continue at this rate. I grabbed the soft gripped handle and locked it in into the fighting chair's rod gimbal, the cup-like device between my legs. The line pulled fast and I fantasized what could be on the other end.

I loosened the drag, so the pull wouldn't break the line. It kept going: a hundred feet, two hundred feet, and as the line inched past another fifty feet, I tightened the drag and pulled. My back strained. The line set and the fish, or whatever monster was on the other end, cut to starboard. I followed it from port, and when the line slacked, I cracked the reel to gather as much as I could before she ran back out.

The elongated bill broke first and what rose from the briny blue stole my breath. The dorsal fin spread in an array of colors I could hardly imagine being in existence. She flexed her pectoral fins while catching air and taking the form of a bird to get rid of the hook in her mouth. A piece of the bonito hung from its bill, igniting my fear that she would toss it as soon as she hit the water. I had seen many grand fish in my time, caught several, but none were as majestic as this.

One for the mantel.

The sun glistened in a sprinkle of ocean water off the dark blue upper body of the sailfish. I sat in awe as my brain paused to take in what I was seeing. Luckily for me, my years of being a fisherman kicked in, and I spun the handle on impulse. The sailfish hit the water and circled back to port. If Kojo had been aboard, I would have instructed him to follow the fish, making the fight easier on me.

Alas, there was no first mate on this trip, and I had to fight alone. The fish soared two more times before sounding, arching my rod over the transom. I allowed her to go, not fighting, but not resting on it either. She sank down thirty fathoms, taking sixty yards of line off my reel, then stopped. The fish wasn't dead or dying, or tired, or playing. She was learning. She was a young fish and although I only had a few specks of gray in my beard, I felt like the Old Man and the Sea.

I cranked the handle and gritted my teeth. My arms pumped, and I pressed hard against the footboard. My feet slipped inside my shoes and the irritation of a blister grew. Flexing my neck, my eyes caught the beauty of the sky. I don't know why, but the words that followed tumbled out as if someone else spoke them. "Oh, what a beautiful day to catch a fish. There's no other beautiful day as beautiful as this."

The panoramic distraction helped to keep my mind off the mounting pain in my body.

I eased back with the rod to see if I could pull her up some. This alarmed the great fish and it took off, heading straight out from stern. Pumping the rod, I let her know I was here to stay, and after taking another sixty yards, she circled around. The tension in the line eased and I worked to bring it back on the reel. My stomach strained and ached, and as I checked to see if I was bleeding, the fish pulled. The rod shot out from me, but I kept a hard grasp to the cork handle.

The sailfish rocketed out of the water, flapping its split tail fin. She jumped and dove, jumped and dove, all while I pulled in more and more line.

Stupid young fish, stupid young fish indeed.

I leaned in, reeling hard, shifting from starboard to port, working her in close. The push and pull of the fight made me wonder if I was leading her or she was leading me. Normally, when I managed to haul a fish to the low platform at the stern, I'd gaff her, pulling her across the rollers. Gaffing took a big chance at damaging such a beautiful trophy, and I didn't want this.

My instincts were to tag and release, but I knew I'd never see one as great as this again. The way I saw it, I had to club her. With her dazed, I could get the wench around her and pull her aboard. That was if she too was tired and not playing coy.

I know a taxidermy man back home. He gonna have a heart attack when he sees what I brung him.

With a first mate aboard, this would be easy, but being alone proved something of a tricky nature. I had to harness the rod to the chair, while trying to club the fish. With the sailfish three feet from the boat, I made my move, keeping one hand on the line, and readying the club high above. This fish was beautiful as any woman or creature could be beautiful and it saddened me to strike such a being. I pulled the line near, hoisted the club, and jerked back.

The wind shifted, stinging with coolness, and I knew this good weather wouldn't last. Heaved off-balanced by the dipping of the tide, I scrambled away from the opening in the transom as the square head of the old red fin emerged, slamming into the sailfish's side.

That Red Fin Devil

Chapter Thirty-Nine

The scarred fin deflected off the sailfish and sank beneath the surface, turning my calmful peace into raging terror. He nipped the sailfish but didn't take a bite out of her, a normal trait for bull sharks who enjoyed testing their prey before eating. Surely, with the force of his impact, he broke a few of her bones and damaged some internal organs.

I released the line without thinking and took the club in both hands. The sailfish darted off, avoiding a second attack from the bull shark, but when the gray beast appeared, I struck. I slammed the club into his head, and he stared up at me with those black, lifeless eyes, provoking my panic. His flat gray head held the width of a doormat and if his length was anything smaller than nine feet, I'd be surprised. I estimated him to be eleven or twelve, but he thrashed about, and I couldn't get a great guess on it. His side struck my roller and the force rocked my boat.

The reel hummed as the sailfish sped away. I wanted to hustle to try and bring the fish in, but I knew better. The shark would kill the beautiful creature before I could get her aboard. If Kojo had been there, we may have been able to do it, but not alone.

You dumb fool. You will get that creature killed as you have gotten others killed.

I batted at the shark until he disappeared below my boat. His fin reemerged, heading off astern and my prized catch leapt against the wave. She ran but my line kept her from reaching full speed. The shark gained on her. My shoulders arched forward with the weight of depression. At the thought of failing yet another task I set forth for myself, my stomach flared.

I couldn't move or think. No one was around and so I let out a cry and slammed my fist against the deck.

"Why?" I screamed out loud; my voice echoing across the sea. I couldn't stand and even crunching over brought thoughts of death to my mind.

Just slip overboard and let that beast do the job. You're the one he really wants.

I rose painfully to my feet and glared out into the distance. The red fin cut back and forth, getting a bead on the sailfish. She leapt again, desperately wanting to survive. The shark closed in on her. The sailfish sprinted into the distance and I never saw her again. Her speed would be too great for the shark and this pleased me. She could have her freedom and I would deny the shark a victory.

I touched my blade to the taut line, and it snapped.

Chapter Forty

Replaying the shark's attempt on my glorious catch, I cursed myself while pacing down the wooden planks of the dock which moaned and echoed under my weight. If Kojo had been there, we could have caught it. The night beat with a chill and a lone lamp cast an eerie rustic glow across the docked ships.

No matter what I've been through, few things managed to creep me out, but the dock at night when all other boats were in, was one. The wind wailed louder and blew colder. Water crashed against the pillars, sounding like a creature emerging from the depths. Haunting memories of war plagued me, but standing here as a grown man, my mind thought of none of these things. Instead, it wondered back to my youth and conjured up one word – monsters.

A foolish jester of a thought, but nonetheless, my feet skittered across the dock. My pace and pulse slowed only when I stood over dry land.

"Where ya goin'?" Kojo called from the darkness, bringing my entire body to shudders and my fists to defense.

"Shit, Kojo. Scared the hell out of me."

"When I saw da AJAX not in port, I tank, where ya be? Ya in no shape to be headin' out dare."

"I'm fine."

"Naw, ya ain't. Dare be blood on ya bandage." I failed to button up my shirt which left my bandages exposed for all to see. I corrected this.

"They bleed from time to time. But I'm fine."

"Catch any dang?"

"Almost." I wanted to tell him about the beautiful sailfish with the blue webbing, but something in me kept it a secret. I didn't share it then or ever with anyone as if it was my own to keep, untainted by the ears of others.

"Ya shouldn't be goin' out dare in ya condition. Ya shoulda called me."

"I wasn't planning on going out, but something in me said to do it and by that time, you were gone with the other fishermen."

"Ya know, wha'ver answers ya seek, ain't out dare." He flicked his head at the dark void of the horizon.

"There's only one answer out there and it's the only answer to the only question I care about."

"What dat be?"

"Peace. Peace is out there."

"Ain't no peace out dare for no damn fool. It's a pause, a break from life. I tell ya dis, no storm of life blows over unless ya face it head on. O'derwise, ya ship sinks."

"There you are." Her voice interrupted our conversation. In a brisk hustle, Mabel came down the path from the White Whale. A sigh accompanied the rolling of my eyes.

"What now?"

"It's Henry."

"It's always Henry. Goddamnit, he ain't my problem." I turned to Kojo. "Good night, friend. I'll see you in the morning."

"Ya ain't goin out dare in da mornin'. Ya need rest."

"Fuck rest." I started to push on, but Mabel seized my arm, halting me.

"He's gonna kill himself." The panic in her voice was real, and I don't doubt she was serious, but no emotion resonated in me. I couldn't care less.

"He's blowing smoke," I said, and tried to step around her.

"No. He's serious. He's been pacing in his painting room all day."

"So? He could use the exercise."

"He's doing it with a gun in his hand, rubbing it against his temples. He keeps talking about life being better off without him. We can hear him saying about losing it all or he lost it all. I don't know. Something bad happened." She stared at me, questioning me with her eyes. I hated her.

"It's not my problem."

"She sounds serious, bro'da."

"I don't want this drama," I said. Mabel brought a world I believed I wanted, but I didn't. I wanted nothing to do with any of them. Their world, their lives were nothing but a fleeting memory in my timeline. A hard lesson I had to relearn.

"Please, you gotta help. He's not right."

"Been down that road already. I know, concussion-like symptoms. Why should I bother?"

"He blames himself for what happened to you."

"That's fine. Like I said, I blame him, too."

"He's not painting, he's not training. Please, I don't want to see anyone else die. If you do this, I'll get them to leave. I'll convince them to leave this island and never come back."

"And never come back?"

"And never come back," she repeated.

"How the fuck are you gonna do that?"

"I," she hesitated. "I have ways."

How could I refuse that offer? The mansion on the hill was in full swing, but no lights touched the top floor, and I knew a man stood there, holding a gun to his head while staring out on the sea.

"I'll drive," Kojo said, walking to the AJAX.

"You're coming?" I asked.

"Yeah, mon. Ya in no shape to be piloting da ship."

"I was just out there."

"And ya a damn fool for it. I drive." The three of us climbed aboard the AJAX and headed to the private dock at the bottom of Henry's cliffs. The tide was up, and the AJAX cleared the reef blocking the isolated beach. We'd have to be out before morning, or the tide would trap us until the following night. Tying off at the dock, Mabel and I vacated the ship.

"You comin'?" I asked Kojo. Standing on the flying bridge, he shook his head.

"Naw, mon. I be here. Dis ain't got nuttin' to do wid me."

"Ain't got nothing to do with me either, but I'm going."

"Dat man, he gonna die if ya don't."

"He'll probably die if I do."

"I don't want no more deaths on my island. Go," Kojo said. Mabel tugged on my arm. I wished she wouldn't touch me. We vaulted up the crooked staircase with wooden boards squeaking beneath our feet. I feared they would give, and we would fall, but Mabel rushed to the top without incident.

The air caught her scent and assaulted me with it. She smelt wonderful. Damn it.

Chapter Forty-One

We entered the backyard with the party in full swing. The scene was all the same; people danced around the lawn and swam in the great pool. A crowd gathered to catch a glimpse of the whiskey guzzling man surrounded in shadows on the top floor. They cheered as a square painting, one inch thick, spiraled through the void of the night. The projectile cut through the light of what stars were seen overhead like a glitch in the sky, blinking in and out of existence.

KA-COW. The report quaked my nerves, paralyzing my muscles. I scanned, looking for a threat despite knowing who the shooter was. None of the guests scattered in fear of the gunshot. Another cheer roared as the painting landed with a puff in the uncut grass.

Had the groundkeepers failed to show for work or had Henry fired them? I wondered. Either way, the lawn grew shaggy and finger-like twigs stretched from beneath the green leaves of the once uniformed bushes. The monster that was this house was slipping back into view, and under the bouncing musical lights, its hideousness shined through its façade. If things kept their course, the mansion would look more like the Addams Family home rather than the White House.

Maybe it should.

Mabel didn't pause to take note and I'm not sure she saw things as I did. Instead, she cut a path, shoving people aside as they beckoned for their idols attention through yet another painting soaring down. I followed close in the gap behind her, avoiding the closure of the crowd by mere inches. Not a single stitch of clothing adorned the people in the pool. Booze and drugs fueled the scene and depravity encased the masses. A potted plant laid toppled over at the top of the stairs and the soil and mulch blanketed the ivory stone steps. No one came to clean it, no one cared to avoid it, no one seemed to notice it.

The dimness within the interior caused me to look for burnt out light bulbs. Large shadows covered the walls, hiding the structure's faults, but a visible crack snaked up from the foundation, sliding behind a portrait next to the back doors, reaching for the ceiling. Below this portrait of a man I didn't recognize and in front of a growing audience, two naked women fondled one another on a parlor couch. Fingers roamed across flesh, exploring areas best left hidden from public view. The ivory white teeth of the dark-haired woman chewed lightly on the earlobe of the blonde. The blonde moaned to the silent delight of the onlookers.

Mabel pulled me along and my eyes shifted to the study where one night, not so long ago, the Edwardian room was garnished with dapper men and cultivated women. Standing in front of the couch, Scott Pound made eye contact with me, but his seductive drunken stare paid no mind as to who I was. His normal guarded stance, to which he used to hide the girth of his body, was gone. His shoulders were relaxed, and from the top two buttons undone on his shirt, a redness grew with the bright flare of desire. He looked away while sinking to his knees. I turned to follow Mabel as an unknown man maneuvered Scott's head into his lap.

No scene rattled Mabel or caused a reaction, and this included the one on the grand staircase. The stained wooden steps held yet another audience watching a man and woman partake in full-on intercourse. They hid nothing from the onlookers, ensuring all had a view, which aided in their arousal. Sweat dripped down breasts and across ripped stomachs. As we made our way past, the woman, bent over, reached out and grabbed me by the crotch. Her pointed tongue licked the fullness of her upper lip. She tried to pull me toward her, but I broke free of her grip, hoping Mabel had not seen.

Apparently, the mansion's grandeur had faded into the dark evening hours where class and dignity vanished, and debauchery and self-indulgence reigned.

"Come on," Mabel said from halfway up the stairs and I climbed to catch her, carefully avoiding the entangled couple or their gawking spectators. We hit the second floor and a voice stopped us.

"Mabel, come join." Nathan filled the threshold of his bedroom. In one hand, he held a glass of wine and in the other, a leather whip. Sweat glistened down his bare heaving chest while on the bed, Alice laid bent over, a pair of black heels accentuating her long legs and firm butt. Her wrists were shackled to a leather rope tied to the bedpost at the head of the bed. She looked at us and smiled. Bright red markings ran across the smooth flesh of her ass and upper thighs. Mabel ignored them as she made her way to the third floor. Nathan laughed. "Oh well, let's finish working on your lines, Alice."

Mabel's stride quickened until we arrived at the third floor. Unable to believe what I had already seen, I worried what else awaited me in this house of ill repute. She pushed open the near hidden door and ran up the enclosed staircase that stretched to a single door. A small crack opened to Henry's private studio. Mabel didn't ease it open, but shoved it, banging into Philip as a loud bang welcomed us.

She flinched and rooted her feet to the floor. The noise may not be familiar to her, but my ears were conditioned to the sound. I rushed past, stepping on Philip who sat by the doorframe.

"Welcome to the party, pal," Philip said with a hard, tired slur. A blue band wrapped around his bicep and a long dark mark tracked a damaged vein in the crook of his elbow. A bent spoon and a used hypodermic needle laid next to him.

"What the fuck are you doing?" I ignored Philip and questioned Henry, my voice echoing in the spacious room. The attic, a loft converted into Henry's painting studio, ran the length of the house. It was air-conditioned, and with the walls sealed in sheetrock, it no more looked like an attic than the first floor looked like a basement.

Standing at the ledge of his balcony, Henry swigged from a bottle held in the hand where a revolver hung listlessly from his trigger finger. The barrel brushed his hair and I froze. A splash of liquid dropped from his lips and as he turned with a heavy gaze in his eyes, he wiped it away with his forearm. Henry thumbed through an assortment of paintings, picked one, then heaved it out the window. Taking a drunken aim, he followed the painting as it disappeared. I charged at him and batted away the revolver before he could pull the trigger and hurt someone.

"Oh, hhee-llo." He swayed. A deterioration of his good looks showed even in the dimness of the room. He was gaunt, eyes sunken in, and his feet shuffled when he walked. His posture wasn't one of a man who carried himself as a king of the world, but one of disappointment. His shoulders sagged and his back arched. His appearance unnerved me.

"I said, what the fuck are you doing?"

"Target practice," he said, swaying. "I guess you hheeaa-rd my business deals on this island are ddee-ad."

"Yeah, we already talked about it at my dock, remember?"

"That's right. We did. I bet you're hhaa-ppy as a pig in shit that those motherfuckers are ddee-ad."

"The way I feel about Jacob and his friends has nothing to do with you. Give me the gun." I reached out to take it away, but he jerked it from me, keeping the revolver at a distance. Liquid splashed out of the bottle and coated the revolver's ivory handle. It was one of the two he had shown me the night of my stabbing. Its glory radiated in the moonlight and any lover of firearms would've been jealous to own it. "You could hurt somebody with that."

He swung around, waving the gun wildly.

"Like whom?" he replied. I gritted my teeth and took a step forward, not backing down. I didn't care if he was a UFC champion, I was ready to fight. I thrust my finger at his face and a flare of pain wrecked my stomach.

"You point that fuckin' thing at me again, and I'll help you along your journey to end yourself." The fire in me caused him hesitation. He turned away, mockingly saying something under his breath, while searching for which paintings he'd throw next. Several hung on the walls, large gashes torn through them.

"Henry," Mabel called.

"Leave me alone," he shouted, refusing to face us.

"Henry." I refrained from yelling and kept my voice calm. His head twitched to the side. I didn't expect to see him this way, but I feared Henry was far worse off than even Mabel understood. "What are you doin?"

"I'm having a drink." He sauntered to the railing and leaned the small of his back against it. A drunken smile proceeded the tilting of the bottle to his lips, and a stream of liquor seeped out the corner of his mouth, which he failed to notice. I feared he would slip over the stone railing to the cement below.

"What's with the gun?" I asked. He whipped it around, the barrel flashing in front of everyone, and brought it to his face for a better look. The intoxicated rhythm of his eyes failed to keep a consistent size.

"I like this gun."

"Put it down."

"Naw, I like it," he said. I stepped forward, halting as he leveled the gun at me. I snarled, refusing to bring my hands up in protest. The last person to level a gun at me got cut wide open. My teeth mashed together, my nostrils flared, and I was ready to attack like a crazed animal.

"Pointing that at me, you must be punch drunk!"

"I'm having a drink, in *my* vacation house, on *my* vacation and it's nnoo-ne of *your* business."

I paused for a moment to let my irritation subside before responding.

"Put the gun away and let's talk."

"You made it ccllee-ar thth-that there ain't nothing for us to talk about."

"You're right. I did. So, what is all this, some way of trying to get my attention?"

"This ain't got nothing to do with you."

"Then stop acting like a fuckin' idiot and put that shit down, Marine." We stood there for a heartbeat, then he lowered the pistol to take another drink.

"Marine." He chuckled. His lethargic eye locked on me. "Why'd you come here?"

"To see what kind of bullshit you're pulling."

"Fuck you. Don't fuckin' stand here and judge me."

"Or what? You'll throw a big fit? You're the Champion of the World and you're acting like this?"

"You ddoo-n't know shit, man. You don't kknn-ow shit."

"What do you have to complain about?" I asked. "You got money, you got women, you got friends, you got the championship, so what? What don't you have that's troubling you?"

"I ain't got shit, man. I ain't got sshh-it. It's all gone. All of it."

"What do you mean?"

"I mean, the fuckin' world has stopped."

"What?" I had no idea what he was talking about.

"Don't you watch the news? Oh wait, you don't watch anything because you're too ggoo-od for it."

"What the fuck are you talking about?"

"There's some crazy fuckin' vviirr-us that has shut down the world."

"What does that have to do with you being an asshole?"

"Because it crashed the economy."

"Really?"

"Not just America, but the world. No flights, no fights, no jobs, no nothing. It's a fuckin' ppaann-demic. The Great Depression all over again. All my ssttoo-cks took a fuckin' dive. I've lost everything. I'm bbrr-oke."

"It will come back." I tried to reassure him.

"Bull fuckin' shit it can. It's all ggoo-ne. My stocks are dead, and Philip started selling. I ain't shit. Everyone drained me of my cash and the stocks took the rest. What money I did have was tied up with that distillery and now that might not happen."

"It might."

"Bullshit. I don't have money. I don't have business partners. Hell, I got a wife who is fuckin' everyone in this house but me and is in love with Mabel over there." He cast a finger past me. Mabel corrected her posture to an unassuming stance, staring at us with that blank gaze, soaking in all she could. "Don't ssttaa-nd there and stare at us all innocent, you kknn-ow what I'm saying is true."

"We've all had our fun," Mabel said.

"No, it's true." From the doorway Alice entered, wrapping tight a red silk robe around her body. She glided across the wooden floor in the same high heels I saw her wearing in Nathan's room. I wanted to throw her down the stairs. She was a leech in my eyes, one of the many sucking Henry dry.

"Alice, you're not helping," Mabel said.

"No, this needs to be said. I do love you, Henry, but no one makes me feel the way you do." She placed a soft touch on Mabel's shoulder and Mabel recoiled.

"I'm not in love with you."

“Yes, you are.” She used a tone indicating she knew better, and I’m sure it persuaded most, but Mabel wasn’t having it.

“No. Love isn’t a part of my equation. It was just sex.”

“It was more than just sex. We had a connection.”

“True, but there was also a connection as your husband plowed me from behind.” Mabel said this to launch shrapnel at Alice, but I caught the crossfire.

“See, bro. I ain’t got nothing. I got no wife, I got no friends, I got no money.” Henry took a long drink.

“What do you mean you got no money?” Alice asked.

“Welcome to the show, babe. We’re broke. Stocks crashed. All our investments, all our money is gone.”

“That can’t be. The house, the cars, the parties?”

“All gone. We were living off credit until the distillery cashed in, but no more.”

“What the fuck?” She spun on her heels to look down at Philip. “This was your job to watch our money. Where is it?”

“Gone. Gone. Gone.” Philip brushed his hand through the air carelessly.

“You owe us, Philip. You and that fat bastard down there. You both owe us. It’s been Henry flipping the bill here and you need to cough up your share.” Philip mocked a cough and then presented her with an empty hand. She turned back to Henry. “Then we’ll sue.”

“With what? We can’t afford a lawyer and it’s a global crash. It’s no one’s fault. No one to sue.” Henry didn’t shout or call her names. Instead, he went back to drinking and sorting through his paintings, the gun still hanging from his fingertip. At my feet laid a beautiful colored portrait of a marlin leaping from the ocean. It curled in mid-air, jumping from a rising wave with a sky full of clouds behind it. The yellow, slightly green, and blue of the fish glowed, and I could almost feel the water it flicked away.

As mad as I was with him, I had to admit, Henry had real skills as an artist. I loved this painting and I couldn’t help feeling sorry for the painter.

“You were right,” he said to me.

“About what?”

“Relying on myself. Never have. You with the bully and getting me a coach. I rely on others to take care of my money, hell, to even spend it apparently and look where it’s gotten me.”

“You still got the title, don’t you?”

“Sure. I’m still the champ, but for how long. The wwoorr-ld is shutting down. There’s no flights or ships out. I don’t know if I can even ppaa-ss a physical to get a license.”

"Come on, man." I found my sympathetic tone. No matter what he did or how mad I was, there was still that kid I had known, that kid I had survived the hard streets with. Henry flung another portrait out like a frisbee, took aim, and pulled the trigger. Nothing happened. "Out of ammo."

"Not quite." He reached into his pocket and pulled out a few casings, slamming them on the desk where his bottle sat. All but two rolled off and chimed against the hardwood floor, and he loaded those two into the revolver. Staring at those bullets, I knew he would kill himself.

"Come on, let's get out of here. Let's get on the AJAX. You and me," I said to him. The acid in my gut bubbled, souring the taste in my mouth. I couldn't stomach witnessing another man's death.

"There's nnoott-hing out there for me either." Henry spoke soft and slow, avoiding me.

"You got the whole world out there. Get on the boat."

"Out there." He threw his thumb back over his shoulder. "Ain't nothing out there but the end of the world. And I got nnoott-hing in here. Shit, I don't even have my wwii-fe."

"Henry, stop this and think. We need to figure out how to get our money back. I mean, what am I going to do without our money?"

"What am I going to do without our money? I like that, Alice. Nice one." Henry's drunken eyes slid off her and landed on me. In their lackluster state, his green eyes studied me. "I'm sorry, Nicky."

The slur abandoned his voice and resembled that of the boy he once was.

"For what?"

"For wronging you the way I did. I don't have an excuse for it. Maybe karma's coming back at me. I'm sorry I did that to you."

"It is what it is," I said. Henry spun around, slinging out another picture and fired. The bullet struck the canvas, deforming the frame, causing it to lose its aerodynamics. It tumbled into space before striking the ground with a thud. His accuracy amazed me. In his drunkenness, he found it troubling to stand, yet could fire. He chugged the last of the bottle and dropped the glass to the floor. It didn't shatter but struck loud and hard, startling the rest of us whose attention was on Henry.

One bullet left.

"Remember going to the range in the Corps?" he asked.

"Sure."

"I was a great shot." A small smile appeared as his eyes glistened over with a memory.

"You still are, apparently."

"I miss those days. I fucked everything up."

“No, you didn’t.” He wasn’t listening. He tapped a finger hard against his forehead.

“I can’t straighten things out in my head no more. I’m sick.” He turned to stare at me, pleading, “I’m drowning, Nicky.”

“You just need to rest, man. Come on, give me the gun. Get on the boat. We’ll relax and give you time to think it all out. You’re the Champion of the World. You made it there and you made all that money. You did it. From nothing. I know. I was there when you had nothing. You can do it again.”

He shook his head, not hearing me.

“Get on the boat.” I extended my hand. He looked at it and sighed. “It’s down at your dock. Get on the boat.”

“I’m drowning, Nicky.”

“I know, Henry.” All my hate washed away, replaced with contempt. “Give me the gun. Come on. Let’s get out of here.”

He sighed again, the sorrow whaling up in his eyes.

“I can’t…I can’t breathe.” He tugged at the collar of his shirt.

“Let’s go see the ocean. The stars are better out there.”

“I can’t see the stars from here.”

“You can on the AJAX. Get on the boat. Remember the peace I told you the ocean gives you? Remember? Let’s go. You and me, bro.” I shook my hand in front of him, demanding the revolver.

“I’m drowning, Nicky.” He planted it in my palm. The revolver wasn’t as heavy as the weight that had been lifted from my shoulders. Air rushed in and a calmness swept through the room. Everyone could breathe.

“Come on, let’s go fishing. Let’s find that peace. Besides, there’s a shark out there—”

“I’m drowning, Nicky.”

I turned to head for the door and the bang that followed silenced the world.

Chapter Forty-Two

I blinked and was aboard the AJAX. Sleep did not welcome me and by the time the first rays of light glinted off the horizon, the party was over. Not in the literal sense, as the drunken festival that developed over the season would continue for several hours before the authorities got there, but the party that entangled the lives of old and new friends, of old and new enemies, had at last come to an end.

Dark clouds held firm overhead, obscuring the light of the stars and moon while also fighting back the approaching dawn. The ocean surged about us and the atmosphere suggested a storm was coming. I didn't know where we were going, and I'm sure Kojo didn't either.

The AJAX's props cut white trails across the swelling sea. My crimson-colored fingers clung on to the marlin painting as if it held some form of reality I needed to protect. Perhaps it did. I looked over my shoulder to find Mabel at the small table in the galley. Her shaking hands scribbled on a pad of paper as the small, dim bulb swung over her head. The light swayed with the motion of the boat, casting her from darkness to light, revealing specks of blood that clung to her face and hair.

My mind paused, stumbling to recall how we got here from Henry's attic. Something pestered my face and I scratched at it, bringing both relief and questions. The texture smeared under my nails and I couldn't distinguish the substance from blood or ocean mist. It was the sight of Mabel and my own blood-stained hands that brought forth my own nagging fear that none of this was a dream.

I'm drowning, Nicky.

Mabel looked up, sensing my stare, and I turned away to face the ocean again. There was no need for a conversation to break the eerie silence of the approaching storm.

The sun breaking over the horizon was like the light of a train coming down a long dark tunnel. It illuminated the tiny peaks and valleys of the rippling water, casting a glow over the edge of the world to see what damage the night had done. There had been none, and whatever tranquility was there, was fading. The air pushed past us, colder than I would have expected, and lightning flashed in the distance. A haunting, yet freeing feeling enveloped me as I stood on the gentle ocean, watching a raging storm approach with the early light of dawn.

The slapping of water against the hull disturbed my ears, but without it, one would go mad. These knocks were loud and hard. BANG, sway, BANG, sway. The boat dipped to the side and a wave slammed against the other. A spray of mist kicked up, but it was the bang which astonished me. The bang that was indeed too quick to protest.

No, not bang, but gunshot. The gunshot was too quick to protest.

Each jolted my shoulders, and I had expected to hear Alice's blood curdling scream. A scream no more than a fleeting imprint on my memory.

She screamed, oh god, how she screamed as his body collapsed.

My hand touched my sore lip and rubbed. Fresh blood coated the side of my index finger. I must have removed a layer of skin from my mouth after the attic. Another wave slapped the wooden hull like a body falling to the deck.

He fell, not dramatic like in the movies, but simply crumbled like all the bones in his body vanished. God, did you see the brain matter on the ceiling?

He had all the riches one could want, and yet one truth prevailed. Henry had what we all have – only a single lifetime to live. His lifespan was short to some, long to others, but ended with the world moving on without him. A life lived in under thirty-five years.

The twin. Why didn't you think about the twin revolver? Why didn't you think to check for the other gun? Why didn't you? Why? Why? This is your fault.

"I'm drowning, Nicky." A ghost crossed my lips.

Pushing all the negative thoughts from my mind, I listened to the sea. It is her love I come back to when my life is at its wits' end. I slithered into my normal habit of not moving, becoming still as a sniper on the hunt. If Kojo and Mabel hadn't known me, they would've believed me to be dead.

A gray and blue sky flashed with each bolt of lightning illuminating the sea. With this light came the flying fish, jumping in schools for their morning breakfast or escaping a larger predator. A gray blanket stretched overhead smothering out the ascending light. It would be dangerous to be out there when those clouds opened, but I had no plans of going ashore yet.

I picked up the painting and studied it. On the back was an inscription in black ink which read, *'To Nicky, with Love, My oldest friend and brother, Henry'*. As the splashing of the flying fish grew, and with my chest seizing under the weight of my emotions, an itch took over me. The painting in my hands flashed memories of the sailfish from the day before. I wanted it or at least, I wanted something like it.

I'm drowning, Nicky.

I pushed opened the cabin door, startling Mabel. We locked bloodshot eyes, but not a word was said. A picture sat next to the pad of paper she had been writing on. She had taken that photo on the first fishing trip we went on with Henry. Both Henry and I were smiling at a conversation I couldn't recall, but we were happy. I was happy.

The cold air blowing in the open hatch sent a shiver through Mabel and she rubbed her bare shoulders for warmth. It was these shoulders that Alice had touched in the attic. Alice ran to her for comfort, but Mabel shook her away.

I placed the oil painting on the counter. She took one look at it and the tears welled up again, but Mabel was no more my concern than Henry was. I stepped back out and flew to my rod and reel. Opening the panel of flooring that was the lid to my bait box, I ran a hook through a large bonito. I festered with the need to have one more crack at something so grand.

The wind tore across the deck of the AJAX with a moaning lurch like the wails Philip produced at the sound of Alice screaming. His heroine haze vanished, and he vomited at the grotesque scene. The iron-rich air which had quickly grew stale in the attic, plastered to the inside of my nostrils and twisted my gut.

The roar of the distant storm took me away from my nightmarish memory and I gritted my teeth. I needed a fight, I needed a victory, I needed the ocean. The world didn't drop off at the horizon, which meant another great fish swam somewhere beneath. Commercial fishing has destroyed the sea life, but the game was still out there, only harder to find. I spent the last ten years tagging and releasing smaller marlins and tiny prize fish, but this day wasn't about that. I was hunting, and today I sought that great fish that would challenge all my knowledge and strength.

The current of the ocean snagged my line and carried it out beyond the prop wash.

"Fishing already?" Mabel greeted the morning air with the wiping of her eyes. Her voice helped to drown out the one in my head.

I'm drowning, Nicky.

"Yeah, early bird and worm and all."

"God. Looks like a storm is coming. Do you think it will break with the morning?"

"Doubt it. Looks like a bad one."

"Should we head in?"

"Nope."

"Do you want some breakfast? I was thinking—" Her mind trailed off with her words. I casted an eye back at her and had a strong hunch she wanted to say something about Henry. I didn't want to hear it.

"I don't want any but ask Kojo."

"I could eat if ya fixin' some."

"Eggs and bacon sound good?"

"Ya. It's in da—"

"I know where it's at. I'll have some fixed up soon." I didn't know Mabel knew her way around a galley and I'm sure it was only a task to keep her mind busy and off the attic. She went back into the cabin, and I'm glad she did. Her pestering voice gnawed at me and I didn't need the disturbance. Kojo was watching me and that was enough.

"Where ya wanna go?" Kojo asked.

"Right here." The limitless ocean held all possibilities and one spot was as good as any. Searching for my line in the dim light of the dark morning, I eased off the drag so no sudden fish attack could break it. The tides grew angry and what was once a gentle slapping now tightened into a steady punch.

Frying bacon filled my nostrils, punishing my stomach for refusing the invitation. The cold air nipped at my hand and the shrapnel still in my body pained me, but I chalked this up to the drop in the barometric pressure. *Oh, this hand, this fucking hand,* I thought.

It had been many years since I lost my finger. Like all things that slip away with time, I don't recall what it's like to have all ten. My deformity didn't prevent me from the duties of a fisherman, but in my mind, the hand was troublesome.

I'm drowning, Nicky.

"Did you find the peace you sought, brother?" I didn't care if Mabel or Kojo were within earshot. The sprinkling of rain and the tussling waves surely masked my whispers. I don't know what propelled me to ask this. Speaking to the dead is about as useful as a white crayon, but comforting, nonetheless.

Standing in the attic, us four were the only one's privy to the death of the Light Heavyweight Champion of the World. Looking at my friend's lifeless body, I knew many would miss him, the fight world especially, but it would still go on. The world always goes on without us.

My line twitched along with the nerves in my spine. I looked into the darkness with a keen eye at my rod which remained erect, but something had teased it. We were too far out to assume it had bobbed across the bottom of the sea. No, something had hit it, which meant something was out there. I adjusted, ready for when the moment came. God and nature could stand by as I took control of my universe.

Waves rolled against the gray horizon, pitching back and forth, and any sane man would head for port. In fact, Kojo made that adjustment, but I cast a stern disproval in his direction, and he corrected. I didn't want to see the port or the island or anything of man. I wanted to be on the AJAX. *Weather and death be damned,* I thought.

"Should I bring it up or are you coming in?" Mabel asked Kojo.

"I'll be there in a second," Kojo said, correcting our course to my approval.

"You sure you don't want anything?" she asked me.

"Coffee, if you don't mind."

"You're in luck. I made some. I'll get you a cup."

"Thanks."

Kojo descended the ladder and stood next to me, eyeing the growing sea and churning storm.

"Could be a bad one," Kojo said.

"Yeah, but the bad part is still far off," I prayed. "I just want one and then we can head back."

I never looked at him, nor he at me. We didn't need to share a stare to read one another. Kojo, now my oldest living friend, questioned my request, but only in his mind. He didn't dare vocalize his objections, for he knew what fishing meant to a man at sea. Our hope or redemption resided only at the end of the world.

"Are ya alright?" He asked of both my physical and mental state. I assured him I was. Kojo patted me on the shoulder and headed into the cabin. A noise caught my ear, one I had not heard in some time, and I listened as his limp trailed behind him. Mabel exchanged positions with Kojo and handed me a ceramic cup. Steam rose over the brim as the temperature continued to drop. The hot cup felt great to the sore tissue of my mangled hand, and so I didn't complain as the heat nipped at my raw lips.

"Thank you," I said. She casted a smile, but I gave her no response. She slipped back into the cabin to sit down and enjoy a warm meal with Kojo. I would have loved a warm meal, but my stomach was of no priority to me. Although they were mere feet away, the vast ocean isolated me. This is what I liked and what I needed most. My moment of truth rode in on the back of a hard breeze and it was *mine* to claim. I would be God of the raging sea this day.

Compressing my abdominal muscles as I crunched forward made my injuries burn. *No struggling. No Complaining.* I readied myself for a fight; injured or damned being no burden to me. I waited for that split-second acknowledgement when hook and fish fused.

It happened, and I lusted.

The coffee's heat dwindled but had yet to extinguish when my line took. Happening so fast and so sudden, I gave a knee jerk startle, and dumped my drink. A brief flash of searing pain in my leg wasn't enough to distract me from my goal. The reel rotated on its axle, buzzing with the release of line into the deep fathoms of the ocean. It pulled, not going out from the ship, but diving deep, sounding. I pulled, and the rod bent low.

It's all the weight of the world which rest between your shoulders. It's plunging deep to take you with it, down into the depths of darkness where evil holds sway.

The rain came in fat drops as the moisture-filled clouds sprinkled us with a predecessor of what was to come.

Increasing the drag helped to slow down the massive fish, but then the line came to a complete stop, drew taut, and strained to the point I feared the microfibers would break. Pressing hard against the footrest, I braced myself and held the rod true. We stood at this stalemate, the fish and I, seeing who would flinch first. I eased the drag a notch, releasing some of its tension. The fish ran.

The line vacated my reel and when the boat dipped, the end of the rod touched the water. My lower back strained, and my shoulders throbbed. I didn't move or pump the crank but watched as the line went out yard after yard and worried the sea had no bottom.

The monster, which kept taking my line, felt much heavier than the sailfish from the day before. Wanting her to slow, I pumped the rod. She gave a little, allowing me to gather some line before she got the yearning to take off again. Despite my resistance, she went from diving deeper to going astern. I wondered if this new movement was from the pain of my hook or the approaching bottom.

I eased the drag, allowing the line to go, but kept pressure to tire the fish. The bearings inside the reel hummed as she headed out toward port side, before circling back to the boat. The line coiled, and I cranked with feverous vigor. Again, she dove, taking the line under the boat, arching the rod over the transom.

We repeated this for over an hour, and each passing minute tired us more. With each pull, a sharp vibrating pain stretched up my chest. I drew back on the rod, then reeled as I leaned forward. Doing this over and over, pumping and reeling, pumping and reeling, I watched my spool grow.

I'm drowning, Nicky.

"Need help?" Kojo asked, spooking me.

"Get the back off this chair and get me the straps. Make hast, I need you up there to turn the boat."

"Is she big?" His movements held an action of fluidity. There is no better a first mate than Kojo.

"Very." He did everything I had instructed before flying up to the bridge to get the AJAX turned about. We didn't pull the fish but positioned it out from the stern, so I could fight it head on, releasing some of the stress in my rod.

"Is there anything I can do?" Mabel asked, placing my Marine boonie cover on my head to keep the rain out of my eyes.

"I'll let you know, but for now, stay out of the way."

We, the fish and I, didn't ease into this fight, and we wouldn't ease out. We charged at one another, two rams fighting for superiority. The harness cut across my shoulder blades but took pressure away from my throbbing arms. We danced that great intercourse of battle between fish and man. The sun rose behind vengeful clouds, casting a gray film over the morning.

All at once, the struggle vanished. My line slacked and at first, I believed it had snapped. The rod bounced, stiffening, and the line curled. I hesitated and hesitation kills. In a panic, I spun the crank to gather it but failed in my attempt to keep it from bird nesting.

I cursed every word I could, but nothing helped. Then, as if spitting in my face, she leapt from the dark water at my starboard side no more than twenty feet away. Her crescent-shaped tail flickered with the rhythm it used to garner speed. The upper body, painted blue, bled deep lines into the fish's white underbelly. Its dorsal fin slicked back.

Her spike-like snout came to a point sharper than the finest sword. Before the great Atlantic blue marlin plunged into the sea, I caught a brief sight of her black hollow eyes. In that frozen moment, we stared at each other, weighing which would give and which would take.

My line coiled still. I could only now fight the fish from taking it any farther. If it reached that part of my line, the tangle would tighten and break. She had to be three hundred pounds at the lightest.

What a trophy she will be. What a trophy, indeed.

I took in more line before she could run off. We pushed and pulled at one another, but I worked her back to the boat. The nest in the line bloomed out, sliding across my hand. When she pulled, the line tightened hard, cutting my knuckles. Blood trickled out.

"You bastard. You bitch," I shouted through closed teeth as I cranked the reel. She swam from starboard to port and I followed her. The battle raged into its third hour and no longer could she flee. Pausing between rotations, Mabel wrapped a handkerchief around my bleeding hand. "Thank you."

S*he had cried for Henry.*

The first time since I had known her, she had shed some form of emotion for another person. I had seen her eyes, glistening in the dim light of the attic, and the outline of two streams of tears running down her cheeks.

Mabel stayed behind my fighting chair, moving when I moved. The blue marlin jumped and pulled, taking several feet of line with her, but never getting near the bird nest. I pumped and reeled, bringing back the line she took. Another hour slipped by and my stomach growled. I don't remember my last meal, but I was hurting for it.

"Want da gaff?" asked Kojo.

"No but get the club. I don't want this thing gaffed. I want it whole." Kojo slid down the ladder and grabbed the baseball bat from above the cabin door while Mabel sank beneath the flying bridge to shield herself from the rain. The fish went port side, then starboard.

"Stay with her." Kojo yelled and I did. Her long tail slapped against the hull with enough force to rock the boat against the growing swells. Mother nature was furious.

"My god. Look at dis tang," Kojo said. I wanted to stand and look over the side to see it again. She was beautiful in my mind and I couldn't wait to pull her aboard. Kojo raised the club, ready to strike her in the head to daze her.

"Mabel, grab that wench." She didn't hesitate to pick up the steel cable and get in position near Kojo. The fish pulled out again, easing away from the AJAX's stern, putting up a last moment of resistance. My shoulders strained, but I eased the pain in them by giving her some line. Allowing her to think she was loose, I sat down on it, and pulled as hard as I could. The great fish flew out of a large swell, shaking with the vigor of a wolf tearing meat from a carcass.

The water rose high and dropped low and the fish which emerged from one tall hill of water, dove into another. It slapped its head against the surface, trying to dislodge the thing which kept it from freedom. I pumped and reeled until the fight went out of the fish. She floated there on top of the water, not diving or running, but slithering like a serpent over the rough sea. The current pushed us toward one another.

Mabel patted my throbbing shoulder and said, "You got it."

I dreamt of this glory and the long hours of conversations it would garner as a trophy decorating my wall. My mantel at home laid bare, reserved for something worth memorializing. This great fish and this great fight deserved such an honor. By some chance, I would take a key from Hemingway himself and write a story about it. My mind filled with child-like glee and my body jazzed with satisfaction.

The pain in my back didn't bother me, nor did the sting on my hand. A numbing sensation throbbed at my stomach. The cold weather neutralized the warm blood seeping between the stitches.

Our great battle, between man and fish, was nothing more than two old warriors slugging it out to the finish. I smiled and looked up at the Heavens as the clouds unleashed their full force upon us. The cold rain felt euphoric.

"How about another cup of coffee?" I asked Mabel. She nodded.
"Do you have a travel mug so the rain—"
She paused as Kojo shouted from the stern, "Shark!"

Chapter Forty-Three

In the distance, the scarred fin of my old adversary rose as my stomach sank. With fighting the marlin, I completely forgot about that damned bull shark that refused to leave me alone. I wanted to grab my shotgun and blast the shark, but if I let go of the reel, the marlin would get away. I tried to keep an eye on the shark while reeling, but the ocean's swells grew, and tossed us about.

"No, no, not now." I cranked the reel as fast as I could as Kojo hustled up the flying bridge. He reached out for the throttle, but his shoes slipped on the wet rung and he crashed to the elevated deck. His fake leg popped off and slid across the flying bridge, teetering on the edge, threatening to tumble into the ocean. Kojo reached for it, his fingertips grazing it, giving it enough momentum to fall.

"No, no, shit." He screamed and laid stretched out on his belly, head resting on the wet wooden deck in defeat.

I couldn't look back to see what was happening. The marlin moved, sensing the predator in the water coming near her. She came back to life, cutting to port, then hurried back to starboard. I fought on, keeping her from sounding. I had lost my last catch to this beast and I would not lose this one. The shark closed in as I pulled the marlin near.

Kojo spun, accepting the loss of his leg, and slammed the throttle into reverse. The boat jerked and pushed us at the fading blue marlin. The bull shark thrusted its tail, kicking up a splash of water behind him, speeding our way. My teeth gritted and I pushed with all my strength to reel the marlin in.

"You need this?" Mabel said behind me, but I didn't know what she was referring to. I didn't look, keeping all my focus on the marlin and the shark. Mabel crept up the slick ladder to the flying bridge and in her hands, to Kojo's surprise, was his prosthetic leg. "Thought you might want it."

"How did you—"

"Saw it going over and caught it before it went into the water." The rain and mist from the sea washed over Mabel's face, but this didn't stop her from giving Kojo a wink.

"Holy shit, thank you."

The marlin's tail flicked at the rear of my ship and I unshackled the rod from my shoulder harness, securing it to the chair alone. "Hold this."

Mabel was there and grasped the rod. She sat in the chair and clenched the rod with everything she had. Holding on to the transom, I snagged the cable leader, cutting my fingers in the process. Neither the injury nor the blood bothered me. I wanted my fish, my trophy, my catch.

"Pull, damn it, pull." Kojo shouted from the bridge. The marlin's eyes no longer registered the danger she was in for our fight had left her exhausted. I pulled the spear-like snout over the rollers, catching an eyeful of the red dorsal fin slicing the water.

"Gaff," I ordered. Mabel fiddled about for a second then charged at me with the gaff as if it was a spear. The curved hook rushed by my head and I caught the wooden shaft. "Get back to the rod."

I didn't want to damage my prize catch with the gaff, but I didn't want to lose it to that demon either. Sticking one side of the marlin would allow me to still come away with a beautiful trophy. I reared back with the gaff, losing sight of the shark who I knew was only yards away. There was no time.

I swung the gaff, arching over my shoulders like swinging a club on a downed enemy. The AJAX slammed into a swell, and artic-cold water electrocuted me. We lunged off balance, like passengers in a car that came to an abrupt halt. I slipped on the water covering the deck, landing on my ass, and sliding into the opening of the transom. With a knee jerk reaction, I threw my head to the side in horror a split second before the marlin's sharp snout shot past my head.

In her last-ditch attempt to finish me off, I avoided certain death, but didn't rest in my survival. She teetered on the roller, threatening to slip back into the briny blue. The rocking of the ship aided in throwing off my balance and I had to make a quick decision. Either push off the fish which would lose her into the water or drop the gaff and try to save myself. I released the wooden gaff, digging my nails into the painted wood on top of the transom to keep from plunging overboard.

Mabel pulled back on the rod, working to keep the fish stable while protesting my failure with a loud yelp. A few stitches popped, tearing the flesh they strived to hold together, and warm blood flowed down my cold stomach. My nails clawed at the wood and my arm strained to hold me from falling. Scrambling to my knees, I slapped a hand on her back, but the mucus covering all fish caused my arm to slip into the dark water, elbow deep.

Saltwater stung the open laceration across my knuckles. I roped my fingers under the marlin as she kicked her tail, slapping to get away from me. I lifted, foolishly wanting to pop the fish aboard, but she weighed too much and the only thing I managed to pull was more stitches. The pain in my stomach and hand grew incidental as the ridged teeth of the shark tore into the flesh of my arm and I lost sight of my own appendage in the dark bloody water.

Chapter Forty-Four

The water frothed with red and white bubbles, but the blood that splashed up with the waves wasn't mine. It poured out of my great fish as the shark jerked its head from side to side. His jaws were locked and his serrated teeth grinded the meat of the marlin, tearing sections from her.

My own blood, dripping from an opening that tore from my wrist to the scar tissue of my missing pinky finger, splashed and mixed with the marlin's. It hurt, but my mania boiled, numbing my pain. I grabbed the gaff at my feet and swung it. No swell or raging weather would throw me off this time. I went for his mouth, aimed for his snout, jabbing for his head. I wanted to hit him in the eye, to blind him, to pierce his brain, to kill him.

I sank the curved hook into the shark's jaw, hoping to free the marlin from his death trap. The shark didn't let go, and instead, thrashed with the gaff. I struck him again and again, striking with everything I had in my torn body. No matter what, the shark kept chewing, ruining what should have been my greatest prize. She was a beautiful fish and deserved to die with respect and grace.

I slapped the gaff into the eye of the shark. A quake jolted through him and he whipped both me and the wooden gaff into the transom's small opening. The wooden shaft snapped under the combined pressure of my weight and the force of his assault. I stumbled back and fell hard to the deck, striking my head on the metal bar of the footrest. Mabel rushed to me, but I was on my feet again with the broken gaff in hand.

"Nicanor, don't." Kojo shouted, but I heard only the roar of the ocean, the crunching of my fish, and the beating of my own heart. Snapping hard, the marlin broke her bill against the ship, leaving a gash in my boat. More blood rushed into the water and my beautiful blue fish slowed to move. I cursed that shark, that damned beast of burden. The shark ripped a large chunk of meat free, circled about, then hit her again.

I stabbed down like a whaler from long ago, ready to strike their money. I'm sure to a literary person like Mabel, I looked as mad as Captain Ahab. Perchance, if there were such a character, his spirit possessed me, for in that moment, I too was mad.

Plunging the spear into the shark's back, I could've sworn it howled at me. For the first time I had the satisfaction of hurting this enemy as it had hurt me. He released his hold on my blue marlin but left a more than sizeable hole, nearly tearing the fish in two. There was no trophy to salvage from bone and torn meat and this served me right. I should have never wanted a trophy and the sea gods were punishing me for it.

The marlin pleaded with me, through dying eyes, and I saw not the fish on my transom, but my friends who had fallen in combat. I lost this fish as I had lost them; unable to save her as I was unable to save them. Then a single thought rubbed out all others. I saw Henry.

I'm drowning, Nicky.

I couldn't save him as I couldn't save my friends in Fallujah who died on the roofs and in the alleys. I couldn't save them as I couldn't save this fish. This fish's life, all it was and all it ever would be, was no more as those Marines were no more. As Henry was no more.

The marlin stared at me, her mouth twitching under her broken snout. Her blood washed across the deck as the AJAX dipped. I grabbed my 1911 sidearm from the cabin and squatted in front of this glorious creature. A tearful moan echoed, and I hated myself for doing this to her. A single round ended her suffering.

The AJAX dipped again, and a rising swell swept her away from my stern, laying her to rest in the depths. I watched her as long as nature allowed, my vision's range limited by the dark clouds above. The gory water engulfed her in its murky cocoon, to deliver her to a place I'd never see, to feed fish I'd never catch.

I left with my head down in disgrace and now watching this fish sink felt like my life sinking.

I'm drowning, Nicky.

In front of my eyes, the red fin shark swam mockingly before me. His mouth appeared to stretch into a smile, either by evolution or by imagination, infuriating me. He wasn't hungry but had killed the marlin out of spite. All the pain I felt meant nothing now. I stood, blood seeping through clenched fists, ready to fight. No more shame, no more running. We were here together, the shark and I, and this was our day.

In haste, I pulled at the seams of my shirt, popping buttons which flung out to be lost at sea. Spotting what remained of the gaff still impaled into the back of the beast, I took aim and fired. I ran through the entire clip, always leading the wooden gaff. I knew this wouldn't cause much harm to the shark, but any small jab weakened a chin for a knockout punch.

The wind bit at my bare skin and I fetched the trench gun from the cabin. This shark pushed me to this point, and a youthful surge of vigor coursed through me. I saw through the eyes of the young me, who lusted for blood and death. I stuffed the buttstock into my shoulder and fired. The shotgun's pellets kicked up small spurts of water. I pumped the forend and fired again, repeating this until my trench gun ran empty.

The shark swam on, diving and hiding beneath the surface. Recharged and breathing hard through my widening nostrils, I reloaded the pistol and shoved it into my belt. Mabel stood clear of me; Kojo mirroring her look of terror. I opened two white buckets of chum and dumped them overboard. The greasy substance normally left a visible trail behind the boat, but in the mist of the approaching storm, the dark clouds prevented such a sight.

"Why are you doing that?" Mabel asked.

"This should keep that bastard here. No way he'll leave with that chum sending his senses into overdrive." Throwing the empty five-gallon buckets to the side, I marched without rushing to my other rods. In the middle of the assortment, shining like Excalibur in the stone, stood my rig specially designed for big shark fishing. Nothing thrilled me more than the foam grip of the bent-butt custom edition rod in my hands…

Like the twin revolver in his waistband you had failed to notice.

…and the fury of nature surrounding me. The six hundred yards of eighty-pound line would hold this beast, and I highly doubted he could bite through the top shot and wire cable. The hook was large, but there was no way this shark would toss it once he got a taste of the baby squid I kept in the bait box.

Mabel grimaced at the sight of the dead creature, but I paid her no mind as I drove the hook through the squid with delight. Who was she to judge me anyhow? She had enough skeletons in her closet to fill a cemetery.

"Come get some, motherfucker."

The shark circled the AJAX as I readied my rod. One would think the prized marlin would've filled his gut, or he'd follow it to the dark depths of Davy Jones' locker, but I knew the truth. This shark didn't care about eating. He lived to torment me, to reward itself with my agony. He cared not about others, but only about its own gluttonous desires.

The taste and smell of this squid would incite an insatiable fury, firing every nerve-ending until the uncontrollable temptation gnawed at his brain and he was forced to take the baby squid. One way or another, either Red Fin or I would die this day.

Or both.

Chapter Forty-Five

His dorsal fin followed the broken gaff and together they slid to my line. I'm sure he thought I had caught something else and was ready to ruin that as well. I danced the bait, enticing the shark until he took it. He snatched the squid, sucking it in, chewing on it, but I made no move to set the hook. The squid was only in his teeth, so I waited, allowing him to swim on in his perceived victory.

Aiming the tip of my rod at that vexing dorsal fin, I inched on the drag and the reel tightened. The braided line stretched, but I wasn't scared of it snapping. This rig was near perfect for the job I had to do. I waited, ensuring the bait was in the beast, then jabbed the rod upward. The shark gave and with the second jab, the circle hook impaled into the corner of his upper jaw.

No amount of chomping would break this steel. The freedom it had known, to swim and to terrorize, was no more. He was mine.

He jerked and thrashed, pleading for release, but nothing would free him from my grasp. I believed for the first time in his life, the shark knew what it meant to be in real danger. The lifestyle he'd always known and was accustomed to was under attack. An island full of fisherman had tried to catch him. Foreigners with boats came by the dozens to cash in on the shark terrorizing the tropics. People brought guns, harpoons, and even explosives.

At the height of his terror, I watched a boat explode with all hands-on deck going down with the ship. It seemed like nothing could stop this leviathan of the deep, and here I was, bringing him in on rod and reel. With another hard pull, I confirmed the hook was set, then cranked furiously enough to blister my hand.

Dark clouds continued to blanket the sky, blotting out the sun. Several lightning bolts flashed at once, creating in the sky a mirage of the great Pantheon. The mystic structure flicked into existence, shielded by intervals of dark sky, announcing that the Gods had arrived to watch our struggle.

Swells grew larger and we rode the massive water roller coaster, never losing sight of our mission.

"You're mine now, you bastard." A maddening shrill escaped me. My stomach ached not from the lack of food, but from the strain I put on the stitches. The wind kicked, slapping water at me. The shark cut out, its tail striking the hull with a loud thud that rattled our bones.

"By God, ya feel dat?" Kojo shouted, spinning the wheel, and staying with this beast. The shark didn't dive as most do once hooked but stay near the top of the water. The light above the clouds wasn't strong enough for me to see my line. At times, the broken gaff sank beneath the surface, then rose out of the water to show me where he was. The AJAX pitched and rolled as rain came screaming across the surface of the ocean.

"I'll die for this." I proclaimed to no one and everyone.

I pulled hard on the rod, knocking off my hat. Rain and sea splashed in my face as I bore down and reeled. On shaky legs, I pushed myself to my feet like a man climbing out of a wheelchair for the first time. Beaming hatred at the fin, I shouted a line memorized from a book long ago, "As he was a bachelor and in no one's debt, no one trouble his head any more about him."

Mabel pressed my hat firmly back on. This helped to keep the rain out of my eyes, so I could see to fight, but I would fight this damn fish blind if I had to.

"You're bleeding," she said.

"I know. That damn shark bit me."

"It bit you?"

"It ain't bad."

"No, but your stomach." She pointed at the red smear seeping into my shorts. Several of the black stitches had popped and one wound gaped. The iron in my blood reached my sense of smell. I touched the wound and was stunned at how much blood covered my fingers. Snarling, I flicked my hand, tossing specks of blood into the water.

"Is this what you want?" I shouted at the shark as I pumped the rod, popping another stitch. "You want my blood? Well, come and get it. Come and get it you bastard, you damned beast, you sonofabitch."

I screamed incoherently.

As if hearing me, the shark spun around. I reeled as the slack grew larger in my line. It couldn't chew through the hook, but I feared it could sever the cable wire. His head rose from the water, waves rolling about, and he opened his massive square jaws as he came straight for us.

As I stared down into the belly of the beast, I thought of Claire. How I wished she could be here. I would tell her how she had damaged me, but I was still strong. Strong enough to outgrow her and take on this death machine that approached. Mouth open, he sank his teeth into the roller at the back of my ship. I would be lying if I said I wasn't alarmed.

This beast wanted this fight. He thrashed his head from side to side, snapping the bolts holding the roller to the stern. I pulled free my pistol and fired.

If you're gonna shoot, shoot to kill. The haunting words echoed from my father. The pistol kicked, producing a blinding light from the muzzle. The projectile struck the side of the large shark but did little to truly harm him. A mere jab in a slugfest.

If my father could see me, what would he say? I chewed the inside of my lip for I knew the answer. A man of few comforting words, we weren't as close as I later wished we would've been. But he was dead, and I wasn't, and so, I don't know why this troubled me, much like not knowing why this shark seemed to only target my boat.

I'm drowning, Nicky.

The shark slapped the hull again, pulling me from my inner monologue. He swam out as if retreating, and I eased on the drag without putting up a fight. I wanted to be rid of this fish as much as I wanted to be rid of the burdensome ghosts of my past. The suffering overshadowed the pain in my belly. I held back the pressure building behind my eyes until I felt the popping of two more stitches.

Pain flared and I grunted as I wondered how many more stitches I had left. When the shark circled again, I reeled, wanting to pull him in as quickly as I could, but the rod bent, and he went back out. I stopped reeling, fearing too much would break the line, the reel, the rod, or all three.

This fight continued with my only baby squid resting in the belly of that bastard. My arms cramped at having fought the marlin for so long. Another stitch popped as I leaned back in my fighting chair. The leather strap of the harness cut into my back, and the trickling blood warmed me. I would reel this bastard in, and his jaws would adorn my ship.

You're hurt. Cut line and go. Cut this fish loose. Get back to the island. Don't be stupid. Don't be a fool. Are you trying to get yourself killed?

The dark inner voice poked at the walls of my skull, but I only laughed as I bathed in flashes of lightning and moaning wind.

"This is war," I called out to the shark. We would fight until we died. This shark fought me as hard as I fought it. We were one in this crazy universe, brothers in a strange way, and I understood that I needed him as much as he needed me.

An hour of fighting rolled by and the storm refused to relent. On we danced like tired prizefighters too stupid to fall. He circled in front of my vision, mocking me, enraging me, and twice now I pulled the pistol from my belt and fired.

Everything the two of us had been through accumulated to this point and now it was time. I fired again.

The bang of the pistol rippled in my ears as it had when Henry killed himself. The champion of the world was no more a god, no more a mortal man than any other.

I'm drowning, Nicky.

"We're all drowning, Henry. We're all drowning," I shouted out into the storm.

We had been closer than anyone I was ever close with and yet he had no real love for me. He betrayed me only as a bastard could betray another. Coke's men stabbed me in the front, but a true sonofabitch stabs their brother in the back. Henry was indeed a true sonofabitch, but I knew this and still allowed him back into my life. I loved him as much as I hated him. He was as jaded and foolish as any other man and this led him to take his own life.

No one can pass judgement on a man who takes his own life because none of us living know the pain of the dead. I know only my own pain and because of this, I couldn't cry for my old friend. He desired a fame and a love that seemed to always be out of his reach. With death, the media would feast on his name. People would wonder why a man on top of the world would do such a thing.

I cranked the reel, churning away the revolving images of Henry's disfigured head. I ignored the pain in my stomach and cared nothing about the bruises on my face or my injured hand. The blood oozing from the wound created by the shark bite was of no matter to me. A wave smashed with such a loud bang I mistook it for a mortar explosion.

My legs throbbed at the thought of shrapnel and I hated the injuries which forced my exit from the Corps. I was once at fate's mercy, not knowing if I would live or die, but now that wasn't the case. The war-wounds that made me vulnerable had long since healed. I was the master of my fate, master of my life, master of my death. I wouldn't allow anything to take away from the glory that would be to live or die in such a struggle of man versus nature.

A laugh escaped me as I thought about all the people who had wrong me in this life. Their faces morphed into one another, passing before my eyes in a daze of delirium. They hadn't hurt me in some spiteful manner. They were only trying to make it in this world as I was.

The laughter continued as the rain drilled a coldness into my bones that I hadn't felt since Fallujah. My teeth chattered and my muscles contracted, but hypothermia was far from my mind. Somewhere, deep in the recesses of my heart, I surrendered. I didn't quit or give-in but surrendered to the understanding of my life. The pain and heartache, the war and losses, and mistreatment from others, all were a part of my story.

They made me, gave me strength, and for that, I couldn't hate them. I couldn't hate Claire or Mabel, for they were people making it in the world. I couldn't hate Jacob or Henry for they were both dead and nothing would change that. I couldn't hate the war or the struggle, but mostly I couldn't hate this shark. This shark was only doing what its damaged mind allowed, and although we had to kill one another, I couldn't hate him.

I no longer felt the cold as my laughter warmed me.

I pumped and pulled, cranked and reeled, revived with a new surge of energy to survive. I turned the handle, not thinking about Henry, or of my father, not thinking about Jacob Coke, or Mabel, or even the dissociated trio of Henry's entourage. Nothing troubled me. Not the wind or the ocean nor the pain or the glory of a catch. None of it.

I wouldn't allow it, for my soul, my body and mind, the very essence of my spirit resided with this shark. He surfaced, his dorsal fin as tall as a rowing oar standing on end, and I swear he smiled at me again. My bones ached and my muscles tensed.

"Do you want more coffee?" Mabel called through the rain.

"Fuck the coffee. Bring me a bottle."

"What kind?"

"Rum. Bring me rum."

"Ya shouldn't be drinking da hard stuff," Kojo said.

"Fuck that."

"Ya shouldn't wid dose wounds. We be turning back for shore."

"Don't you fuckin' dare. I won't stop until this fight is over."

"Ya hurt."

"I've been through worse and you know it." But Kojo was right. The pain grew to the point that I couldn't push it from my mind forever. As it rose, the fight in me weakened, but I cranked on. The shark came at the ship again, slamming headfirst, cracking and straining the hull.

"He'll sink us," Mabel said, passing me the bottle.

I'm drowning, Nicky.

The top was off, and I took a hard pull from the burning liquid. It warmed my bones, but the blood seeped from me still.

"No. He can't," I lied. She leaned over me and noticed the blood.

"You're bleeding worse now. We should go back."

"Fuck that. Go back inside and don't bring your negativity out again." She made a move to turn toward the cabin, but I grabbed a fist full of her wet shirt. She paused, unsure of what I was doing, and the surprise beamed off her face as I pulled her in for a hard kiss. I released her shirt, slightly pushing her away, and she returned to the comfort of the cabin.

She was a fascinating human being and a wonderful lover, but her heart died years ago, ruined for anyone. This was why she could watch without judgement and this was why we couldn't be together. There was nothing else the two of us could share with one another. She would go on to spread the word of Henry and write many best-sellers. In doing so, she was like Henry and Alice and all the others in my life. They would get exactly what they wanted.

I wasn't *in love* with her, the mystique of her charm having faded, but I did love her.

Hurt, but not defeated, I shoveled on, refusing to quit, and forcing her from my mind. The ocean kicked up and showered me. I spat out the saltwater and blinked away the sea, the warmth of her lips disappearing. The liquor splashed across my chin, mixing with the seawater clinging to my beard. "Fifteen men on a dead man's chest, yo-ho-ho, and a bottle of rum."

The shark gave a hard, victorious tug, and I leapt to my feet to meet its challenge.

"Come on you bastard, you sonofabitch. I am here. Finish me. Finish me or I swear I'll fuckin' kill you." And as if accepting my offer, he slammed against the hull again. I lost my footing but caught the transom, which kept me from spilling over into the water. The shark swam from starboard to port and charged across the stern with jaws wide to nip at me. A third time I fired the pistol and again put two holes in that fish. He swam on, unfazed.

He sounded, going down, but he didn't stay long. The fight was fleeing from him as well and he resurfaced, broken gaff riding high. Several dots bled from his side and back, but he fought on.

"You're mine now, you bastard," I screamed and the pain in my stomach brought me to my knees. Two of my wounds were completely torn open. The blood poured hard from them. Still holding the rod, I couldn't bring myself to crank the reel. I wanted Henry or my father, or any one of my Marines to help me stand, but with Kojo steering the vessel, I was alone on the deck.

I'm drowning, Nicky.

The red fin shark pulled the line and with the rod still attached to me, I slid toward the opening. Freedom was far from his mind. He was trying to pull me in, sensing I wasn't secure in my own boat.

"He'll go over." Mabel screamed. I planted my feet against the half walls of the transom, flanking the opening hatch, and pushed back. He swam off the stern, unable to take me or my line with him. Circling and swimming back and forth, the youthful behavior to sink low and take my line with him was gone. I knew this now because he knew it and we were one.

I reeled. He circled. I pumped. He swam. I bled. He bled.

"Come on, you sonofabitch. Have at thee." We clung to our death struggle, the only thing keeping us alive. The swell kicked the AJAX to the side, slamming hard and forcing our rotation. I pulled back on the rod.

"I'm taking us back," Kojo said.

"You do, and you'll never step foot—" The pain stopped my words. The exhaustion wrapped me up in its unhealthy embrace. I was a Marine. I was a man of the storm. I mustered through the agony. "You'll never step foot on this boat again."

Of course, I wanted it to end, but I wouldn't retreat from the fight.

You'll die. You'll die if you don't let him go. You'll die.

"Then I'll die." And with that, the inner voice vanished. This shout confused Mabel and Kojo, but I didn't worry about them. I drank and bled into the storm. My energy drained, but I thought of the trio in Henry's house and my anger warmed me and fueled my fight.

"You're mad," Kojo said.

"As mad as a hatter." I laughed. Mabel ran out and placed her hands upon my shoulders.

"Kojo, get us back." I felt the boat change directions.

"No! You can't. Not until this is over. You can't, Kojo. I need this."

"Nicanor, you can't do this." Mabel's fingers squeezed into my cold flesh.

"Don't doubt me now." I whispered into the wind. My legs trembled, refusing to stand, and so I receded to sitting on the deck. I was cold. I was tired.

"You look dead," Mabel said from behind me.

I get that, I wanted to say, but I didn't. I couldn't get the strength to speak. I pumped the rod and cranked the handle. The shark swam no farther than the port edge to the starboard edge. He, too, tired beyond all measure. I kept him at the stern, right outside the transom and, gathering all the strength I could muster, made my lunge.

In my last effort to kill this beast, I leaned over the side, risking all, and plunged my trusty blade into the shark. He bucked and with the help of a swell, toppled over the broken rollers, and onto my stern. The wave shoved him through the opening on the transom and he slid to me. Sensing my triumph was near, Nature wouldn't be denied a victory over man. The rocking of the ship hurled me back and I collapsed. Together with the shark, we two warriors sprawled out on the deck. Water and blood swirled around us.

There came a moment's pause where we stared at one another. It lasted only for a second, if not less, then we knew our battle wasn't over. His tail whipped and his teeth snapped. The ocean spun the AJAX. Mabel, off-balance, managed to scurry away from the shark's stained teeth and reached the safety of the cabin.

My blade rested in the shark's back and I seized its leather handle. I ripped it free, bringing with it blood and ocean water, before plunging it back in six more times with wet thuds. His fight was far from over too. Jerking his head to the side, a serrated tooth caught my arm and tore open a bad gash. Blood didn't ooze or seep but spurted. I screamed, leaving my blade in his back, and jerked the pistol from my belt one final time.

His body flopped and his massive pectoral fin slapped the pistol from my grip as I swung it around to finish him. The AJAX tilted hard one away, then rocketed back the other, and we slid. The shark slammed into the hull and I into him. If it had been the opposing side, the beast would have crushed me.

A row of top teeth caressed my shoulder, opening a fine laceration. I grunted and went for my knife. The boat swung about again and Kojo fought to keep it afloat. The propellers churned and he headed for shore. I didn't mind now, that this beast was aboard. Mabel screamed from somewhere behind me and the engines roared louder. The current tossed us about and we spun across the deck.

I clung onto the knife, riding with the shark as his snapping jaws reached for me. The force flung me away, but I kept a hold of my knife while scrambling around the fighting chair to avoid him catching me. The shark slammed into the chair and the bolts strained but kept him at bay.

The transom's door slammed shut, then popped back open. I went for the pistol, but the AJAX dipped the other way, and the gun went from my grasp. The ocean nailed the ship, and again the shark launched at me. He slammed into the fighting chair but this time the bolts snapped the wood beneath it.

He came at me, mouth open, teeth bare, but the chair deflected the shark, giving me a moment to slide out of his way. The pistol skidded toward the open transom hatch. I slipped across the wet deck and snatched it before the pistol could go overboard. Our eyes stared at one another, an inch apart, and I squeezed the trigger.

I fired again and the shark flopped, gaining traction to get me. I fired again and again until the hammer fell on an empty chamber. One last-ditch effort, he snarled and came at me. Still holding to my knife, I growled. I ripped back as he crashed into me and buried the Ka-bar blade of my trusty knife into the top of his head. The pointed tip slid with ease between his eyes. My blood poured into his mouth as two of his teeth punctured my side.

I stabbed again, trying to strike the y-shape makeup of his brain. He fought on, snipping, trying to force me into his mouth, desperately needing to kill me. With one final drive, carrying the weight of my body behind it, I plunged my knife in, finishing the fight.

The great beast, the terror of the red fin, the shark of all sharks I had ever seen, was dead. I laid back, exhausted. Each stitch that held my three wounds closed were no more. Together, our blood mixed with the rain and the seawater on the deck. I laid there no longer moving but staring at my shark.

Its lifeless eyes were as familiar to me as the eyes of my own reflection. I loved this shark for he was the best opponent I had ever faced, and I had bested him. I had won.

I couldn't speak, nor could I move. I didn't hear Kojo or Mabel as they spoke to me. I simply watched my shark with the relief of a man who had gone five rounds with the greatest of all time. I didn't register the cold water splashing on me. I had no fear of hatred or anxiety or worries. A strange elation came over me. I had finally found what I had been searching for all these years.

A calming peace washed away any concerns I had for this life or the next. I laid back, elated in my victory.

As graceful as the marlin leaps into the air, breaking free from the confines of the ocean, I found peace in this world.

Semper Fi

Author's Notes

I wrote the first draft of this story in under three weeks. Although it was shorter, the main idea was there – that we all suffer from some sort of PTSD. One can live in a tropical paradise, have the freedoms every person wishes for, but still suffer from their own demons. PTSD isn't the only theme of this story. It's also about accepting your life and fate and understanding that everyone gets what they deserve, even if it's not what they thought they wanted.

This story was written with my love of many things. At the time, I had fallen in love with the roaring twenties, Great Gatsby, Hemingway, and art deco. Many of these are used in the story. I also have a love for MMA, fishing, the stock market, and the idea that freedom is not necessarily related to having wealth.

Then there's Mabel. I love this woman. She is a mixture of three real women: Tamara De Lempicka, Zelda Fitzgerald, and my wife, Jennifer Nix, who drew all the pictures and the cover for this book. Three very free-spirited women.

This book was finished during the Pandemic of 2020. After being inside all the time, it's nice to get out, even if it's only in your head. Maybe you can't go to the beach as of now, but you can feel like you are there. Experience this book; sit outside in the sun; pour a glass of your favorite drink and enjoy. It's meant to bring on that tingling feeling of summertime, when the waves are crashing upon the warm sand, and the breeze blows gently about the surf. *Can you hear the seagulls in the sky and smell the salt in the air? Can you?*

THANK YOU

PALS

I wanted to say thank you to everyone who read this book. It was a three-year labor of love and I hope you all enjoy reading it as much as I did creating it.

Thank you to Margie Teamann for proofreading.

And most importantly, thank you to my first editor, reader, and wife, Jennifer. For the countless re-reads and edits, the endless sketching of the cover and pictures in the book, and the excitement in your eyes when you read a sentence that you find truly impressive. I love you, today.

Author Biography

Chance Nix was born and raised in Pleasant Grove, Dallas, Texas, before enlisting in the Marine Corps. With two tours of duty, which includes the Battle of Fallujah, Chance came away with a sense of pride, a Purple Heart, and a few stories to tell. In between his two tours in Iraq, Chance volunteered to drive a seven-ton truck through the murky waters of Louisiana to aid in the relief of Hurricane Katrina.

After being injured during his second tour, Chance spent some time getting short stories published while working on his novel, *Kill! Kill!*, about Iraq. Being a lover of 80's action movies and macho tough guy films, he wasn't content with making the book some sappy autobiography. He may be all too familiar with self-deprecating humor, but the thing that really gets Chance going is writing some kickass action.

Chance spends his time between writing, veteran activities, and raising his kids. He may be a little older, a little slower, but he can still shoot a tick off a dog's butt at 300 yards.

www.ingramcontent.com/pod-product-compliance
Lightning Source LLC
Chambersburg PA
CBHW020500310726
48979CB00016B/2738/J

* 9 7 8 1 7 3 4 0 8 8 4 2 7 *